Maria Trench

Charles Lowder

A Biography

Maria Trench

Charles Lowder
A Biography

ISBN/EAN: 9783337009854

Printed in Europe, USA, Canada, Australia, Japan

Cover: Foto ©Raphael Reischuk / pixelio.de

More available books at **www.hansebooks.com**

st. A

ND EDITION

PREFACE.

—◦◦◦—

"I CALL a man remarkable," Carlyle says, "who becomes a true workman in this vineyard of the Highest." If this be so, Charles Lowder was certainly one of the most remarkable men among those who have lately passed away. "His work has made 'Lowder' and 'St. Peter's, London Docks,' household words in this our Western land," were the words of Dean Stansbury, of New Jersey, in a sermon preached soon after that work was ended by death. It is hardly necessary to say that his life has been written by the wish of his brother and his sisters, without whose generous confidence the task would have been an impossible one. To his eldest sister, especially, the writer is indebted, not only for all information as to his early life, but for constant and kindest help while attempting to

carry out the wishes of his family. Their desire
that the book should be written (at the cost of a
sacrifice of private feeling) has been wholly from the
belief that, for the sake of others, it was well that
the story of his life should be told, although knowing
that he would himself have shrunk from it while still
amongst us. Had he ever contemplated such a
record being made, he would certainly have left
more material for the purpose; but there is not, in
his letters or papers, the slightest token of their
having been written for anything but the immediate
purpose of the moment. His book, " Twenty-one
Years in St. George's Mission," now out of print,
was placed in the writer's hands by his brother, the
Rev. William Lowder, to be used as might seem
best ; but with the exception of the account of the
cholera in St. Peter's parish, only a very few short
extracts from it have been given. We are therefore
the more indebted to those who have most kindly,
and at considerable trouble to themselves, supplied
information, both in writing and in conversation,
without which this memoir could not have been
written.

While heartily thanking all who have thus
lightened the writer's task, it is impossible not to

mention with especial gratitude the clergy and
Sisters of St. Peter's-in-the-East, the Rev. James
Skinner, Rev. H. Rowley, Rev. J. E. Swallow, Rev.
Bryan King, and last, but not least, the Rev. Robert
Linklater. To him, and to Mr. Skinner, both the
writer and readers of this memoir are most largely
indebted. For Charles Lowder's life was his work
in London ; and to the men who lived and worked
with him in London, the one as his leader, the other
under him, we must turn to hear the story of his
labours.

It may very probably seem to not a few that
too many details have been given in the following
pages, at least of Mr. Lowder's last days. But this
will be forgiven, if it be remembered that the book
is written, first of all, for his mourning parishioners
at St. Peter's-in-the-East. They long to follow his
last wanderings after his departure from England,
to hear his last words before he passed into the
silence which cannot be broken, and to stand by his
death-bed.

Whatever has been said, in the following pages, of
the fearful misery that almost touches the splendour
of West London is very far within the truth. What
are the words of John Martin, the poet schoolmaster,

who had been rescued from direst misery by the St. Peter's clergy, and had himself drunk to the very dregs the cup of want and suffering ? Here is a passage from his note-book :

One who lives amidst the courts and alleys of a great city, and sees the filth of human life that the very houses have in them ; one who can see, as I just now saw, girls of twelve and thirteen lost to all shame and decency, proceeding on their way to infamy, and no hope of a friendly hand to stay them in their downward path ; no hope, except perhaps for one or two who will be as brands from the burning fire ; one who knows that, as rats undermine a building, squalid crime is at work upon the very foundations of morality and law, cannot, must not, till he has left these scenes for peaceful nature, be an optimist.

I pass through the filthy lanes, not in imagination, for I have been through them bodily just now, and I see the most squalid beastliness, oaths, quarrels, fights, drunkenness. To know that the image of God can fall below the level of the brutes is grief enough. To know that that state is its highest joy ; to know that life in all its circle of intellectual and bodily pleasure holds no greater amusement or attraction, is enough to take the edge off all joy. The dreadful, weird phase of uncivilization presented ever to me makes me dejected—a dejection increased by my bodily languor. What avails it that this is Christmas Eve ? What avails it that Christ, the Divinely pure, was born as to-night, when I know that there are thousands of souls that reject and despise the hope of everlasting life, for the reason that they are not fit to live now ? At the best, the life of this people is very mournful. There is such an utter absence of any desire to achieve immortality to be discovered in them. They pursue daily the same dull,

never-thinking course of existence; the only variation to which
they look forward being that of hard drinking. The children
grow up just in the same way; at four years old they can "swear
like troopers," very often being taught by their parents to do so.*

These outspoken opinions are, as Mrs. Craik
has well said, "valuable both in themselves, and as
coming out of what is the usually silent class—silent
both because it is educated neither to think, nor to
express its thoughts. Emphatically one of the
people, born and living to the last amongst the
lowest class of the people—this man, with his rarely
clear brain and righteous heart, pure from first to
last, amidst surroundings absolutely unspeakable
in their vileness, John Martin has a right to be
heard, the more that his voice comes out of the
grave."

Surely he is right that the very foundations of
our national existence are being undermined. Let
any thoughtful person drive from our beautiful West
End parks, past the palaces of our Princes, to Ratcliff
Highway, and then say whether there do not exist,
among ourselves, the elements of a retribution more
terrible even than that of the French Revolution.

It was in the midst of such scenes that Charles

* "A Legacy," by the author of "John Halifax," p. 140.

Lowder lived and laboured to the last. There are those whose time and talents are almost wholly given to the important task of influencing the educated, the rich, and the great, and who feel that in gaining one such, they benefit many poor. Their work leads them into pleasant paths—to the fair homes of England—amidst all the charm and grace of the most perfect and intellectual social intercourse. There is the pleasure, which it is impossible for any man not to feel, of knowing that they influence those upon whom the fate of kingdoms depends, and of being mixed up with all that is most interesting in the history of our own time. But the Vicar of St. Peter's-in-the-East chose literally his Master's task, —to preach the Gospel to the poor, and to bring healing to their bodily ills. No marvel that one who worked chiefly among the rich and noble of this world should have been stirred by his example, and that, seeing his calling, he should have exclaimed, "I long to go and cast myself into that Mission." *

A leading champion has fallen in the battle ; but if England had but three hundred men as good as he, East London might yet be reclaimed and saved. Will not some such men volunteer ? Why do they

* See p. 135.

not rather press forward to the high emprise, as they gallantly do for foreign military service ?

" I fear more for the rich than for the most degraded poor—more for Belgravia than for St. Giles' ; for the more light there is, the more responsibility." Words of mournful foreboding from one to whom East London has been a subject of deep anxiety for half a century, Dr. Pusey. Knowing the horrors of those dark places and cruel habitations of our land, he yet fears more for those who dwell at ease, surrounded by outward refinement, beauty, and culture. " For when He maketh inquisition for blood He remembereth them, *and forgetteth not the complaint of the poor.*"

If there be anything which brings still more sadness to the heart than the degradation of the ignorant, it is surely the thought of those, called by their own hearts, by education, and the needs of others, to some noble purpose, who are yet content to dream away their lives,—indifferent spectators of the sorrows, sins, and wrongs of men, when they might have been leaders in the battle against evil.

There is a field in East London for as noble and knightly adventure as ever was achieved by England's chivalry. Even as the hosts of Midian were

of old delivered into the hand of the chosen three
hundred, so, even now, it may be, and our country
may yet be saved. The age of heroic deeds is not
gone by. Charles Lowder has shown us what may
be done. It *cannot* be but that a ready answer will
be given to the voice, as of a trumpet-call, from
his grave : *Et nos vincamus aliquid !*—" Let us, too,
conquer something."

CONTENTS.

————

CHAPTER I.

1820–1840.

CHAPTER II.

1840–1851.

CHAPTER III.

1851.

CHAPTER IV.

1852–1857.

CHAPTER V.

1854, 1855.

CHAPTER VI.

1856.

CHAPTER VII.

CHAPTER VIII.

CHAPTER IX.

1856-1860.

CHARLES LOWDER.

CHAPTER I.

BIRTH AND EARLY YEARS.

1820-1840.

"Go, mark the matchless working of the Power
That shuts within the seed the future flower."

AMIDST the many problems discussed in public and in private there is one which, in some form or other, is continually brought forward by thoughtful Churchmen— "How to gain the masses of our population to the Church?"

Whether the practical results of such discussions have been anything but meagre may be doubted, but it is impossible to doubt the interest which the subject must possess for any Christian heart to whom the facts of the case have been brought home.

And therefore it may be well to record the life of one who did not in mere words discuss the question of converting our English heathen, but who solved it in action, and who, passing from amongst us, has left a Christianized population in the worst slums of London to be the living answer to the question about which so much is said and

B

written. He speaks to us, but only through patient action ; he has written for us, but his " epistle " is to be found in the souls and bodies rescued from degradation, " seen and known of all men."

Charles Fuge Lowder was born at 2, West Wing, Lansdown Crescent, Bath, on June 22, 1820, and was baptized the following month at the parish church of Walcot. He was the firstborn child of his parents, Charles and Susan Lowder. His grandfather, John Lowder, a retired naval officer, had, some time about the middle of the last century, bought a piece of ground on Lansdown Hill, Bath. There he built a house, to which he brought his family from Southampton.

This house, afterwards occupied by Mr. Beckford, the eccentric author of "Vathek," was the first beginning of Lansdown Crescent, then the highest inhabited part of the city. Here John Lowder spent the remainder of his life, and here he died in 1810, leaving a widow (daughter of Dr. Glass, a well-known Exeter physician) and several sons and daughters.

The youngest of the family was Charles, the comfort and delight of his widowed mother, whom he tended with dutiful love and care during the eleven years of her widowhood. Two years before her death he had married Susan, second daughter of Robert Fuge, of Plymouth ; and at the invitation of his great friend, Johnson Phillott (brother-in-law to his wife), he made his house their home until the birth of their firstborn child.

° This child had indeed an inheritance of rare goodness, as well as of personal comeliness.

I had opportunities of knowing his parents (writes one who in after years had indirectly some influence on the destinies of their son), and I have never known any who, under heavy trials, so perfectly exemplified the difficult character of "patient in tribulation."

There are few afflictions really harder to be borne without flinching in the face of our fellow-men, than the loss of wealth and worldly position, even when it comes without leaving any room for blame. Such an affliction befell Mr. and Mrs. Lowder at a moment when they were in the high day of health and vigorous usefulness, and in the full enjoyment of social popularity in Bath; but it remains with me still, as an abiding lesson which I shall never forget, how they both impressed me with their calm, unruffled gentleness of temper, and the sweet dignity of their resignation to the will of God. They were a remarkably "beautiful" couple, in that true sense of "beauty" which bespeaks nobility of character sanctified by grace, as well as in the ordinary sense of physical form; and no one could spend an hour in their company without feeling refreshed by intercourse with such good and winning people.

Mr. Lowder was partner in the Old Bath Bank, and a comparatively rich man; and his unwearied exertions to promote the welfare of others, especially of those whose circumstances were less happy than his own, had won for him in his native city the name of "the poor man's friend." And not undeservedly, for to the poor his thought, leisure, and money were ungrudgingly devoted, and in all benevolent efforts he received sympathy and encouragement from his wife.

Most good men have had good mothers, and have been encompassed by their prayers, and it is touching to read, in the light of her son's life, the daily prayer used by Mrs. Lowder for the yet unborn infant: "Bless it, O God, in mind as well as in body; endue it with an understanding capable of knowing Thee, with a heart strongly bent to fear Thee, and with all those holy and good dispositions that may make it always pleasing in Thy sight. Make me a joyful mother of a hopeful child, who may live to be an instrument of Thy glory, and by serving Thee faithfully and doing good in his generation may be received into Thine everlasting kingdom."

Thus she prayed for her child, and truly God gave her the petition which she asked of Him.

Before the birth of his eldest daughter, Mr. Lowder had made a home of his own at 9, West Wing, Lansdown Crescent, and here his three elder daughters were born. A fourth daughter was born in 1830; and in 1831 the family was completed by the arrival of a son, William Henry, who, coming after four girls, was welcomed by his elder brother with infinite satisfaction. On hearing the news, he insisted on the whole family marching in procession into the courtyard, where he ordered them to clap their hands in honour of the event.

Family affections seem to have had a more than common hold on Charles Lowder, and to have been, throughout his career, the softening influence of his life; and these affections were doubtless greatly fostered by the circumstances of his boyhood, families of relations both on his father's and mother's side being settled close around his home, all living on the most loving terms with each other, while a large circle of valued friends, many with young families growing up, supplied abundance of playfellows for the children. An old friend speaks of Charles, in these early days, as a " most sweet, bright, and courteous little fellow."

The careful moral and religious training given to their children by such parents as Mr. and Mrs. Lowder need hardly be mentioned; but there was this special advantage in their education, not so common then as now, that they were trained in *definite* religious principles. Their father, born in a time of Church laxity, and educated in a Moravian school, had, early in life, studied the claims of the Church of his baptism, and intelligently submitted himself to them ; and, his wife being of one mind with himself, their children were early imbued with fixed principles as to their religious position and privileges. Nor did any day pass without a Bible lesson from their mother, besides the too often neglected rule that some portion of Holy Scripture should daily be repeated by the children.

Charles was sent, at seven years old, to a day school kept by the Rev. Harvey Marriott, and soon after to a school kept by the Rev. Edward Simms in a farmhouse lately built in the Park, then being laid out at Bath.

One of his first letters shows the little boy's interest in politics, which became very keen in his youth and early manhood.

Bath, Aug. 5, 1829.

MY DEAR MAMMA,

I went to Mr. Simms's on Monday. I like him very well ; he wears his gown. We are to learn Cæsar and Greek Delectus, and to read Goldsmith's " History of Rome." O'Connell is to sit in Parliament.

Other letters show how eagerly the schoolboy read newspapers, and with what interest he followed the passing of the Emancipation Bill through Parliament, and the exciting public events connected with it. Later on, his energies in this line had full scope during the exciting election at Bath in 1838, when, after severe exertions made by his father and other members of their committee, two Conservative members were returned. Charles found very congenial occupation in bringing up the voters, and ran some risks, so great was the uproar on the occasion.

His bodily strength and activity kept pace with his mental growth; he was foremost in sports; and his sister recalls his "bright radiant face, as he marched out with his schoolfellows, armed with wooden swords, to defend or attack 'The Lion's Den,' in the pretty little village of Charlecombe, near Bath."

After a few months at Bruton School, he passed, in 1835, to King's College, London, of which Dr. Major was then Head Master. When consulted after a time by Mr. Lowder as to the advisability of preparing Charles for a University education, Dr. Major wrote of "the steadiness of character and fixedness of principle, based," he adds, "I am convinced, upon a firmer foundation than mere human strength, which will enable him to resist successfully the temptations with which that career may be beset."

There can be no doubt that his character had been greatly strengthened by his confirmation, which had taken place in October, 1836, just as he entered the senior department of King's College; and in after years he referred to it as marking an important era in his spiritual life.

The honourable position which he won at his final examination proves that he must have used his natural abilities well and conscientiously while a student at King's College.

You will be happy to hear (Dr. Major wrote to his father) that your son stands *first* in theological subjects, second in classics, sixth in mathematics, second in German, and ranks among the most distinguished in Professor Dale's department (English literature).

He had the advantage, while in the College, of being brought into contact with distinguished men, who succeeded each other as principals—Hugh James Rose and Dr. Lonsdale, afterwards the venerable Bishop of Lichfield.

Charles left King's College in 1839, and was rewarded for his steady perseverance while there by being allowed to make his first acquaintance with the Continent. Very early letters discover the passion that remained with him through life, to be his greatest refreshment at intervals of hardest work—the intense love for and enjoyment of fine scenery. And now a little trip to Belgium, in the summer of 1839, in company with his father and an old friend, was the first of a long series of interesting and sometimes important tours, ending with that which brought his whole earthly pilgrimage to a close.

In February, 1840, he entered at Exeter College, Oxford, of which Dr. Richards was then rector, and Mr. William Sewell one of the tutors. In the previous year, he had tried for a scholarship at University College, to which the following letter refers :—

MY DEAR BROWNE,*
    It is due to you as well as to Mr. Lowder that I should send you a few lines to say that he acquitted himself with

* Now Archdeacon of Bath, then Classical Professor at King's College, London.

great credit in the course of his examination for our scholarship, though his competitors were too strong for him. He performed most of his exercises in a manner which did him great credit. We were so much pleased with his examination and his general demeanour, that we offered to admit him and give him his rooms next Easter if he wished to reside so early, and I should have been very glad to have had him a member of this College. But his destination was already fixed at Exeter. We were obliged to you for sending us so good a candidate.

Yours very truly,

F. C. PLUMPTRE.

Charles Lowder came to Oxford when the Tractarian movement was in its very flower and vigorous freshness, and was amongst those on whom it worked most powerfully. The three great leaders were in the prime of their labours and influence : Mr. Keble was Professor of Poetry, Dr. Pusey was startling the University by his sermons and incisive teaching of forgotten or overclouded truths, and the hermit of Littlemore held spellbound and fascinated the students who weekly thronged St. Mary's to hear from him what he had learned and received himself in the silence of prayer and study. Their teaching was no novelty to Charles, but rather the strengthening and filling in of outlines already familiar.

He mentions a sermon of Dr. Pusey's on " The Duty and Benefits of Fasting " as "containing much good advice to those who were endeavouring for the first time to act up to the principles which the Church has laid down for the present season."

A few sentences may be given from another letter, as anticipating the consistent practice of the future priest in his after life :—

I heard a most excellent sermon yesterday from Newman ; the text was from St. Jude, "These are spots in your feasts of charity." "A danger of the present time," Newman said, "arose from what might be called the *luxury of religion.*" None could rejoice more than the preacher himself at the increased regard to ecclesiastical architecture, music, the ornamenting of our churches, etc., but still it must be recollected that these required to be accompanied by *personal holiness*, and that even the spirit of devotion might become little better than a luxurious pleasure, unless we maintained a spirit of self-denial in it, to remind us that we are not to make everything so much a gratification to ourselves, as a sacrifice to God.

The consistent practice of Charles Lowder was, indeed, a meet outcome of such instruction ; for his mind seems to have seized upon and assimilated whatever bore on the necessity for self-sacrifice as the only true and right result of more than ordinary means of grace.

He writes of having been especially impressed by a sermon of Archdeacon Manning, "On the Danger of Sinning amid Religious Privileges ;" and another sermon of Manning's * seems to have sunk very deeply into his heart and memory. Indeed, his life was but the working out of its concluding sentences :—

The Church asks not for yours only, but for *you*. This is the return she would demand for your spiritual nurture here, that you give up *yourselves ;* it is your *own selves* that she requires. You must expect to labour in season and out of season, trials, crosses, disappointments, the opposition of enemies, the lukewarmness of friends, slights and misconstructions, ingratitude and rebuke. But all these are light things compared to that heavy load of responsibility which every minister of God has laid upon him, viz. to answer for the souls of his flock. Great, then, is the probation

* On St. John xviii. 16.

here of those who would take upon them these sacred functions, but great shall be the reward hereafter of all who, in meekness and singleness of heart, aiming only at God's glory and the salvation of souls, put their hand to the plough, and, with God's grace resting on their endeavours, desire not to look back.

CHAPTER II.

"The end proves all, and that is still to come."

THE first year of Charles Lowder's residence at Oxford was marked by the publication of Tract XC., and the next by the suspension of Dr. Pusey.

On the latter subject he writes to his father—

I think the present persecution of Dr. Pusey may all turn out for the best, for even moderate men cannot deny the gross injustice of condemning him unheard. It is generally believed that the Board could come to no collective judgment, for they differ from one another in their views, and so the Vice-Chancellor has no reason to give for his sentence. Wall has taken a very active part, and I was talking to him yesterday about it, just after the Vice had sent him an answer to the Requisition, viz. that he could not assign any reasons. The sermon will be published to-morrow, and so the heresy, if there is any, will spread like wild-fire. I heard it at Christ Church, but did not remark anything objectionable, but of course I cannot be answerable for hearing all that he said or understanding it.

Whilst thus interesting himself deeply in the movement to the practical results of which amongst the heathen of London he gave his life, Charles was diligently reading ;

relaxing himself meanwhile by long walks, rowing, and the society of friends. With his high spirits, popular manners, and thorough enjoyment of innocent amusements, it was indeed well that he had never lost sight of the serious aspect of life and of its duties, and that he had early desired to devote himself wholly to God's service as a priest of His Church. For before half his Oxford career had passed, a severe and searching trial befell him and his family in the failure of the Old Bath Bank, in which his father was a partner. Although it was caused by misplaced confidence in others, and not the slightest reflection was cast on the integrity of any of the partners, yet the fact remained that the bank had failed and that the means of providing for their families were gone.

Universal sympathy was felt and abundantly expressed at so unlooked-for a calamity.

All who know you (one friend wrote to Mr. Lowder) grieve indeed that your generous confidence in others should have been so deceived, whilst they justly exonerate yourselves from blame.

If (says another) in the hour of trial it be a consolation to know that you possess the esteem, the love, and the confidence of all to whom you are known, you have that consolation in the highest degree.

Nor were the expressions of sympathy confined to words; most generous and delicate acts accompanied them. An old family friend, who had been proved in joy and sorrow and never found wanting, requested that he might undertake the charge of enabling Charles to conclude his University education, at the same time offering a home to the whole family till future plans could be considered and matured.

Charles himself proved to be an apt scholar in learning the lesson of courage and Christian patience afforded by his parents' example. There is no trace in his letters at the time of any irritating or crushing effect from this reverse, but rather every token of the wise and religious spirit in which he accepted it, consoling his parents, and manifesting the desire which never left him of becoming the support and mainstay of his family.

I doubt not (he writes) that if we are spared to look back on the trials which it is now our lot to go through, we may think these the happiest, because the most instructive, days of our life. . . . Although, from circumstances, we were not thrown into pleasures and amusements which would keep all sober reflections from our minds, yet still there were many habits which one quiet routine of duty would engender, not altogether consistent with the feelings which a Christian should always keep uppermost in his mind, viz. that he is but a stranger and a pilgrim upon earth. . . . I think therefore that we may learn to acknowledge the wisdom of God, who, in this important period of our lives, has taught us not to look here for a certain abiding-place.

Through the kindness of the friend who was maintaining him at College, Charles spent the Long Vacation of 1842 with a reading party at Heidelberg ; denying himself, in order to save travelling expenses in England, the pleasure of seeing his family, who were then living at Chudleigh, near Exeter.

His father writes to him—

Chudleigh, June 21, 1842.

It is fitting, my dearest Charles, that you should receive a father's blessing on your birthday. May God bless and preserve you, and keep you ever in holy living, and by His grace fit you for holy dying whenever that solemn hour come upon you. May your intended travels be both agreeable and instructive, and may the great object which you have in view in this excursion be completely accomplished, viz. the attainment of honours in your academical career, in order that you may more successfully minister in God's Church, and thereby promote His glory on earth and the temporal and eternal welfare of man. This is the sincere prayer of

YOUR AFFECTIONATE FATHER.

After three months' steady reading Charles returned to Oxford, and from thence writes to his mother—

I now feel quite settled down to work, for though there was not a very long interval between leaving our books at Heidelberg and taking them up again here, yet our journey home was a break which I think we really required; for a pretty steady application for three months tells upon you, and really demands a little rest. I look forward to my next break, though not with impatience, as there is something to be done before it, but with the pleasant anticipation of seeing you all again, for I have never been absent from you so long as from April to Christmas. Mr. Willis has been up here, and I have been engaged in going about with him. We walked over to Littlemore yesterday, as he wanted to see Newman, who took us into the chapel.

At Easter, 1843, he took his degree, and, after most despondent forebodings, he was not displeased to find his name in the "classical list" among the second-class men.

My rooms (he wrote) look out on the schools, so I could see the men collecting as the time drew near for the list to come out, but I could not muster up courage enough to go and wait for it myself. . . . When from the cheering and running off with the news, I saw that the list had come out, my heart began to beat rather more quickly than usual, but at last, when I saw Powles running towards my lodgings, I thought it must be all right, and so it proved.

Of course (he adds), it is a great relief to my mind that I have got some substantial proof that I have not wasted my time up here, and that I have turned my reading to good account. All our dons are well pleased, as we have one first and three seconds from Exeter.

Later on, alluding to his appearance in the fourth class for mathematics, he thus accounts for it :—

I hoped that I had succeeded in taking my name off altogether, but having unfortunately done two questions, they must needs give me a fourth, much to my disgust.

After obtaining so honourable a position in classics, he was advised to try for a College Fellowship.

You may easily fancy (he writes) that I am quite sick of examinations; luckily, on the present occasion I do not feel very anxious, except to acquit myself well in the eyes of the College. I do not feel that I have any chance, as there are several good men in for it.

The disappointment, consequently, was not severe when he found that the present Lord Chief Justice (Lord Coleridge) was the successful candidate.

Soon after taking his degree, he accepted the offer of a title for deacon's orders from Lord John Thynne, Rector of Walton-cum-Street, near Glastonbury, and Sub-Dean of Westminster, who required his curate to be also tutor to his three sons; and on September 24, 1843, he received deacon's orders from the Bishop (Denison) of Salisbury (ordaining for the infirm Bishop of Bath and Wells), and at once began his duties at Walton.

In his first letter from thence to his father, he writes—

It was a great comfort to me, I assure you, in taking upon myself the solemn vows which I have just done, to think that I not only shared in the prayers of the Church in general with those who were with me admitted to this office in the Church, but that there were also many friends and families by whom I was more especially called to mind, and commended to the guidance of God's Holy Spirit. It required indeed such an assurance to support me in the thought of the great responsibility which particularly in the present state of the Church) is laid upon the shoulders of its ministers, and I can only pray and desire the prayers of others also, that the same Holy Spirit who has led me to seek this office, may give me grace, in the words of St. Paul, so to use that office that I may purchase to myself a good degree.

In the same letter he describes his first entrance on his public clerical duties, which (on the first Sunday) consisted in reading prayers and preaching and taking a funeral in the evening.

Entering on his tutorial duties in his usual bright and happy temper, he writes, after a little experience—

I am going on very pleasantly, and like my prospects much. I had no idea I should feel so well disposed towards my tutoring, but having nice boys to deal with makes a great difference.

His fellow-curate at Street was Mr. Merriman, now the venerable Bishop of Grahamstown, who was then preparing himself for his devoted missionary labours in South Africa. His example and conversation were contagious, and exercised a life-long influence on the younger curate, whose own distinct desire for mission work may be dated from this time. This desire grew and strengthened with years, and, as we shall see, caused him on more than one occasion great searchings of heart before he could decide on his path of duty. The zeal which he would so willingly have employed in foreign lands was, however, to be concentrated on the teeming thousands of his native land, and the large sympathies of his heart were to find their vent in the unattractive slums of the great Babylon of England.

So earnestly, however, had he set his mind on missionary labour that, after a few months at Walton, he proposed to his family that they should all emigrate to New Zealand, and work there as a Christian family for their maintenance, while he should devote himself, under the noble Bishop of that new diocese, to the spiritual duties of his calling. It was (as Mr. Ernest Hawkins, the energetic Secretary to the S.P.G., remarked in answer to the proposal) a novel one. " I see no difficulty," he added, " but in the means of support, though this is a serious one ; nevertheless I would urge you not hastily to give up the plan, which seems a most wise and Christian one."

The scheme was submitted to the Rev. J. H. Pinder, then Principal of the Theological College at Wells, an interested and valued friend, who gave it his approval ; and Archdeacon Brymer of Bath wrote an introductory letter to Bishop Selwyn, setting forth the qualifications of his old friend Mr. Lowder, senior, either for educational or agricultural duties in a new colony.

Some extracts from a long letter addressed to the old family friend before mentioned, will best express Charles's motives in proposing the scheme :—

I have now for some time felt a growing desire to engage in missionary labours. The more I reflected on the subject, the more I felt what a vast field of labour lay before us in Christianizing our colonial possessions—what need there was, not merely

of money and resources, but of labourers in the Lord's vineyard,
and that, however insufficient the present number of clergy in our
own country may appear, and really is, for the wants of the population, yet that in the colonies, whose interests, both religious and
political, we are bound by all the ties of duty to protect, the
deficiency is most awful.   With these views, I could not but
desire to offer my poor services in the great work.   I feel that it
is the highest sphere of duty to which a clergyman can be called,
far from the temptations to ease, luxury, and seeking for pre-
ferment which surround him in this country, and affording opportunity for the entire devotion of all his mental and physical
powers to the service of his Master.   But entertaining as I did
most sincerely these feelings, which I cannot but think were
implanted in my mind by God's grace, I also reflected that I was
not, in the peculiar circumstances of my family, free to entertain
them.   I remembered that I had a plain, straightforward duty
to them; that, as long as I had it in my power, it would be my
duty and happiness to share with them whatever means of support
the Almighty might see fit to afford me.   It was not with me a
mere *family affection*, which it would perhaps have become me to
forget in the thought of the higher duty which I owed to God,
but whether I was not bound to turn my labours to the best
account in England, consistent with my ordination vows, in order
to afford them the *means of support*.   I felt the force of this
latter consideration, and therefore endeavoured to stifle my
missionary desires, which, I can assure you, was a source of great
pain and no little difficulty to me.   The thought, however, at last
suggested itself that my father and the rest of my family might
be not unwilling to engage in similar labours according to their
several abilities, and I felt how much assistance they might afford
in carrying out the object I had so much at heart.   I accordingly
proposed it to them; my father and mother both consented, the
former entering into it most warmly, as well as Susan and Mary.
After due consideration, we determined to make an application to
the Secretary of the S.P.G., who encouraged our views and advised

us to make them known to the Bishop of New Zealand. This I have done, and we now await the result of our application.

It can be easily understood that a scheme of this nature did not commend itself to all members of the family, and one especially, whose excellent judgment always carried great weight, saw many practical and prudential objections to its accomplishment. To him Charles writes—

Prospects must not be confounded with duties ; every one has a right to give up his worldly expectations, provided he injures no one but himself by so doing; nor can I subscribe to the principle which I have heard maintained, that those only who have no prospects in England should go out as missionaries. May we not be allowed—indeed, are we not called upon?—to make sacrifices, and does it not increase confidence in the purity of our motives to feel that we are not consulting private ends in the course we adopt? I cannot, then, but believe that, as far as I am myself concerned, I have a perfect right to give up my own worldly expectations, and I feel the highest pleasure in being able to do so in behalf of so holy a cause. . . . The reasonable prospect of making ourselves useful will, I doubt not, support us through many trials, and if, by God's grace, we may be made the instruments of turning others to salvation, what greater reward can be desired? It has proved sufficient to rouse the energies of many before us who will be noble examples for our imitation, and may we not hope to follow in the same path? Though I trust it may please God to smooth the way for the accomplishment of this object which we have so much at heart, of course it must depend on the encouragement which the Bishop gives us whether New Zealand be our destination.

Considering the amount of thought and anxiety which this scheme must necessarily have occasioned to its origi-nator, and this in addition to his constant daily work with

pupils and parish, it is not surprising that the strain should
have told on mind and body.

After some months he writes that he is "feeling unequal to his duties," and ás the conclusion of his diaconate
is drawing near, and he cannot obtain a title for priest's
orders at Walton, he wishes to resign his duties there, and
take some temporary work till the expected answer from
the Bishop of New Zealand shall arrive. The result was
that he applied for, and obtained, the office of Chaplain
to the Axbridge Workhouse, the Bishop consenting, as a
favour, to accept the position as a title for priest's orders.

Although the connection between the young pastor and
his flock at Walton had been of such brief duration, he had
succeeded in winning much sincere affection, and the severance was not effected without painful emotions on both
sides.

I felt much (he writes) at leaving. I had doleful partings with
parishioners, and I trust I have left many who will pray for my
future welfare.

This hope was fully realized, for to the end of his life
his visits to Walton were heartily welcomed by all who
ould remember the time when the young deacon began
his ministerial duties among them. In his first Rector, also,
and his family, he found true friends through life. Lord
John Thynne, writing seven years later about Charles's
application for work in London, says—

So far as I know, and can speak with certainty of any other
person, I believe Mr. C. F. Lowder to be a sound English Churchman, and I have much respect for him.

And as late as June, 1881, the present Rector of Walton-cum-Street, Mr. Hickley, replies to an inquiry for any traditions about his short career there—

There is no memorial of Father Lowder's work at Street or Walton. The old people here remembered him kindly, and he used to visit them when he came to see us. I have only heard one saying respecting him, that he used to say prayer in church by himself on the week-day : no small thing for a young curate forty years ago. From that acorn grew St. Peter's, London Docks.

Before entering on his new duties, Charles received priest's orders in Wells Cathedral (December 22, 1844), Bishop Denison, of Salisbury, again acting for Bishop Law. During the incapacity of this aged prelate, his son, Chancellor Law, was acting as Commissary and residing at Wells, and it devolved upon him to offer hospitality to the candidates for Holy Orders who came to Wells. But from the circumstance that Mr. and Mrs. Lowder had undertaken the charge of the Bishop in his infirmity, the Chancellor had many other opportunities of seeing and forming an opinion of their son. He writes, some time after, of the "high promise" which Charles gave at the time of his ordination, and expresses a desire that he might " be placed in some position where his talents and worth might be fully drawn out and exercised."

After his ordination, the young priest at once entered heartily upon his new duties, which, though only meant to be temporary, were diligently discharged. The improvement of the workhouse schools was his special care. He began the practice of public catechising, useful to old as well as to young, and in all ways laboured to reach the hearts of a class whose circumstances required much patience and love.

His resignation of the Axbridge Chaplaincy was
hastened by the death, in September, 1845, of Bishop Law,
which relieved Charles's parents from the charge, for
three years tenderly and assiduously fulfilled, of tending
his declining age ; and although Chancellor Law was most
anxious that the family should settle near him, yet it was
judged more desirable that the eldest son should now be
allowed to accomplish his wish of making a home for them
himself.

The Rev. James Frampton, Vicar of Tetbury, in the
diocese of Gloucester, was just then in want of a Senior
Curate.   Charles Lowder accepted this curacy, and the old
Vicarage House became for the next five years the happy
home of the once more united family.   He went up to
Oxford to take his M.A. degree, at the beginning of 1846,
and immediately afterwards took possession of his new
home.

Tetbury is an old-fashioned country town, with about
3000 inhabitants, perched on the tops of the Cotswolds, in
Gloucestershire, bare and bleak, with stone walls separating
the fields instead of hedges.   It has a history dating back
to ancient British times, and the old names are still attached
to certain divisions of the town.   The church (St. Mary's),
just opposite the Vicarage windows, is a large lantern-like
building, with the old tower and graceful spire of its predecessor remaining.

In a letter dated January 16, 1846, the new curate
writes—

I slept in my own house for the first time yesterday, which
is an era in one's life, and to-day I managed a little visiting of the
sick, so I shall get my hand in by degrees.

He did indeed "get his hand well in," not only in visiting the sick—a duty ever most conscientiously and tenderly
fulfilled—but in all parts of the priestly office. Young and
old, rich and poor, felt his influence, and were stirred by his
zeal. His visits to the schools were regular and his teaching systematic, and both teachers and scholars welcomed
him with pleasure. He took great pains in preparing the
young for Confirmation and Holy Communion, teaching
them both in classes and by individual intercourse. Many
were brought to the Sacraments who, from ignorance or
scruples, had been deterred. In one instance the family of
a leading tradesman were all admitted to Baptism at the
same time, through his teaching and influence. In the
public services one improvement followed another ; and
when a beautiful little chapel-of-ease (St. Saviour's) was built
by the Vicar, in 1848, daily matins and evensong were
introduced.

For several years the Senior Curate had as his coadjutor
an earnest priest, the Rev. T. L. Williams, now Rector of
Porthleven in Cornwall, who was like-minded with himself
in desiring to bring Church teaching and practice more and
more fully before the people; and Tetbury people still look
back to this time as one of the brightest and most pro-
gressive in their recollection. He drew up for their use a
little book, which has been found useful elsewhere. "The
Penitent's Path" was intended to supersede a favourite
manual much in use, but whose teaching was the reverse of
orthodox. Accordingly, this is arranged as much as possible
on the same plan, while conveying sound Church teaching.

Amongst those who, besides parishioners, look back
with pleasure and thankfulness to those Tetbury days, may

be mentioned his sister's pupils, some of whom he prepared for Confirmation. Others, too young at that time to be thus specially brought under his spiritual influence, were yet not too young to remember with gratitude his bright, cheery ways with them, nor his playful kindness.

I remember so clearly about Tetbury (writes one of these), and the first time I saw that beautiful, noble, kind face. He was not only a perfect saint in his life, but he was so good to little children, and full of kind playfulness towards them. I remember how he used to amuse Carrie and me in that old orchard ; and all the time he was leading a life of holiness quite different to other men.

His love of children was a characteristic feature all his life. As a lad at school, he used to print letters in large type, that his little brother might have the pleasure of reading them himself, and entered into all his childish interests. Even babes were quiet and happy in his arms, and at the infant schools the little ones flocked round him while he played with them. In the school treats and excursions he was ever the ruling spirit, full of joyous life himself, and shedding brightness on all around. "God made flowers and children," he would say, "to make the world beautiful ;" and his love for both never cooled. To the last he had a child's love for gathering flowers, but then it was to send them to those who had seldom a chance of seeing them grow in the fields.

No wonder that children were devoted to such a friend, and that the most pathetic incident in that last sad, wonderful scene was the grief of the little children who helped to swell the sobbing multitude lining the streets of St. Peter's parish on the funeral day.

Some time after the family had been fairly settled at Tetbury, each member having taken up work in the parish as well as at home, the expected answer arrived from the Bishop of New Zealand. Circumstances had quite changed since the application was first made, and even if this had not been the case, the Bishop's answer as to *financial* prospects (an important matter where so many were concerned) was so discouraging, that no room was left for regret that a settled home had meanwhile been provided in England. Bishop Selwyn cordially thanked his correspondent for his offer of help in that far-off diocese, but he felt himself in duty bound frankly to set forth the very uncertain condition of his own financial position, " being by no means sure," he writes, " that I may not be obliged to betake myself to the plough for the maintenance of myself and my family."

Charles plainly saw that this particular scheme could not be carried out, but his missionary zeal was by no means abated ; and when, in the following year, an offer was made to him by the Bishop of Cape Town to take the charge of Port Natal—" a most spiritually destitute place, but a most promising opening for missionary labours "—he felt it necessary to consult a friend, who knew his circumstances and who also knew by experience what mission work is, before he could make up his mind to decline the offer.

If (he says) my parents were in prosperity, and consented to my going, I should feel at liberty to do so ; but I fear very much lest my own feelings on the subject should lead me to forget positive duties at home, and it is therefore that I so much desire the counsel of one who can look calmly upon it. You know that I have long felt a great desire for missionary employment, and this, instead of diminishing, has become stronger and stronger : and I have always hoped and prayed that if it were right for me to undertake it, it would be providentially pointed out, and the feeling has grown upon me that it would be. The present offer was made quite without my seeking it, as I had no idea that Merriman would mention me to the Bishop, and therefore I the rather desire to be taught if this must be considered as a call.

As before, he yielded up his inclinations to the judgment of those whom he considered better able than himself to decide, and the post was declined. Looking back over the history of the then infant colony, we can see how much suffering he was spared in having escaped the episcopal authority of Bishop Colenso.

The Bishop (Monk) of Gloucester at this time offered him the living of St. James's, Gloucester, but on inquiring he found that the position required a man of means to keep the very excellent schools in an efficient manner ; and besides this objection, there being no house for the Incumbent, he felt obliged to decline it.

The great interest which he took in education led him to seek, in 1849, the recently founded office of Government Inspector of Schools ; but this he failed to obtain, in spite of letters of high recommendation both from his Bishop and Vicar, and he remained at Tetbury for two years more before the call came which was to lead him to that wide field of missionary work in "the largest heathen city in the world, except in China," to which the rest of his life was to be given.

CHAPTER III.

1851.

"Meet is it changes should controul
Our being,—lest we rust at ease."

IN after years, giving some account of his work, Charles
Lowder wrote : *—

There are a few personal matters, which the writer thinks it
well to mention here, as they may help to show how the missionary idea first grew in his mind. He remembers well, as
Curate of a country town in Gloucestershire in 1851, reading one
evening by the fireside the account of the farewell of the Incumbent of St. Paul's and St. Barnabas', the touching words which
he spoke, and the sad leave-taking of his much-loving flock.
The whole history was not to be read carelessly, or reflected
upon without many burning thoughts. Those which arose in his
mind were of deep sorrow for the parish which had lost so devoted a priest, of prayer that his place might be supplied by one
who would faithfully carry on his work, and of ardent longing that
if it were God's will he might be permitted to take a part, however humble, in aiding such an object.

He felt that, in his own parish, he had reached the end of his
tether; after nearly six years of parochial labour, he could not

* " Twenty-one Years in St. George's Mission."

induce his Vicar to move further in advance, and St. Barnabas' offered a most inviting field for more congenial work. Here the experiment of winning the poor to the Catholic faith by careful teaching and services was being successfully tried, and proved the soundness of the system which Mr. Bennett originated in that parish, and which, by a remarkable Providence, was, in spite of all opposition, maintained and perpetuated.

There was another who, at the very time these prayers for St. Barnabas' filled Mr. Lowder's heart, was equally full of desire and prayer for help in the same work :

" To each unknown his brother's prayer."

It is just thirty years ago (he writes) when I was permitted to share with Mr. R. Liddell the honour of introducing Lowder to the diocese of London. In March, 1851, Mr. Bennett had been driven from his post, as he expressed it, by the Prime Minister who had temporal authority, by the Bishop who had spiritual authority, and by the *Times* and the mob who had no authority ; and Mr. Liddell, his successor, determining to live at S. Paul's, committed the charge of St. Barnabas' to me.

A few months' experience of the difficulties, not to say dangers, of the position convinced me that it would not be possible to meet them without the opportunity (which Mr. Liddell's generosity at once conceded) of choosing the men who would co-operate with me in the work.

To an advertisement which Mr. Skinner accordingly put out, he received, with many others, the following answer :—

Highbury Park, St. Barnabas' Day, 1851.

REVEREND SIR,

Having been away from home, I only saw your advertisement in the *Guardian* yesterday, and I take the earliest opportunity of placing myself in communication with you.

I have been for nearly five years and a half the Senior Curate of a country town of more than three thousand in population, the chief pastoral duties of which, including preaching, parochial visiting, the care of souls, etc., have devolved upon myself, aided by another Curate, in consequence of the weak health of my Vicar, who is, however, resident. During that time daily service, the Holy Communion twice a month in the two churches, and other services have been commenced or continued. I am particularly desirous of entering upon no other sphere of duty where at least the same privileges are not offered to the parish, and ·I should prefer an increase. . . .

My opinions are perhaps best expressed, as we must use terms of distinction in these days, by the name of Anglo-Catholic, being decidedly those of firm attachment to the Church of England, with the earnest hope of being an humble instrument in bringing her Catholic character more closely home to the hearts of her members. . . .

Although I have entered into this detail, yet I must now explain that I am only placing myself in communication with you, without making a formal application for the curacy advertised ; as I should only resign my present charge with the hope of entering upon a more important and promising sphere of labour, and should probably sacrifice pecuniary advantage in a change, my present stipend being much larger than that of most Curates.

I should mention that my present curacy is that of Tetbury, Gloucestershire ; my Vicar's name, the Rev. J. Frampton ; but as I have not given him any notice of leaving, I should not wish him written to before I had heard again from you as to the circum_stances of your parish, and the probability of a wish on your part to form an engagement.

I might, in that case, also refer you to a former Rector, the Rev. Lord John Thynne, Sub-dean of Westminster, Archdeacons Brymer of Bath, and Thorpe of Bristol, and the Rev. J. H. Pinder, Principal of the Theological College, Wells.

I remain, reverend sir, yours faithfully,

C. F. LOWDER.

In a letter to his sister, written June 19, he mentions that he had answered an advertisement in the *Guardian* (on St. Barnabas' Day), "not knowing that it referred to St. Barnabas'," and that he received "a letter from Mr. Skinner, the senior and responsible Curate of St. Barnabas'," in reply. This letter was quickly followed by an interview, as Mr. Lowder was in London, and it was arranged that he should take part in the services at St. Barnabas' on the following Sunday.

I remember, as if it were yesterday (Mr. Skinner writes), the impression made upon me by his striking (even then) almost hairless head and radiant face, with the bloom upon it which bespeaks purity of soul. I felt at once—"Here is the very man we want." The testimony of his work, from that day to this, is all the evidence needed to prove that the rapidly formed impression was true.

This impression was confirmed by letters from several friends, notably from Lord John Thynne and from Mr. Pinder, Principal of the Theological College at Wells, who wrote of his "having known Charles Lowder from boyhood," and of his belief that, "under the guidance which he will meet with, he will prove a valuable helper in parochial work." His letter ends with the prayer, which was indeed answered—

"May it please God to overrule your communication with him to the best interests of our Church, and to the usefulness of my young friend."

It is impossible not to be struck, in looking over the letters written about Mr. Lowder at this time, by the *confidence* with which he seems to have universally inspired those who knew him, and which is not common in the case of a young man whose sympathies were all with a school antagonistic to popular Protestantism, and even to safe and easy-going Churchmanship.

Archdeacon Thorpe, of Bristol, writing to Mr. Skinner to "welcome him with best wishes and earnest prayers into his new and responsible position," mentions Charles Lowder, and expresses his "strong conviction that he is very particularly suited to the place proposed for him." He adds—

I scarcely know on what grounds I can speak so decidedly. I believe it is from what I knew of him before, and what I have heard of him from many different quarters.

To Charles himself Mr. Pinder wrote—

Southsea, Hants, July 4, 1851.

MY DEAR CHARLES,

I concluded from the letter addressed to me by Mr. Skinner that the situation would probably be offered you, and it gave me very great pleasure to add my testimony in your behalf. Judging from the opinions expressed by him, I cannot imagine a more desirable person to act with and under—one who would not consider the essence of religion to be in a lighted candle or a surplice, but one who, by bringing his people's minds to the reverence and love of Christ's Church, or Christ in His Church, will, no doubt, in due time find from them a ready co-operation in all things tending to order in the service.

I greatly honour Mr. Bennett, but I would have yielded the point to my Bishop. I may be wrong.

Pray let me hear what the plan of your mother and sisters is. Knowing the intensely domestic character of your good father, I can easily understand how great the trial of separation has been to him, and I shall like to hear all their plans. I would humbly

hope in God (referring to the Exeter Synod) that this new
symptom of life in our Church will stay the impatient spirits,
who have been looking to Rome for security, and make them
pause and learn yet to love their Church as she deserves. . . .

Believe me, ever yours very sincerely,

JOHN H. PINDER.

To his mother Charles writes—

London, St. John Baptist's Day, 1851.

. . . It was a great comfort to me, while assisting in the
beautiful services of one of the most beautiful churches in England,
to think that I was joining in prayer on my birthday with those
who, I doubt not, were praying for me.   I enjoyed above description the hearty and devotional character of the services, and took
part by singing the Litany in the morning, assisting at Holy Communion, and saying part of the prayers afternoon and evening.
I have now just returned from preaching there, and I believe Mr.
Skinner and myself are mutually satisfied one with the other.   It
quite rests now with the answer which I shall make after consulting with you and my sisters, whether I have the privilege of joining
in the great work which is being carried on at St. Barnabas' or no.

His mother's choice was soon made.   Neither she nor
any of hers could bear to stand in the way of the work
upon which her son's heart was set.   They arranged to
live at Enfield ; Charles became one of the curates at
St. Barnabas', and went into residence at the college on
September 30, 1851.

This is not a history of St. Barnabas' Church and
College, yet it is necessary to say a few words as to the
state of matters there while Mr. Lowder was on its staff,
since it was the school in which he learned to use those
weapons which he afterwards wielded with signal success

during his long battle with vice, ignorance, and misery in the east of London.

It would be impossible to do this with any accuracy, were it not for the kindness with which correspondence on the subject has been placed at the writer's disposal, and the information supplied by those who kept St. Barnabas', through the burden and heat of those troublous days, as a stronghold of faith and devotion.

In 1851 (the then Senior Curate writes) St. Barnabas' was at the head of the movement. The success of Mr. Bennett's work in Belgravia, of which it was the fruit; the *éclat* of its consecration festival the year before; the novelty of its constitution, administered by a college of clergy and choristers living in community, with multiplied services day by day; the free and open access to it for rich and poor, the beauty and symmetry of its structure and furniture, and the perfection of its music, had combined to make it an object of public attraction, in a year, too, in which the first "Great Exhibition" brought the world to London.

But among those who were drawn to it by mere curiosity and love of excitement, there were many who came with avowed feelings of hatred and hostility; and during the whole of that memorable year it was only held, as a beleaguered city is held, by armed men, against the violence of enemies who battered at the doors, shouted through the windows, hissed in the aisles, and essayed to storm the chancel gates.

It is not without difficulty, at this present time of writing, that I bring myself to believe that such experience of the Puritan *furor* as fell to my lot in 1851 could really be possible.

The moment of the papal aggression was the lucky occasion for which some had been anxiously seeking to make a deadly onslaught upon the restored propriety of our English public worship. The butler of the Irvingite Apostle, Mr. Henry Drummond, was the ringleader of the malcontents. And Lord

D

Shaftesbury unhappily contributed to the fray by announcing, at an excited public meeting in the parish, that he would prefer worshipping "with Lydia by the banks of the river side" to joining in such services as ours, while another leader made pious declaration of his conviction that our church had mistaken its patron saint in choosing the Apostle Barnabas rather than the robber Barabbas, to whom we more properly belonged.

No doubt the disturbance had reached its climax on Sundays, November 10, 17, 24, 1850, when the poor and the timid were actually driven by bodily terror from worshipping at St. Barnabas' altogether, and the religious people of the district were so horri- fied by the blasphemous cries of the mob, that they were fain to keep within their houses.

But in 1851, when Mr. Bennett had already been sacrificed and cast out, as a "sop to Cerberus," the spirit of unreasoning Puri- tanism was as unsatisfied as ever; and the excited passions of the multitude continued to be employed by interested people, all through the spring and summer of that year, to make our position as dangerous and difficult as it could be made. It was only by keeping a large body of gentlemen—regular members of our flock —on the roll of sworn special constables, that we were enabled to preserve order during divine service; and Sunday after Sunday we had to post some chosen ones by the chancel gates, to prevent the ringleaders from breaking into the sanctuary.

The notion of any place in the church being reserved as specially sacred, much more of being barred off, for the special accommodation of the clergy and other ministers, was abhorrent to the general mind of those unruly people. It was a strange thing to see how the spirit of disorder seized upon many persons, apparently good and earnest in their way, and forced them into the ranks of the rioters, as if only for disorder's sake; even clergymen were often amongst the most troublesome. The most difficult thing was to persuade people to sit down when their appointed seats were shown to them. Some loudly protested against dividing the sexes; others claimed a right to perambulate the church, to examine the painted windows, and criticize the Latin legends which enriched the walls.

On one occasion a respectable Irish clergyman sought me out in the vestry, and, in great anger, appealed to me against one of the vergers, who, he said, had insulted him by imputing to him "ignorance of the Greek alphabet." I begged him to tell me how the Greek alphabet had anything to do with his refusal to be seated during divine service, which was the verger's complaint against him.

"Well, sir," he answered, "it was just this way: Being in London for the Exhibition, I came to see St. Barnabas'; and if I had taken a seat, I wouldn't have seen it a bit; so I just wanted to walk round, through the crowd, and examine it at my ease. This man here kept harrying me about taking a seat; and then I said to him plainly, 'Are you not ashamed of yourselves to be worshipping the Virgin Mary here? For there,' said I (pointing to the keystone of the chancel arch)—'aren't they the very letters, V. M.?' 'No,' said he, '*we* are ashamed of nothing here; but it's *you*, and the like of you, that should be ashamed, not to know the first and last letters of the Greek alphabet when you see them.' Now, sir, I appeal to you, was that a right and respectful thing for a menial to say to a Protestant clergyman like myself?"

I acknowledged that it was not very respectful; but begged him to consider that it was true that the letters in question were not V. M., but A and Ω, and also that it was true that during divine service a church is for worship, not for idle curiosity; and that had he taken a seat when asked to do so, the imputed insult would never have happened. We thereupon shook hands, expressed forgiveness all round, and the Irish clergyman departed.

On another occasion, a man came into the vestry when I was just beginning the choir prayers, in a state of frenzy, demanding why he should be asked to sit apart from his wife, "contrary," he declared, "to the laws of God and man and all decency." I tried to explain that the church was built free for all to enter it who willed to worship in it; but that, of course, now, and in London especially, we could give no possible security that all who are free to enter are fit to enter, and therefore that a division of the sexes, as far as it goes, was some protection to women, and, at any rate, it was all that we could afford.   I omitted some older and better reasons for this separation; but, for the respect due to his wife, what I had said might suffice.   The man went away pacified and reconciled.

By this time, 1854, with the exception of the troubles arising from Mr. Westerton's ambition to be the Protestant champion of England as churchwarden of St. Paul's, and the persistently aggressive theology of a certain colonel of militia, who assumed to influence Bishop Blomfield, and to claim for the Church of England the simplicity of but *one* Sacrament, we were able to carry on our work in comparative peace.

But, it will be asked, what was the ritual which roused such a storm and provoked such outrage at St. Barnabas'?

It had reached the stage of daily choral worship, and the simplest rule of reverence and order in carrying out its details.

Bishop Blomfield had stopped in great measure the choral worship at St. Paul's, and he had ordered it to be stopped at St. Barnabas'.   I honestly tried to obey him, but my first attempt at "saying" instead of "singing" the versicles was received by the congregation with so loud and determined a burst of song in the responses, that I felt obliged to go to the Bishop, and to tell him plainly that, if choral service was to be discontinued at St. Barnabas', I must decline to have any responsibility for keeping order there.   The people were *determined* to assert and use the liberty given in the Prayer-book.   I told him so distinctly, and the Bishop did not persevere.

The points of ritual to which we had attained, and which roused such fury against us, were very simple :—

1. Procession of clergy and choristers from and to the vestry.

2. Obeisance towards the altar on entering and retiring from the sanctuary.

3. The eastward position.

4. Coloured coverings proper for the season on the altar.

We had been compelled to yield one or two points upon which Mr. Bennett had insisted, *e.g.* the invocation of the Blessed Trinity with the sign of the cross before the sermon, and the position eastward of Epistoler and Gospeller; also to adopt the black gown in the pulpit—for which, indeed, the Bishop was not responsible—and to say the daily prayers in the midst of the people, outside the chancel.

But Bishop Blomfield never treated these matters from a legal or canonical standpoint; he simply enforced his arbitrary will, which was, no doubt, influenced by his well-known terror of a London mob. When he was entreated to reconsider his order to say the prayers outside the chancel, and it was pointed out to him that the priest was less well both seen and heard there, than on the higher platform inside, he replied, " But those poppy-heads are in the way." I had the poppy-heads sawn off instantly, and so got back to my stall. When he was respectfully called upon to prescribe the collect, for which there is no rubrical authority, which he ordered to be used in the pulpit before the sermon, and asked to appoint the particular side of the polygonal pulpit at which it should be said, he answered, " I have no power to do either of these things, but if you don't say a collect, and don't say it to the west, I will withdraw your licence." When asked to give an example of our " excessive Ritualism," he instanced our communicating the choristers before the people.

He allowed the procession of clergy into choir, for the daily office, as a right thing; he forbade their proceeding to the celebration, with the vessels in their hands, as intolerable. The clergy might bow to the altar—indeed, " it would," he said, " be well for them to set an example, in this respect, to their congregations," whom he thought " far too inobservant of outward expressions of reverence;" but they might not bow in reciting the " Gloria Patri."

The question of the metal cross upon the re-table over the altar was treated with singular violence. The Bishop ordered the churchwardens to remove it: only one would obey him. The other, refusing to allow the legality of the removal, instantly replaced what his colleague had taken down. This unseemly struggle between the churchwardens went on till, at the suggestion of a distinguished counsel, the cross was *nailed* to the table, on the supposition that its legality depended on its fixture; the Bishop meanwhile declaring, " If it costs me my see, I will have that cross removed." The subsequent litigation proved how wrong, as to law, everybody was, including the Bishop, and that the cross, in its original position, was as secure as it remains to-day.

I mention these details, and record the episcopal policy of the time, in order to show the position under which Charles Lowder began his apprenticeship to " Ritualism;" and to indicate the whole amount of it in its most advanced stronghold, when the persecution which we endured was such that, for a time at least, the church and its ministers were in daily danger from the mob.

Since 1851 there have been all sorts of decisions by the Ecclesiastical Courts and the Committee of Privy Council upon ritual questions, many of them clean contradictory one of the other, but all of them more or less elaborately argued. We have had, moreover, the Public Worship Regulation Act, framed expressly to " put the Ritualists down." The danger is no longer to life, but to liberty. Men are not threatened now with personal violence by an infuriated people; they are only sent to prison in cold blood by three " aggrieved parishioners." Liberty of law is made to yield to the tyranny of judgments. But the principles which triumphed over Lord John Russell's " No Popery" mob at St. Barnabas', and Publican Thompson's rabble at St. George's-in-the-East, are more deeply set and more widely prevalent than ever. The degrees of ritual practice vary according to the circumstances of each parish in which it is used; but there are few churches (not absolutely belonging to the Low Church school) in which the measure of ritual, *now*, falls behind the St. Barnabas' of 1851.

CHAPTER IV.

THE BATTLE AT ST. BARNABAS'.

1852–1857.

"The strength of resolute undivided souls
Who, owning law, obey it."

IT is certainly not without interest and instruction, as bearing on our own time, to recall the history of an "advanced" Church thirty years ago, and to remember that there was nothing in its ritual or arrangements which is not carried out now, without comment or objection, in the most "moderate" English Churches, and even amidst the Puritanism prevailing in Ireland.

In order fully to understand the difficult position in which Charles Lowder learned the lessons which he afterwards nobly put in practice, it is also necessary to say that there were other obstacles, besides Bishop Blomfield's policy, through which the clergy of St. Barnabas' had to fight their way. There can be no doubt that in these, as in other things, the future missioner in East London was gaining, by experience, some of the wisdom which made him set great store upon those principles of internal discipline which cemented the work of the clergy engaged with him into the unity of one mind.

The church and college were in a difficult and anomalous position ; not independent as now, but legally a chapel-of-ease to St. Paul's, Knightsbridge, served by curates, under its Incumbent, while its whole constitution and *raison d'être* tended to force the clergy who ministered there into an independent course of action.

This was not, perhaps, lessened by the difference in character of the two noble-hearted men on whose leadership matters chiefly depended :—the one gentle, in every sense of the word, and generous to the core, with a keen prevision of the disastrous consequences which imprudence might bring, and a not unnatural dislike to being dragged through the dirt by imprudences, or what he deemed such, of those for whose acts he was responsible ; the other absolutely fear-less, unless he may have been said to fear cowardice and its consequences, referring everything to certain fixed prin-ciples, and possessing, with warm sympathies and affection, an unbending will in maintaining the legitimate issue of those principles.

Both, remaining true and loving friends to the last, have been spared to see the happy results of their work ; but while desire for the glory of God and salvation of souls ruled in both hearts, there were evidently secondary considerations, different in each, which influenced their respective lines of action. Loyalty to the Bishop who had greatly trusted him, and committed a difficult post to his keeping at a critical moment, governed Mr. Liddell's course ; while the Senior Curate of St. Barnabas' was chiefly led by loyalty to the congregation who, deprived of Mr. Bennett's leadership, turned to him, and demanded from him that he should guard that liberty in worship and devotion which they were determined not to yield.

It was indeed well for those liberties, not only at St. Barnabas', but throughout the whole Church, that in the beginning of the battle which still lasts, the stronghold most hotly attacked was held by one able to perceive that the struggle was not for this or that detail, but for a principle at stake—that the question was whether lawful liberty or tyrannical coercion should prevail. He and his fellow-workers also knew that to give up a multitude of small things, each one of which might in itself be called trivial, was to give up something considerable, which would permanently lower the whole standard of teaching and of worship which they had found established, and which they felt it right, if possible, to maintain. For indeed that outward order was but the outcome of the people's devotion. They were wise enough to remember that their congregation, being composed of men and women with faults and weaknesses, were not angels, or even wholly saints; and that if everything outward, which either gave expression to devotion or nourished it, were given up, grave consequences would quickly follow. Souls would not only be chilled and repressed, but the poor and ignorant, on whom warm energies were expended, would fall away.

It was for their sake that by entreaty, argument, and persuasion, the Senior Curate struggled against the Incumbent's original desire to assimilate the services at St. Barnabas' as closely as possible to those at St. Paul's, a policy which would have obscured the whole principle of freedom in details, and made the young and vigorous daughter a source of weakness, instead of strength, to the mother church.

Knowing the practice which now prevails in the latter,

it is certainly curious and instructive to find such prohi-
bitions issued to the Curate of St. Barnabas' as, *e.g.*, on
March 9, 1852 :—

> Let no flowers be placed on any occasion on the altar.
> Let the celebrant stand, at the *commencement* of the Communion
> Service, at the north side of the table.
> Let the Commandments be read distinctly, not chanted.

And so on, through twelve injunctions, the fulfilment of
which would greatly astonish the present congregation of
St. Paul's.

The position of affairs would have been still more
difficult, had it not been for the personal kindness and
generosity of Mr. Liddell, and the warm affection and
gratitude which he always expressed for the Curate of
St. Barnabas', even while feeling that he was responsible for
that church as much as for St. Paul's, and that he was
placed in a false position by seeming to maintain that of
which his own judgment disapproved.

At this distance of time there will be no breach of
confidence in giving the following letters, while the judgment of so distinguished a layman as the late Baron
Alderson on the question at issue is interesting and
valuable.

St. Barnabas' Parsonage, Pimlico, July 4, 1854.

DEAR SIR EDWARD ALDERSON,

Though a stranger to you personally, I feel a sure
hope that you will allow me to consult you in the present emergency; for indeed it *is* an emergency of great gravity to the
Church in this parish and throughout England. I beg to be
allowed to say that I presume to write to you only because I
know how steadfastly your heart is bound up in the English

Church, and because I have the highest confidence in your learning and judgment.

The Incumbent of the parish (in which this church is a chapelry), with, I am sure, the most loving sincerity, has seen fit to yield up to the Bishop that liberty to adjust the internal affairs of his own church which the law allows him. He thinks he has only yielded certain specific points; and this, for the present, may be so: but I fear that what he *has* yielded is the principle of freedom within the Church's law, and I cannot but apprehend the very worst consequences from a sacrifice of which the Bishop of London will be too ready to avail himself, for carrying out his own private wishes and opinions.

As yet, the church of St. Paul's is the only one involved; but is it possible for the Incumbent to retain a position in one of his churches which he has yielded in the other?

The Bishop has threatened us with a visitation. How is he to be met?

I have begged Mr. Liddell to decide whether he is to be met on the ground that changes may be made here simply because he (the Bishop) wills it, or on the ground that no changes shall be made from an existing state of things which is edifying to the people and lawful in the Church. He has made no decision; I fear he is already committed to the former side of the alternative.

The body of clergy licensed here, for the work of this church and district, have resolved to be the instruments of *no change whatever*, and to take their stand upon the ground that their people's spiritual interests ought not to be sacrificed by them; that if our worship here be indeed unlawful in the English Church, the sooner it is put down the better; that if otherwise, they can be no parties to such an act of tyranny and oppression.

Is this a course which we may take, and still act with loyalty and fidelity to the English Church? If the Bishop holds a visitation, may we request that it be by a solemn and formal court, and that we ourselves may be heard by counsel?

There is another side of the case which, if you will allow me, I would present to you.   The necessary disadvantages which belong to this church and "college," from its present constitution, are very serious; the Incumbent being, practically, non-resident. . I enclose a case for reference, which will show you what I mean; and from which I doubt not you will gather that the perils from within, to a work like this, are at least not less grave than the perils from without.

The Incumbent is strongly impressed with his own inability to do justice to the two works (as I may now call them) of St. Paul's and St. Barnabas'; and he feels that if the two could be separated, neither would interfere with the prosperity of the other.   This, I may add, is, under present circumstances, the opinion also of Mr. Bennett, and of others who are anxious to see some way of saving our work here.   But the possibilities of this depend upon questions of law with which I am not acquainted. Would you kindly consider them?

I would only say, in conclusion, that I have no personal motives whatever in submitting these matters to you.   I cannot, of course, disclaim the most keen and loving interest in this church and district, but I do not seek for anything for myself; I am anxious only for the stability of a work which is looked up to from all corners of England, and for the strength and glory of our own beloved Church.

> Believe me, dear Sir Edward Alderson,
> > With the deepest respect,
> > > Your most faithful servant in Christ,
> > > > JAMES SKINNER.

> > > > > 9, Park Crescent, July, 6, 1854.

MY DEAR SIR,

I sympathize with you in your difficult position, which seems to me to require a mixture of firmness with prudence rarely found together, but which, I hope, will not be wanting in your case. . . .

From my knowledge derived from an intimacy at school and

College,* I begged him † not to yield to the Bishop, but to take his stand on the ecclesiastical law — the best for Mr. Liddell, and *for the Bishop also.* A coward, as the Bishop is and always was, will give up much protection by quitting the shelter of the law. It is an easy answer to complainers, *" the law allows it."*

But Mr. Liddell has the right of altering St. Barnabas' as well as St. Paul's, and I don't see how you can prevent him. Yet I deprecate your all refusing to act if he does so. Your remaining may prevent much evil, and I don't see, if it be known, as it must be, that you disapprove, why you should not remain to do as much good as you can. . . .

I deprecate your resolution against *all* change, though I believe it would be wisest to make none. ¯ Nothing seems to me to be more unadvisable than, at this time, to separate St. Barnabas' and St. Paul's.

You will have, in the present state of things, no security for a proper appointment. I don't think Mr. Bennett's prudence so great as his zeal in advising it.

I am at a loss to know what the Bishop means by a special visitation. He will have enough to do if he undertakes such matters throughout his diocese. If he does, I should certainly put him, as far as the law will allow, at arm's length, and appear by advocate at it ; but I don't believe that it will happen.

In the mean while I advise you in patience to possess your souls. Sail with as little sail as you can conscientiously ; the

* Bishop Blomfield was born in 1786, and Baron Alderson in 1787 ; they were at King Edward VI.'s School, Bury St. Edmund's, together from 1801 to 1804, the Bishop having entered it, at eight years of age, in 1794, and the Judge in 1801, having migrated thither from the Charterhouse ; they were at Cambridge together from 1805 to 1809, as the Bishop entered at Trinity in 1804, and the Judge at the same College in 1805 (afterwards migrating to Caius) ; they took brilliant degrees, the lawyer, however, beating the ecclesiastic, the latter in 1808 as Third Wrangler and First Chancellor's Medallist, the former in 1809 as Senior Wrangler, First Smith's Prizeman, and First Chancellor's Medallist. They were both Fellows of their respective Colleges.

† Mr. Liddell.

tempest will soon pass.   People at present are making political capital, as it is called, out of Romanizing Protestants, as they call them.   I have the greatest contempt for all such people and their attempts ; but I fear lest some of my earnest-minded friends should not be so quiet as I am.   Sooth to say, Belgravia has produced some extravagances of devotion.   There has been a good deal of gesticulation, very pardonable if it did not do so much mischief to others.   We suffered here, at St. Mary Magdalene, from it when Dr. Pusey preached the other day.   But as we are quiet people we are recovering the effects.   I wish people not to feel one jot less, but to express it much less outwardly.   This is what we ought to aim at, and if we can accomplish it we shall keep all that is good, in spite of all the Westertons in the world.

I have read the enclosed paper with, I own, some satisfaction that you are not so strict in your discipline at this moment as you ought to be.   I should not wish it permanently to be so, however.   For I agree with you that you want a head to govern.   But don't begin your repairs in the hurricane month.

If I can be of use I shall be glad, and shall be always ready to talk it over with you.   A short conversation is worth a quire of writing; as, in conversation, I see and appreciate your difficulties, which it is not so easy to do in a letter.

Very faithfully and truly yours,

E. M. ALDERSON.

To the Rev. J. Skinner.

A memorial had been presented to the Bishop, entreating him to reconsider such commands as were contrary to lawful liberty.   Mr. Richard Cavendish * wrote to Mr. Skinner :—

I have written to the churchwardens to append my name, but for fear of any mistake I write also to you. . . . Words cannot

---

* Afterwards Lord Richard Cavendish.

express my indignation, especially at the Bishop's conduct. It is sad, too, with such a constant trial pressing upon you, to have all the misery of this wretched struggle with the Bishop, to whom you ought to be able to look for your principal support. It is most needful that a stand should be made against the unlawful commands of a Bishop, issued ·merely in the vain hope of " satisfying a public " who will never be satisfied with anything short of the abolition of all Catholic doctrine and worship in the English Church. The notion of your having on any account to leave St. Barnabas' fills me with dismay. I dare not think of it. May God be merciful unto us !

Throughout this struggle for liberty, Charles Lowder was, as will be seen from the foregoing letters, of one mind with the Senior Curate, joining heartily in his efforts to preserve what had been gained. In all that has been related he shared by sympathy, counsel, and co-operation, so that it forms part of the story of his life. Nor was it an unimportant part. He was polishing his armour, never on earth to lay it aside, for the hard and life-long battle which was before him ; and learning, even through his own or others' mistakes, lessons without which he would have been lacking in much of the experience which he brought to bear upon his future work. Of his life at this time Mr. Skinner writes :—

His whole heart was centred in *work* for the poor; his districts lay in the slums to the west of Ebury Square, which are now improved out of existence, and he had special charge of the day and night schools. In these two spheres of labour, he devoted himself to the task of raising up the ignorant and vicious and oppressed to a higher and truer conception of God and of themselves. He learnt by experience how much a warm and bright and beautiful ceremonial contributed to this end; and therefore he valued it, while, for its own sake, he cared little about it.

No man had less of mere æsthetic sentiment about his religion. He was weak, rather than otherwise, in imaginative power ; but he had considerable intellectual, specially logical, force, and a strong will, combined with indomitable courage. His appreciation of ritual, as the handmaid of devotion and the expression of faith, was from the conviction of his understanding that it is a logical necessity of the case, as well as the fulfilment of a natural law; that—given a human soul and body for the instrument, the creeds of the Catholic Church for the subject, and Almighty God for the Object of faith and worship—ritual is the only process by which Christian homage can be outwardly paid. As to the ritual of St. Peter's-in-the-East, men may well be allowed to differ in their criticism. But in one thing all must be agreed, that Charles Lowder knew what he was about when he began it; I mean that it was the result of principles learnt at St. Barnabas', and of long and diligent experience among the classes for whose souls he painfully watched, and for whom he actually found it to be a stay.

If it be said of the long battle at St. Barnabas' in which he took part, that it was a struggle for trivial details, unimportant to real work, the answer is that, besides the *principle* of preserving liberty which was involved, each detail was only trivial in the same sense in which the colours of a regiment are in themselves unimportant— a piece of embroidered silk, no weapon of war, and yet so precious in their symbolism that a soldier counts blood and life itself well lost to save them. Nay, the very fierceness of the attack upon outward order and reverence was the most striking acknowledgment of consciousness, on the enemy's part, of their power and importance,—even as the splendour of military ritual can never be witnessed without forcing us to feel its influence, and the power which it must possess, especially with the rough and un-educated, to kindle enthusiasm and create unity of feeling and of action.

Time, after all, brings relief to most difficulties, if only they can patiently be borne; and so, for St. Barnabas', time and patience wrought out the solution of nearly all that contest, of which a brief notice has been attempted here, and of which the end may be as briefly told. In a letter to the *Times* of July 13, 1854, the Senior Curate wrote :—

God knows, sir, our work — our real vital work — here is but hardly begun. There are yet a thousand strongholds of Satan to be stormed, which may make the boldest heart tremble. But who hinder us? Who weaken our arms and baffle all our efforts? "A Belgravian" and such as he. We cannot build up poor men's souls, and fight against such foes as these at the same time. . . . The outcry has gone forth, "The worship of St. Barnabas' is Popish." I deny it. The worship of St. Barnabas' is the worship of the Church of England. We challenge this issue in the courts of the Church of England, if any such there be. If it is not the worship of the Church of England, the sooner it is put down the better."

The distress of litigation, to which the questions in dispute were at length referred, was enhanced by two unfavourable decisions ; but it was not without compensation. The logical issues of the first—the Lushington judgment—were plainly these: (1) That the reformed Church of England is a new thing—the creation of the sixteenth century, without continuity or dependence or affinity or

E

descent beyond three centuries.   (2) That what the present
Prayer-book of the English Church has prescribed is a
virtual prohibition of everything else, *ejusdem generis*, parity
and tradition having no value even as explanatory in
cases of doubt.   (3) That the usages of the ancient Church
are absolutely repudiated.

The judgment was an attack upon the essence of the
Church of England in its character as a portion of the one
Holy Catholic and Apostolic Church ; it was an effort to
abolish that ceremonial worship of God which has ever
been the correlative of sacramental grace in the Catholic,
as previously in the Jewish Church.

The appeal to the Court of Arches, under Sir J. Dodson,
did little to remove the stigma.   But the cause was submitted, on appeal, to the Committee of Privy Council, and
on March 21, 1857, it received such a different, because
fairer, construction as (if that Committee had but adhered
to *its own* sentence) might perhaps have satisfied the
Church, and finally settled those disputes as to ritual
and ceremonial which still continue to burn.

The use of the cross as an ornament of churches from
the earliest periods of Christianity was plainly confirmed ;
the credence table and the embroidered and coloured
cloths of the altar were pronounced lawful ; the use of
lights at the celebration of Holy Communion was not
disturbed ; and, generally, the construction of the word
" ornaments " in the much-canvassed rubric at the opening
of the Prayer-book was declared, after much consideration,
to apply and to be confined to those articles, the use of
which in the services and ministrations of the Church is
prescribed by the First Prayer-book of Edward VI.

It is important to note here that it was under the sanction of this first judgment of the Privy Council (whatever its worth may be) that Charles Lowder introduced his "ritual" in the East of London; and that he conscientiously felt it to be right for him to persevere in it, as being the Church's law, in spite of the fact (which he left them to reconcile with consistency) that the Lords of the Council had changed their minds.

The following extracts from letters will give some notion of the depth of feeling which these judgments excited amongst the congregation of St. Barnabas'; and as they practically settled the troubles of the infancy of that parish, they may interest many to whom the excitement and anxiety of those days are only now matters of history.

The two first are from an able Chancery barrister, of condolence on the Lushington judgment, and of congratulation on its reversal; and the last is given, with Mr. Liddell's kind permission, as containing the account of the final peaceful settlement of affairs at St. Barnabas'. It was written to his former coadjutor after broken health had forced the latter to retire from his post.

. . . I beg to offer you my most sincere sympathy on *the* event of this day (December 5, 1855). Indeed, I can assure you that I feel it myself, personally, quite a blow; though, of course, much less so than you must, whose whole life has of late years been so bound up with all that a godless world is seeking to undo, and who have with such labour brought St. Barnabas' to be a model of a Christian sanctuary.

But pray be not discouraged. I am well aware how discouraging and heart-sickening this day's proceedings must be to you, but you have still left the lasting encouragement of a congregation of attached and grateful people. . . . I grant the judgment was an able one as a piece of reasoning from his premises, but these I think sadly far from being those from which a judge in such matters ought to start. . . .

I much dread, nevertheless, the effect of to-day's decision upon the minds of many of the clergy, specially of those labouring in humble imitation of St. Barnabas', of whom I know several, in country districts, where they have not the sympathy and encouragement of kindred minds immediately to fall back upon. Never do I remember to have read of any judicial decision which has so avowedly inculcated sacrilege as this in the removal of crosses; or which will produce such incalculable mischief, especially in the minds of the ignorant, whom it will take years to persuade (if ever they can be persuaded) of the valuelessness (really) of doctrines stamped with legal authority.

But I hope and believe you will be sustained under this trial, and abate not a jot of that steadfastness you have so invariably shown.

Forgive all this from a layman; but I cannot refrain from speaking out, things have come to such a pass.

My other object in troubling you with this (after conveying to you my heartfelt sympathy) is, in case (as I hope devoutly it may) the decision is appealed from, to offer you my *free* and willing professional services in helping forward the case in any way in which I might be of use. . . .

March 24, 1857.

Though of course, through your friends, you have heard of the glorious news of Saturday, I cannot help troubling you, mixed up as I have been so much of late in the contest, with a few additional remarks upon it.

.I hope you are satisfied with it. I think we all ought to be. I myself am overjoyed and filled with thankfulness for it—so much more than we could have expected, looking at the constitution of the court, and the two adverse judgments to work against.

I cannot, in fact, help recognizing God's especial providence in thus "turning the hearts" of the most unlikely to so decided a step in our favour as a *reversal* on *three* important particulars.

I believe also that the longer and more calmly we look into it, the more reason for joy we shall discover in it. I can hardly yet bring myself to realize its importantly beneficial ultimate effects, and all disappointment at private losses should surely be merged in the vindication of the principle *at large* for which we have been contending. Mr. Liddell has again and again said he has been fighting the Church's battle, and not a mere local battle. Well, he has won the greater; can he not afford to give up the less? He has set free every clergyman, every architect in future to decorate their churches with the "servilely imitative" and "meretricious ornaments" which we have heard so much about. And the intense sophistry which Dr. Lushington has done his best to circulate, and the groundless imputations he has charged you with, have been scattered to the winds. . . .

It really was the greatest treat (merely intellectually considered) to hear each quicksand that wrecked us before, now passed in safety—though it was in fear and trembling that one listened to it. A more exciting scene I seldom remember.

Wilton Place, Wednesday in Easter Week, 1858.

Let me ask you still to rejoice with me that St. Barnabas' is, with the blessing of God, going on so very prosperously. . . . In spite of all the obloquy from without, and many acknowledged infirmities within, it has gone on, doing, as I believe, a great and mighty work for God. And having my eye on *you*, who worked there so hard and above your strength, I may say to those who succeeded you, while I wish most gratefully to appreciate their exertions also—still I may say, " Other men laboured, and ye are entered into their labours."

I think that judgment of the Committee of the Privy Council broke the neck of the opposition here. We soon settled down into a state of blessed quiet, interrupted now and then by a little trouble, but nothing to speak of; and the work has gone on thriving progressively ever since. Whenever there is any discussion before the Bishop of London, I find it so much easier to stand up to him and tell him my own exact mind and determination, than I did with the last Bishop, whom I had known intimately from a child, and from whom it gave me the most intense pain to differ; though *that* latterly, as you know, was not seldom. He, towards the end of his career, used to take one's opposition as a personal insult; whereas the present Bishop is very good-tempered, and being no older than myself, and with no parochial experience, he is easier to deal with, even though we may not agree. I stand, as steadily as I can, upon the law of the Church, and he has had in several arguments with me to end by knocking under, or letting me alone, which is the same thing. You may have perhaps heard that some time after the delivery of the judgment he visited my churches, with a view, as he said at first, of exercising his discretion as Ordinary upon the use of the altar-cloths, and next upon the disposal of the stone altar after its removal. I had to tell him *tout bonnement* that, as I was advised, he had no power whatever, either in the one instance or the other; and he said he would consider it, and wrote in a few days to say I was right. I have had two or three cases of dispute between me and Westerton brought before the Bishop, in all of which he has ended in giving sentence in my favour. We had a great tussle, by the way, at first, because he withheld White's licence unless I surrendered to *him* the discretionary power which the law of the Church gives to an Incumbent in reference to the details of divine service. But there, again, he was so entirely in the wrong that in the end he had to give way.

But enough of these matters. The blessing is that *now* we are *established* and swimming in deep water, and each day only strengthens our position.

This Lent was very devoutly kept, and I speak of course more of St. Barnabas' than St. Paul's. The attendance throughout it has been most remarkable, and on Easter Day the throngs of worshippers were such that the church was quite incapable of containing them; they stood out in the street, opposite the west door, quite across to the opposite side of the road. There were three celebrations—6 a.m., 159; 8 a.m., 137; 11 a.m., 187; total, 483.* I was there in the evening, and I never saw such a congregation in my life, and so reverent and earnest! . . .

We have just got over our Easter Tuesday election of church-wardens with unwonted quietness and brevity. Ten or twelve minutes concluded the whole affair, *mirabile dictu.* Westerton had, and I believe with sincerity, expressed his wish and determination to resign; but his party could get no one else to stand. The influential people of the parish stand aloof, and so he was urged by his party to stand again, and at last consented. I agree with you that we really now need not care who is in the office, and it is doubtless better that they should have their fling, to show at last how little they can do or have done in obstructing the truth; for God in wonderful ways overrules human violence or party spirit for the ultimate furtherance of His own work. Bad men seem always on the *point* of prevailing, but somehow they don't. For my part, as long as Churchmen are remiss about putting a worthy man into this office, I am profoundly indifferent who fills it, and would just as soon have Westerton as any one else, if not sooner, for I have got to know his ways now. He cannot hinder one morsel of our real work, and the field of controversy about externals is greatly narrowed by the recent judgment. . . .

In the mean time, thanks to God, we are carrying on our services and regulations with increasing order and efficiency, and agitation against us has burnt itself out, without having shaken us from our steadfast position. . . .

I ought to tell you that, being most anxious to spare the devout feelings of our people to the uttermost in the necessarily painful matter of removing the stone altar, I took that responsibility entirely upon myself. By Cundy's advice, and after a beautiful simple design by him, I employed Myers, the great building con-

* On Easter Day, 1881, there were 761 communicants at St. Barnabas'.

tractor in Lambeth, to make a very massive one in carved oak, on six pillars, of exactly the same dimensions as the original stone one, so that all the vestments fitted, of course, perfectly. The stone one was then most carefully taken down by first-rate work-men. The beautiful slab was laid down on a level with the floor, so as to form the basis on which the new altar had to stand, and was thus secured *in situ* as much as was possible under the circum-stances. The rest of the structure was set up again in the crypt, immediately under the altar, with a new slab of plain Portland stone. So if at any future day that absurd prohibition of a stone altar be repealed, then the whole thing is capable of being re-stored as it originally was. . . .

Ever, my dear friend, yours most truly and affectionately,

ROBERT LIDDELL.

CHAPTER V.

" The strawberry grows underneath the nettle. "

WE have broken the thread of our story in order to learn briefly the issue of the contest at St. Barnabas', and must return to the Easter of 1854, when Westerton was a candidate for the office of churchwarden at St. Paul's Knightsbridge.

To the crypt at St. Barnabas' there is an underground passage from the choristers' vestry, where the boys occasionally lurked and larked. Among these was at this time a cousin of Charles Lowder, a Christ's Hospital boy, who was on a visit at the college. He was inflamed by the sight of " Vote for Westerton " carried on a board by a man, "sandwich-wise," through the streets near St. Barnabas'. He and the other boys conceived a fierce desire to do battle with the innocent bearer of the obnoxious placard, and he entreated his cousin to allow them to throw something at the man. Charles bade him not throw dirt or stones, but gave the boys sixpence to buy rotten eggs. They were not slow in using them, carrying the war into Ebury Street, and the bespattered " sandwich " complained to his employers, who speedily invoked the aid of the law against the assailants. Charles was interrogated, and took all the blame of inciting the boys to bedaub the inscription. Before the police magistrate, he repeated publicly the admission of indiscretion, and sorrow for it, which he had already made privately, and the case was dismissed, with more than acquiescence on the part of the prosecution.

He expressed nothing but deep regret and self-blame for his thoughtless and wrong action, and, it need scarcely be said, made liberal private compensation to the placard-man; but, in the state of matters at St. Barnabas', his fault was more than ordinarily full of mischievous conse-quences, and of distress to his colleagues and superiors. The newspapers of course made large capital out of the occurrence, proclaiming a Puseyite conspiracy to put down Protestant churchwardens by force. Bishop Blomfield took the matter up, and the following letters will show how he dealt with it.

The Bishop of London requests the Rev. C. F. Lowder to call at London House to-morrow, at half-past ten o'clock.

London House, May 3, 1854.

London House, May 6, 1854.

DEAR SIR,

I am sorry to be under the necessity of stating that I consider it to be my imperative duty to mark my sense of the scandal occasioned to the Church by your late indiscreet conduct.

I had at first thought it would be necessary to revoke your licence; but in consideration of your having made, though some-what tardily, a public acknowledgment of your fault, I shall content myself with suspending you from the exercise of your functions, as Curate of St. Barnabas', for the space of six weeks, dating from this day.

It is with extreme pain that I visit you even with this censure; but my sense of duty to the Church will not allow me to do less.

In the way of *punishment*, I am sure that your own feelings will have been enough. I trust that you may be able to regain, for yourself and for the Church, the ground which you have lost.

I am, dear sir,
Your faithful servant,

The Rev. C. F. Lowder.   C. J. LONDON.

Lansdown House, Ryde, May 9, 1854.

MY LORD,

I have just received your lordship's letter, which I found awaiting me here. I am most thankful to your lordship for having so far listened to the kind intercessions of Mr. Liddell and Mr. Parke, of which I only to-day heard, as to mitigate the term of suspension first intended.

But feeling, as I do most deeply, the sin of causing this scandal to the Church, I am almost thankful to be allowed to bear some ecclesiastical punishment at your lordship's hands. I trust that, by God's blessing, it may be the means of effectually quickening my endeavour, for the future, to labour more heartily and patiently for Him against whom I have thus sinned.

If I failed to express to your lordship as earnestly as I felt my sorrow for this transaction, I trust that your lordship will ascribe it rather to the shock that my mind had sustained, than to a wish of justifying my conduct.*

London House, May 10, 1854.

MY DEAR SIR,

I hasten to acknowledge the receipt of your letter, which is in all respects what it ought to be: and I assure you that what has happened, painful as it has been to me and to your

---

* The copy of this letter ends here.

other friends, will not alter my opinion of you, as a zealous and conscientious Clergyman.

I am, my dear sir,

Your faithful servant,

C. J. London.

Mr. Bennett wrote to Charles :—

Frome-Selwood Vicarage, Somerset, May 8, 1854.

My dear Friend,

Take heart and be not dispirited. . . . I do not see that anything done by you in this matter, as far as I have heard of it, involves one iota more than thoughtless indiscretion. . . . It may be any one's turn next—*my* turn perhaps—to be overtaken in a fault.   I have no doubt I myself have done, or might have done, a similar thing.   You have acknowledged your mistake and made atonement.   We must pray for your peace and restoration, and God will hear our prayers ; and after you have suffered a while, all will be peace again.

Would you like to come *here* for a short time ?   There is room for you, and we shall all be *glad* to give you shelter.   I who was myself a refugee from dear St. Barnabas' am the fittest now to shelter *you*.   Come here then, and in this comparatively quiet place seek peace, and God will give it.

Charles went to see his family at Enfield, and his brother wrote : " I never saw any one look so broken-hearted."   The little episode of his " ovation," as Bishop Blomfield playfully called it, was for long a sore subject with him, and one of which he was heartily ashamed.   It led, however, to circumstances which influenced his whole after life.

He went abroad during his six weeks' suspension, and spent some days at the Petit Séminaire of Yvetôt, in the diocese of Rouen, where he was hospitably entertained. The superior, M. l'Abbé P. L. Labbé, had lived much in England when his father was an *émigré*, and took the more interest in his English guest. Charles writes to his mother:—

Rouen, May 22, 1854.

. . . I have been on the move since landing at Havre, and so have not been able to sit down quietly to write before to-day. I left Ryde on Wednesday morning for Southampton, took the steamer for Havre about 2.30, p.m., and after a quick passage arrived at one the next morning. I spent Thursday in Havre, and the next morning started early on foot, sending my carpet-bag by train. It was a very good day for walking, not too warm, and I made a good use of it. Leaving Havre about 7.30, I got upon the heights of Andelys, whence there is a very fine view of the town and the Seine, and then continuing on the heights to the interesting old church and remains of the Abbey of Graville. . . . At Yvetôt, a station on the Havre and Rouen railroad, I found my carpet-bag, and we both journeyed on to Rouen. After going about hunting for lodgings, I at last fixed upon my present humble abode, a small room and a bed-room, for which I give ten francs a week. . . . I have an introduction to the Archbishop, but he is unfortunately absent, confirming. I am, however, to be introduced to him when he returns. Mr. —— also has given me an introduction to a friend of his at Yvetôt, whom I must try and find out, as it is lonely knowing no one.

It is a great privation to be away from dear St. Barnabas' during this festival season which is coming on; however, I must bear that patiently, as it is my own fault. The Rogation Days are kept here by processions through the town, and I suppose Ascension Day will be observed with great solemnity; but of course, although one tries to enter into the spirit of the services, it is not like one's own home. . . .

Yours very affectionately,

CHARLES.

Vernon, Department of Eure, May 27, 1854.

On Tuesday I went to Yvetôt, a station on the Havre and Rouen railway, and arrived at the Petit Séminaire, a large school for boys, in the afternoon. I was received very kindly, though M. Labbé, to whom I had introductions, did not return till the evening. They begged me to sleep there, which I did, and I hope to spend a part of next week quietly there, and so see something more of the working of the French clergy and their schools.

Thursday, of course, being the Feast of the Ascension, was kept very solemnly, by immensely crowded churches. It is indeed very striking to see the reverence and hearty devotion of the people ; I wish we had anything like it in England. Friday, I took a walk to Mont St. Catherine, which you may remember —the beautiful hill above Rouen, where there is a most lovely chapel, though the ornaments are not yet finished. . . . It will be much richer than St. Barnabas'. . . .

I hope to spend a quiet Sunday to-morrow. I wish I had St. Barnabas' a little nearer. It is very trying to be so long without Communion.

Yvetôt, May 31, 1854.

. . . I spent a very quiet Sunday at Yvetôt, partaking, I hope, in spirit, with my friends at St. Barnabas', in my own room, and thoroughly enjoying afterwards a ramble and rest in a delightful park near this, the Parc de Bigy, formerly belonging to Louis Philippe, where I lay on the grass, and thoroughly enjoyed myself.

Vernon is very prettily situated on the Seine. I left on Monday morning and walked to Les Andelys, enjoying on my way the views of the valley of the Seine, especially an old ruin, on a most commanding height, called Chateau Gaillard, built by Richard Cœur de Lion in a year. . . . I slept on Monday at Le Grand Andely, and walked thence yesterday to the *Côte des Deux Amants*, called so from a very romantic lay, of a lover dying in carrying his beloved up the hill. . . . I walked on to Pont de l'Arche, where I took the train, having completed a very good day's work by twelve o'clock. I met M. Labbé in Rouen, and we came on here together by the train, arriving about six o'clock. I shall probably stay here over Whit Sunday, and then I shall begin to think about returning. I should like very much to be back on St. Barnabas' Day; but perhaps, as I could not do any duty till the Sunday after, it would be better not. I shall still want a little more holiday, to make me perfectly strong, though I now feel a great deal better, but still not able to encounter any great anxiety. My friends here are very kind, and I have plenty of French conversation, as well as time for quiet thought and recreation.

Yvetôt, Whitsun Monday, 1854.

I have enjoyed my visit here very much, having received very great kindness from all the clergy. It is a school for almost all classes, on a strictly religious footing, under the Archbishop, called the Petit Séminaire; the Grand Séminaire at Rouen being entirely for education for the priesthood. Here they are admitted, rich and poor, paying what they can, from £10 to £20 a year, but without any difference being made in their treatment. There are about eighteen masters, all Priests, except a Deacon or two. They live on the happiest terms with the boys, dining, sleeping, playing together, as one family. I have a good deal of opportunity of studying their character, both in school and out, and it is very interesting to see their well-disciplined tone.

On Thursday I walked with an English boy to Jumièges, a beautiful ruin, the nave Roman, the choir middle pointed, a great deal of polychrome remaining on the walls; it was desecrated at the Revolution.

Yesterday, though I missed grievously the Great Blessing, yet I had a great deal to interest me; for a College Service it was very impressive, from the number of Priests—seven officiating, to represent the Seven Gifts of the Holy Spirit. About one hundred boys communicated at a Low Mass, said before High Mass. In the afternoon I attended Vespers and Compline at the parish church, between which one of the Professors here, a very nice man, preached a very good sermon from Acts ii., on the sanctity of the Church and her members. . . .

His enforced exile from the spiritual home, after which he yearned, was to bring forth abundant fruit. For he was at this time brought under the influence of one who, though dead, had the greatest power over his future life, suggesting to him fresh fields for conquest, and strengthening him for the emprise.

He seems to have taken up, in the library at Yvetôt, the "Life of St. Vincent de Paul," by M. Abelly ; and, after he left it, M. Labbé writes to him :—

Yvetôt, 9 Juin, 1854.

Mon cher M. Lowder,

Comme vous n'avez pas eu le temps d'achever chez nous la lecture de la vie de S. Vincent de Paul, qui paraissait vous intéresser, je prends la liberté de vous l'envoyer, et vous prie de la lire en mémoire de vos amis d'Yvetôt, et encore plus en mémoire du grand saint dont elle retrace les actions. . . . Pour moi, cher Mr. Lowder, je me ferai un devoir de vous mettre chaque jour dans mes prières, afin que Dieu, qui vous a donné une si grande droiture et humilité de cœur, achéve son ouvrage en vous.

Croyez moi bien,
Tout votre,
P. L. Labbé.

Long afterwards, Charles wrote of "the deep impression" made on his mind by "the sad condition of the French Church and nation in the sixteenth century, and the wonderful influence of the institutions founded by

St. Vincent in reforming abuses and rekindling the zeal of the priesthood."

The heart must be dull indeed (he said) which is not stirred with emotion at the self-denial and energy with which the saint gave himself to the work to which he was called. . . . The deep wisdom which sought out the root of so much evil, in the unspiritual lives of the clergy, and provided means for its redress . . . was well calculated to impress those who seriously reflected on the state of our own Church and people, and honestly sought for some remedy. The spiritual condition of the masses of our population, the appalling vices which prevail in our large towns, and especially in the teeming districts of the metropolis, the increasing tendency of the people to mass together, multiplying and intensifying the evil, and the unsatisfactory character of the attempts hitherto made to meet it, were enough to make men gladly profit by the experience of those who had successfully struggled against similar difficulties.

Thus, being dead, St. Vincent de Paul yet spoke to the heart of an English clergyman and gave a new impulse to his life. For Charles Lowder was not one to receive vividly such impressions, without working them out to any practical result. His life of labour in the schools and district of St. Barnabas' might have satisfied most men desiring work for the poor. Each of the assistant curates had two rooms in the College, as it was then called, living at a common table. They lived to minister in the adjoining church, and to serve the poor and ignorant; but there are traces in Charles's letters of his feeling even this simple and devoted life too comfortable. A mingled cry of suffering, agony, miserable laughter, mad blasphemy, rang in his ears, and entered into his soul,—that cry which

F

day and night goes up from the streets of East London, but which most of us have neither ears to hear nor hearts to consider.

He returned to St. Barnabas' at Whitsuntide, but the thought of joining some kind of community of missionary-priests had taken hold of his mind, and he was evidently trying to collect information on the subject. M. Labbé writes to him :—

Yvetôt, October 7, 1854.

MON CHER MONSIEUR,

. . . Je regrette de ne pouvoir vous donner les renseignements que vous désirez sur les Constitutions des Prêtres de la Mission ; je ne les ai jamais eues en ma possession, j'ignore même si elles sont du domaine public, et n'ayant aucune rélation chez les messieurs de S. Lazare, je ne puis pas même être renseigné sur ce point. Je ne suis pas surpris, mon cher monsieur, du plaisir que vous avez trouvé à la lecture de la vie de S. Vincent de Paul. Après les livres saints, je n'en connais aucun qui me fasse une impression plus salutaire. On sent, en le lisant, un désir ardent de lui ressembler, et il semble que cela ne soit pas trop difficile. C'est ce que j'éprouvais encore la semaine dernière, en entendant lire pendant le repas (nous étions réunis tous les prêtres de la maison pour notre retraite annuelle) la partie qui traite de ses vertus. Je voudrais, mon cher monsieur, que vous fussiez si épris de S. Vincent de Paul que vous ne voulussiez pas demeurer plus long-temps hors de l'Eglise qui a produit un si grand saint. Vous avez du remarquer en lisant sa vie qu'il accueillait avec grande charité les Prêtres *Hibernois* (comme on disait alors) persécutés pour leur refus de se conformer à l'Eglise établir d'Irlande, qui est sœur de la vôtre, et la seule dans le monde en communion avec elle. Ne vous fâchez pas de ce que je vous dis cela ; mais je suis si triste de voir qu'un homme si désireux de tout ce qui est bien, ait les yeux fermés à la première de toutes les vérités catholiques, celle de l'unité :—*et unam Ecclesiam.*

Soyez assuré que je ne vous oublirai point, et que personne ne désire plus que moi votre bonheur en ce monde et en l'autre.

Je suis, avec une respectieuse affection,

Votre dévoué serviteur,

P. L. LABBÉ, Pr.

One great interest of Charles Lowder's life was his younger brother, as the following letters will show :—

Ryde, September 4, 1854.

MY DEAR MOTHER,

You will be glad to hear that I saw Willy off on Saturday, . . . but did not arrive till after the steam-tender had taken her first trip, and Willy among her passengers, to the *La Plata.* I was therefore obliged to wait for her last trip with the mails, about 2 p.m. On reaching the *La Plata* in Southampton Water I saw Willy on the look-out, though he had almost given me up. I had about half an hour to spend with him, during which we enjoyed our walk together on the noble deck, which extends the whole length of the vessel. . . . He hopes to reach St. Thomas's in eleven or twelve days, and Barbadoes about the 21st. And there seems every probability of their doing so with this splendid weather.

St. Barnabas' College, October 14, 1854.

MY DEAR WILLY,

I am very much obliged for your note which you wrote from St. Thomas's. . . . After leaving you on board—which I was very glad I had the opportunity of doing, for I was able to picture to myself better your life at sea, and I know what a comfort it is on such occasions to have some friend to see you off—I returned to Southampton, and arrived just in time to catch the Ryde steamer. . . . I hope you will give us as accurate accounts of the climate and your arrangements at Barbadoes as you did of your voyage, as they will be very interesting. Give me some idea of your school, and the various professors and masters, and of the tone of the place. We have, of course, been kept in a state of great excitement by the news from the Crimea. The landing of the troops, as well as the preparations made for it, are so graphically told in all the newspapers, that there is nothing left for me to tell you. . . . I fear the false rumour of the taking of Sebastopol must have been brought out to you by the last mail; we are now expecting to hear of it in a day or two—the news will probably arrive in time for this mail. You will see that Sir W. Young was killed in the 23rd, which suffered more than any other regiment; it must be a very heavy blow to his mother. His brother is, I believe, out with the Artillery, which must make her more anxious. I have not heard of the death of any one else whom I know, but the loss in officers has been very great. . . . We are going on quietly here, yet with a little trouble now and then from our agitating friend, ——, who behaved very improperly in church last Sunday, for which he had to apologize. I fear Denison's trial must come on. I hope to send you a form of prayer to be privately used on the subject, which you might give to any who are really interested about it; only it is not a subject to be discussed too freely in your position. I trust the gambling propensities. which were so rife among your fellow-passengers, are not indulged in to the same extent in the West Indies. At least you will have the satisfaction of leading a collegiate life, which will keep you from having to do with such people. I have no doubt the hot weather has a bad effect in this way on many, enervating their minds, and laying them more easily open to temptations.

We are just commencing a branch of the Guild of St. Alban in this district; I trust it may be of great service to us in binding together, by a more religious tie, many young men who are anxious to serve the Church according to their opportunities. . . . With my sincere prayers for your health and spiritual welfare, believe me,

Your very affectionate brother,

CHARLES.

St. Barnabas' College, December 1, 1854.

MY DEAR WILLY,

I have heard of you, though not from you, as your letters have been constantly forwarded. I am sorry to find that you have not yet become reconciled to the climate and annoyances which you must of course expect. I trust, however, that time, and the interest which I hope you will find in your new duties, will enable you to bear patiently what might otherwise seem unbearable. Make up your mind to it as a point of duty, and then doubtless you will have more strength than you would have supposed.

As to climate, just think of our soldiers at present in the Crimea, and how much officers brought up delicately have to endure, and that will be a great help; I find it is so with myself whenever I am tempted to complain.

The war gives us a great deal of anxiety just now, especially when it seems that the weather is putting a stop to the siege operations. They will have a hard time during the winter, and there will be need of very large reinforcements to give reasonable hopes of success. We expect a very trying winter in England, as the war is raising the price of provisions, and there is very little work going on. You will have heard that Lady Young has lost both her sons, William at Alma, and the other from cholera at Balaclava. It is quite wonderful how rapidly recruiting is going on, so that the losses in the army will soon be made up, and probably many new regiments raised from volunteers out of the Militia. . . . As to home news, I mean from St. Barnabas', I have not much to tell you, as we are going on quietly. Skinner is away, spending the winter in Egypt; he was last heard of from Alexandria, after a very bad passage. There have been some heavy storms in the East lately, in one of which several transports were lost in the Black Sea—a sad loss to our troops in the Crimea, who require every possible addition to their comfort. . . .

—— called a short time ago, but I was out of town at the time, on a visit to Sir Frederick Ouseley at Langley. He is now building a church and college at Tenbury in Worcestershire. The

Bishop of Hereford allows him to do almost all that he wishes, and, amusing enough, hoped that he would have Gregorians, as he said he had persuaded his son in his own church. Ouseley is a great anti-Gregorian. . . . God bless you, and guard you in His keeping, and enable you to do your duty in the state of life in which He has placed you, is the sincere prayer of

Your affectionate brother,

C. F. L.

My dear Willy,   St. Barnabas' College, February 16, 1855.

I received your letter before the last mail went out, but had no leisure to answer it as I could wish, and indeed now you must excuse any want of clearness from the pressure of other work. I feel very happy at the thought of your course having been so far prosperous, and that you seem to have been led on towards the attainment of the object for which you went out. I quite sympathize with you in the difficulties which you feel under the Bishop's roof; but I think, if with openness and straightforwardness you combine that modesty which becomes a young man in stating his opinion on all points, especially doctrine, before a Bishop, you need not compromise either your conscience or your prospects.

With respect to your preparation for Holy Orders, the books you mention will be very useful to you. You should certainly read Hooker's fifth book, as most valuable on the ecclesiastical system, sacraments and ceremonies. With respect to the Holy Communion, the nearer you keep to the words of Holy Scripture and the formularies, as well as of some of our soundest divines, the better. Wilberforce's book has been most valuable, however much we may lament his defection; and if you found any account of your belief you may be called upon to give, on our Lord's own words, "This is My Body," "This is My Blood," not pretending to explain how it is His Body or His Blood, either by transubstantiation or consubstantiation, or any other substantiation, but as being so "verily and indeed" in a supernatural manner, beyond our comprehension, explaining that the spiritual benefits accrue only to the faithful, whereas the ungodly receive the Sacrament to their condemnation, I do not think your views can justly be questioned.

But the less we attempt to dogmatize on the manner of Presence, so long as we really believe it, or on that which the ungodly receive, as Denison, I think the better, in the present state of things. The truth is rather learnt through prayer and holiness of life, and we must especially guard against the sacramental system blinding us to our need of a heartfelt loving religion, or of a change of heart towards God. The Sacraments are means towards an end, and they are necessary to salvation, but we must not rest on them as the end; and there is the greatest danger lest we should forget the need of personal holiness, either in our own lives or in our teaching.

I fear there are many persons very reverent in outward behaviour, very constant in their attendance on the ordinances of religion, frequent at Holy Communion and daily service, and regular in private prayer, who yet have not that experience of peace and comfort, and joy in believing, which we may hope and trust for, because they do not seek Jesus Christ as the end and object of their prayers, and strive after that love for Him which can alone satisfy our souls.

I would therefore recommend your reading such books as Thomas à Kempis, or Sutton's " Meditations," and giving some time daily, besides your morning and evening prayers, to prayer and meditation, especially in reference to our ordination; the morning is always the best and quietest, and I should think the warm climate which unfits you for violent exercise would be favourable for quiet and contemplation. You need not doubt being remembered in my prayers, that you may be guided by God's Holy Spirit to an earnest and painful discharge of your duties, and that if it pleases the Lord Jesus to call you to the ministry of His flock, you may be a good and loving shepherd of the sheep for your own and their salvation.

I saw Mr. Butterfield yesterday. He made particular enquiries for you, and was very glad to hear that you were putting your talents to a good account in the way of architecture, or rather building; he thought you would find it very useful in the colony. He hoped very much to hear from you.

We are now in some anxiety in consequence of Westerton's bringing an action in the Consistory Court to remove our altar, credence, screen, etc., but I trust it will all be for the best, and that this may be the means of settling the disputes on these subjects. . . . . We have some young members of the Guild of St. Alban's who are working the night school and lending library, and assisting us in other ways. I trust they will be a great help to us in time; it gives a definiteness and regularity to their work.

We have been suffering from a long and very severe frost; it was prophesied to last six weeks, and it will have been five weeks to-morrow. The crowds on the ice have been very great, and a captain in the Guards drove on a sledge the other day.

——, about whom you must have heard as giving us so much trouble, is in prison for fraud: he has been going on in a dreadful way, poor fellow! I believe he is mad, but he has done a great deal of mischief.

And now, my dear Willy, I must bring my letter to a conclusion, and with every prayer for your future welfare, and that God's blessing may attend your labours and studies, believe me,

Your very affectionate brother,

CHARLES.

CHAPTER VI.

MISSION TO ST. GEORGE'S-IN-THE-EAST.

1856.

"Who, not content that former worth stand fast,
  Looks forward, persevering to the last,
  From well to better, daily self-surpast."

THE time had now nearly come when Charles Lowder
was to realize that life of which he had so earnestly
dreamed in his retirement at Yvetôt. The ship of St.
Barnabas' was finally gliding into smooth water ; and the
brother priests who since 1851 had together striven to
steer her through the storm, were called to leave her about
the same time.

By the end of 1856 the question of internal authority
was settled, though it was not the will of God that the
men who contended for it should continue to reap its fruits.

One thing we are all agreed upon (Mr. Liddell wrote in
October, 1856, to the Senior Curate), that it is *headship* and local
supervision which St. Barnabas' wants. It pains me most deeply
to add that I, more and more, fear this is what you cannot give
it, from the weak and broken state of your health, which it seems
to me must impose upon you entire absence, or preclude you, if
present, from leading and taking the labouring oar in the pastoral

and ministerial work.   And this evil will not be mitigated by a fifth or sixth man, even if we could supply them, because he would be subordinate to, or equal with, the men already there; whereas the admitted want is a man with capacity to lead.

Influential friends, such as Bishop Wilberforce and Dr. Pusey, had strongly advised Mr. Skinner to hold on at his post, even if he could only give the help of a general superintendence.   But the imperative orders of his medical advisers forced him at length to give up his home, and the work to which for five years he had been devoted.   "You yourself," Mr. Liddell wrote, November 7, 1846, "know how I had anticipated availing myself of your services at St. Barnabas'; but, disabled as you are by the Sovereign Will of God, I must bow my head, and seek for another coadjutor."

Of this time Charles Lowder wrote :—

Five years in St. Barnabas' only proved what might be done among the poor in London, and gave time to reflect on how much remained to be accomplished.

It was so ordered also, by God's good providence, that a society of priests had lately been founded in London, called the Society of the Holy Cross.   Its objects are to defend and strengthen the spiritual life of the clergy, to defend the faith of the Church, and to carry on and aid Mission work both at home and abroad. The members of this society, meeting together as they did in prayer and conference, were deeply impressed with the evils existing in the Church, and saw also, in the remedies adopted by St. Vincent de Paul, the hope of lessening them.   They all felt that the ordinary parochial equipment of a rector and curate, or perhaps a solitary incumbent, provided for thousands of perishing souls, was most sadly inadequate; that, in the presence of such utter destitution, it was simply childish to act as if the

Church were recognized as the mother of the people. She must assume a missionary character, and, by religious association and a new adaptation of Catholic practice to the altered circumstances of the nineteenth century and the peculiar wants of the English character, endeavour, with fresh life and energy, to stem the prevailing tide of sin and indifference.

Whilst this small society of earnest priests was thus desirous of attempting some missionary enterprise in addition to their own duties, there was in the East of London a priest, the Rev. Bryan King, Rector of St. George's, who, almost unaided, in nominal charge of thirty thousand souls, had for a long time anxiously looked and longed and prayed for help from others to make some religious impression upon the masses of heathen souls committed to his care.

I had been more than usually oppressed (he writes) by the hopelessness of my position, the leader of a forlorn hope indeed, during the Advent season of 1855, when, in the ensuing season of Christmas, the Rector of the adjoining parish of St. Paul's, Shadwell, conveyed to me the glad tidings that a band of clergy in the west of London were looking out for a suitable sphere for the experiment of a preaching Mission, and that the Rev. F. H. Murray, the Rector of Chislehurst, was in some way connected with the clergy in question.

Upon this information, which had been derived from Mr. Thomas Charrington, a resident of Chislehurst and the conductor of an extensive business in Shadwell, I immediately wrote to Mr. Murray, offering a warm welcome to such an agency in my parish of St. George's East.

The Rector of Chislehurst was one of the first members of the Society of the Holy Cross, and he had mentioned to Mr. Charrington, who was his churchwarden, his own and his brethren's desire to find some sphere in which to bring their plans for Mission work to the test of experience.

At first little more was contemplated than a preaching Mission, for they all had their own parochial duties, and could give but little time to anything else. St. George's-in-the-East was to them a *terra incognita*, and one member of the society was despatched on a voyage of discovery.

The result was that on the evening of Ash Wednesday, 1856, Charles Lowder and the Rev. Newton Smith went to Mr. King's rectory, from whence, with two or three members of the choir, they walked to a room in a court leading out of Ratcliff Highway, which had been used by Mr. King for a Sunday school. Here an old servant, who still serves the Mission, rang a bell at the entrance to the court, and a few were gathered together. Her account of them is that they were mostly, if not entirely, of the respectable and religiously disposed sort, who already went to church when they could. This went on for a fortnight, two clergy going there three times a week. Among the first were the Rev. G. Cosby White and the Rev. Francis Murray.

It does not appear that at this time Charles Lowder contemplated taking charge of the Mission, or any more prominent part than others in working it. The following letters to his mother, written during Lent and Easter week of 1856, contain mention of the undertaking, of which his heart was evidently full, but none of any severance from St. Barnabas' :—

St. Barnabas' College, February 25, 1856.

I write to let you know that I returned to St. Barnabas' on Thursday night, having spent four happy days with a few other clergy in quiet and retirement at Chislehurst. It gives one great strength for one's duties at this season. . . . Our service at 5.30 is progressing ; we had more working-men yesterday. The Mission at St. George's will, I hope, succeed in time. . . . I hope you will all say the third collect for Good Friday daily, for the success of the Mission at St. George's-in-the-East.

St. Barnabas' College, Saturday morning, 1856.

You must not think because you did not hear from me on Saturday last that I had forgotten Mothering Sunday,* but the truth was I was so busy preparing for the meetings, which I have been holding daily, and sometimes twice a day, with the people of my district, for prayer and singing and instruction, that I had not time to get the cake, so I thought it had better be kept till the Octave, and sent it to-day. I trust you have received it ere this, and will believe it is not a mere form, but a remembrance of the love and duty which one who wishes he were a more loving and dutiful son desires to offer to you. I trust the present may prove as sweet as the pleasure of sending it.

I have spent a very happy week in constant meetings with my people, who seem to have appreciated the opportunity of spending one week specially in religious duties. I have been speaking to them of the Christian life, first in the heart, then in the Christian family, then in the world, in doing good to their neighbours, in church, in sickness and death ; and to-morrow I conclude with the Christian in heaven. It has brought me in contact with many whom I had in vain striven to win before, and it has been very delightful to see how regular some have been in daily or even more constant attendance. I trust it will help to prepare us all for Easter. . . .

We are making progress with the Mission, and are hoping to plant two clergy there to take charge of it, and are preparing to

---

* Mid-Lent Sunday. There is a Devonshire custom that absent children should on this Sunday send a cake to their mother, a custom which Charles Lowder seems always to have observed.

collect funds. . . . If I give up the *Guardian* will you be able to send one to Willy? I should like to know before I settle to do so.

March 26, 1856.

I am much obliged to you for your letter received this morning, especially as I fear you wrote it amidst many other occupations. I had wished to have written before, to say how sincerely I have prayed that you might receive all spiritual blessings at this happy season. I am glad you have enjoyed the privilege of having its joy brought out in the services in Church, for thus we can really rejoice together. We have had a very delightful Easter, more so than any I have spent here before. The greatest comfort of all was the large number of communicants; there were two hundred and seventy at the early Communion at seven, a great number of them poor, and two hundred at midday. It was a beautiful sight in the early morning, the procession chanting the hundred and eighteenth Psalm up the aisle, and, as it happened, we came to the nineteenth and twentieth verses as we entered the chancel gates. The church was, of course, nicely decorated with flowers. And then to find so many prepared, at so early an hour, for Holy Communion was very comforting. It was far more than a recompence for one's labours in preparing them during Lent. I had seen about fifty or sixty of them privately, one by one, during the last fortnight of Lent, besides hearing a great many confessions. Our congregations during the rest of the day were very large—in the evening more crowded than I had ever seen before; very many obliged to go away for want of room, and persons standing close in all the aisles. I am happy to say I have stood my work very well, and though, of course, feeling tired now, yet after a little rest shall be able to get on for the confirmation at the end of next month.

We have not succeeded in getting rid of Westerton. My love to my sisters, and believe me,

Your dutiful and affectionate son,
CHARLES.

P.S.—My love to Janey,* and tell her how sorry I am to hear of her illness.

The Mission scheme had now been brought before Bishop Blomfield, and Mr. King wrote in April to Charles Lowder :—

I enclose you the very gratifying reply of Mr. Green to my request. I think we might well append to our statement something to this effect :—

"The Bishop of the diocese has expressed his approval of the above scheme, and has promised a contribution towards it for the next five years, should it please God to spare his life so long."

MY DEAR MR. KING,   London House, April 5, 1856.

The Bishop of London, to whom I have read the paper respecting your proposed Home Mission, directs me to inform you that he approves of the scheme, and is ready, should it please God to spare him, to contribute £10 a year for five years towards the carrying of it out. Praying God to prosper you,

I remain, yours very truly,

T. K. GREEN,

Chaplain.

The operations of the Mission were, after the first fortnight, removed to one of the worst lanes in the parish, Lower Well Alley,† near the Thames, in the cottage of a poor woman whose husband was at sea.

* His old nurse, who for fifty years had lived with different members of his family. She entered his father's service when Charles was an infant, and remained until her death, a beloved family friend. When Mr. Lowder lost his fortune she at once drew £100 from her earnings in the savings' bank, and gave it to Mrs. Lowder, not knowing if it would ever be returned. She refused to leave them, though they could no longer give her wages, but worked as hard as ever to the end for love of them.

† It is now the centre of the parish of St. Peter's, London Docks. Mr.

She herself was just confined (Charles wrote), and unable to take much part in our arrangements, or otherwise to secure order than by expostulating with disturbers from the top of the stairs. And disturbance certainly there was; for as soon as the hymn, which was sung in the alley, the better to collect a congregation, was commenced, a violent opposition was displayed by the Irish, who swarmed in the houses around, and on the first evening interrupted and almost frustrated all attempts at preaching by their clamour and violence. Many dangerous missiles were thrown; for as the court was paved, and so no loose stones came to hand, they soon sacrificed a large beer pitcher, whose fragments were hurled at our heads. An attempt also was made to catechize us as to our acquaintance with the Latin of the Nicene Creed.

After about a fortnight of more or less energetic disturbance, the missioners were left in peace by the Irish, and the baptism of a sick child was among the first fruits of their work. But the longer they worked, the more they felt that little good result could be obtained from desultory efforts, and that some regular and local agency must be established. "Scarcely any impression," Mr. Bryan King said, "seemed to be made upon the people, so that one, if not more, of those clergy who had joined the work at first, now gave up the attempt on account of its apparent hopelessness. It was under these circumstances that a member of my family said to Mr. Lowder, 'Oh, I hope and trust, Mr. Lowder, that you will not be disheartened and induced to give up the work,' when he replied, 'No, you need not fear that; it would take a great deal to dishearten me.'"

King writes: "I was struck with the great improvement of the outward aspect of this court as I walked through it on the day before Mr. Lowder's funeral after landing at the Tunnel pier."

In Calvert Street, a small street running out of Old Gravel Lane, and about five minutes' walk from the river, there is an old and tolerably large house, ugly beyond description, but possessing the advantage of standing in what was by courtesy called "a garden." The wall of this enclosed space forms one side of the street, the house itself being part of the wall. The line of the window-sills, which have given way considerably, show how bad and insecure are the foundations. There are two entrances to the house, one at each end, reached by a steep little flight of steps, and admittance is gained from the street by two grimy doors in the blank wall.

This house was vacant at the time when the band of missioners determined to offer to the Rector of the parish the services of a curate to live amongst the poor, although doubting whether they could raise £100 a year for the purpose. The venture was made, a clergyman of some experience in missionary work was chosen and approved by the Rector, and the house in Calvert Street was secured as his residence. It has been occupied by the Mission ever since ; being now divided into two houses, one occupied by the clergy of St. Peter's, the other by the Sisters.

Mr. King has kindly supplied some account of the beginning of the Mission ; of this time he writes :—

The missionary priest was most zealous and devoted to his work, but he was young and somewhat *erratic*. His ecclesiastical position was that of a licensed assistant curate of the parish church; that position, however, was little more than nominal. It was neither practicable nor desirable that I should exercise more than a very general control over a work which was of the nature of an experiment, and one in which I myself had had no experience ;

G

and yet, in spite of this, I could not of course divest myself of all responsibility, still less could I exonerate myself from all the consequences of any acts of indiscretion which might be committed by one who was in fact my own representative in all his ministerial work.

And hence it was that I wrote to Mr. Lowder, representing to him that the Mission had now assumed the character of a permanent work, and that it was essential that it should be placed under a responsible head, to whose charge I might commit a conventional district of my parish.

From all that I had seen and known of him, I had the most implicit confidence not only in his self-denying zeal, but also in his sobriety and discretion ; and I may with perfect truth assert that never since he accepted my proposal did the conduct of the St. George's Mission cost me a moment's anxiety, nor ever, so far as I now remember, did any cause of difference or even of discussion arise between Mr. Lowder and myself respecting it.

Here are Mr. King's letters, asking Mr. Lowder to take charge of the Mission :—

Rectory, St. George's East, Rogation Tuesday (April 29, 1856).

. . . Now, upon the commencement of our scheme (for I am perfectly certain that we are only commencing), it is necessary that we should fix the *principle*, and, so far, the *precise system* upon which this Mission is to be based and carried on.

We begin, then, with two clergymen and two districts. It seems to me to be quite out of the question that these two (and the other six or eight to follow) should lodge each apart in his own district. In this there is no provision for unity, co-operation, sympathy, etc. But over and above this objection there is no provision in it for the discharge of my responsibility through the missionaries. By the ordinance of Christ Jesus in His Church, the paramount cure of the souls of this parish is vested in my (most unworthy) hands. And the ecclesiastical position of the missionaries will be—assistant curates of the parish church; nay (as you are aware), I shall be amenable to the law for any ecclesiastical offence into which any of them may fall. Our system, then, must be based upon these fundamental principles of the Church.

But then, when the missionaries are not living under the same roof with me, I can only exercise a very general and indirect control. The necessity of the case seems to me to require that there should be some clergyman intimately associated with myself in the duties of the parish church, who yet should preside over the Mission House, and exercise a general (though of course most delicate) superintendence over the members of the Mission. Now, two months ago I was unable (I now believe providentially) to fill Mr. de Burgh's place at the parish church; that place is yet vacant (Mr. Richards being a temporary occupant of it).

Will *you* come and occupy this post, with the superintendence of the Mission House?

You seem to me to be *the one man* wanted. You would have in such a post the entire confidence both of myself and of the members of the Mission, and you are the only man to whom I can look, as Mr. Nicholl is evidently not sufficiently robust for the duties of my very large church.

You will see that the system which I suggest for our Mission is no new and untried one; it is precisely that which has worked so well in all our colleges for centuries, where we have a general Head, and a Vice or deputy living with the Fellows and exercising superintendence.

Notwithstanding Mr. Nicholl's views (and I had a short talk with him on the subject last evening), I still think that we could not do better than take the (comparatively) large house which I spoke to you of before. It, and the one which adjoins it, are the only houses in the whole district which could accommodate four or five clergymen. It is close to our present field of labour, and it is a *respectable* house. I think we should do wrong to take a house which did not admit of the expansion of our work in six or twelve months' time, and I know of no other house in the neighbourhood which would admit of this.

Then we should very probably find that a commercial day school for the sons of the small shopkeepers (Woodard's lower middle class) would answer well in the house (twenty such boys would cover the support of another priest to conduct the school). This, I believe, would be as great a blessing as any branch of the Mission, and would, by God's blessing, bring the parents to the Mission services, and for this obviously a respectable house is essential.

Then the house in question is let at a very moderate rent, the rent being £35 per annum, and the taxes £12 in addition. If we allow this house to pass out of our hands (it will be vacant next quarter day), I fear we shall long have cause to regret it.

My general notion of the scheme for the Mission is this : The two clergymen to hold preachings two or three evenings in the week in different courts of their respective districts ; then, as they gain some hold on the attendants, to say to them, "We have morning and evening service, and Sunday evening service, at the Mission House : will you come there when you can?" then, from *that* service, they will be prepared for the service and sacraments of the Church.

We must try to *begin* upon sound principles, for, I doubt not, our present two will soon become eight or ten missionaries. Pray weigh well the above, and specially the part which concerns yourself.

Should you entertain the proposal, my path (under God's mercy) will be cleared.

Believe me, yours very sincerely,
BRYAN KING.

Rectory, St. George's East, May 2, 1856.

Will you kindly take with you to Titchfield, etc., to-morrow a packet of some fifty of our circulars? I wish to distribute them in my church next Sunday, collecting alms for the Mission on Whit Sunday. I shall not get more than £6 or £8, but I think that some of my people may become interested in the Mission. Mr.

John Knight will give £10 per annum towards it (he already gives me £25 *per annum* for curate's stipend). I enclose a rough sketch of the lower part of my parish, containing nine hundred souls, and well divisable into three missionary districts. A modification of my former plan occurs to me thus : You come and head the Mission as one of them, all the clergy of the Mission officiating with me occasionally at the parish church (this seems to be essential on other grounds); we shall then begin with three clergymen, instead of two, at the Mission. I shall be able to dispense with a special brother curate with me at my church, and to divert some £50 or £60 *per annum* to the support of the Mission, which now goes to my brother curate. I am sure you will take my proposal into your serious consideration. I really do not at all see my way to the establishment of this Mission in my parish unless *you* can come and conduct it.

Believe me, yours very sincerely,
BRYAN KING.

Rectory, St. George's, Friday afternoon.

. . . At Mr. Hubbard's request I have just had an interview with him. He thinks he knows of some two or three clergymen who would like to join the Mission. I said that I should prefer not adding to our staff for some few months, in order to feel our way.

The £40 additional curate's grant was not made for the Mission, but for parish church, so Mr. Knight's contribution must stand at the original £10, instead of the £25. Mr. Hubbard seems much interested in the Mission.

To his parents Charles wrote on receiving Mr. King's letters :—

MY DEAR FATHER, St. Barnabas' College, May 6, 1856.

Will you read first the larger and then the smaller note from Mr. King, enclosed, and then Mr. Bennett's letter ; and then judge whether I can do otherwise than accept the call?

Altogether I feel that our connection with St. George's has been very providential, and as I have in no way sought the appointment, so I cannot but think that the time is come when I may have an opportunity of carrying out the work which I have so long had at heart. I pray that it may be a good work for the Church ; my desire is to make it a thoroughly Catholic one, a life of poverty, and self-denial, and dedication to God's service, and, if it may be, the revival of a really religious order for missionary work—men trained in holy living for the work of winning souls.

Dr. Pusey and the other members of the Mission wish me to go, and we have had already sufficient promise of support to justify our commencement. We have about £130 or £150, mostly annual subscriptions, and Dr. Pusey has about £150 or £160 at his disposal, which he will give to it. And this is only from the few we have asked. . . .

My duty to my mother and love to my sisters, and believe me,
Your dutiful and affectionate son,
CHARLES.

P.S.—Please return the enclosed. Of course I shall have to arrange the details somewhat differently. I shall stipulate for the virtual, if not legal, freedom of the Mission.

St. Barnabas' College, May 15, 1856.

MY DEAR MOTHER,

. . . I suppose my father has told you of the subject of my last letter to him, though you do not say anything about it. Will you tell him that I am very much obliged to him for his kind letter, and that it is a great comfort for me to think that, if I am privileged to begin this great work at St. George's, I shall go there with the full sanction of both my spiritual and natural fathers.

I am now arranging with Mr. King the position of the Mission clergy, and negotiating for a house. I will let you know as soon as that is arranged. I shall hope to be at home in July, so as to get some rest before I begin the work. . . . I am glad to hear Janey is better; my love to her.

> Believe me, your dutiful and affectionate son,
>
> CHARLES.

The letters which follow from Mr. King evidently deal with Mr. Lowder's stipulations for " the virtual, if not legal, freedom of the Mission," and are interesting as showing the first tentative lines upon which the experiment was made.*

Rectory, St. George's East, May 14, 1856.

MY DEAR LOWDER,

I have not yet heard from Mr. Woodbridge, the land-lord of our proposed house. My offertory last Sunday (including £3 or £4 from friends) amounted to £12 12s. 3d. ; then I have received information of a grant of £40 *per annum* from Mid-summer, from the Additional Curates' Society, for the parish church. Very probably Mr. Hubbard has obtained this for the Mission—at all events, I think I can appropriate it to that object ; then, as I resign Mr. Knight's contribution to a curate's stipend, he allows me to transfer this £25 per annum to the Mission (I presume in lieu of his promised £10 per annum). Pray let me have a list of our present donations and subscriptions, and I will apply to my college for help. I should like to interest them in the matter. We may well be thinking of a third member of the Mission. Would Nicholl join it? and has he health for it? If he would, you, or rather we, should (D.V.) form a united and happy family.

Upon the question of ecclesiastical districts I do not think that I should hereafter object to them, provided that on the formation the *Bishop would or could withdraw from me my cure of souls within such districts.* My deep objection to the present arrangements of such districts is this, that without in the least

* The answers to these letters have been lost.

absolving the parish priest in conscience from the responsibility of their charge, they now only interpose obstacles in the way of his discharge of such responsibilities.

I *think*, however, that you may implicitly rely upon my anxiety to meet *your* wishes and those of the other clergymen who may join us, in everything within my power, but I confess that I would rather not anticipate future contingencies. If we begin this work, simply trusting (and confident as we may be) that God will take charge of us and it, shaping its direction for the best, then He will *certainly* take charge of its success ; whereas if we forecast, and are careful about the future, I fear 'we shall find our wisdom to be foolishness.

Do not, dear Lowder, suppose that in so saying I am in the least blaming *you*. I wish to confirm my own faith, and I am certain that you will quite agree with this principle.

Rectory, St. George's East, May 16, 1856.

. . . Though I fear I cannot acquiesce in your *theory* as to the position of the proposed Mission in this parish, I believe that in *practice* we should be quite at one.

I am fully convinced of the necessity of the members of this Mission being as free and unshackled as possible, *i.e.* as is compatible with their ecclesiastical position as *assistant priests in the parish*, and for that reason I begged you to superintend it, because I knew that, under your superintendence, any ordinary control or interference on my part would be quite uncalled for. I should be perfectly ready, when circumstances permitted it, to resign my paramount cure of souls over the districts into the hands of the Bishop, with a view to their formation into distinct parishes.

But so far as I understand your theory, it is that the members of each Mission should be at liberty to exercise their ministry in a parish *in entire independence of the parish priest.* Now, such a position seems to me to be almost as schismatical (and much more fatal to the unity of the Church in the parish) as is the position of a Wesleyan or any other mission. The fundamental constitu-

tion of the Church of Christ with reference to its parochial distribution is this : there cannot possibly be more than *one priest of
the parish* who, in the language of the Canonists, is the *Persona
Ecclesiæ Parochialis*, or *Sponsus Ecclesiæ Parochialis*, any more
than there can be more than one Bishop of the diocese. In the
one case there may be suffragan Bishops, as in the other there
may be assistant priests; but anything like independent jurisdiction in either case is impossible, or absolutely fatal to the unity
of Christ in His Church. I cannot but feel strongly, then, that
if such Missions as we propose are to be employed at all in
the Church, they must be constituted in harmony with the parochial systems, or rather with the fundamental constitution of the
Church Universal, and not upon any scheme devised by you or
me. The paramount cure of the souls of the parishioners of
this parish, which I received on my knees from the Bishop of
this diocese at my institution, I cannot but regard as a spiritual
reality, and not as a mere legal fiction. It is, then, simply impossible for me (or indeed for any other parish priest) to divest
myself of my spiritual control (however remotely and rarely it
may be exercised) with respect to the districts to be occupied
by the members of the Mission.

But could I (independently of the question of duty and conscience) debar myself from the *exercise* of such control? You
speak of building a chapel and having it licensed for divine
service at once. Well, for any irregularities in the service of such
chapel both the Canon and the common law will hold me alone
to be responsible. Is it then reasonable that I should debar
myself from the possible exercise of that ecclesiastical control
which is essential to the discharge of such responsibility?

And further, is it *desirable*? We contemplate eventually the
erection of several such chapels, and the addition of some six
or eight missionaries. Suppose, then, some one missionary to
commit grave irregularities in the celebration of service in such
chapels, or in the conduct of his Mission. I must, of course, in
such a case, protect myself and my parish from such irregularities;

but I should have no power to interfere, scarcely even by way of remonstrance (and the head of the Mission would have no *ecclesiastical* jurisdiction whatever). I should therefore be compelled at once to adopt the extreme measure of requesting the Bishop to issue an inhibition against such missionary, and to withdraw his licence. I should scarcely consent to place either myself or the members of the Mission in a position in which such a course as this would be my only alternative.

It is, then, I think, *absolutely essential* that such Missions as we contemplate should be constituted in *entire harmony with the fundamental ordinances of Christ in His Church, as those are fixed by the Canons* of the Church Universal. If you think that such a Mission could not efficiently be worked in connection with myself as the parish priest, then of course you will seek for another sphere ; if you have any *doubts* on this point, then you can try the experiment (say, for three or six months) ; and that you may be perfectly unshackled at the termination of such period, I will, if you wish, take upon myself the responsibility of taking the house in Calvert Street for the temporary purpose. Nay, further, as we are beginning a very eventful experiment in the Church of England, it is most important that we should begin upon a sound and safe basis.

Both you and I may be deceived or biassed : you may regard the Mission too exclusively from your point of view, as of course I may from mine. Send then your letter and this to Dr. Pusey for his counsel ; he, in Oxford, has the advantage of consulting far better and wiser heads than yours or mine, learned Canonists and earnest and experienced parish priests.

Beg him to draw up an experimental scheme or constitution for the Mission, giving it as free and unshackled a position as is compatible with my responsibilities, and I doubt not that such a scheme will meet the wants of both of us.

Believe me, yours very sincerely,

BRYAN KING.

P.S.—I do not advert now to the minor matters alluded to in

yours of Whit Tuesday, as *e.g.* your objection to the members of the Mission discharging any stated duties in the parish church, and your objection to undertake at present the charge of the *remotest* district of the parish, because (however anxious I may feel on this latter point) I shall of course be ready to defer to your wishes in all such matters.—B. K.

Rectory, St. George's East, May 19.

. . . Collins spent yesterday with us, and from some talk which I had with him as to the Mission, I think it possible I may have misapprehended your meaning when I supposed you to propose that I should *absolutely* give up the district to the Mission. He thinks you wished only for the arrangement which is carried out in Leeds under Dr. Hook, who says to a clergyman of a chapel, "I give up this district to you (delegating to you my charge over its people), but I must take it out of your hands should you commit any grave irregularity." Now, should this be your meaning, I presume there would be no difficulty about the matter; only to the *latter* part of the above proposition I should much prefer the following understanding—indeed, I should in every respect prefer saying—"I give up this part of my charge to you, having entire confidence in you ; only let there be the fullest confidence between us. So pray don't enter upon any *new line of action* without first apprising me of your intentions, and so affording me an opportunity of consultation with you about it."

Collins thinks it would be better were you to give me at first a written plan of your proposed scheme of working the Mission, to prevent all future misunderstanding; but as our plan is at present utterly experimental, and must be modified almost from day to day, this would hardly be practicable. And I confess I do not like the thought of it, as it seems to imply distrust, of which I feel not the slightest shadow, either with respect to him or yourself.

Rectory, St. George's East, May 21, 1856.

. . . There is no difficulty in the least about the assignment of a conventional district with the consent of the Bishop. This I have done for several years in the north-west portion of my parish, but then, of course, such an arrangement is necessarily terminable at any time, at the option either of myself or the clergyman in charge.

I cannot possibly make such an assignment *absolutely* until I be formally discharged from my *legal* and ecclesiastical responsibilities in respect to such districts. However, it seems right upon all accounts that we should apprise the Bishop now in the first instance of our progress and prospects. I will therefore write at once to Mr. Green, informing him of our present position, and requesting him to consult the Bishop upon the question of the assignment.

Rectory, St. George's East, May 27, 1856.

. . . I have just heard from Mr. Blomfield, in answer to my application to the Bishop through Mr. Green, who writes on the subject as follows :—"His Lordship desires me to say that the clergymen who are to act as missionaries in your parish will be licensed as your assistant curates, and although it will be in your power to give them any extent of pastoral charge which you may think proper, they will still be amenable to your authority as much as an assistant curate would be, for their position as missionaries cannot affect your jurisdiction as Rector. While therefore you may give them a great liberty of action, and more than you would give to an assistant curate, you cannot resign a district absolutely to their charge, so as to give up your right of interference in any matter or at any time which might seem to you to require it. As Rector you will, therefore, be responsible for their proceedings.

" The Bishop also desires me to say that if Mr. Lowder comes to him, appointed by you, and with the usual testimonials, he will be prepared to license him."

The above remarks upon the necessary present ecclesiastical position of the Mission, in *any* parish, is, you will see, very much as I anticipated. I have not a copy of my note to Mr. Green, but if you would wish to see it, I dare say that Mr. Blomfield could lend it you. I repeat that I do not anticipate *the least practical* difficulty between us. You would, of course, inform me of any new line of action upon which you were about to enter before you committed *me* to it, and with that limitation (which is essential to my responsibilities in the case) you would be free in your action.

May 31, 1856.

. . . You misapprehend the Bishop on the points of a conventional district. I wrote to say that I proposed to assign one to the members of the Mission, and he does not say a word against it; he only speaks *of the position of the clergy* in charge of such conventional districts. Upon the *principles* of your scheme for the Mission, of course, I quite agree; as to the *time* for carrying some of them out, and the Christian *economy* and *reserve* to be observed (respecting some of them), of course that must be left to the members of the Mission, and I trust that they will always be in the habit of the fullest and most fraternal consultation with myself, upon all *religious* questions affecting the parish, whether more directly relating to the parish church or the Mission. I need but allude to two points of the scheme in question.

First, I fear that it will be no more legally practicable to use the licensed chapel for other services than those of the Prayer-book than it would in the case of a consecrated building.

Secondly, as to churchings and baptismal services, I much doubt whether churchings or baptisms could be legally celebrated in such chapel at all.

On the point of "fees" (I hate the word in connection with religious services), I presume that you mean strictly "*fees*," and do not mean that people should be taught that they *can* return God thanks without making to Him *thankofferings*." The enclosed, which I circulated some twelve years ago, will explain what I mean.

The openness and simplicity with which Charles laid his wishes before his parents proves his confidence in their readiness to join with him in the offering of his life, and

in his choice of poverty and self-denial. He writes to
them without passion, without any enthusiastic expressions, and without using arguments to support his wishes,
betraying unconsciously his knowledge of their greatness
of mind. One to whom the writer is most indebted for
information concerning " Father Lowder" writes thus of
his parents :—

It was my privilege to know these two charming persons
very well. They lived * and died at Frome, and I was one of the
curates of the parish church for four years. I see now the bent
figure of this dear and venerable old man, Mr. Lowder's father,
climbing the hill to church, each morning, to be present at the
daily celebration.

I think he communicated every day. It was a picture that
always moved one's heart, to see him kneeling, in rapt prayer, in
the beautiful side-chapel of the parish church. Often his wife was
with him, whenever her health permitted, and one could not see a
more lovely old couple in all Christendom.

It used to delight me to walk with him in his garden, and
let him pour out all his heart in praises of his son. He was so
proud of "Charles," and it was a pride that one respected and
loved.

I never met a more gentle, unselfish, noble-hearted old man.
It was no wonder that our Mr. Lowder should be what he was,
the child of such God-fearing, saintly parents.

Their devoted daughters made a home for them at
Frome, taking pupils ; and Charles probably wished to
talk matters over with his own people at this crisis of
his life. In his sister Susan's journal there is the following
entry :—

* From 1854.

June 22, 1856.

Charles appeared unexpectedly at church this morning.*

25th.

After service, Charles brought Dr. Pusey to see us, and asked him to say something to our pupils. He spoke to us of the doctrine contained in the sermon we had heard from Mr. Richards, and gave us his blessing.

July 2.

We all, with Charles, went by train to Westbury, and there clambered up to the "White Horse," by a very steep, slippery way, where we enjoyed the fine views.

It may, perhaps, have been during this gathering of clergy of Frome-Selwood that it was determined to attempt some sort of revival of Retreats for the clergy, and that Dr. Pusey, with his wonted hospitality, offered his house for the purpose. For the next letter from Charles to his mother gives an account of the first beginning of what has since then become an habitual practice with a large body of the English clergy.

To know that it should have had its cradle in the home of the venerable man to whom the Church owes largest gratitude will be, in these his days of calm retirement, a tender gratification and interest to many.

My dear Mother,   Oxford, July 12, 1856.

Writing from the Union to you reminds me very much of thirteen or fourteen years ago, for though the room is a new one, yet the associations are in many respects the same. . . .

---

* He remained during the Festival of St. John Baptist, when the chancel of Frome Church was opened. Amongst the preachers during the Octave were Dr. Pusey, Rev. Upton Richards, Dr. Evans, and Dr. Woodford, now Bishop of Ely.

We have spent a very happy and, I trust, profitable week at Dr. Pusey's. There have been at one time and the other seventeen or eighteen clergymen present. We met together about half-past six to prepare for Holy Communion, and say Prime, the first Hour. Then we went to Holy Communion at St. Thomas's at seven, remaining in church for prayer about half an hour after the service; then came back to say our Thanksgiving, and Terce; after that breakfast, at which a very beautiful book of meditations for a Retreat like ours was read; went to the Cathedral, or Magdalen Chapel, at ten, and, on two days, after that to a chapel in one of the cemeteries for private prayer; then returned to Christ Church for Sext, and then our conference: consulting together on points of interest, such as conversion and confession, or on some book of the Fathers. After that, dinner about two or three, when there was also spiritual reading.

After dinner Nones and prayers at the Cathedral; a walk before tea, and after tea another conference and reading, and Compline before bed. I have given you a full description, thinking you and my father might be interested in what, I trust, has been a very useful week for those engaged in it; being an attempt to revive a kind of Retreat for Clergy, that they might be able to give more time to prayer and common consultation in quiet and away from distraction. It has been an especial help to me before entering upon the Mission. Dr. Pusey has entered very kindly into it, and given us the greatest assistance, besides lodging and boarding us all.

This account that I have given you is meant to be private, so do not let it go out of the house. I am going to preach at St. Thomas's to-morrow in the morning, and at Littlemore in the afternoon, and shall leave by an early train on Monday morning, and probably sleep at Mr. Knight's, York Place, St. George's East, on Monday and Tuesday, getting off if I can early Wednesday morning. My duty to my father, and love to Aunt E., Rose, and Willy.

Believe me, your dutiful and affectionate son,

CHARLES.

It is certainly remarkable that the first attempt at a Retreat for Clergy in the English Church should have immediately preceded the first organized and real attack upon the heathenism of London.

Mr. Lowder left St. Barnabas' on August 22, and took up his abode at the Mission House in Calvert Street, in the parish of St. George's-in-the-East.

It is not without its own interest and importance, at this crisis, that among the last anxieties of Bishop Blomfield's long and active life was the question of Charles Lowder's licence to St. George's, which gave rise to the following letters from the Rector of the parish :—

Felixstow, Ipswich, August 9, 1856.

MY DEAR BROTHER,

I think that I can hardly ask the Bishop yet for a licence, either for the clergyman or (on that account) for the *room*. In consequence of some remarks of the Bishop in Mr. Blomfield's letter to me of May last, respecting the importance of great prudence and discretion on my part, as well as on the part of the clergymen acting as missionaries in my parish, I was led to reply that I should not ask the Bishop to license any clergyman for such duty, until he had the experience of at least *two months'* work as a missionary.

Again, your form of licence will hardly do. I can hardly undertake the payment of £80 *per annum*, and it does not seem right that I should in terms undertake what I do not intend *personally* to fulfil. We must settle the form of nomination with the Bishop when the time comes.

Should you wish an immediate licence, of course I will write to Mr. Blomfield upon the subject, but I think it would be better to waive this point at present.

P.S.—I am very glad to hear from St. George's of the successful commencement of the Mission services by Collins.

H

August 12, 1856.

. . . I think that you have quite misunderstood me in the matter of the licence ; I never distrusted your fitness for the Mission in every way. I do not in the least object to nominate you *to-day*, as indeed I fancied I had sufficiently indicated in my last note to you, nor indeed do I object to nominate Collins. The simple fact is this : In the letter to me in question, the Bishop was evidently nervous and anxious about our experiment, warning me about my responsibility, and desiring me to be very cautious, etc. Well, he had behaved so kindly and generously at first in giving us his confidence and countenance—he was suffering from severe illness at the time—that I thought I could not do less than attempt to tranquillize him and satisfy his apprehensions by replying that, should he wish it, I would not nominate any clergyman to the Mission until he had some couple of months' experience in the work. I presume that this *did* satisfy him, and simply on this ground I wished you (as I still do) to waive your wishes for the present about your licence. At the same time, I repeat that I shall be ready *at once* to apply to the Bishop for permission to nominate you to the assistant curacy should you still wish it. I assure you that I have not personally *the shadow of a feeling* on this subject; it is to me a matter of indifference whether I nominate you now or two months hence ; but I am sure that you will agree with me in thinking it right to consult the feelings and even prejudices of our poor worn-out Bishop in such a matter. You know that we have it under his hand that he will be ready to license you on my nomination. Well, under such circumstances, no successor of his (be he who he may) *could* hesitate a moment to carry out that intention, when you had left your former cure and entered upon your duties at St. George's in consequence of such expressed intention of the then Bishop.

However, judge for yourself in the matter ; only pray do not conceive that there is any distrust on my part. I shall be, I repeat, perfectly ready and willing to do what you may wish.

August 16, 1856.

I did not inform you of the circumstances in question, because in the first place the Bishop's cautions, which gave rise to my proposal, were intended solely for myself; and, secondly, it seemed very undesirable that I should unnecessarily inform you of a circumstance which might bear the appearance to you of the Bishop's want of confidence in yourself; and I may here say that Dr. Pusey (who was informed by me of all the circumstances) *fully agreed with me* in this view. However, I much regret that I should (however unintentionally) have caused you any pain or annoyance. I write to-day to the Bishop (through Mr. Blomfield), but I will not in the *first instance* say that you make his immediate licence a condition of coming to St. George's, as he might construe that as a kind of threat. I will merely at first say that you are naturally anxious that the thing should be settled before his resignation, adding too my own request on the same ground. I don't think that you will need any testimonials for this transfer of your licence from one cure to another.

August 21, 1856.

The Rev. F. G. Blomfield informs me that "the Bishop is prepared to license Mr. Lowder and Mr. Collins as your assistant curates," through the Archdeacon acting as his commissary; but in reply to my query as to the statement of stipend, he writes as follows :—"The Bishop would not feel himself at liberty to alter the usual form of nomination, which I enclose. The amount of the stipend may be agreed upon between yourself and Mr. Lowder and Mr. Collins, but in law you will be responsible for the payment of it, from whatever source the funds may be derived." Now, I presume that if we mutually agree upon the stipend of £4 per annum each, and I pay you that sum quarterly, this will meet the above requirement (for the present year, you can return me £8 out of the £10 which I paid as my subscription for this purpose) ; this arrangement comes within the *letter* of Mr.

Blomfield's direction, and I should think would be accepted by Archdeacon Hale under the circumstances of the case.

The two letters which follow are the last from St. Barnabas' and the first from Charles Lowder's new home to his mother.

St. Barnabas' College, August 18, 1856.

MY DEAR MOTHER,

You may suppose I am fully occupied, as I hope to get down to St. George's on Wednesday, when my address will be Mission House, Calvert Street, St. George's East.

Yesterday I took my leave of most of my flock, though I take a last Communion with them on Sunday morning next.

I am going to send down a small box of books which may be useful to Willy, and some note-books ; if there are any which he does not want and Annie does, she can have them. Some few are yours ; the box is also yours.

I am busy paying farewell visits, which is not a happy occupation.

Duty to my father, and love to all.

Believe me, your dutiful and affectionate son,

CHARLES.

Mission House, Calvert Street, St. George's, August, 1856.

MY DEAR MOTHER,

I was very glad to receive your letter this morning. I arrived here about five o'clock, and we had a service at eight, at which, although a very wet day, there were a few people. We hope to begin our temporary church very soon, although there are delays from the Metropolitan Board of Works, who have to approve of every building before it is commenced.

I shall be glad to see Willy, who I suppose will make his appearance here soon. We might give him a bed in a day or two, but, you may suppose, we are all in the rough. This letter is the first I have written in my own room, having only just got the table in. You may tell Annie I have her scroll up behind me, over the chimney-piece, and a picture of the Crucifixion and her drawing of St. Laurence before me. It was, of course, very painful wishing good-bye to all at St. Barnabas'; however, I got through it better than I expected. I met the people of my district in the school-room on Sunday afternoon, and I am going to receive Holy Communion with them next Sunday at half-past seven. I hope you will remember us at your eight o'clock Communion. Wishing the school children good-bye tried me most. However, it is not as if I was quite cut off. There seems a great work to be done here, if God gives us grace and strength to do it. Duty to my father, and love to all,

From your dutiful and affectionate son,

CHARLES.

So, with single heart, he gave himself to the work to which he was called. He had looked steadily, during his missionary visits to East London, into the great gulf of misery and sin ; and, no longer content to stand on its edge, giving a helping hand here and there, he cast himself boldly into the midst of it, if by any means he might save some.

CHAPTER VII.

FIELD OF THE MISSION.

"Where all life dies, death lives, and nature breeds
Perverse, all monstrous, all prodigious things,
Abominable, unutterable."

WHEN Charles Lowder gave his life to the Mission of St.
George's-in-the-East, he had reached the age of thirty-six,
a time of life when a man's character is no longer imma-
ture, although it can never cease to grow and to be modified,
in one direction or another, until the end.

What was the work for which, in the very prime of
manhood, he thus gave up everything else on earth? And
what manner of man was he who chose this work, and
how did it re-act upon his own heart and outer bearing?
What is the image which he has left in the hearts of his
people?

It is difficult, nay impossible, to draw a truthful picture
of the field which he voluntarily chose as that of his life's
work. The shadows would be too black and unrelieved.
There is a long street within five minutes' walk of the Mission House where Charles lived. It has been said that—

A full volume would not suffice to exhibit the records of debauchery and crime with which the history of but one street in

the East of London is associated. That street is the Ratcliff Highway.* Houses of call, dancing and concert rooms, brothels and spirit shops, furnish a *rendezvous* for the lowest types of humanity of almost every nation.

This Highway runs through the parish of St. George's-in-the-East, from west to east. Foreign sailors from every country— Greeks, Malays, Lascars, Dutch, Portuguese, Spanish, French, Austrians—may be encountered everywhere; so that, with the German sugar-bakers, the population is as mixed as any in the world.

The street is laid out, as it were, for the reception, entertainment, and amusement, *tale quale*, of sailors, and is filled with boarding-houses, slop-shops, and all the attendants of a seafaring population. Amongst them are two or three collections of foreign animals and birds, Mr. Jamrach's wild beasts and curiosities being the most famous.

But in what words is it possible to speak of the unhappy beings who absolutely throng this street, lying in wait for their prey?

Alas, alas! we are content that vice and misery should be removed from our sight, as something which offends our so-called refinement and culture. The streets of West London are, as it were, swept clean of the outward hideousness of sin. What would be at once put a stop to by the police in any of our "respectable" thoroughfares is permitted to go on unchecked within an hour's drive of Rotten Row. We are careful to guard our high-born wives and daughters from at least those outward scenes which might shock their eyes and corrupt their morals; but though we talk sentiment about the brave tars of merry England, we

---

* Now called St. George's Street.

do little or nothing to save them from ruin, in every sense, when they return to our shores.*

St. George's-in-the-East forms a part of that eastern London little known to dwellers in pleasanter quarters of the metropolis. And yet, to quote Charles Lowder's own account of those parts—

St. George's contains one of the main supplies of London's wealth and commerce, as well as one of its most curious sights— the London Docks. The extensive basins, in which may be seen the largest ships of the world; the immense warehouses, which contain the treasures of every quarter of the globe—wool, cotton, tea, coffee, tobacco, skins, ivory; the miles of vaults filled with wines and spirits; the thousands of persons employed—clerks, custom officers, artisans, labourers, lightermen, and sailors—make the Docks a world of itself, as well as a cosmopolitan *rendezvous* and emporium. Those who merely catch a glimpse from a river steamer of its forest of masts can have little idea of the busy scenes which are daily to be witnessed within its high walls. Here are vessels swarming with labourers lading and unlading; powerful hydraulic cranes, lifting their tons; gaugers measuring and testing the wines and spirits; porters shifting hogsheads : coopers hammering; clerks busy entering the freights; the trim American clippers, the fast tea-ships from China, or the Mediter-

---

* While these pages are passing through the press, a Mission House and Restaurant for sailors has been opened at 42A, Dock Street, London Docks. It is under the same admirable management which has already done so much for working-men by opening Restaurants, where they are well and cheaply fed, in different parts of London, notably in Harrow Road, off Edgeware Road, and in Paternoster Row. The large and widespread missionary labours of these Sisters in the worst parts of London, make us feel that they need nothing but material support to enable them to reclaim thousands, and to found real havens of refuge for sailors. Those whose hearts are touched with pity for these men cannot do better than visit the establishment in Dock Street, and judge for themselves. It is outside St. Peter's parish, in one of the worst parts of Wapping.

ranean steamers, warped out of the river through the dock-gates
into the wide basins and taking up their berths. Then, of course,
this commerce brings a vast amount of traffic into our streets.
Waggons laden with merchandise—heavy casks of sugar or wine,
bales of cotton or wool, tea-chests, bags of coffee—to be dispersed
throughout the metropolis, the country, and the world; huge
boilers, engines, or machinery to be shipped to the colonies or
foreign countries—all this life and animation give a special character to our streets and thoroughfares.

Here, therefore, the sailors swarm, and here, in Mr.
Lowder's words, " are to be seen the poor denizens of the
neighbouring brothels, flaunting their finery and their persons, and plying their hateful trade by night and day. . . .
The recklessness of vice, the unblushing effrontery with
which it is carried on when the lowest of every country
combine to add their quota to the already overflowing
stock, can scarcely be conceived. The public-houses are
chiefly kept by foreigners, as are very many of the lodging-
houses, whilst most of them live upon the vices of the
sailors ; and publicans actually keep wretched girls in their
pay to entrap the poor sailor, who is soon stripped of his
all when he falls into their treacherous clutches. A staff of
prostitutes is, in fact, part of the stock-in-trade, and instances
could be adduced in which houses of ill fame have been
attached to the public-houses, or rented by their owners.
At one time the publican interest was so powerful in the
parish, that for years one at least of the churchwardens was
a publican.

" In the midst of such scenes of sin and misery the
children were brought up, the school of too many being the
streets, abounding in temptation, echoing with profane and

disgusting language, and forming a very atmosphere of vice; their examples at home a drunken father and mother, with brothers and sisters already deep in sin; and abroad thieves and prostitutes a little older than themselves. Thus they were early taught to thieve, to swear, to be bold and immoral in their manners and talk, and so to fall in with sins which they beheld in others at the most precocious age."

This was no exaggerated description of this parish, for it had few redeeming features; scarcely any residents of education and respectability to foster a better spirit, unless we except a few professional persons whose ties confined them to the spot, nearly every person of this stamp having given up his residence in the parish that his children might not be contaminated by evil sights and sounds.

Never can the writer lose the haunting memory of that Highway—the evil faces of men, the poor lost women sitting with uncovered heads in groups on door-steps, or walking with sailors; the sickening brutality, degradation, and open vice with which the very air seemed thick. And ever, within sound of this very murmur of hell, the daily cry ascends from the altar of St. Peter's: "Thou that takest away the sins of the world, have mercy upon us."

Ratcliff Highway is outside the bounds of St. Peter's parish; but we have been lately told that twenty years ago that street represented the condition of a whole parish, in which "all the elements of degradation—poverty and improvidence, drunkenness and prostitution, robbery and violence, ignorance and unbelief, were active—a whole parish in which many of the most 'respectable' found their interest in supporting vice, while the police were both unwilling and afraid to interfere."

And the worst is that what is seen in the streets is the least part of the wretchedness which exists. To know and write of these things it is necessary to have lived amongst them. No apology is necessary for long extracts from the accounts most kindly supplied by one * who worked for eleven years in those streets and lanes. He writes :—

The most graphic picture of the narrow courts and alleys, as seen through the murky atmosphere of fog and dust, with all the horrors of sight and sound and smell—scowling brutal faces of men, degraded monsters of women ; poor little children half clad except with dirt, with naked feet and dishevelled hair, playing in the gutter, many of them stunted, half-witted, and deformed, and all wan and sickly looking ; the air filled with the bruit of quarrels, shameful words, and curses—no mere passing experience of such outside features can give any adequate knowledge of the life that is lived within, in the wretched hovels that go by the name of home.

Thanks to the *London Labourers' Dwellings Society*, many of these houses are now much better cared for, at least in those parts where the society has property, but at the time of which I write I suppose that the average of the parish would give thirty souls to each small house.

A whole family in each room : one room for day and night, for living and dead, for all sexes and all ages. Think how hard it is to teach children and grown-up people the respect and reverence due to themselves as part of the Body of Christ, amidst such surroundings of their daily life. How almost impossible it is to train up the young in habits of decency and purity under such degrading conditions. It half drives one mad to think what it is in the sight of the purest Heaven—the mad riot and shameful

* Rev. Robert Linklater.

wickedness of souls that have been redeemed by the precious
Blood, who by the foulest sins desecrate their bodies which are
part of Christ, who day by day grieve the Holy Spirit of God and
drive Him from their hearts.

And these, the many of them, are sailors rescued from the
waves. Sons and husbands for whom have gone up from many
an English village, ay, and from homes throughout the world,
the earnest pleading of brave women's hearts. Men who through
the long night watches have paced the deck and thought of the
days gone by, the happy times when they were pure and innocent,
kneeling at their mother's knees. Or who have seen God's
wonders in the deep, who have "cried unto the Lord in their
trouble," and were half persuaded for the rest of their saved lives
to "praise the Lord for His goodness, and declare the wonders
that He doeth for the children of men." And now, when to their
straining eyes appear the cliffs of dear old England, and when
with grateful hearts they land, they are seized upon by harpies,
liers in wait for blood, who rob them of all their hard-earned
gains, and worse than rob them, spiritually murder them.

I have heard the most piteous stories of large sums of money
thus squandered in a day or two. And the mother or wife, who
waits at home, has to starve. Ordinary people cannot believe
what fools sailors are. Now and then an exposure of the
"confidence trick" opens our eyes. Their very simpleness, which
makes them such easy dupes, shows how easily they could be led
to good, and is an appealing cry to us for protection and help.

I went down to Southampton, some little time ago, with a
sailor who had just been paid off. It had cost him five pounds to
get from Tower Hill to Waterloo Station. I asked him how he
could possibly have spent so much money. He said, "Well, I
wanted first to go to the shipping office, and I didn't know the
way, and you can't ask your way in London for nothing." I said,
"Why did you not take a cab?" He answered, "So I did at last,
and that was the cheapest turn I had." The cabman had only
charged him *sixteen shillings* for the journey (about a two-shilling

fare), and the poor sailor then felt he had to treat him, as he couldn't charter him all the way to Southampton.

To return to St. Peter's-in the-East : let me try to describe a visit to one of the dens which are the homes of our poor. Having struggled up the narrow rickety stairs, and passed lower regions peopled with men, women, and children, who open their doors in curiosity to gaze at us, and thus reveal the hideous misery within, we come to a garret where a poor woman lies dying on the floor, huddled into a corner on a bag of straw, covered over for the sake of warmth with all the rags which constitute the property of .the place. One is half stifled with the intolerable smell. At a glance we take in the awful poverty, for literally there is not a stick of furniture, save the crazy-looking table and one broken chair. The children—well, I have seen them quite naked like savages. Perhaps even in the depth of winter no fire in the grate. Of the horrors of vermin one cannot speak. We are told, and we could have guessed it from their faces, that they have not tasted food that day.

God only in heaven knows the awful poverty and suffering that beneath His pitying gaze is bravely borne by thousands and thousands of our unhappy brothers and sisters in these dark corners of our land. And in the place of which I speak only a dock wall separates them from the food and produce of the world, and, a little higher up the river, only a railing shuts them out from the Royal Mint, where all the money of England is coined.

And I am speaking, not of lazy vagabonds, but of those who either cannot get work, or are too ill to work. How the heart of the missionary is stirred to give to these poor sufferers the " such as I have," the treasures and joy of heaven. What a cruel pity it is that, having such a life of misery here, they should miss the Life of Joy hereafter.

But it may be said, " Poor creatures ! what do we pay our poor-rates for ? Why do they not go into the workhouse ? " Why not, indeed ? I suppose because to go into the workhouse is to give up for ever the battle of life, is the snapping of the last thin thread of hope, the for ever drowning themselves, body and soul, in the dark waters of pauperism. How can we marvel that these poor creatures cling so tenaciously to the dear life, that they suffer any privation rather than break up their little home and sink for ever the prospects of their children?

The *Guardians* of the Poor so carefully fulfil their trust, which they consider to be the keeping down of the rates, that the respectable poor would rather die than enter their dreaded walls; and as now all outdoor relief is stopped, unless the charity of the Church can help them, sickness and bad times to them mean simply starvation and death.

The great industry of the Docks and river-side is lading and unlading ships. The regular payment of such work is fivepence an hour, making one pound a week, if lucky enough to be employed the whole week. For many days and weeks contrary winds may keep the ships down channel, and then there is nothing to do. It is quite a common thing for men to be for weeks without work. And yet out of this precarious labour a man has to pay his weekly rent, and clothe and feed himself and his family. How can he put by anything?

And as the arrival of ships is uncertain, so when they do come it is in great numbers; consequently extra hands have to be employed to unlade and get them ready for sea again, and thus more men are required for these spurts of trade than can be regularly employed in ordinary times. If these considerations affect even prosperous times, it may be imagined how the poor have suffered during the months and months of commercial depression through which England has lately passed.

I do not know any more pitiful sight in London than that which can be seen any early week-day morning at the dock entrances. Thousands of labourers waiting for work, and waiting day after day in vain. The official whose duty it is to select the men required has often told me that it has cut him to the heart to see this surging mass of eager upturned faces struggling to get near him, to have to meet their imploring eyes, and yet to be obliged to deny them and shake off their appealing glance and cry back into their despairing hearts, knowing but too well what it all means in the starvation and suffering of their homes.

What I have said can give but a faint notion of the atmosphere of pain and want and sin which Mr. Lowder had to breathe for twenty-three years. No wonder it broke down his splendid health and saddened his heart. Think what it is to have to live in the midst of such suffering lives and to be unable to relieve them all. Only those who have tried it know how living in such a depressing place, and having constantly to grapple with the same difficulties, the same hopeless puzzle of degraded life and multiplying degradation, break down the stanchest heart. And Mr. Lowder's heart when he assayed the work must have been stanch indeed.

CHAPTER VIII.

PORTRAIT OF THE MISSIONER.

> " For of the soul the body form doth take,
> For soul is form, and form doth the body make."

" TELL us what he was like," is a child's demand concerning the hero of a story. And older children wish for a word-painting of " Father Lowder's " outward appearance and character. But the colours must be gathered, here and there, from those who knew him well.

He was tall, rather slight than otherwise, but remarkably well made, and with that grace and elasticity of movement which marks strength and muscular power. His head was singularly fine, bald in early manhood, and well set on his shoulders, the organs which phrenologists assign to the moral qualities being largely developed. His features were regular and finely cut ; the calm steadfast grey eyes, keen and fearless, shaded by somewhat large lids, could look cold or tender, or light up with a merry roguish twinkle, as occasion arose. The strongly moulded mouth and chin and tightly closed lips gave evidence of a strong will ; but the lips could relax into a very sweet smile, and of late years this was their general expression, while the clear complexion and fresh colour betokened health of body and of mind.

This is a picture of him in his prime, before oppressive cares furrowed his brow, and ill-health and premature age robbed him of his freshness. It was a thoroughly sculpturesque head, and was said to resemble a carved portrait of Canning in St. Mary Redcliffe, Bristol. Dr. Wolff used to say, "I love Lowder's face; it is like one of the old Passionists;" and one of his curates said, "If the Father were to get up into the pulpit and say nothing, you could not help being the better for the sight."

His manner and address were dignified and courteous, though as a rule he was silent and reserved, except when out of harness, when he was full of spirits, and always talked freely and made friends. He walked at a swinging pace, and never allowed himself a moment more than necessary to reach his proposed point. He was full of energy in all manly exercises. "I can hardly believe," a friend writes, "that it is only fifteen months since I put on his skates for him. We went off one frosty morning to have a quiet day on a pond in the country."

His "outward fairness was all the more fair because it was but the ambassador of a most fair mind," but all who write of him say that his character is one difficult to describe. And yet there is the greater reason for attempting it, because his letters reflect little of himself.

This is certainly, in part at least, owing to the absolute want of self-consciousness which must have marked his character to a very unusual degree.

His letters have been placed, in great numbers, at the writer's disposal, and rare indeed must it be to find a collection written with such sincere simplicity, without the faintest trace of self-consciousness, or of occupation with

I

self. They are in one way the less interesting; for people with some self-consciousness cannot help expressing their inner selves in their letters; even excellent people are more or less occupied with their own emotions, and, unconsciously, their pen paints themselves.*

But really Charles Lowder seems never to have thought about himself, certainly never contemplated himself. If he ever passed through that "stage of piety" which Fénélon says most good people traverse, the stage of self-introspection, there is no token of it in anything he has left. He seems always to have been thinking of others, and, even in his constant correspondence with the mother to whom he was devoted, to have no need for *épanchement* about his own feelings and wishes, simply because he was not thinking about them. When he did feel anything touching himself keenly, as his exile from St. Barnabas', he expresses it to his mother, but in simplest and shortest words. There is no dwelling on the subject, as if it were one which interested him. Most people are interesting to themselves, but it almost seems as if Mr. Lowder did not find himself so; what evidently occupied his mind, as far as earthly interests went, were his own family, his work, and natural scenery.

The more his letters are read the more they convey the impression of one wholly truthful, wholly to be trusted, without any inner folds—expressing far less than he felt, far less than he was prepared to do.

Those nearest to him say that he was naturally excitable, but was so deeply impressed with the danger and evils connected with such a temperament, that the severe self-dis-

* Of this, Bishop Patteson's letters will recur to many as a striking instance.

cipline used to keep it under, gave an impression of coldness ; so that to some he might appear a man of highest religious character and principle, with a stern sense of duty, an iron will, and a dogged perseverance in doing what he felt to be right, but lacking tenderness or *humanity.* Certainly this is the impression which he made upon some outside his own family. One who lived and worked with him for many years says that he thought he was "*naturally* a cold, stiff, stern man ; and that it was the conquest of grace over nature which so wonderfully softened him in later years." But he goes on to say :—

Another friend of his, with whom I have discussed this point, thinks that the tender heart was always there, and that as his natural strength decayed its warmth was manifested.

I do not know that these two views are necessarily antagonistic —the one may look deeper beneath the surface than the other ; but I am sure that my view is the more true one as regards very many people who have known and respected Mr. Lowder through long periods of his life. Much as they respected and admired him they could not all at once get at his heart. But when they did, how rare and true and deep did they find his love. All the more precious because such an unexpected find.

My own theory about this is that the desertion from which he had suffered,* a stab to his inmost heart, had added to his natural reserve, and chilled and kept back for a time the flow of genial and confiding love.

The turning-point came in the death of his father and mother. I know that Mr. Lowder came back from their death-beds quite changed and softened. Indeed, he told some of the poor people that he was afraid he had not before entered sufficiently into their sorrows, but that now a new light had been let in upon his soul.

* When three curates suddenly left him to join the Church of Rome. See Chapter XV.

And he was a man who, when he changed, changed for ever.   He was as determined and persevering in this as in everything else. He set about it in a mechanical and business-like sort of way, but he succeeded.   He became wonderfully gentle and kind before his death.   I have often been amused and edified in watching the manifest effort it cost him to sustain the attempt : one could see the workings, and nothing showed more the real goodness of the man than this difficult conquest over natural reserve.

And my opinion is that this was all as it should have been. Had Mr. Lowder been other than he was he would never have done the work he did.   It wanted a stern, determined man to make anything of the sort of people he had to do with.   Gentleness and tenderness would have been mistaken for weakness by the poor enervated lives he had to cultivate and raise.   His firmness was like an anchor to their shifting, changing, easily discouraged hearts.   He shamed them into consistency and pluck by his undaunted steadfastness.   They saw this noble figure stand like a lighthouse amidst overwhelming waves of desertion, treachery, disappointment, and rebuke, and they were abashed that small trials of their own estate, and unworthy attractions of sins they had abandoned, should undermine their determination and sap their perseverance.   They feared and admired him, and I dare say his great example of stern duty-doing, sticking to his purpose through thick and thin, had more effect on the savages amongst whom we had to live, than if he had been tender and soft.   It really was a noble picture they looked upon, "a good man struggling with adversity."

And if they quailed before his determined and rebuking eye, yet they tasted the tenderness of his love and pity in their hour of sickness or spiritual need.   He never could have won the intense love of his people if they had not found out that beneath that cold exterior beat the warm true heart of the friend they could trust, the priest they could revere.

It is quite the feature of their lasting regard for him, this mixture of admiration for his courage and gratitude for his love.

"Ah! the Father, he *was* a man and no mistake," is still said with trembling lips, and looked from eyes beaming with tenderness and pride. Nor do I believe there is a more united parish in all Christendom than St. Peter's-in-the-East; from the youngest choir-boy to the oldest worker, all caught from Mr. Lowder that keen interest in the work and sense of personal responsibility which was his special characteristic.

One spirit animated all, churchwardens, school teachers, choirmen, down to the youngest choir-boy.

I cannot bear to speak of ourselves, we the curates, who for six years were unbroken in our ranks. His generosity to us, and trust in us, are too sacred subjects to go beyond our own hearts. But I ought to say that in a great measure the peace and quietness of St. Peter's parish was due to the generous and Christian conduct of the Rectors of the various parishes which girt us in on different sides—St. George's, Wapping, and Shadwell. It was in their power to have made it otherwise, and it was really their large-heartedness and nobleness of mind which guided them, for they did not agree with us on theological questions.

I think they recognized the goodness of Mr. Lowder, and respected the man, although they did not approve of his principles. At any rate, the result was peace.

Another, who worked in the parish for some years, writes:—

My first introduction to Mr. Lowder was at the Calvert Street Mission House, where I went with the view of joining the Mission as a schoolmaster, and of doing such other work as a layman might properly perform. I cannot say that his manner was encouraging, for he appeared to me to be a cold unsympathetic man naturally, and although I joined the Mission, I was afraid that I should find it very difficult to live with him. I had reason for modifying this impression afterwards, for he was far less unsympathetic than he seemed to be, and when you understood him, and he understood you, it was easy to work with him.   Unfortunately, some did not understand him, for he practised a reserve of speech and manner which I know led more than one of his associates to misunderstand him and to leave him.   I did not wonder at it, for during the whole time I was with him I cannot recollect that I ever received a word of sympathetic encouragement from him ; he did his work, and shunned and shrank from anything like unnecessary talk about it, and he expected others to do the same.   .

"I am sorry you are going," said Mr. Lowder to me as I was leaving, "for I think we have understood one another."

"I think we have," said I, and so we parted.   But I felt sure that while life lasted whatever feeling he may have entertained for me would remain, and it was so.   I saw it and felt it whenever I met him in after years.   And as time went on he appeared to me more genial, his face irradiated with a smile when you met him, and the expression was softer, even, at times, to sweetness.

One who perhaps knew him best of all says—

He had two different sides to his character ; the one he was most known by, I suppose, was distant and stern.   On the other hand, he was gentle, kind, and tender ; his sternness came. often quite as much from shyness (for he was very shy), and his distance from great reserve, as from anything else.   You should have seen him with the sick and dying to know what he was.   His whole face softened, and the gentle tone of his voice, and the movement even of his hands, as he touched the sick person, must have been soothing.

I was sent for (another writes) to be with a woman dying of typhus fever.   She was a good woman.   I saw she was just passing away, so I sent for Mr. Lowder.   He came at once, and never shall I forget his tenderness.   The sick woman was, to use the poor people's expression, "dying hard"—quite deaf and speechless.   He fanned her and bathed her lips, while I was attending to other things; and he literally *prayed her away*, each prayer fitting in as she was gradually passing on, and when at the last I touched him, almost a burst of thanksgiving broke from him, for she had indeed a wretched home.

One of the Sisters who worked for him in Calvert Street told the writer how greatly she was struck by his tenderness on one occasion. It was New Year's Eve, just after the midnight service, and she had locked up the house and gone to bed, when there was a ring at the gate. She went down, and found Father Lowder waiting at the door with a poor miserable woman whom he had saved from throwing herself over the bridge, and whom he had brought to the Sisters for shelter. It was a terrible sight, for the poor creature was tearing, screaming, and throwing herself about—a sight which few could look upon without their faces expressing horror. But in the midst of their struggle with the poor thing, the Sister said she could hardly help staring at Mr. Lowder, for his face was absolutely shining with love, compassion, and tenderness: there was nothing else to be seen there ; it seemed, she said, as if fatherly pity and yearning affection streamed down from his countenance upon the poor lost one, as though he saw nothing but one suffering and enslaved, felt nothing except longings to comfort and to save her. "He came back again," the Sister said, "the first thing in the morning to see after her, and try and persuade her to something better."

No wonder that another should write : " I used long ago to say to myself that if I were sunk in the depths of sin and degradation, I should never fear him, or think that he would turn from me."

After his death one of his cousins wrote from Yoko-hama :—

I never have forgotten and never shall forget the day when first Cousin Charles came, and, singling me out from among my eight hundred school-fellows, took my hand in his and made himself my friend.   That day, and the days I spent with him at St. Barnabas' and subsequently at St. George's-in-the-East, are among the few happy recollections of my school life.   I loved him, because I always felt that he loved and sympathized with me though I was but a child.   He never was angry with me, or rebuked me, though I needed it often enough ; but for that very reason I dreaded to grieve him, and so was unconsciously led by him.   I feel that I owe more to him than to any one with whom I was brought into contact in my early days, for he it was who first implanted in my heart a manly spirit, by teaching me the true courage of a good conscience.   Thus has his influence been carried to the very antipodes of his life's work.

How interested he used to be (another says) in all my little silly affairs, ball-going, and nonsense of that sort, because it interested me.   I think the strongest point in his character, and one not often met with, was his great " large-mindedness "—I do not know how else to express it.   I always think of him as one ready and willing to "eat with publicans and sinners," and be friends with them as well as with worldly people.   Some good men get on with worldly people, and like their society and that of great people, but Mr. Lowder, without liking it or enjoying it particularly, made himself one with all.   What a simple, grand, *selfless* nature it was ! his few faults all on the surface, and altogether coming from his eager, buoyant nature.

It was this single-hearted simplicity which seems to have most of all impressed good laymen who knew him well.   One of these, Mr. Charrington, who had been his fellow-student at King's College, and through whom, eventually, he came to St. George's, says of him—

He never turned about—always went straight before him. If people opposed him he did not argue, but went on, turning neither to right nor to left. He had all the odds against him when he began his Mission, and I think one secret of his success was his genial *bonhomie* and gentleness combined with perfect courage. He knew what he meant to do, and went straight to his point. I never heard him speak in a tone of complaint or irritation; he always made the best of things, although he must have had very much more than falls to the lot of most of the clergy of misrepresentation and obloquy to contend with. He possessed immense moral courage, and when once he had determined to undertake any particular work, he persevered unflinchingly, unless compelled to abandon it for want of sufficient pecuniary support. How Mr. Lowder succeeded in maintaining all the works of St. George's Mission (including the erection of the beautiful church of St. Peter's and the schools) is almost miraculous. Doubtless the incessant anxiety inseparable from the work he had undertaken very materially weakened his constitution, and shortened a life which, had it been passed in the ease and natural charms of a country living, might have been prolonged for many years. No one more thoroughly enjoyed the beauties of Nature than Mr. Lowder. To him London had no natural charms, and he was too glad when the opportunity presented itself to him of spending a portion of the last two or three years of his active life in this place,* for which, and for its Rector and inhabitants, he always felt a very sincere regard.

In Mr. Lowder the Sisters found a man they could work with, and they have changed the whole character of the district where they live.

Another layman, who knew him well, writes :—

* Chislehurst.

It is now about thirty years since I first met Lowder.   I was
then living at Stoke Newington, where the new district parish of
St. Matthias' had been formed, and we were intent upon building
a church.   Mr. Brett, the founder of that work, drew round him,
at our anniversaries, many well-known Churchmen, and among
them, more than once, came Lowder.   He was then a tall,
handsome young man, having the fearless eye and firmly set
mouth, the high spirit, combined with a genial sense of fun, that
we like to associate with our idea of the typical Englishman.
When, soon afterwards, we heard that he had left his West End
curacy, and had been sent to set up the banner of the Cross in
the most neglected quarter of the East of London, we felt that
he had many natural qualifications for the arduous task.   He
attacked the strongholds of vice in Ratcliff Highway with the
same straightforward sense of duty and disregard of self with
which, had the weapon of his warfare been carnal, not spiritual,
he would have stormed an enemy's fortress.

One natural qualification, however, and that among the most
potent, he did not possess, and on that account, perhaps, the seal
of God's hand was the more clearly stamped upon his work.   He
had no pretension to eloquence.   He spoke earnestly, but often
with apparent difficulty.   In the slow, discouraging process of
gaining the confidence of a people ignorant of religion and
suspicious of its ministers, he owed much to his transparent
sincerity, and to a *bonhomie* which helped them to realize that,
in his mouth, the words " my brethren" were no mere conventional form of address, but the expression of the love and
devotion of a life.

On the rare occasions when I was able to gain a few minutes
of his society in my own family circle, there was a delightful
geniality in his manner that made his little visits bright spots to
look upon ; and his affectionate interest in my wife, whom he had
known as a schoolgirl, and in our children, never flagged.

He was a very energetic worker.   Frequently he would dash
into my office in the City, when abroad upon the never-ending

labour of obtaining funds for his Mission works, write a few lines, or in a few brief words give his message, and then depart as rapidly as he came. I cannot remember one occasion on which he was persuaded to remain for a few minutes' rest and refreshment. And yet, withal, he never appeared despondent or impatient. It was always the same brave, cheerful countenance.

He used to make me feel ashamed by the cordial way in which he always acknowledged my assistance, which was, in truth, very trifling. It was almost entirely in connection with the accounts of the income and expenditure of the Mission. These we had to furnish annually, and sometimes it was a little difficult to arrange them. I always had the most comfortable position his rooms offered, and often he would place himself by my side in a constrained attitude, and, with the perspiration standing on his forehead, pore over the puzzling figures till we had reduced them to order. This was very uncongenial work for him, and might have been expected to bring out any latent pettiness of temper, had such existed, but I can truly say that I never took leave of him without feeling for him an increased love and veneration. Of late years I noticed, with deep concern, that he suffered a good deal from indigestion, and I think that he began to fear lest his strength for the work, which still crowded upon him, should fail him; but his Master knew His faithful servant, and spared him the sorrow of laying down his arms while life remained.

If one may so describe it (they are the words of another friend), he had a way as it were of looking neither to the right nor to the left, but *straight on*, with the one end always before him, God's greater glory. I remember one anniversary six or seven years ago; things were rather gloomy and funds very short: when he was making his speech he said, "It makes no difference to me whether I go away, or stay here and continue my work; I merely wish to do God's will." This was no technical form of speech with him, but the moving principle of his whole life in small as well as great matters.

He was always fair, and always a gentleman, and therefore he was always respectfully listened to (another said, speaking of his attendance at public meetings). He entered enthusiastically into all schemes for strengthening the Church, or promoting the social happiness and welfare of the people, and he was keenly interested in all the great questions of the day. He used to hesitate a good deal in speaking, but his hesitation was with a purpose, for he brought out the right word in the proper place, which cannot always be said of those who are more fluent.

One of his most marked qualities was his love for children, and they were devoted to him. They never were afraid of him, but always ran up to him whenever he stopped in the street to speak to them, which he constantly did. There was soon a little group round him, and he used to gather the little ones inside his cloak. The day before he left the parish for the last time, he was playing with some tiny things in the street, and, wrapping his cloak round them, he brought them into the Clergy House, and gave each some strawberries which had been sent to him, to their great delight. At such times, or when he went away for his holiday, he threw off his cares and was another man. A layman who helped him occasionally says—

One day, during the Mission of 1874, I saw him come out of church after Evensong. There were a number of children in the church—not trim little country children with rosy faces, but the poor little half-clad children of the London Docks,—and they came crowding round him. Three or four took hold of the corners and edge of his long cloak, and spread it out like a tent, while half a dozen more crept underneath, laughing and shouting and struggling ; and so he went down the street with all the rest at his heels, to the utter amazement of two rather precise-looking country parsons who had come to see what was going on at St. Peter's, and who stood watching him and exclaiming, "Why, they're all round him!"

In the Guild of St. Katherine, which was for the elder girls, and of which he had the charge, he took the greatest interest, drawing up their rules and the office which they used once a month. He used to come to their meetings and keep them all merry with odd dry jokes or amusing stories. On their annual festival he spent the whole evening with them, entering into all their amusements with almost boyish freshness; he was full of fun when once he threw off his cares, and in teaching them how to get up charades used to become almost as excited as they were.

One of his curates who travelled with him wrote—

No one could say he really knew Father Lowder who had merely seen him within his own parish. *There* he was indeed "the Father," to whom every one looked up with mingled reverence and love; but to most, at least during the latter years of his ministry, he was a man absorbed in his work and ascetic in his habits, though underneath that apparent frigidity not a few had learnt how warm was the heart that beat, and deep the power of sympathy with the sorrows of others. Still it was necessary to have seen him far away from the oppressing cares and anxieties of his parish to discover what he was made of.

I had the pleasure of travelling for a month with him in the summer of 1873. It was my first visit to the Continent, and I found in him an excellent cicerone.

What struck me most in that tour was the complete change which came over the man; he was the high-spirited, light-hearted, congenial companion, at one time fairly beating the guide by the pace he walked (the man actually refused to go further with us), or, as on that same day, after eight or nine hours' hard tramp, and after having been wetted through and through by a terrific thunderstorm, running the whole way down the zigzag path leading from the summit of the Breven into Chamounix. Yet, despite the unclerical garb he assumed in walking, consisting of a white flannel suit and straw hat, no one would have doubted what he was, and I felt not a little proud of being companion to one who, wherever we went, attracted so much attention on account of his noble, saintly face, and dignified, courteous manner.

"The Father" was certainly the bravest man I ever met; I do not think he knew what fear was. He was passionately fond of all athletic exercises, such as riding, rowing, and skating, and above all of mountaineering, in which he frequently won the admiration of his guides. This natural gift of courage supported him in the tremendous difficulties of his work at the Docks. The half-savage denizens of that part soon learnt to respect a man whom they had seen stopping many a street fight, or facing an infuriated mob, or ministering to the bodily and spiritual wants of the victims to Asiatic cholera, sometimes carrying the sufferers in his arms to the hospital. It was true courage, and of the highest type, the spirit of the Christian martyrs of old, which enabled him to live down the fanatical opposition that raged against the introduction of Catholic truth into their midst, and to stand firm when his own fellow-workers more than once deserted him. He despised popularity, and never shrank from anything he considered a duty for fear of man on the one hand, or to secure good opinion on the other. An old friend, in allusion to this, has instanced the calm way in which he would say his office with uncovered head in a crowded railway carriage, or "say grace" in some equally crowded dining-room in the City. And yet, with all this, he took the lead, and men of all grades in society naturally gave way to him, and were ready to follow him, trusting to his intrepid spirit and undeviating rectitude of purpose.

Among his own people he was *king;* he took the lead in every work, and when not actually engaged in it—away, it might be, on the Continent—it was felt that he overlooked and directed us all. The secret of his ascendency over his subordinate workers, clerical and lay, was that we knew he never asked another to do what he would not do himself, and that he never shrank from any work because he knew that it was not exactly that in which he shone. As an instance of this, I remember one Lent he showed us an anonymous letter he had received from some one in Old Gravel Lane, suggesting that the congregation would be better pleased if he were to ask either of two of the assistant clergy, whose names were mentioned, to preach the "Three Hours' Agony" on Good Friday instead of himself. He said so humbly, and without any expression of anger towards the writer, " I know I cannot preach as well as you, but I think it my duty to preach on that day." In the same spirit he would always listen attentively and humbly to the sermons and instructions of his young curates, and hardly ever criticised what he had heard from them.

He never shrank, however, from administering a rebuke when he thought it was required, and sometimes, as we thought, at inopportune times ; but I am sure it cost him real pain, and was done from a stern sense of duty. It was no slight tribute to his personal character that men would take such *public* rebukes from him, which they would have resented keenly from any one else.

In all religious ministrations he was intensely reverent ; never rapid or hurried, a matter of great importance when the congregation was chiefly composed of poor. They often spoke of the difference between him and others in this respect. " I never knew before how beautiful that chapter is," one of his people said ; " when I went home I read it for myself, but it was nothing the same. I wish the Father would always read the lessons ; he makes the Bible speak." The poor people used to say, " I don't like to come in late to church when the Father is there, for even if his back is turned I feel he knows it." He used to impress upon them to be very careful about their thanksgiving after Holy Communion, and not to hurry out of church directly the service was over.

One of his curates who worked with him to the end has written the few notes of recollection which follow :—

His extreme reverence in prayer at all times was most remarkable ; his attitude at such times, and especially when kneeling down for his prayer before preaching, was in itself a sermon ; at such times a very calm and sweet smile would play on his features.   A priest who saw him on the last Sunday that he spent at St. Peter's, said to me that he had often observed this, but never so strongly as on this last Sunday.   I remember some years since, when walking with him on Chislehurst Common, he proposed our saying our office together : he was just as recollected and devout then as if he were in church or in our oratory at home.   And this reverence was ever the same, however great his fatigue, especially during the last year of his life.   Shortly before leaving England, when much wearied with a school excursion, we said our Evensong and Compline together; in spite of his fatigue, there was no lounging or want of the same reverent posture which always so remarkably distinguished him.

He was scarcely ever to be seen really vexed ; but I remember once, in 1874, when there was a serious overflow of the Thames, and he had been working up to his knees in water for some hours, carrying the children out of school, we had got him some hot brandy and water : he seemed really annoyed at what he thought any fuss being made.   But his care for others was as great as his want of care for himself; if he thought any of the clergy in the house were ill, he was always the first to make them rest.

To know him was indeed to love him ; and the *more* you knew of him the greater grew the love.   The name of "the Father" but expresses what he was to all, priests and people too. He was always the same—stern, people often thought him, but never so in reality, full of warm love and sympathy for and with all.

He thoroughly hated all unreality, and "Ritualism," *so-called*, was extremely distasteful to him; he loved a grand ceremonial because it was to him the outward expression of truths he held most sacred, and a means of impressing them on the uneducated.

He never passed over any fault or mistake in those who worked with him; and would, perhaps weeks after, abruptly and in the middle of the meal, ask why this or that was done or not done, as the case might be, something he had noticed, but had omitted to speak of at the time. He was so thoroughly just and fair, that one could always receive in good part anything he might say. He never shrank from speaking what he thought, whoever the person might be whom he had to reprove.

This sketch of Charles Lowder's character may be concluded in the following words of his only brother, and of the friend under whom he first worked in London :—

In writing freely of my brother, I may say what I think others have said elsewhere, that his natural gifts, though of a high order, would not have won him the esteem or the success which he attained. Though a sufficiently good classical scholar to take a second class, his tastes were not literary. He talked comparatively little, and was not great at general conversation, though he was neither uninterested nor unacquainted with what was going on around him. It was a real pleasure to him to be in ladies' society, and no one was more courteous. In the early part of his clerical career, which really began at Tetbury, his chief interest was shown in the schools, and in the teaching of the elder boys, some of whom turned out remarkably well. I do not think he had any special taste for ritual as such; it was to him a means of teaching the great Catholic verities. It was an iron will, exercised first on himself, and a constant control over himself in both word and deed, which made him all that he was. Hence he had, to the

K

best of my belief, none of these sins which overtake young men in their college days, either of extravagance or self-indulgence, or worse, to trouble him with their remembrance. He was essentially pure, upright, and conscientious, and also very simple and really devout; as a boy I noticed this. He erred in judging others, in his early days at least, by his own standard, and thus appeared often severe, brusque, abrupt, and wanting in sympathy. He was too true to pay compliments, or even to appear to be giving praise. Hence he often made people afraid of him, without cause. After he solemnly gave himself up to his Mission work, he never looked back. He chose poverty, misery, and unsightliness for his sphere, and he only indulged his love for scenery in his holidays. His choice made him a celibate; it was, I believe, a real self-denial to him, for he was not without those natural feelings which make a man desire companionship, a home, and the pleasure of children. But the secret of his life was the simplicity with which he obeyed his Master's call: "Take up thy cross, and follow Me."

All who knew him intimately knew another thing about him— that, while one secret of his influence over others was his almost habitual joyousness, his solid piety was the secret of his joyousness. "Out of the same vessel," as an ancient writer puts it, "flowed forth oil and honey—the oil of goodness, the honey of joy." With that writer, we cannot but admire the spiritual warrior, how "from the rock of patience he drew forth, at one and the same moment, honey and oil; how his mercy towards the vicious suffered no diminution from their vice, and his joy in labouring for them lost nothing by his own suffering; nay, how his mercy and his joy were alike increased—*ex dolore delectatio, ex passione compassio.*" This was eminently the case with Charles Lowder. He was a workman who did his part, for God's glory, and not for man's approval; and he did it promptly, bravely, patiently, and humbly.

CHAPTER IX.

" To love and bear ;. to hope till Hope creates
From its own wreck the thing it contemplates."

SOON after Charles Lowder had made his home in Calvert
Street, he was joined by two clergymen, Mr. Collins and
Mr. de Burgh, and by two laymen intending to take orders.
They lived, indeed, " in the rough " at first, and perhaps it
may be said that from this time Mr. Lowder never lived in
any other way.

There are just two rooms, one on either side of the
little entrance passage of the house in Calvert Street where
the clergy of St. Peter's still live ; one of these was Mr.
Lowder's sitting-room and library, the other the common
dining-room. Over these are two rooms occupied by two
curates, and on the third story two more, one a curate's
room, the other the Vicar's bedroom. It is hard to imagine
anything more homely, simple, and without ornament than
this Mission House. But in 1856 it formed one with what
is now the adjoining Sisters' house, and the first thing done
was to open a room in the latter, licensed by the Bishop,
for daily prayers and frequent preaching. " Here," Mr.

Lowder wrote, " was gradually gathered a little congregation."

This room is now used as the Sisters' oratory, and on the altar lies the little wooden crucifix which the priest at Zell-am-See placed in Charles Lowder's hands after his death, and gave to his sister.

A little choir of boys was formed ; the first choir boy, who was caught in the street, tamed, taught, and brought to Confirmation and Communion, is still living, with his wife and children, in the parish.

But a larger place of worship was urgently needed, and on the Thursday before Advent in 1856 a temporary iron chapel, which had been built in the garden of the Mission House, was dedicated, under the name of " the Chapel of the Good Shepherd." Here, from the first, the daily Eucharist was celebrated—on Sundays at eight and eleven, on week-days at seven. The chapel was soon thronged, and the band of communicants whom Mr. Lowder left at St. Peter's began gradually to be formed as, one after another, those whose hearts had been touched were carefully taught in classes held for Confirmation candidates, and for instruction in the Holy Scriptures.

There seems to have been no excitement connected with these conversions, but when once Mr. Lowder got hold of a man, he did not let him go, and the work became real and solid. Mr. Bryan King wrote of the " overwhelming force " with which the issue of twenty-four years' labour and trial was brought to his heart on the day of Mr. Lowder's funeral, September 17, 1880. " I could only call to mind," he added, " some five or six communicants of the church as resident within the present parish of St. Peter on the formation of the Mission, whereas at present their number is, I believe, about five hundred."

To his mother Charles Lowder wrote :—

Mission House, February 6, 1857.

I was obliged to be at St. Barnabas' again on Wednesday, and in the evening I was presented with a most beautiful testimonial, in the shape of a complete service of gilt Communion plate for private celebrations, but large enough for our present use in the chapel. The box itself forms an altar with a consecrated slab, and super-altar with candlesticks and cross. Some of the pieces are gifts of particular friends : the cruets are given by the poor ; Mr. Liddell gave the chalice ; so that it forms a very interesting memorial of my connection with St. Barnabas', and, as we shall use it here, a connecting link between the two. When you come up I shall like to show it you. Mr. Liddell's speech in presenting it was so kind that I really felt completely overcome, and scarcely knew what to say. The thaw commenced here yesterday, and of course the streets are dreadfully dirty. It is of no use asking you to be careful in walking out, for you seem to enjoy your tumbles, but you may meet with one too many.

Your dutiful and affectionate son,

CHARLES.

From this time Mr. Lowder went every year to the feast for rich and poor at St. Barnabas' on the dedication-day. A friend who was always present said that it was most remarkable to see how all faces beamed when he entered the room, especially those of the poor, and how one shout of welcome and applause greeted him. Hardly any other name was cheered at that feast as his was, and just as warmly after he had been absent for years as on his first reappearance after leaving St. Barnabas'. "I can see him now," his friend says, "catching up our tiny M—— on his shoulder, and carrying her round the room to make the *quête*, after dinner was over, for the poor children in the schools to have their day in the country. Mr. Lowder always made this *quête* himself."

Women's help was of course needed, and this was given at first by two ladies, who took lodgings in the districts, where they taught a small school, and also visited the poor. They tried to persuade mothers to bring their children to be baptised; but the ignorance of the people was so great that they seemed to think that Baptism was something like vaccination, and asked if it would hurt them.

In the spring of 1857, Dr. Neale's sister offered her services, and began to form a Sisterhood in connection with the Mission. There was indeed much to cheer on the brave Missioners. They had begun their work in the south-east part of St. George's parish, in a district cut off from the rest by the Docks, and, with part of Wapping and Shadwell, forming an island.* About six months later, a promising beginning of another Mission was made in the western part of St. George's parish, at Wellclose Square. Here a church, originally built for a Danish congregation in 1696, became vacant; and, being admirably situated for Mission purposes, Mr. Lowder determined to secure it for the Church of England. He rented it from the trustees, and began services in it in Lent, 1857. Soon after Easter, it was formally opened, when the sermon was preached by the late Dean Stanley. Mr. Lowder seems to have thought that this would eventually form the head-quarters of the Mission. It fell out otherwise, but at this time, just nine months after he had left St.

* Now the parish of St. Peter's-in-the-East.

Barnabas', there were four clergy working in the Mission— two at Wellclose Square, and two at Calvert Street. He determined, to save the expense of two establishments, that the clergy should all live in the Mission House which had been taken in Wellclose Square ; so, abandoning his first quarters in Calvert Street, he gave them up to the Sisters, some of whom have remained there ever since.

It was just at this time that Bishop Wilberforce wrote to Canon Butler :—

I quite long to go and cast myself into that Mission ; . . . if only now we had a Bishop of London who would go and spend a day or two in Wapping with those zealous men, what might we *not* do ? *

To Mr. Lowder the Bishop wrote :—

The Athenæum, May 21, 1857.

MY DEAR MR. LOWDER,

I enclose you a letter from a young man of whom I know nothing but that he has written to me stating that he is a Roman Catholic, highly connected, but penniless, who longs to enter our Church's Orders and work on Catholic grounds.

You will remember that I *know nothing of him.* But if you can inquire (which I have no means of doing), a zealous work-man seems to me too precious a thing to be lost.

I cannot write this without adding that I have received from my dear friend, W. Butler, a most deeply interesting account of his visit to you. I beseech you, for Christ's sake, whilst you give all possible liberty to this great movement with which you are so identified, yet zealously to watch to keep it truly Church of England.

If there is anything in which I can aid you, without in the slightest degree interfering with the Bishop of London, call upon

* "Life of Bishop Wilberforce," vol. ii., p. 341.

me for aid. Two things only occur to me—*secret* alms and secret intercessions; for the first, call on me when you want help; for the second, I will try to offer them for you; for even though you are not in my diocese, you may count on my hearty sympathy in such a work as yours.

I am, ever very truly yours,

S. OXON.

Nothing could be kinder than the words with which the new Bishop elect of London had welcomed and sanctioned the missionary movement in the diocese to which he had just been called, as his first letter to Mr. Lowder will show :—

9, Plain Parade, Brighton, November 13, 1856.

MY DEAR SIR,

Let me thank you for sending me the earnest expressions expressive of the feelings with which you have undertaken your difficult part in St. George's-in-the-East.

I sincerely trust that God may bless all earnest and single-hearted efforts to spread the Gospel of His Son through the masses of the metropolis. You certainly may rely on my readiness to give what aid my guidance and advice afford.

I doubt not that God will so direct the zeal of those who seek Him earnestly in prayer, as to save them from any dangerous errors in doctrine or practice.

And though there may be many zealous men in the diocese to which God has called me, from whom I must greatly differ, I still trust that I may be a fellow-worker with all who love the Lord Jesus Christ in sincerity.

Mr. King has communicated with me respecting the chapel to be opened. I have put him in communication with Mr. Lee, of Dean's Yard, and I hope all the legal difficulties may speedily be arranged, when I shall be very glad to see the chapel secured as a chapel-of-ease.

Yours faithfully,

A. C. LONDON (Elect).

P.S.—It seems to me that you are right not to defer the commencement of your work in your new chapel longer than absolutely necessary. My engagements with the candidates for ordination, and with the sermons I have already undertaken to preach, fill up my time till the close of this year. I hope to be settled at 37, Lowndes Square, after the 23rd, my consecration. On the 24th, 25th, 26th, and 27th, I shall be occupied from eleven to three with candidates for ordination, but I would gladly arrange for an interview with you at any other time after my consecration, say on Monday, the 24th, at a quarter before eleven. I should wish, if possible, that Mr. King and you should see me together, and explain the connection of the Mission with the parish church. I therefore name the day and hour when Mr. King is to see me respecting the new chapel; but should you prefer a longer interview, I shall keep myself disengaged on Wednesday, the 26th, at three.

No one can fairly charge Charles Lowder with disloyalty to that much-abused principle the "law." So anxious was he to act honestly within the limits of the judgment of 1857, that he applied to Sir Frederick Thesiger, Q.C., afterwards Lord Chelmsford, and to Dr. Deane, Q.C., for an opinion as to how far the vestments and lights were covered by it, before continuing to use them. It is only necessary to give the conclusions of the opinion which is published *verbatim* by Mr. Brooks on "Disputed Ritual Ornaments and Usages," under sanction of the E.C.U.

1. Upon the question of Dress, we are of opinion that the present Prayer-book, taken in conjunction with the First Prayer-book of Edward VI., sanctions the use of the Vestments worn by Mr. Lowder in the ministration of Holy Communion, and that he may, in executing the holy ministry, lawfully put on a white Alb plain, with a vestment, and that such dress is according to the

form prescribed in the Book of Common Prayer, made and published by authority of Parliament.

2. On the whole, we are of opinion that two Lights on the Communion Table are not forbidden by Law, and that Mr. Lowder may continue the use of such Lights. But in this matter, as well as in that of Dress, usage to the contrary has so long prevailed, that we do not consider that he is liable to punishment or censure for celebrating the Holy Communion without Lights.

(Signed)　　FREDERICK THESIGER.
J. PARKER DEANE.

Temple, May 23, 1857.

There were, however, those who were on the watch to stir up difficulties, and in May, 1857, the Bishop wrote to him, saying that representations had been made to him concerning " dresses and ceremonies " used in the Mission chapel and in the church at Wellclose Square ; and he desired that no " dresses " except the ordinary surplice should be worn at Holy Communion, that candles should not be lighted unless the darkness required it, that no " coverings " should be placed upon the altar except such as he (the Bishop) personally approved of, that no cross should be set upon the altar or " depicted on the wall behind it," and that no processions should be made " without the church or chapel."

The Bishop wrote that these instructions were not grounded upon the law of the Church—indeed, he had but lately officially concurred in the Knightsbridge judgment, affirming the legality of vestments—but upon his fears of " approximation to Romanism " and " mimicking of Popery ; " and he expressed his opinion that " those foolish ritual observances necessarily tend to confound our ministrations with those of Roman Catholic priests."

It is necessary to say thus much as to the Bishop's action, in order to explain the following letters, which are important, as giving Mr. Lowder's convictions in his own words. The copies of the letters are in his own handwriting; the first is undated, but the reference to Mr. King proves that it was written about the same time as the second letter.

. . . Mr. King informs me that your lordship has expressed some doubt as to the legal obligation of the chasuble and altar lights. I trust that we may be enabled to remove these doubts when we next see your lordship. But without waiving this point, I think we may claim some attention on the ground of expediency. Here, my Lord, are a few clergy undertaking a work of acknowledged importance, of vast difficulty, and requiring self-denial, patience, faith, and hopefulness. They have been invited in a very providential manner into a parish, of which before they knew nothing, but where there is a wide and unoccupied field for their labour, where they have the entire confidence and good will of the Rector, who approves of their principles, and who would not willingly give his sanction to the carrying out of any others. Those principles I have already set before your lordship; they are the principles of the Catholic Church, as taught in the Creeds, Liturgy, and ritual of the Church of England. Our system is a consistent one, to preach the whole Gospel of Jesus Christ as the Church has ever received it; not only in our sermons, but in the visible teaching of sacraments and ritual observances. To narrow our liberty in carrying out this system, or to mutilate it in points which to your lordship may seem unimportant, but which to us are most important, is to weaken and abridge when we so much need strength and elasticity—is to deprive those who have the work to do of that spring and energy which result from confidence in the truth and consistency of their teaching.

To put it even on a lower ground, the Church permits us these ceremonies and outward expressions of devotion; and we like them, and find them a help to our own devotion and that of our people. Is it too much to claim from your lordship and the world in general that we should be allowed the comfort of them in a work which requires us to give up other comforts, so that what we willingly resign in our own houses we should enjoy in our churches? We adopt a system which we conscientiously believe the Church gives us; we adopt it as a whole; why should we be continually fretted by the denial of parts which, in our conscientious opinion, are necessary to the unity of that system?

Your lordship has received the charge of an immense diocese, containing hundreds of thousands of unconverted souls. We, in all humility, offer to do what God in His mercy may enable us for a few thousand of these. We desire to do it as the Holy Spirit leads us in the Church's way. We neither judge nor hinder others who may be led to try some other way. We do not ask your lordship to commit yourself to any principles of which you may disapprove, but merely to permit an experiment, not forbidden by the Church, to be carried out by those who have the heart to do it. Surely, in such a diocese, in such a work, there is room for us all without hindering one another. Evidently something more elastic and energetic is wanting than the old parochial system; are we to fall back upon Wesleyanism, or on the Catholic teaching of our Church?

If your lordship fears lest such a system should lead to Romanism, I can only say that I have had some experience of these principles, having taught them as well as I knew for thirteen years, during which period I do not remember more than two instances of persons belonging to the working classes being induced to leave the Church of England for the Roman communion: one was a young person who had been led to the Oratory out of curiosity, and whom I succeeded in convincing of her error; another, a poor woman, who was induced by secondary motives, but has so far acknowledged her fault as to leave her children in the Church of England, and will probably soon return herself. No, my lord, I find that with all our ritual and dogmatic teaching we have great difficulty in raising them to the standard of good and consistent members of the Church of England; there is not much fear of their getting beyond that. Protestantism is still very strong in England. That your lordship may be guided by the Holy Spirit in encouraging rather than checking a work undertaken in all sincerity for the glory of God and the salvation of souls, is the sincere prayer of, etc.

Mission House, Calvert Street, Wapping, E., May 2, 1857.
MY LORD,

Having understood from Mr. de Burgh that it is your lordship's wish that the chasuble should not be worn in the celebration of Holy Eucharist by the clergy of St. George's Mission, I beg most respectfully to submit to your lordship that we have always worn it here, since the opening of the Iron Church, in entire conformity with your lordship's strict injunctions to us, at our first interview, that we should obey the law. The Privy Council, in the late judgment, having expressly laid down that the rubric in the First Book of King Edward was the rule for ornaments and dresses of the ministers, and since that directs that, "At the time of the Holy Communion, the priest that shall execute the holy ministry *shall* put upon him the vesture appointed for that ministration, *i.e.* a white albe plain, with a vestment or cope, and the assistant priests and deacons *shall* likewise have upon them the vestures appointed for their ministry, *i.e.* albes with tunicles," and since also the present rubric before Morning Prayer directs "that such ornaments of the ministers at all times of their ministration shall be retained and be in use," I do not understand, my lord, what alternative is left for us. We are simply obeying the law, a law directly binding upon our consciences, and, moreover, involving a principle for which I am prepared—and, thank God, not myself alone, but very many others of the most earnest clergy in the Church of England, are prepared also — to sacrifice everything, the honour and dignity of the Blessed Sacrament of our dear Lord's Body and Blood.

The Church of England has ruled that this holy service should be distinguished from all others by the dress of the celebrant and his assistant ministers. Can your lordship really desire those who are conscientiously resolved so to distinguish it both by their teaching and devotion, to break the law of the Church in this respect?

It is not, my lord, a question now of forcing changes of ritual upon an unwilling congregation; we have an entirely new congregation to form, and I can truly say that I have never heard of a single person in this district being offended by our wearing the chasuble. On the contrary, our solemn celebrations of the Holy Communion, especially at seasons like Christmas, New Year, and Easter Eves, have made great impression on those who had never thus felt Christ preached to them; and we trace many conversions from these occasions.

We are making a great venture for the salvation of souls; the only prospect of permanent success is, so far as I can understand, in carrying out those principles which I submitted to your lordship in my second letter—the setting forth, in all its fulness, the love of Jesus Christ and His grace in the sacraments and ordinances of His Church. I should have no heart myself to work on any other principles, nor could I expect God's blessing were I to attempt it. I believe that the measure of success with which God has prospered us, has been entirely owing to our faithful adherence to these principles in the spirit of love and charity. I desire not to judge others; thank God I have never interfered with any who were earnestly striving to win souls; but I do ask your lordship to extend to us that liberty in keeping the Church's laws which the world claims for those who are continually breaking them. Some of us may err sometimes in excess of devotion, but surely this is better than chilling neglect and careless irreverence. I trust, my lord, that I have said nothing in this letter inconsistent with that respect for your office and person which is sincerely felt by

Your lordship's faithful servant,

C. F. LOWDER.

P.S.—I should perhaps mention to your lordship that I had

intended to leave London as early as I could next week for a
fortnight's rest, which I believe is necessary for me, but of course,
if your lordship wished it, I would delay my journey.

Ultimately no change was made in the manner of conducting divine service at St. George's Mission.

Mr. Rowley, who was afterwards ordained, and went
with Bishop Mackenzie to Africa, had joined the Mission
in Calvert Street early in 1857, taking charge of a school
for boys in Old Gravel Lane, while the girls and infants
were taught by the Sisters. The story of those early days,
which he has been kind enough to supply, is too interesting
to be omitted. He writes :—

When I joined the Mission I did not expect to lead an easy
life, yet I had not thought that the domestic arrangements of the
Mission House would be so well calculated to make one endure hardness. The furniture was scanty and of the plainest description,
and until I became used to it my bedstead was a trial to the flesh,
for the mattress was so thin that the iron laths were painfully
perceptible to the touch. But there was not a more luxurious
couch in the house.

The members of the Mission had their meals in common. There
was food enough, yet very little room was left, either in the quantity
or quality of it, for the practice of self-denial. Nevertheless days
of abstinence and fasting were not ignored. As time went on it
was found that a more generous diet was needed in order to maintain health and fitness for work, the physical atmosphere of the
Mission districts being most depressing. For instance, a large
soap and candle maker's establishment was just opposite to the
Mission House; the dust-yard of the parish was close to it; an
animal charcoal maker's premises were not far from it; the water
of the Docks, which in the summer sometimes seemed to putrefy,
almost surrounded it; from the sewer gratings there came the

most abominable of odours, for, the district of Calvert Street being below high-water mark, twice a day the debouchments of the sewer were closed, and the smells from the houses were generally most unsavoury.

But the place might have been a paradise of sweetness for any manifestation of discomfort that Mr. Lowder made; yet, as I afterwards discovered, his olfactory nerves were exceedingly sensitive.

Just before I joined, the forces of the Mission had been divided. The Rev. H. Collins, the Rev. Hubert de Burgh, and a Mr. Fletcher, a Cambridge man, who then intended to take Holy Orders, had removed to a house in Wellclose Square, in order that the services in the Danish Church, which had been rented by the Mission, might be the more conveniently under-taken, and the district nominally assigned to this church be the more conveniently worked. With Mr. Lowder in the Calvert Street house, there were the Rev. W. Burn; Mr. H. Martin, who also was staying at the Mission with the view of there passing the time between the taking of his degree and his ordination; a Mr. Drew, an elderly gentleman who acted as chief of the commissariat, etc., and myself.

Between the clergy at Wellclose Square and at Calvert Street there was at first a not infrequent interchange of duty, but gradually it became apparent that a more serious division than that which was made by dividing the forces was to be feared. Not one word on this subject to my knowledge escaped Mr. Lowder's lips, but the adherents of Messrs. Collins and De Burgh were not so reticent.

The Rev. H. Collins was a remarkable man, an enthusiast, and able to excite enthusiasm, a sweet-dispositioned man, with winning ways and great readiness of speech. His very peculiari-ties—and he had many—were attractive, for though with reference to dress he sometimes set at nought all conventional ideas, he did so with such simplicity that, even while tempted to laugh at him, you were drawn more closely to him. He regarded the so-called "religious life" as indispensably necessary to satisfactory work amongst the neglected people in the East of London; but in the cultivation of that life he sought the aid of the masters of devotion in the Romish rather than in the English Church, and his preaching and manner of life exhibited a similar tendency.

Mr. Lowder's appreciation of the value of the "religious life" was, I am sure, as intense as that of Mr. Collins, and in his fervent desire for the unity of Christendom I think he might have been willing to make concessions to Rome which very few English Churchmen would think desirable; but he had no desire to leave the communion of the English Church, and he held on his way sturdily and steadily, working and praying, and hoping that by his work and prayers some approach to that unity for which he longed might be made.

I do not know this from any formal communication from him to myself, but I gathered it from occasional observations of his, and from the whole course of his life during the time I was appointed with him.

The congregations in Calvert Street and at Wellclose Square were not large; that of the former was drawn from the immediate neighbourhood, while that of the latter was mainly composed of people, mostly young men and women, drawn from other districts. Every effort was made, by means of outdoor preaching on Sundays, frequent daily services, and personal invitations, to get the people to come to church, but for a time it seemed almost without effect. Now and then a poor soul borne down by care, hard work, ill usage, or poverty, having been touched by the kindness shown by the Sisters or other members of the Mission, or pricked to the heart by what had been preached in the streets, would slink into church; but it was long before what could be called a congregation was really formed in Calvert Street. Mr. Lowder was not an eloquent man, though he never preached written sermons, and for months after I joined the Mission the substance of his sermons seemed to me to be ill·calculated to attract the kind of people amongst whom we lived. Self-sacrifice, the giving up all for Christ, was his constant theme, and it was

L

treated in such a way that I was not surprised when a man who sometimes attended our services said to me, " You men are very good men, I dare say, but your goodness is not for such as we. You make religion too hard. Why, you preach to me as though I was all soul and no body, when I know and feel every day of my life that I have got a body, and that it makes claims upon me that I can't set aside."

His sermons were frequently more suitable for the dwellers in the cloister than for the inhabitants of one of the most degraded parts of London. It was his life, then and afterwards to the day of his death, which influenced for good the people about him. He lived amongst them, and he was ever seeking their welfare. See him when they would, come to him when they might, he was always the same, always before all things desirous of leading them from the lower animal life in which they lived to the higher life in Christ. They may have found it difficult to understand his sermons, and probably they were often puzzled by the seeming impossibility of the life he set before them, when they thought of the life which, as it would appear to them, they were ordinarily compelled to live ; but he was a good man, at all times and upon all occasions ready and willing to help them and their children ; they could understand that, and in the end they learnt to trust him and to love him.

Various circumstances combined to make it necessary that the members of the Mission living in Calvert Street should remove to the Wellclose Square Mission House. The Sisters had need of a more convenient house than that in which they lived. Messrs. Burn and Martin had left the Mission in order to work in the districts connected with the parish church, and it was manifestly desirable that there should not be in any sense a divided responsibility—that the real head of the Mission should have the control of it. This change, however, soon led to others, for Messrs. Collins and De Burgh, finding it difficult to fall in with the new arrangement, left the Mission, and some time afterwards were received into the Roman Communion.

This was a severe trial to Mr. Lowder, but no word of complaint escaped his lips. He rarely afterwards spoke of his former colleagues; and when he did so, it was never to their disparagement: he seemed to be grateful to them that they showed so much regard for the interests of the Mission as to allow a space of time to intervene between their going away and their joining the Church of Rome.

The burden that their departure placed upon him was very heavy. The daily services of two churches, besides much other clerical work, had to be provided for, and for some time no regular aid could be procured. The pecuniary affairs of the Mission suffered, and he was responsible for liabilities incurred in its behalf. He bore up bravely for a long while, passing more time than usual in the oratory in prayer; but at last his strength failed him, he became ill,—and at this critical juncture, when it seemed that there was danger of the Mission being given up, the Rev. R. M. Benson came to its aid, and did not leave it until Mr. Lowder was restored to health and strength, and some regular clerical help had been secured.

Then there came a period of hard work—very hard work, for the Mission was much under-manned—during which the day and Sunday schools were largely increased, the congregations were enlarged, a refuge for fallen women was opened, night classes for young men were established, and a greater hold upon the people who had been brought under the influence of the Mission was gained.

Mr. Lowder did not frequently visit the schools; he reserved himself for the religious instruction of the children by catechisings in church. I did not think that he had a very happy manner with children; nevertheless, by constant hammering away at them, he managed to make them acquainted with the first principles of our holy religion. I was talking not long ago with a man who as a child attended the Mission schools at this period of which I am writing, and he distinctly remembered the results of Mr. Lowder's catechisings, and could repeat word for word, though not learned from a book, the formulæ in which he was taught to utter Christian truths.

Mr. Lowder recognized the fact that the absence of definite religious teaching, the failure to build up our children in a clear and definite knowledge of divine truth, was the main cause of the sad diversity of opinion upon religion which prevails amongst us, and also of that indifference to religion which is even more prevalent. The doctrine of the Incarnation of Christ, and the extension of the Incarnation through the sacraments as a means of union with Christ and as channels of grace, usually formed the basis of his catechizings, and indeed of his religious teaching generally. But I do not remember a single instance where, in enforcing this, he, as far as I was able to judge, went outside the lines of the English Church. He kept within the covers of the Prayer-book, though he left nothing therein unused, if I except the Articles, concerning which, considering the material he had to deal with, he was judiciously silent.

His teaching was never controversial. He expressed the truth as he had received it, as though there was not and could not be any other view of it than his own, but he assailed no one. In this he was consistent with himself, for I cannot recollect any instance of his speaking against any person, or against any view of religion with which he did not sympathize. I confess that I should have had more sympathy with him myself had he shown less reticence in these respects, yet I have not unfrequently had reason to be thankful for the example he thus set me.

His clerical coadjutors after Messrs. Collins and De Burgh had left him were the Rev. C. Anderson and the Rev. J. W. Temple, who remained at the Mission until just before the Rev. A. H. Mackonochie joined it. With the accession of the latter gentleman there came what might be called a revival. He took charge of the Wellclose Square district, and soon gathered around him a set of enthusiastic men and women. Mr. Lowder's exertions were mostly confined to the Calvert Street district, where his life and work were beginning to tell for good in many ways.

Soon after Mr. Mackonochie joined the Mission the riots at the parish church began.   I do not think that it can be said that any one connected with the Mission was responsible for these riots. A certain amount of antagonism existed in the minds of some of the inhabitants against the Mission, but it would never have manifested itself in violence and indecent attempts to interfere with the services of the Church.   But though the missionaries did not provoke these unmanly disturbances, they were affected by them.   The Mission chapels were sometimes invaded; the Mission House was once attacked; both Mr. Lowder and Mr. Mackonochie were required by the Bishop of London to officiate at the parish church, and were consequently exposed to the assaults of the mob.   But I don't know that Mr. Lowder on any occasion lost his equanimity.   He was summoned before the magistrate and fined for shutting the vestry door of the parish church upon a man who, having no right to be there, insisted upon trying to force his way in; but he made no comment upon this beyond mentioning the fact, which he did with a smile at the incongruity of his being fined for protecting God's house, while it seemed impossible to get any one punished for desecrating it.

In any other part of London I do not think that these riots would have been tolerated for a month, but St. George's-in-the-East is removed from the quiet thoroughfares of the metropolis; violence and disorder were chronic there, and months were allowed to pass before the authorities showed themselves to be in earnest in putting them down.   I am sure, however, that the great majority of those who Sunday after Sunday congregated at St. George's Church for the purpose of creating a disturbance, were not parishioners of St. George's; they came from other parts of London.

Of the parishioners who made themselves conspicuous in fostering and carrying out the disgraceful scenes in the church, it would be absurd to suppose that they were urged thereto by a zeal for religion.   One of the most conspicuous of them (I believe that he was the original "aggrieved parishioner") was fined at the Middlesex Sessions for keeping houses of ill-fame, and the rest

were not famous for their purity or their piety.   The character of
some of these men was thus set forth by a young man who
attended the night school in the Calvert Street district : " It's all
a question of beer, sir, and what else they can get.   We know
them.   They are blackguards like ourselves here.   Religion ain't
anything more to them than it is to us.   They gets paid for what
they do, and they do it like they'd do any other job."

Upon the whole, the riots aided rather than injured the Mission,
for at their close I believe Mr. Lowder was more popular in the
parish than he had ever been before, and it is certain that they
won for it in other parts of the country many friends.

Very soon after the Sisters had begun their work, they
had taken a few penitents into their house in Calvert Street ;
but it was soon found to be both too small for the numbers
collected in it, and too near their old associations.   The
work was one of absorbing interest to Mr. Lowder, and in
June, 1858, he took a house at Sutton, in Surrey, having
room for about eighteen penitents, who were tended by the
Sisters, their head-quarters still remaining in Calvert Street.
He felt that the connection of the Refuge with a particular
district gave it a special importance, as auxiliary to the
Mission, by helping to foster a public feeling against the
prevailing sin of those parts ; as the inmates were nearly
all girls from the district, the Highway, or neighbouring
streets, who, either through the Sisters' intervention or the
effects of open-air preaching, were drawn to ask for assistance.

Some of these were gathered in through a sermon,
preached in the open air, on the occasion of a girl having
committed suicide by throwing herself into the Docks ;
others by a similar sermon after a murder, originating in a

quarrel between two men about a poor girl. A crowd was always collected at such times, a large proportion being sailors and other men. It became a great refreshment to Mr. Lowder, after leaving the sad scenes of Ratcliff Highway, to go to the Home at Sutton, and to see the rescued ones employed usefully in the laundry and kitchen, or, in their time for recreation, in the garden, enjoying country sights and sounds which some had never known, and but few since the days of innocent childhood. Better still, as he himself wrote at this time, it was his joy " to join with them in their prayers and hymns, in their little oratory, where their hearts seemed indeed to unite with their voices ; or to look at the attentive faces, and very often streaming eyes, with which they listened to assurances of a Saviour's mercy, and calls to repentance and faith in a Saviour's blood."

But his work with them was one of extreme difficulty : they had been used to such brutal treatment from the sailors and thieves who were their former companions, that it was long before they could bear restraint or curb the violent tempers long indulged ; while the dreadful atmosphere of their former homes, the oaths and blasphemies which formed their conversation, had blunted their feelings, and tended to harden them in sin. " It is scarcely possible," he said at that time, "to describe the violent outbursts of passion with which the Sisters have had to contend, or the frantic rage into which the poor girls at first lashed themselves at some trivial remark."

All this made him the more earnestly desire to use measures of prevention in the case of innocent girls under his care. At this time, two years after the opening of the

Mission, between three and four hundred children were being educated in his schools ; and thus a way was opened for a very humble beginning of an Industrial School for girls, under the Sisters in Calvert Street. The work had been forced upon them by the necessities of the case, for, as Mr. Lowder wrote soon after the school had begun—

How could the clergy or Sisters go out on their daily visits among the poor without meeting with very many pressing cases ? Young girls, perhaps still in the school, or just out of it, living in the greatest peril with a drunken father who might at any moment cast his child adrift; an idle, unfeeling stepmother, who would send her out to nurse a child she could scarce carry, and be a drudge in a house to a large family ; and if she came home worn out, or was sent away because it was too much for her, would tell her, "Then you may get your living on the streets." Some, already in workships, factories, and even dust-yards, where they shrank from the contamination to which they were exposed, gladly sought a shelter under the wing of a loving and religious house. Some were admitted for their very importunity, because they prayed so earnestly to be saved from the danger and wretchedness by which they were surrounded at home. One, whose temper often made it difficult to keep her, would say that if she were sent out she was sure to be tempted on to the streets. Another had lost her mother, and, during her father's absence at work, would get the meals for her brothers, who were thieves themselves, and would bring home their companions with them. A third was in danger of temptation from her own father, from whom her mother was separated. Others had been starving at home, or were driven from home by aunts or other relations who had undertaken to keep them, and must have gone to the work-house if we had not admitted them.

There was no room for an organized Industrial School in Calvert Street; and, after many difficulties, buildings at

Hendon, originally almshouses, were taken, and there a school was formed for girls rescued early from the temptations around them, and was called St. Stephen's Home. It stood on a high and healthy spot, three miles beyond Hampstead, and thither also the penitents were removed, as their numbers had now outgrown the Sutton house.

The day of the dedication of the Hendon Home was one of great joy to Mr. Lowder. The old buildings had been fitted up as laundry, kitchen, and nursery; while the newer part was devoted to a chapel, chaplain's rooms, Sisters' rooms, and dormitories for penitents. It was dedicated, on June 21, 1860, a procession being formed in the courtyard and passing through the building to the chapel, while prayers were offered in each part of it for God's blessing on the Home. The sermon, of which Mr. Lowder wrote as "very impressive and eloquent," was preached by the then Dean of Westminster, now Archbishop of Dublin.

Early in January, 1859, Charles Lowder went to Frome, to attend the sick bed of his old nurse, who had been rather a second mother to him than a servant. It was the first time that death had visited his home circle, and he felt it keenly. Writing on January 11th, his sister says—

She had been suffering for some weeks from a complaint in her foot, which proved to be mortification. At ten p.m. Charles celebrated Holy Communion in her bedroom—Janey perfectly sensible, though much exhausted. None of us went to bed; but R——, K——, and I watched by her to the end. About 1.15 a change came over her; all were summoned, and while Charles was offering the commendatory prayer, the spirit quietly departed, and the poor wasted house of clay was all that remained to us of our dear, faithful old nurse, the loved watcher and guardian of our babyhood and childhood, the friend of our riper years, to whom we all went with all our concerns, sure of sympathy and interest. The weary old pilgrim of threescore years and fourteen is gone to her rest. We cannot grudge her; but we weep for our loss—a blank which none other can supply.

It is difficult to say whether the existence of such unusual relations between masters and servants are more honourable to the former or to the latter.

The two following letters were written to the brother whose career Charles had watched with loving anxiety, on his ordination (Trinity Sunday, 1859), when he received his title from the late Rev. Thomas Keble, Vicar of Bisley; and on his receiving priest's orders a year later.

Sutton, June 9, 1859.

My dear Willy,

I fear you will think that I have been very neglectful in not writing to you after your ordination, but I did not know for certain that you were ordained, until I saw the lists in the *Times* on Wednesday, and since then I have not been able to write much. However, I hope you will accept my most sincere wishes that God's blessing may abundantly rest upon your ministerial life, and that you may have a full supply of those gifts and graces which may make your ministry profitable, both to yourself and others. You have indeed taken Holy Orders at a time when it needs great searching of heart and faithful courage, for these are days when those who will do their duty fearlessly must expect much tribulation. We are cut off from the world, so far as its pleasures and honours are concerned, though our very duties bring us into close contact with it. May we learn to despise its vanity, even while in love we seek to convert it to God.

I trust you will have much happiness in your work at Bisley, such happiness at least as may be good in encouraging you to go forward as a good champion of the Cross. I shall be glad when you have time to send me a few lines about your work, and be assured that you will never be forgotten in the prayers of

Your affectionate brother,

CHARLES.

Mission House, Wellclose Square, E., June 3, 1860.

MY DEAR WILLY,

I ought to have written to you last week or before, to assure you of my prayers and good wishes at your ordination. I have indeed prayed that you may be a faithful priest—none but priests can know what an awful burden the priesthood is ; and as you come to learn what the priest's responsibilities are for each individual soul with which he is brought into contact in confession and spiritual intercourse, as well as his solemn duties in offering the Blessed Sacrifice—which I am sure I never realized (imperfectly as I do) until I began to approach it daily—then you will indeed feel how much you need all the prayers that can be offered for you. And yet the graces of the priesthood are very wonderful, for how otherwise could we be saved ? That the great High Priest may abundantly bless you from above with the manifold gifts of His Holy Spirit, is the sincere prayer of

Yours most affectionately in our Lord Jesus Christ,

C. F. LOWDER.

CHAPTER X.

THE LINES OF THE BATTLE.

"Here and there you may meet with those who recall you at once from the accessories to the essence of our existence; who instead of spelling its little syllables, interpret its great meaning; who do its work, not from a menial point within it, but from a lordly position beyond it, and rather *pass through* the present than are imprisoned in it."

AT the time when Mr. Lowder was left single-handed, through the defection of Mr. Collins and Mr. de Burgh, Mr. Mackonochie, then curate at Wantage, went with a friend to see the Mission. This was in November, 1857. He had no thought then of doing more than seeing a work which interested him; but he was so much moved by the sight of the brave, lonely soldier, that he offered to come and help him as soon as he could; and in November of the following year he took up his abode at the Mission House in Wellclose Square. He had a heart which stirred at the trumpet's summons, and it is impossible to tell what the blessing of his presence for the next four years was to Mr. Lowder. No one, probably, could have been of the same help and comfort to him at this time.

They lived together in Wellclose Square, though Mr. Lowder's chief work was in Calvert Street district. It will be seen, from his letter to his father when asked to head the Mission, that his first thought was to try and form a "religious" (in the technical sense) brotherhood, with the hope that this organization might extend to other parts of London where hard missionary work was needed. But it was ruled otherwise; circumstances did not lead in the direction he had aimed at, and in the end little more was attempted than a Parochial Clergy House. Probably his strength lay rather in that direct missionary work among the lost souls of heathen London, in which he became of renown, than in the formation and ruling of a society of men.

He says himself that "the amount of active duty required of the clergy was a bar to the adoption of a stricter or more monastic rule." But a rule they had, and one which left little time for anything but prayer and hard work. Here is his own sketch of the daily life in the Clergy House in Wellclose Square :—

The first bell for rising was rung at 6.30; we said Prime in the oratory at 7 ; Matins was said at St. Peter's and St. Saviour's at 7.30; the celebration of the Holy Eucharist followed. After breakfast, followed by Terce, the clergy and teachers went to their respective work—some in school, some in the study or district. Sext was said at 12.45, immediately before dinner, when the household were again assembled; and on Fridays and fast days some book, such as the "Lives of the Saints" or Ecclesiastical History, was read at table. After dinner, rest, letters, visiting, or school work, as the case might be, and then tea at 5.30 p.m. After tea, choir practice, classes, reading, or visiting again until Evensong at 8 p.m. After service the clergy were often engaged in classes, hearing confessions, or attending to special cases. Supper at 9.15, followed by Compline, when those who had finished their work retired to their rooms.   It was desired that all should be in bed at 11 p.m., when the gas was put out; but, of course, in the case of the clergy, much of whose work was late in the evening with those who could not come to them at any other time, it was impossible absolutely to observe this rule.   In an active community the rules of the house must yield to the necessities of spiritual duties.

This kind of rule went on to the end.   Once, for a short time, the clergy were somewhat separated—indeed, one of them was a married man—but from 1872 all were united in a Clergy House.   Mr. Lowder laid much store by this arrangement; he had dreamed of it, though on more monastic lines, at St. Barnabas', where the way of life was not poor or strict enough to satisfy him.   He writes of having "great reason to be thankful for the blessings of such a community-life for himself," and of "believing that his brethren equally. felt the advantages of being linked together in all the details of their daily life, especially in prayer and constant intercourse."

If the outer details and circumstances of the Mission are somewhat minutely described, it must be remembered that Mr. Lowder's *life* was really his *work*, and that more than common interest belongs to it in the eyes of all who would fain join the battle against ignorance and vice. And for this reason: because, as even those who were far from agreeing entirely with him acknowledged, his Mission was the first which made any real impression upon the heathenism of the worst parts of London.

It is therefore worth asking, what were the lines upon which he worked, not only as to outer organization, but also as to inner principles?

He has told us himself that, in order to lay a sure foundation for the missionary work of the Church at home, "it must be built up, stone upon stone, like a breakwater, where a vast amount of labour is spent on that which will never appear till the judgment day, and where, after these stones have been carefully laid, they must be strongly cemented together until they can be left to buffet against the angry storms and waves of the ocean."

Words of truth and soberness, as well as of eloquence, were spoken in the early days of Father Lowder's work :—

Although the Church throws herself upon the masses, she deals with each individual soul as if it alone were entitled to all her love. Never, while the Church has comprehended her mission, has she affected to win souls by general measures which ignore the needs of each. The soul of man is not a mere part of a machine, which moves because you set the machine in motion. It is a living force, a centre of undying life. . . . Open your metropolitan cathedral on Sunday, and fill its aisles with multitudes, who listen if they do not pray. It is well ; but what if the seed lie upon the surface, when there is none at hand to cover it with soil, and, ere Monday morning comes, the fowls of the air devour it ? . . . The Good Shepherd calleth His sheep by name. Individualizing work is a matter not of taste, but of necessity. A religion which does not attempt this may succeed in adding to the stores of the understanding ; it can never win the heart. It may cover the wounds of society ; it can never bind and heal. . . . The St. George's clergy live in the centre of a dense population ; they are always on the spot. They are there ready to make the most of every opening, and to guard against each threatening of danger. They are surrounding themselves with services, schools, reformatories. They are winning penitents and gathering in communicants. Their object is not only to diffuse an influence, but in the name and in the strength of Christ to save. Around them are those who *have been* saved—saved from lies, and prayerlessness, and lust, and despair, and hell. Such, of course, *may* fall away and be lost, as may any Christian on this side the grave. But, as it is, God "has called them to this state of salvation" by the entreaties, and toils, and sacraments of the St. George's missionary clergy. He will call others.*

Father Lowder did not feel that his object was gained "merely," as he said, "in bringing people to church, or in inducing large numbers to make some outward profession of religion without a real change of heart and life." We have seen how he warned his younger brother of the danger of allowing even diligent use of sacraments to take the place of this vital change. Still less did he believe in the regenerating power of attempts to brighten the surface of society by plans of social recreation, by lectures, concerts, or tea-meetings, while the festering sore is left untouched; although fully acknowledging the value of such things in their proper place, and gladly using them.

He described what he strove to effect—"to bring home to consciences the guilt and heinousness of all sin in God's sight; the love of God, making sin what it is, and alone giving hopes of pardon through the precious Blood of Jesus Christ."

"We believed," he said, "that though it were a much more difficult work to win souls to Christ in the sorrowful ways of true repentance, and in the fruits of penitential discipline—to build them up and train them in the whole faith of the Catholic Church, and in the duties of the Christian life; yet that thus only were we fulfilling our special obligations as missionary priests of the Church—

* Sermon by Rev. H. P. Liddon, D.D.

thus only were we feeding our flock in the rich pastures of their Christian inheritance—and thus only enabling them to contend against the manifold trials and persecutions amidst which they lived, to be a witness for the faith in a wicked and perverse generation, and thus to be truly missionaries themselves in bringing other souls to Christ."

He spoke openly, and with no bated breath, to those who were awakened and troubled, of confession and absolution ; not as a dangerous remedy to be used in extreme cases, but as freely offered to all requiring more comfort and counsel than they could find without it. He spoke of it in the spirit of that Canon of the Irish Church, now swept away by those who rose up against her ancient faith, saying, "Let us root out the remembrance of it from off the earth." *

"I wonder," one of Mr. Lowder's former fellow-workers says, "how people who object to confession would deal with the sort of cases which form the principal part of Mission work in East London and places of the same kind. Without confession they would be working entirely in the dark ; without confession these poor straying souls would not have perfect assurance of forgiveness—would not realize that the

* Addition to the 19th Canon made by the Irish Convocation of 1634 :—

"And the minister of every parish shall, the afternoon before the said administration, give warning by the tolling of a bell, or otherwise, to the intent that if any have any scruple of conscience or desire the special ministry of reconciliation he may afford it to those who need it. And to this end the people are often to be exhorted to enter into a special examination of the state of their own souls ; and that finding themselves either extreme dull or much troubled in mind, they do resort unto God's ministers to receive from them as well advice and counsel for the quickening of their dead hearts and the subduing of those corruptions to which they have been subject, as the benefit of absolution likewise, for the quieting of their conscience by the power of the keys which Christ hath committed to His ministers for that purpose."

M

past is really wiped out, and that the future is clear before them. I have still ringing in my heart the cry of two poor labouring lads who had just made their first confession, and who came to me, their hearts bursting with joy too great to bear : 'Ah, sir, if we could die now!' I could tell the most wonderful stories of changed and rescued lives of lads and men who have been brought by God's grace to seek His pardon in the ministry of reconciliation."

But chiefest, and above all, before souls converted and rescued, the Holy Communion was set forth both as the great act of worship and the great means of spiritual grace. It is best to give in his own words his belief and practice on this awful subject.

If it be asked, as it is by some, why the Holy Communion is made the great central act of worship, the answer is that it is the one great service ordained by Jesus Christ Himself—" This do ; " —the Liturgy of the Church ; that it is a commemorative sacrifice, the great means of showing forth that which it most concerns us to show forth as the means of our salvation, the Death of our Lord and Saviour Jesus Christ; that it is the communion or communication of the inestimable blessings which are derived from the Incarnation, Passion, Death, Resurrection, and Ascension of our Blessed Lord.

Nothing could exceed his care lest souls committed to him should approach this Blessed Sacrament unworthily. For this reason, amongst others, he valued confession, as helping the poor to perform that duty of self-examination enjoined in the Prayer-book, but of which the difficulty, even intellectually, is so enormous to the uneducated. He has left on record his belief that he would have been unfaithful, alike to his vows and to those under his care, had he ever allowed any outward opposition to wrest from his hands this most powerful weapon against the enemy of souls. The careful preparation of his candidates for Confirmation, both young and old, also gave occasion for close spiritual intercourse and for individual instruction. The classes for Confirmation generally went on for three or four months every year, and communicant classes for the greater part of the year.

The value of instruction to individual souls, as compared to that given in sermons, has been likened to the different results attained by throwing a bucketful of water from one side of a wall over empty vessels set in a row on the other side, and by pouring water into the same vessels one by one. In the one case, some drops of water would probably find their way into the vessels; in the other they would be filled to the brim. Certainly Father Lowder's flock were fed on the latter principle, as we may learn from the following words of one who stood by his side in the battle-field, as to his manner of waging war, and the result :—

It was surely a great act of faith in the Almighty power of the Holy Ghost, ever present in the Church, and ever young, that in planning his campaign against this region of darkness and heathenness, "this common sewer of all the realm," Mr. Lowder should elect to fight with the old Church weapons, and operate on the old Church lines. The spiritual victory of St. Peter's is a witness to the power of the old faith and ancient ritual of the Church of Christ to reach the hardest and most abandoned hearts, and win them back to purity and the love of God.

All that I have said of the condition of things in East London generally, and the neighbourhood of Ratcliff Highway in particular, is of value, not so much to excite sympathy with Mr. Lowder and help Churchmen to understand his life-sacrifice, as to try to paint the circumstances of human life with which, in the lowest depths of infamy and mire of bestial habits, the Almighty power of grace has grappled, and lifted up into the sacred associations of the Body of Christ. It is, indeed, most wonderful, this manifestation of the Presence of God in the Church, this proof of the Church's power of reaching and elevating souls lost in sin whenever her true teaching is faithfully put forth, and her spiritual powers fearlessly made use of.

Now that the experiment has been tried upon the very dregs of our national life, and is acknowledged even by enemies to be an astonishing success, it is easy enough to say that it is only what one ought to have expected. But we must never forget that it was Mr. Lowder who first had the faith and courage, and love of souls, to stake his life on the realities of those principles which we now accept. Others had preached before the love of the Crucified Lord and the sinless Humanity of Christ. Mr. Lowder brought this within the hope and reach of the most straying sin-stained soul. He made them feel that they could be taken up from their sin, and all the fearful surroundings of their spiritual darkness, into that same pure Body of Christ, by means of the sacraments which Christ has left to His Church; that the Church *is* the Body of Christ, and that God the Holy Ghost dwells in the Church, and that He operates by means of those organs of the Body which Christ had ordained—bishops, priests, and deacons—in their exercise of the spiritual powers · He had left them, and their administration of the sacraments He had ordained.

And this is what I can bear faithful witness to as the experience of my eleven years' work amongst them, that the people of St. Peter's *do* believe that when their children are baptized they *are* "regenerate and grafted into the body of Christ's Church," and that therefore, being made part of Jesus Christ, they are bound to follow His holy example and live His life, in union with Him by prayer and meditation and reading God's Word and receiving

RESULT OF TEACHING.165

Holy Communion. They believe that the Bishop *does* give them the Holy Ghost in Confirmation by the laying on of hands. They believe that our Lord *has* "left power to His Church to absolve all sinners who truly repent and believe in Him." And so, when they cannot quiet their own conscience, they go to the priest and open their grief, that they may receive absolution. They believe that the Blessed Sacrament *is* a sacrament—is not only bread and wine, but that there are *two* parts, and that the invisible part is the " Body and Blood of Christ, which are verily and indeed taken and received by the faithful in the Lord's Supper."

And what has been the result of all this teaching and holy discipline? Not only that open professional sin has been swept away from the streets of St. Peter's—that there is not one known house of ill fame in the whole parish, when within a quarter of a mile streets are peopled with these poor outcasts ; but also that the communicants of St. Peter's have been lifted above their suffering life into joy and peace. They are able to accept the sorrows of life as incentives for clinging nearer to the heart of God ; they can rejoice in tribulations, because thus they are more like the " Man of Sorrows." They have learnt and proved that it is the most blessed privilege of our union with Christ to bear the Cross with Him, and sympathize in all the sufferings of His Body for His Church's sake. And in consequence they are the most united congregation I have ever met with. They really do feel that they are "members one of another," and are bound together in the Body of Christ by the love of God the Holy Ghost. It is an astonishing exception to the usual London congregation in the real *family life* which characterizes it.

We therefore owe to Mr. Lowder's memory a deep debt of gratitude, in that he has proved the power and life of the Church of England, and its ability to reach and reclaim the lost lives that lie hidden in our slums. Dissent has never been able to touch this class of life. Especially as Churchmen are we grateful to him in that he has done it by the simple preaching of the great truths of the Incarnation, and the use of the means of grace which flow from it.

It is a marvellous fact that now, as in old time, the faithful declaration of the highest truths of our religion, and the common-sense application of the powers entrusted to the Church—by which not only are souls told to " come to Jesus," but also told where to find Him, namely, in the Blessed Sacrament of His Body and Blood ; not only told that the Blood of Christ cleanseth from all sin, but also that by the command of Christ the pardon of that Precious Blood is applied to the penitent soul in absolution— should have raised up, from most unhopeful materials, this stanch and noble army of communicants, five hundred strong, rescued from slavery, and restored to their lost heritage. It is a fact which demands the attention of all who care for missionary work.

Let me tell one story, of which the hero is a little child nine years old, just to show the missionary spirit which animates even our children, and how their young hearts beat with the love of God. This child, one of my St. Agatha's choir-boys, was very ill, and had to be taken to the London Hospital. The ward of a large hospital is not a cheerful place for a young homesick affectionate child, and yet this brave little fellow found work·to do. He made friends with the men, and when the Bishop of Bedford came to preach in the chapel, he collected a band of eight big men and marched them off to the service. They would not have gone but for this child ; their hearts had been touched by his prayers and his pretty innocent ways. They called him " our little master." One day, he was telling his mother of the number of deaths there had been in the ward since he arrived. His mother said, " My dear, you ought to pray for them when they are dying." He answered, " Mother, I always do."

As with doctrine, so with ritual. Mr. Lowder determined to model the services of St. Peter's on the old Church lines, in the true spirit of the Prayer-book.

He had virgin soil to work upon. He had this advantage, that his people did not know what the inside of a church was like. There were no Puritan prejudices to consider. Hence it was but the instinct of a true Churchman and Christian to make the great service of the Holy Eucharist the central act of worship on the Lord's Day. To his poor people, whose minds had not been warped by controversial bitterness, it would seem the natural fulfilment of our Lord's command : " Do this in remembrance of Me." Therefore, with all that could make the service bright and beautiful, the Holy Eucharist was solemnly offered every Sunday and holy day.

I suppose there is not a more beautiful service in London or England than the High Celebration at St. Peter's, London Docks. And it is entirely a labour of love, a religious service, on the part of those who form the choir and who assist at the altar. Besides the ennobling feeling thus engendered by a service offered willingly and not for money, the reverence and solemnity of the whole sacred act has had a surprising influence for good on the lives and tone of mind of those who take part in it. Indeed, this is the practical value of such a service, apart from its aspect towards God as our " bounden duty," that it raises the hearts of the poor out of the miseries of their earthly lot into the majesty and peace of heaven. The beauty and the brightness of the services, the glorious music, the solemn dignity of the ritual, all these contrast with the squalidness and nakedness of their homes, and make the church to them the very house of God, the gate of heaven.

They have told me so more pathetically than I can hope to write it.

And it must be remembered that at the time Mr. Lowder inaugurated this order of service, there was no doubt that he was acting strictly within the liberties of the Church of England—nay, according to the express ordering of the rubric. The Privy Council had given judgment in the case of Westerton *v.* Liddell, that the ornaments of the church and ministers as used in the second year of King Edward VI. were sanctioned by the first rubric of the Prayer-book. It had not then been attempted to invert the plain meaning of words. It was not surprising that the new wisdom of the Court of Final Appeal, in its contradictory judgments of later years, made no difference in the order of service at St.

Peter's.   The people had grown to love and value their beautiful services, and Mr. Lowder's principles did not urge him to attach any special weight to the decisions of a secular court which had usurped the spiritual jurisdiction of the Church.

It will be seen that in later years his action in this matter was not allowed to remain unchallenged by the Church Association.

CHAPTER XI.

1859–1860.

> " Loco d' ogni luce muto
> Che mugghia, come fa mar per tempesta,
> Se da contrari venti è combattuto ;
> La bufera infernal, che mai non resta,
> Mena gli spirti con la sua rapina,
> Voltando e percotendo li molesta."

IT was fortunate that during 1859 and 1860 Mr. Lowder had a fellow-soldier by his side, the Rev. Alexander H. Mackonochie, who, like himself, did not know what fear was, and who cared nothing at all for mob violence or mob law. For at this time they had to work through the riots at St. George's-in-the-East, once infamously notorious, but which have scarcely been heard of by the younger amongst us.

It so happened that Mr. Bryan King entered upon the charge of his parish just after a celebrated Charge by Bishop Blomfield, in 1842, in which he strongly urged upon his clergy obedience to several very plain directions in the Book of Common Prayer. Probably, and fortunately, neither he nor his hearers in the least anticipated the opposition which this obedience would provoke ; an opposition which seems to us almost incredible, since it was directed against practices about which no one would now think of raising any question.

Mr. King was amongst those who carried out the directions of that Charge, beginning to do so on entering upon his cure. He had succeeded to a *régime* of terrible neglect ; his predecessor had only appeared once in the parish church during the seven preceding years, and had only one curate. It can easily be believed that this system was well pleasing to such a population as the parish contained ; that no riots disturbed the peaceful slumbers of their Rector ; and also that the first tokens of an active ministry roused opposition amongst those whose wretched interests it was sure sooner or later to invade. They found a fit representative in one of the churchwardens, Mr. Thompson, who kept a public-house at the corner of Cannon Street. However, after a time the hostility seemed to die away, and as Mr. King said, " I was permitted in comparative peace to pursue my almost hopeless work in the midst of this dreary wilderness of human souls."

Fifteen years passed in this cheerless peace. Then came the Missions, attacking the very strongholds of Satan, and bringing new strength to the mother church. In 1859 six clergy at least were labouring in the parish, besides a large staff of lay assistants ; fifty-four services were held weekly in place of the four per week which Mr. King had found established, and six hundred children were under instruction in the six schools which had been set on foot.

No wonder that the cry arose that Mr. King had

"alienated" his parishioners. There is a letter to Lord Brougham, published as a pamphlet at this time, by one signing himself "an Englishman," in which he makes an eloquent appeal to justice and common sense on behalf of clergy whom he says he neither knew nor had ever spoken to. "Alienation, indeed!" he indignantly exclaims, "what more convincing evidence of the depth and reality of the work now being carried on at St. George's than the rancorous hostility which it has encountered from the advocates and doers of Satan's work in that benighted parish? The parishioners were quiet enough so long as the one curate with his four services a week essayed feebly to arrest the overwhelming tide of vice and crime; but, now that the Rector of St. George's has directed a more powerful armament against the stronghold of sin, its defenders cry out like Demetrius of Ephesus, for their 'craft' is in danger. But the alienation in this case means the severance of the tacit alliance between the Church and sin—her clergy and the tempters to sin—the rending and repudiation of that unnatural amity which was the growth of long years of neglect and unfaithfulness."

The result of this neglect may be imagined from one fact. The East London Association, formed for the suppression of at least outward vice, caused a careful survey to be made of a considerable section of the population, contained within a parallelogram of four streets within which St. George's Church is situated. This section was found to contain 733 houses, of which 40 were public-houses and beer-shops, and 154 were houses of ill fame. It was not wonderful that amid such a state of things should be found the elements of fierce opposition to any

form of religious earnestness, and of readiness to make
the church a scene of outrage and blasphemy. The marvel
is that for ten months a lawless mob was allowed to do
this with perfect impunity, and, as official documents show,
with too much, on the part of many in authority, which
appeared to be a source rather of encouragement than of
repression to the rioters.

The members of the vestry of St. George's were elected
by the inhabitants of the whole parish, and it is enough to
say that more than one were owners of a large number of
houses used for evil purposes, while several were notorious
for the moral scandals which they had occasioned. Upon
this vestry devolved the duty of electing a lecturer at the
parish church. In December, 1858, they elected the Rev.
Hugh Allen, who was remarkable for the extravagance of
his Puritan tenets. He had lately been elected lecturer of
the parish church of Stepney, but the Rector had succeeded in excluding him by interposing his veto against
his being licensed by the Bishop. Mr. King attempted
the like course, and, on its failure, appealed to the Bishop
against the licence, on the ground of circumstances which,
four years previously, had induced Mr. Allen to resign
his lectureship at St. Luke's, Old Street. The Bishop,
however, did not again communicate with Mr. King, and
licensed Mr. Allen on May 17, 1859.

His entrance upon his office gave the occasion for the
breaking forth of the long smouldering fire. The vestry
were well aware of the victory they had gained, and of
Mr. Allen's violent antagonism to the teaching and worship
carried out in the parish church. He entered it, amidst
shouts of " Bravo, Allen ! " from the mob, on May 22nd,

insisting on superseding the ordinary service. The Act under which he was appointed * enjoined that "the lecturer should be admitted by the Rector, to have the use of the pulpit from time to time," but Mr. Allen apparently claimed the right of using it whenever he was so disposed. He entered the pulpit, triumphantly brandishing the Bishop's licence in his hand, and was greeted with shouts of applause. He had a band of devoted and noisy adherents, who filled the church with uproar, and, elated by their success, invaded it on the next Sunday, during the usual service, the clamour and violence reaching such a pitch that the clergy and choir were with difficulty extricated from the mob by the police. This was the beginning of the riots which for ten months, more or less, made a Christian church a disgrace to England—the vilest of the vile, the very scum of the most degraded parts of London, men, women and boys, going there for "a lark," and rioting almost unchecked by the law.

The Bishop now "earnestly recommended" Mr. Allen not to attempt to preach in the church until his rights and Mr. King's should be respectively decided by law. The Court of Queen's Bench, to which the vestry had appealed, decided that Mr. Allen's act on May 22nd was an "intrusion," and recommended that he should be allowed to have a service of his own after the usual Sunday afternoon service. However, Mr. King yielded to his wishes, and allowed the lecturer's services to *precede* his own. The consequence was that two or three hundred of Mr. Allen's congregation remained in the church, taking possession of the choir stalls in order to prevent

* 2 Geo. II. c. 30.

Mr. King from officiating, and he was persuaded by the churchwarden to give up the attempt.

The battle had now fairly begun, and the mob regularly attended the ordinary Sunday afternoon services, invading the stalls, shouting, hissing, and yelling. On August 14th the cry was raised, "Let us attack the choir boys." They had taken refuge in the baptistry, and the door was held by force against the mob by a few friends of order. One of these was prosecuted by the publican churchwarden for having struck the hat of one of the assaulters, the vestry paying the expenses of the prosecution.

In the middle of August, both Mr. King and his curate broke down, their health giving way, and they left St. George's for a time, when the whole burden of the parish fell upon the Mission clergy, chiefly upon Mr. Lowder and Mr. Mackonochie. The riots continued unabated, the churchwardens never giving a single offender into custody. On one occasion Mr. Mackonochie was assaulted by the mob, and was with difficulty rescued by the police.

It is impossible to read without shame for the authorities concerned, the documentary evidence as to the history of these riots.* The Chief Commissioner of Police, to whom application was made for protection, simply replied, "The law does not authorize the employment of the police inside the Church of St. George's-in-the-East, as you request." In another letter to Mr. King he wrote :—

I have seen this morning one of the churchwardens of the

---

* It is to be found in the "Copy of all Correspondence that has taken place between the Clergy, Churchwardens, and Inhabitants of *St. George's-in-the-East*, with the Home Office and the Police Authorities, relative to the Disturbances in the Parish Church. *Ordered*, by the House of Commons, *to be printed*, 8 February, 1860."

parish, who stated, in his own and his colleague's opinion, that the introduction of the police on duty in the church is calculated to excite persons who may attend the church, and in case of collision disastrous consequences may ensue; and that it would be better to apply for assistance, when absolutely required, in the event of the commission of any legal offence of which the police can take cognizance.

The church and congregation were thus given over to the pleasure of a howling and blaspheming mob; and the police authorities and the Home Secretary having been in vain appealed to for sufficient protection by the clergy in charge, the church was closed by an order from the Bishop to the churchwardens on September 25th.

The immediate consequence was a rush to the Mission chapels by the rioters, who gathered more than a thousand strong in Wellclose Square, attempting to break into the church, and seriously threatening the Mission Houses. On September 25th Mr. Lowder's life was in danger from their violence, as, baffled by the effectual measures which had been taken to barricade the gates, they turned their rage against him, and attacked him when he left the church, trying to seize and throw him over the bridge. His friends made a *cordon* at the entrance to the bridge, and held it against the mob until he reached the Mission House by a back entrance.

But the rioters were at length met with a strong firm hand. The congregation were admitted to the church only by tickets, and on the following Sunday, October 2nd, some of them succeeded in forcing their way through the crowd, and the service was carried on without actual interruption. "No one,' Mr. Lowder wrote, " could easily forget the ·

sense of awe created by the solemn stillness within the church, contrasted with the noisy hum of voices indistinctly heard without."

Writing to his father, he says—

I ought to have written before to acknowledge the receipt of the parcel, which arrived quite safely, but my time has been entirely taken up, and this week very unpleasantly, as the rioters from St. George's came down to Wellclose Square in the evening. I hope to prevent any disturbance in the Mission Church next Saturday by admitting our congregation by tickets, and I hope we have caught a ringleader, against whom we shall apply for a summons to-morrow. Mackonochie is gone for his holiday, so I am by myself.

A few days later he wrote :—

Sunday, October 2, 1859.

. . . I send you these few lines by the morning post, to say that all has gone off quietly to-day. We had no disturbance of the services; there was a large crowd in the evening, but the police kept them in perfect order, and the ringleaders have been alarmed by our proceedings against them. My father will, I dare say, like to read a letter of mine in the *Times* of Saturday. We are in much better spirits, and hope that the rioters have received a check.

October 3, 1859.

I hope you received a letter yesterday afternoon which I sent by the day mail. . . .

It was a great mercy to get over the Sunday so well. The police acted very well, for the first time all through the rows; I wrote to one of the commissioners myself, and he sent down satisfactory orders. The prosecutions in the police court and the magistrate's declaration have also been of great service in alarming the ringleaders; but, above all, the many prayers which have been sent up to the throne of grace have produced this happy result. I came out of church by myself, and walked through the lane which the police made in the crowd, and could only hear a few boys hissing. Our services were without the least interruption, thanks to our tickets, which have annoyed the disturbers amazingly. I trust that this check may do something for the production of peace when the parish church is opened. The Rector is come home, but I fear that we have much to go through as regards the parish church before the parish is quiet again. However, I do not think they will dare to do much against the Mission, and what has been done is all tending for good in drawing sympathy at home and abroad. We had several defenders yesterday, amongst others Thomas Hughes, the author of "Tom Brown's School Days." It is quite a comfort to see a Monday paper without any account of alarming riots in St. George's.

Both Mr. Lowder's anticipations were fulfilled ; after a Sunday or two there was no more trouble at the Mission chapels, and the services were carried on from that time without interruption. But a long, weary battle was still to be fought at the parish church, of which the practical burden fell chiefly on the Mission clergy. The vestry had applied to the Bishop to interfere with the long-established mode of worship at St. George's, especially choral service and the Eucharistic vestments, which had been presented by the congregation, and used for two years, many members having pressed the use of them upon the Rector. The legality of the latter had been but lately affirmed in the Knightsbridge judgment, and the Bishop of London had expressed his official concurrence with that judgment.

Unhappily, as it seems, for peace, a letter appeared from the Bishop in the newspapers, dated September 5, 1859, in answer to the vestry, in which he characterized the use of

N

the vestments as "this childish mummery of antiquated garments," and assured the vestry that though, in consequence of the legal decision in their favour, he would not appeal to a court of law upon the question, yet at the same time he would not hesitate to deprive of his licence any assistant curate who should use them, who had not the legal protection enjoyed by an Incumbent. The vestry met, and enlarged their demands, requiring nothing short of a return to the exact way of performing the services when Mr. King became Rector, seventeen years before.

Ultimately, Mr. King consented to be bound by the Bishop's decision as to the two points of the hour of the lecturer's service, and the vestments, "so long," he wrote, "as the parish did not disturb me in any of the other matters complained of; but that if they took an adverse course in these respects, I should consider myself at liberty to, and should, repudiate the decision as to the lecturer and the vestments." *

The Bishop decided both points in favour of the disturbers, and the church was reopened under this arrangement on Sunday, November 6th. It is needless to say that the concessions made were but as fuel to the flame ; and, even before the sermon, the morning prayers were more seriously interrupted than they had ever been before.

Writing of the impression received by him "from those who, on the part of the Government, are charged with the preservation of peace," the Bishop expresses his belief at this time that "the chief cause of remaining irritation and disturbance is the practice of turning round in the pulpit with the back to the congregation after the sermon." He

* Extract from the record of the Arbitration of the Bishop's legal secretary.

desired Mr. Lowder and Mr. Mackonochie "to drop the practice alluded to." Those who were really acquainted with the lives and interests of the people who promoted the riots, could not but know that the practice of turning eastward at the ascription of glory to God had no more to do with the offence taken than that of turning eastward at the Creed ; and that every attempt to remove supposed causes of irritation was followed by a fiercer outbreak of blasphemy and passion. The Bishop was requested to come and preach in the church, but he declined ; however, he seconded Mr. King's renewed appeal to the Home Secretary for the attendance of police within the church ; and, on November 10th, Sir Richard Mayne, who had refused his request in June, wrote to acquaint him "that a sufficient number of police shall be sent (to St. George's Church in the East) on Sunday next, to maintain order." This first real attempt on the part of the authorities to enforce order was successful ; attempts at interruption gradually became less serious, and by Christmas Day had almost entirely ceased.

On December 24th Sir Richard Mayne wrote to Mr. King : "I have to acquaint you that after next Sunday, the 25th instant, the police can no longer be employed inside the church of St. George's-in-the-East." No reason was given for this measure, but Sir Richard added that all the accounts he received of the sentiments and motives of those who took part in opposing the mode of performing divine service at St. George's induced him to believe that an alteration in some matters of merely ceremonial obser-vances would allay the lamentable excitement. He was in vain entreated to withdraw the police gradually, and assured that a sudden withdrawal would be certain to provoke a recurrence of the outrages, especially as Mr. Allen was to officiate for the last time in the church on January 1st, 1860, when a strong demonstration from his followers was to be expected. The police were withdrawn, and the field was left open to the rioters.

They took advantage of it, and from this time the riots became worse and worse, until, by the middle of February, they had reached their climax. The whole service was interrupted by hissing, whistling, and shouting; songs were roared out during the sermon and lessons, and cushions, hassocks, and books were hurled at the altar and its furniture; while the clergy were spat upon, hustled, and kicked within the church, and only protected from greater outrages by the efforts of sixty or eighty gentlemen from different parts of London, who, unasked, came to the rescue.

Mr. Lowder wrote long afterwards of a little self-elected guardian to the Mission clergy at this time :—

During the riots in the parish church, when the Mission clergy assisted the Rector in his time of need, and were themselves in considerable danger from the mob, while returning from the church to the Mission House, we generally found on our way home a little girl from the school, trotting close by our side, as though to protect us from the violence of the people, who were pressing and shouting around us. She would take up her position near the church, and often wait a long time until we appeared; and if we did not recognize her before, we soon heard a little voice by our side, addressing us by name to show that she was near. This child, a wild little thing, living in an unfavourable atmosphere at home, was afterwards taken into St. Stephen's Home and sent out to service, and is now married.

At length public feeling was aroused; and the Home Secretary was appealed to in newspapers, by several members of Parliament, and by a deputation, fifty London incumbents and about a hundred other clergymen of every shade of opinion joining in the memorial. On February 6th, and 7th, Lord Brougham rose in the House of Lords and spoke on the subject. Two passages from his speech may be given :—

I beg to have it distinctly understood that the question of putting down this disgraceful nuisance has nothing whatever to do with the supposed errors out of which these disturbances have arisen. Be the clergyman ever so much in the wrong (and I do not say that he is in the wrong), this does not furnish an atom of excuse, or even of extenuation, for such scandalous exhibitions. I can only repeat the expressions of disgust at those proceedings which I uttered on a former evening, and my conviction that, whatever may be the merits of the question, whether as to dogma or discipline, it is not to be settled by the outrages of a riotous mob.

The Home Secretary at last gave orders that the police were again to attend at the church. Instead, however, of being dispersed amongst the congregation as at first, a force of sixty was marched into the church with such display as increased irritation, and, notwithstanding the Rector's remonstrances, during the *morning* service, which had not been interrupted for some Sundays. There they remained, inactive witnesses of disgraceful scenes. On February 26th and March 4th, the mob took possession of the choir stalls, pelted and defaced the altar hangings with orange-peel and bread and butter, and threw down the altar cross. On the following Saturday, the Bishop sent an informal monition to the churchwardens to remove the choir stalls, the altar hangings, and the altar cross. His directions were forwarded at so late an hour on Saturday night that it was impossible for the Rector to obtain legal advice. The churchwardens gladly carried out the injunctions, and all the special objects of the rioters' hate were swept away.

It was not likely that they would pause in their career of easy victory. The clergy, deprived of their stalls, had retreated to seats placed within the altar rails, as the only place left free for them ; but the mob soon invaded the altar itself, taking possession of the seats of the clergy and choristers. On the following Saturday, May 19th, an order arrived from the Bishop desiring the churchwardens to remove the forms which had been placed within the altar rails for the clergy, to hinder them from walking into church in procession, and to place them wherever they, the churchwardens, might choose.

The English Church Union became alarmed at the consequences involved in the question of the legality of these monitions from the Bishop, not through his court, but sent as a *personal* act. The question appeared to them to be—Were the services and ritual of the church in each parish to be subject henceforward to the decision of the lawful tribunals of the Church, or to the wishes and commands of any individual Bishop? The executive of the Church Union resolved to take the opinion of several of the most eminent legal authorities on such questions, as to the lawfulness of the several orders made by the Bishop for changes in St. George's Church. A consultation was held upon this point by Dr. Phillimore, with Messrs. J. D. Coleridge, Prideaux, and Stephens. They unanimously expressed their conviction that the so-called "monitions" were "not worth the paper upon which they were written."

The mob continued to use their opportunities. The story of the riots may be concluded in the words of "A Layman" in the letter to Lord Brougham already mentioned, written in April, 1860 :—

Nearly every point assailed has been (unwisely I think) surrendered for the sake of peace. . . . And what has been the result? Why, that the state of things is as bad, if not worse than ever it was. A pretty close attendant at the services at St. George's for some months, I will venture to say that the scene of riot and blasphemy on Sunday, the 8th of the present month, has never, on more than one or two occasions, been equalled, certainly never surpassed. There were the same execrations, hisses, and laughter, the same bursts of groans and howlings, the same stamping of feet and slamming of doors, the same hustling of the clergy and maltreating of helpless little choir-boys, the same blasphemies, the same profanity, the same cowardliness, the same brutality as ever. I can find no words which more thoroughly express my sense of the horrors I witnessed than the language of the reports which appeared in the daily journals (all of them anti-Tractarian) on the following day. "It was left for last night," they say, "to witness a series of the most diabolical outrages ever perpetrated in any church. The conduct of the mob was perfectly fiendish." . . . The most violent outbreaks usually occur during the reading of the scripture lessons, the recital of the Creed, the chanting the "Gloria" or the "Prayer for Bishops and Clergy." . . .

. . . These riots are not a question for argument, for concession, for temporizing : they are a scandal to be put down, an infraction of law and order to be suppressed by the strong hand, *immediately and at any cost*. In a word, my lord, not another Sunday should be permitted to witness these awful scenes of blasphemy and sacrilege. They should be suppressed next Sunday ; not by draughting into the church a large body of police, to be silent witnesses of the outrages, but by giving them instructions to take every individual rioter—the whole congregation if they come within that category—into custody; and means should be taken to compel the magistrates, for once in their lives, to administer strict justice instead of paternal counsels, as is usually the case with persons charged with rioting at this church. Leniency is a fatal mistake in matters of this kind. I have seen and known enough of the riots and the rioters to be enabled to register my solemn conviction that there is scarcely a particle of religious feeling involved in the matter.

. . . Is a consecrated church to be profaned by scenes of riot and blasphemy and violence which would not be tolerated for a moment in a Roman Catholic church, in a Dissenting chapel, in a theatre, a concert-room, a casino, or in Mr. Churchwarden Thompson's public-house at the corner of Cannon Street? . . . I believe that if the majesty of the law had been vindicated in *one solitary case*—if a single rioter had been punished with a short imprisonment and hard labour—anything to stamp the crime of sacrilege with judicial reprobation—the Sunday services at St. George's would not be, as they now are, a weekly scandal. . . . No language which I can employ could convey a stronger censure upon each and all of them—the Home Secretary, the Chief Commissioner of Police, and the magistrates—than the single fact that, up to the very day at which I write, these atrocious scandals, far from being suppressed, are reiterated every Sunday under circumstances of increased atrocity.

On Monday, February 6th, the day after the most awful riot I ever beheld in my life . . . Sir Cornewall Lewis deprecates the use by Mr. F. Byng of the term "outrages" as being applicable to these proceedings. . . . Every act of the Bishop of London, since his first intervention, has resulted in a triumph for the rioters over the Rector of St. George's. . . . And the magistrates. . . . Out of the dozens of cases which have been brought before them, they have not punished a single rioter with imprisonment.

I have shown that for many months the house of God has been desecrated by the most appalling outrages, that His consecrated servants have been refused that protection from personal violence which they have a right to demand as citizens, and that they have been absolutely surrendered to the mercies of a persecuting mob. I have shown that they have vainly appealed to the law of the land, that they have been denied all redress, that they are deserted by the authorities, and that their own Bishop has—well, my lord, that their own Bishop is not on *their* side in the matter. In a word, my lord, I trust I have shown that there is now no earthly tribunal open to them but that to which I confidently appeal—the public opinion of the country, its justice, and its common sense.

In June Mr. Lowder received the following letters from the author of "Tom Brown's School Days ":—

3, Old Square, Lincoln's Inn, June 7, 1860.

MY DEAR SIR,

I venture to apply to you to know if anything can be usefully done to bring about a better state of things in St. George's Church in this fashion.

Arthur Stanley was up last week, and has got the sanction of the Bishop to the plan, if it can be carried out.

Hansard (who is, I think, known to you by name) is now without a cure. He it was who sent me and others to St. George's last autumn. He sympathizes with you all heartily, and is in favour of good music and church decoration ; in fact, for a clergyman who is not professedly a High Churchman, I know no one who more honestly appreciates and respects that section of the Church, and the work they are doing.

If Mr. Bryan King would not object to take a year's rest, the Bishop will sanction it, and Hansard would take the cure for the year. We have *carte blanche* as to funds, so that Mr. King would not be put to any expense whatever, and would receive his full stipend (though I am aware that this would not weigh much with him). I do conscientiously believe that no better plan could be hit upon for getting rid of this scandal; and in the course of the year I am sure that we could so arrange and organize matters that Mr. Bryan King on his return should be able to take up his ministry again, without any recurrence of these disgraceful riots. I am sure that you would all like Hansard, and be able to work well with him, and that he is just the man to deal with this state of things. Can you help us? I do think that if Mr. Bryan King would see and talk with Hansard, they would arrange everything satisfactorily as to what should be done. I should add that this is no plan of the Bishop, though he has approved of it if it can be managed. I do not think that he has acted well in this matter, and would have nothing to do with a plan coming from him, though I am glad to have got his approval for this, which I do believe to be the very best course to be taken just now. Please let me hear from you soon.

Ever yours most truly,

THOMAS HUGHES.

3, Old Square, June 9, 1860.

MY DEAR SIR,

    Thanks for your kind note.

Hansard is unluckily out of town for Sunday, having gone down by special invitation to preach in his old country parish. I will try to bring him down to see you early in the week. You may rely upon it that I would take no part in any plan which I did not think a good one from your point of view. I most heartily respect and sympathize with you, and your work down there is a noble one, and it is a most painful thing to me as a churchman to see it interrupted in this way. I have worked with Hansard in London for many years, and do not know his equal for dealing with the roughest part of a London population, while he makes no secret of his respect and liking for the High Church party, though neither he nor I can be said exactly to belong to it.

I do think, please God, if Mr. Bryan King can make up his mind to take a year's rest, that all may be now set right.

Believe me to remain, most truly yours,

THOMAS HUGHES.

The arrangement proposed by Mr. Hughes was carried out. Mr. King left the country on July 25, 1860, and Mr. Hansard took charge of his parish. The services of the church were, before Mr. King's departure, exactly the same as those in English cathedrals, except that hymns were sung instead of anthems. Still the riots rather increased than abated, and, on November 14th, the Bishop wrote to Mr. King recommending that surplices for the choir should be given up, the Psalms read instead of chanted, the black gown worn in the pulpit, etc. Mr. King was abroad, but answered the Bishop's letter on November 23rd, refusing to sanction these changes in his church. On November 22nd, however, the Bishop had sent a fresh "monition" to Mr. Hansard, requiring him to yield up for demolition and abolition all that had been demanded. On November 24th, Mr. Hansard refused to violate the engagement into which he had entered with Mr. King as to the mode of conducting the service, and wrote to the latter informing him that he resigned his charge, and that the Bishop's chaplain would take the duties of the following day. The struggle was over, a memorable instance of the victory of mob law.

CHAPTER XII.

"To strength and counsel joined
Think nothing hard, much less to be despaired."

IT is a relief to turn from the miserable story of the St. George's riots. But Mr. Lowder believed that, on the whole, they had "tended to consolidate and establish" his work. "The very dregs of the people," he said, "were taught to think about religion. Many were brought to church through the unhappy notoriety which he had gained ; and some who came to scoff remained to worship. Mr. Mackonochie's valuable assistance at St. Saviour's was bearing good fruit. The conversion of many souls in the way of true repentance, the increase of communicants, adults and children brought to Baptism and Confirmation, the better organization and instruction of the schools, and the careful administration of the charities of St. Saviour's, all bore witness to the zeal and power with which his missionary labours were carried on."

A friend to the Mission wrote to Mr. Lowder about this time (the letter is undated) :—

"I have doubled my subscription this year, as I fear the late disturbances may have put you to additional expense, and, perhaps, done you some damage. How far you are involved with Mr. King in the introduction of unusual vestments, in the celebration of the Holy Communion, etc., I do not know, but I should not wish it to be supposed that I at all sympathize with such matters because I give your Mission some little support. Let me say, however, that though we may differ on this point, yet I most thoroughly venerate that spirit which, working in you and your fellow-curates, has enabled you to labour with such self-denial in the desperate haunts of sin which surround you, and I am sure that your present trial, if borne to the end as you have hitherto borne it, cannot but strengthen your cause. Continue to look with a patient and pitying eye on the miserable men who trouble you, for is not the Church somewhat to blame that she has allowed such to grow up within her borders?"

The following letters are too interesting (as showing the change of feeling towards Mr. King), and too honourable to the writer, to be withheld, although, for obvious reasons, names are omitted :—

MY DEAR SIR,

As you were in charge of the Mission works at Michaelmas, 1861, and no doubt heard somewhat of the matters alluded to in the enclosed correspondence, I think it only due to send you a copy, and further to tender an apology to you and the other clergy for everything said by me which in any way reflected on you and them.

Faithfully yours,

Rev. C. F. Lowder.   —— ——.

[COPY.]

VERY REV. AND DEAR SIR,*

I believe you were present at St. George's-in-the-East on the morning when the service was conducted and the sermon

* This letter is addressed to a well-known dignitary of the Church.

preached by me.   I have no doubt you were pained and grieved by many of the expressions and statements I then made use of. I now write to express to you my deep regret for having uttered many of the said things, more especially those which condemned, or appeared to condemn, the conduct and motives of the Rector of the parish.   I have since been led to see that much (I do not say all) of what I then spoke against is the truth and power of God. Will you pardon me if I request that, should you have mentioned to Mr. King what then happened, you will also lay before him this my retractation and apology.   I ought in justice to myself to add : 1. That I write this not at any one's request, or even suggestion.   2. I by no means say that I *ex animo* assent and consent to all that was done during and before the time of the riots by the Rector and clergy of the parish ; but I do feel the greatest respect for what I now believe to have been their integrity and singleness of heart, and I very much regret my ever having been guilty of so ungentlemanly an act (to say the least) of opposition to a clergyman in his own church.   I remain, dear sir, with much respect,

Your faithful servant,

—— ——.

My dear Sir,

I lose no time in acknowledging the receipt of your letter of December 22nd, and thanking you for the very frank confession which it contains.   You are right in believing that I was at St. George's-in-the-East on ——.   My reason for attending the service was this: I was going to see the Bishop of London the next day, in order to talk over with him the future arrangements of the church, and discuss the possibility of the Rector's return.   I could not help saying to the Bishop that all healing of the troubles of the parish seemed impossible while the Rector's absence appeared to be used for the purpose of keeping ill feeling alive in the parish.   I do not deny that I was pained by what I heard from you in the morning, and as much and more so by what I heard from Mr. —— in the evening.   I will gladly avail

myself of your permission to communicate to the Rector what you
have said to me; in fact, it is only justice to yourself that I should
do so.   May God bless you in your work.

Yours very truly,

——— ———.

When, some years afterwards, Mr. King preached in the
parish at one of the anniversaries, he was greeted outside
the church with a round of hearty cheers, many pressing
forward to seize his hands and to assure him of the change
in their feelings towards him.   There were also several
instances of men who had joined the scoffers at St.
George's, but whose very profanity had been the means
of their being brought to a better mind, and who became
choristers in other churches, or assisted priests in Mission
work.   And three, at least, of those young men who came
from other parishes to protect the clergy from the mob
"were induced," as Mr. King wrote long afterwards, "to
give up their situations in commercial houses in order to
seek admission into Holy Orders, from the conviction that
the cause which excited such deadly hostility from the
profane was one above all demanding the devotion of the
servants and soldiers of Christ Jesus."

Another fruit of the riots was the Working Men's
Institute.   A gentleman, previously quite unknown to the
clergy, had come to St. George's at the worst to offer
his help in preserving order, and was so deeply impressed
with the need of all kinds of agencies for taking hold of the
working classes, that he originated an Institute for their
benefit.   It was begun in February, 1860, in the Mission
House in Wellclose Square, the clergy having removed to
another house, but was so soon thronged by members that

it was necessary to obtain larger and better rooms. The new institution was opened with an address by the late Rev. F. D. Maurice, on October 22, 1860, and within a month was joined by 180 members. It included first and second class reading-rooms, and a youth's club, where daily papers, periodicals, chess, and other games were provided, as well as a good circulating library. Besides this, classes were held for those who wished to profit by them in singing, French, and drawing, as well as for more elementary teaching, with the generous help of some of the excellent teachers connected with the Working Men's College in Great Ormond Street. Lectures were given once or twice a month by friends to the Mission — the present Archbishop of Dublin, Dean Stanley, Thomas Hughes, and others. During one year more than four hundred members were admitted, and the Institute did a good work for some years. It was removed, when the work in Wellclose Square was perforce abandoned, to a house in Old Gravel Lane, opposite St. Peter's Church, where it still exists, though somewhat changed in character, being less a literary than a dining club, where cheap and good meals are provided for working men and their families.

In July, 1860, Mr. Lowder had the refreshment of "a very delightful trip of three weeks to the Channel Islands" with his two sisters ; and on January 20, 1861, he was at Frome, where the whole family assembled to celebrate his beloved mother's birthday.

It was a winter of great distress, and he made an appeal in the newspapers. More than £200 was sent to him while he was at Frome, which was carefully dispensed by the clergy in food and clothes. Their intimate knowledge of the district, of course, enabled them to do this far more satisfactorily than it could have been done by any other agency ; still it added to the work, which was beginning to press heavily upon the Mission clergy and to tell upon their health. There were only two priests and a deacon at this time for the daily and frequent services in two Mission chapels, besides all the pastoral work and secular business which fell upon them.

Mr. Lowder felt that, their work having been consolidated, it was high time to form the two Mission districts into ecclesiastical districts, each with its own incumbent. This was the more necessary on account of the uncertainty of his tenure as curate, especially under the circumstances of the parish church. He therefore secured a site close to Calvert Street, in Old Gravel Lane, about a minute's walk from the old iron chapel. On this site now stands the stately church of St. Peter's-in-the-East.

Seven hundred children were taught in the schools at this time ; the Government inspectors reported that the children were "very fairly instructed," but that "new premises ought to be provided," and that there was "want of appliances for teaching." Mr. Lowder's desire was to build a church and use the iron chapel as a schoolroom, "but," he wrote, "we cannot build or make improvements, or get better appliances for teaching, without larger means." And from this time especially, as fresh work opened out, money anxieties and difficulties added heavily to that weight which he patiently bore during the twenty years that were to pass before he gained his rest. He had doubted in 1856 whether £100 a year could be raised to

O

support one missionary curate, and now, in 1861, the expenses of the Mission were between £3000 and £4000 a year.

He himself, it need scarcely be said, continued to live in simplest poverty. A lay friend, who occasionally went to the Mission House to help him in business matters, said to the writer, " When I saw his bedroom I said to myself, ' Any gentleman who is content to live in this way must be in earnest.' The curates' rooms were far better."

The following letter from Mr. Rowley shows that Mr. Lowder must have written to him with much anxiety about this time of the want of means for carrying on the Mission :—

Mpames Village, Manganja Land, Central Africa, March 10, 1862.

MY DEAR MR. LOWDER,

Thank you much for your letters. This is the third time I have tried to get off an answer. Once our brethren carrying them were plundered of all—letters lost ; another time they went to the bottom of the Shiré, through canoe upsetting; and now there is but an hour or so to rest during a long and hurried march to write my answer.

I sympathize deeply with you in your trouble in carrying on the Mission for want of adequate funds. If the work has partly to be given up in consequence, the Mission has done well. It has provoked other good works—think of that. I wish I had time to write more largely; attribute it only to the right cause. Do not think it want of will or affection. My love to all. May God bless you all ; I think of you daily. We are much tried just now ; our Bishop is dead, and we are shut up in the land.

Ever most truly and affectionately yours,

H. ROWLEY.

Will you give my kindest and most respectful remembrances to your father ?

In Lent, 1862, he went to Bedminster to conduct the first parochial Mission in the English Church. His lack of eloquence makes his success in Mission work the more remarkable. It may have been, as the layman just mentioned said, " The people had heard others call them ' brethren ' from the pulpit, but they never saw any one else become really their brother, living amongst them, in poverty, and wholly at their call and service. He was indeed their *servant*, as he was the servant of Christ."

Some of his Mission tracts are, however, written with remarkable strength and telling directness ; they seem to come straight from a full heart, a soul intensely realizing the verities of which he wrote, striking home to souls over whom he yearned.

The Bishop of the diocese opened the Bedminster Mission by preaching the first sermon on Ash Wednesday, and for the ten following days there were constant Mission services, including lectures to two hundred colliers in the schoolroom, and ending with a midnight visit made by the Vicar of Bedminster and Mr. Lowder to a neighbouring coal-mine. They were accompanied by the wife of the Vicar and by Miss Lowder, who wrote the following account of the expedition. After describing their descent, she says :—

We came to a large open space which they said was the stable ; it was now empty, and here it was proposed that Charles should preach to the men. This being arranged, some of the colliers set off to assemble all in the pit, while we continued our journey. One of the colliers explained to us how they worked : they lie nearly flat on the ground, and with their axe dig out from the bottom upwards, so that the upper part gives way, and large masses of coal fall off; or as the collier explained it, "when the legs are cut off, the body tumbles." When we returned to the stable, we found a goodly company of colliers, some standing upright, some leaning against the black wall, while most had seated themselves in rows one behind the other. The effects of light and shade cast by their numerous lights was very striking. The service began with the hymn "Rock of Ages;" it seemed well known to all of them, and they joined in it most heartily. Then they all seated themselves again, and listened most attentively to the sermon. Charles spoke to them of the rock on which they were seated; of the rock over them and all around them; of the Creator of that rock, even God, Who made all things. They could not tell, he said, how long this rock had been buried under the earth; yet there was a Rock before it—the Rock of Ages—the Rock that was cleft for us, even Jesus Christ, Who was before all things, and by Whom all things were made. He told them what He had done for us in His Incarnation and Passion, and then spoke of what sin was— a fresh insult to Him,—of repentance, and a judgment to come. He talked to them of the Hartley Pit accident, and of what those men would have given for a longer time. "Would you not like to see that tin flask," he said, "which bears so simple an inscription, perhaps scratched on it at the very moment when the full danger of his situation burst upon the writer: 'Mercy, O God!'?" Then we all knelt down, and said the Lord's Prayer. The Vicar spoke to them afterwards, telling them of a plan he had formed for their benefit: that he wished to have a room for them, open every evening, where they might go and read the papers, and have tea and coffee, and where lectures, both instructive and amusing, would be given. He told them that his great wish was to serve them in sickness and in health, but that he would much rather serve them in health, for then when sickness came they would know each other the better. He said he had been called but a day or two before to the bedside of a sick man, whom he asked concerning his soul's health; but the man could not answer him. He then told him to say the Lord's Prayer after him; but the sick man was unable to do it. He tried again, asking him to say only, " God be merciful to me a sinner; " the man said " God," and could say no more.

A deep impression was made upon many at Bedminster, and the Vicar, Mr. Eland, writing some time after, said that he looked back upon the Lent Mission with entire satisfaction.

This year of 1862 was in many ways a bright and encouraging one to Mr. Lowder ; the strain of troubles at the parish church was over. His little pamphlet, " Five Years at St. George's," had drawn attention and interest to the Mission, and a heavy debt which had hampered the funds was, at Easter, finally extinguished. He was full of schemes for buying the Danish Church in Wellclose Square, which was offered for £2000, of raising an endowment, building schools, and forming the district into a separate parish. This scheme, which was never to be realized, he seems to have thought easier to accomplish than that which came to pass—the formation of the parish of St. Peter's in the Calvert Street district.

He was the more anxious to establish the work in both districts on a definite ecclesiastical system, because it was suffering severely from lack of sufficient clergy. Mr. Mackonochie had been called, this year, to the charge of St. Alban's, and Mr. Lowder lost in him one whose place could never be entirely filled. He was now left alone to carry on the work once allotted to three priests, with only the help of two deacons, having lost the Chaplain of the House of Mercy at Hendon ; and he writes of himself at this time as " trying to hold his ground till relief comes."

In the end of August he took a much-needed holiday among the Swiss mountains, and crossed the St. Bernard, visiting Milan, Turin, Verona, and Como, returning by Trent and Méran, Innspruck, Salzburg, and Munich. It was his first visit to the Austrian Tyrol, where his last days were to be spent.

I feel all the better for my holiday (he wrote to his mother from Bruges on September 15th), and hope to get on with my work when I return, as I shall have plenty to do. I fear I shall be the only priest, though there are two deacons. One of them, I think, will be a great help, though he has only determined to remain till Christmas. This will probably be the last of my long letters, as I shall not have much time for writing, and I quite dread the sight of a month's correspondence which I shall find on my return.

CHAPTER XIII

FOREIGN TOURS.

1862.

"O there is sweetness in the mountain air,
 And life that bloated ease can never hope to share."

ON the first Thursday in Advent, 1862, the "Confraternity of the Blessed Sacrament," of which Mr. Lowder was one of the founders, was inaugurated.

Of other works in his Mission he could write in 1863 that "the great bond of these associations is the Holy Eucharist," "forming more and more the life of the Mission." The communicants steadily increased, and on some festivals there were choral celebrations for the schools, interspersed with hymns sung by the children, to whom this service became full of brightness and heartiness.

Mr. Lowder used to be asked sometimes by those experienced in education, how it was that children and young people in his schools seemed to grasp and carry away with them the faith, far more than those in more advanced schools. His answer was that he thought it was the result of the effort made in the Mission schools to lay a deep and sound foundation of elementary dogmatic teaching. The first principles of the Creed were impressed over and over

again in the catechisings in church, which were addressed
to all, even to the youngest. He found that this teaching,
coming with authority and the associations of the services,
was very effectual in impressing sound Christian doctrine.

The children themselves did not agree with Mr. Rowley,
that Mr. Lowder had not a happy way with them. It was
a great offence if one of the curates took the catechising,
and one little girl, remarkable for expressing her feelings,
used to say aloud on such occasions, " There now, *it 'tain't*
Mr. Lowder ; 'tis a shame."   One of the infant school-
mistresses writes :—

I was working down there from 1860 to 1870, ten of the very
happiest years of my life, and I will speak as I ever then found
him.   I could go on for ever speaking of his love for little
children. He was rarely seen alone in the streets; generally he had
a train of tiny children after him.   Many is the time I really
wished him further off, when I was very busy with a lesson, or
playtime was " just up ; " for as soon as he appeared there was
nothing but fun. He used to take the skipping-ropes out of their
hands and say, "Come, you can't skip. I'll show you how; look at
me," and gravely skip away amidst peals of laughter ; then burst
out and laugh till he looked at his watch, then : " Oh, hush ! or
we shall be put in the corner," and off he would run.

But the catechising—how I wish others could do the same—he
riveted the children's attention.   I never heard any one catechise
as he did.

Children's funerals were made the occasion of teaching
and comfort to their parents, everything connected with
them being made bright and beautiful. A little child, early
in 1863, was going home just after the Litany and catechising in church, when she stayed to play with a school-

fellow, and slipping from the kerb, fell under the wheel of a coal-waggon, which crushed her head and killed her on the spot. Mr. Lowder came up a moment after, took charge of the little body, and then went to break the tidings to her mother, sending for a Sister to comfort and support her. He had the little coffin reverently laid out in the school-room, where the parents visited it, and on the funeral day there was a choral celebration in the Chapel of the Good Shepherd, the funeral service being sung at eleven. Nor did he leave his little one till she was laid at rest; twenty-five of the clergy and choir, with three hundred school-children, bore her to the Tower Hamlets Cemetery, a violet pall, with its cross and crown of snow-drops, covering the coffin, the bier carried by girls from the Industrial Home, while many hymns were sung during the procession and at the grave. The great delight of the child had been, on coming from school, to sing the hymns and repeat the Creed she had learnt, and to try to teach them to a tiny brother. And now the mother began to prepare for her own Confirmation and first Communion.

Thus the foundations of the spiritual temple were carefully laid, stone by stone, before those of the material structure had been begun; and Mr. Lowder could feel that as soon as ever the church he hoped to build was consecrated, he could transfer to it a congregation already trained to value its blessings.

The following letters to his mother were written in Lent, 1863, and during a short autumn holiday:—

Mission House, Wellclose Square, E., March 7, 1863.

. . . I am now simply alone until Palm Sunday or Easter; depending upon what help I can get, with Lent services and work,

and sixty or seventy to prepare for Confirmation, besides, of
course, looking forward to Easter Communions, but I am happy
to say I have been remarkably well since the beginning of Lent,
having had no indigestion for three weeks, and feeling well up to
my work.   We are very poor just now, but depending, I hope,
upon our good God, who has never yet failed us.   I am reading a
very interesting life of the Curé d'Ars, which is very encouraging.
To-day we are fortunately out of the bustle, but I expect we shall
have some of the Danish royal family at the Danish service on
Mid-Lent Sunday, when we shall have to pay them some attention, which, being a Sunday, we can do.

Interlaken, August 22, 1863.

. . . I am ashamed to find that though my intentions were
good, they have been so badly carried out, and that it is now a
fortnight since I wrote to you, but the truth is we have been
moving about so much and taking so much exercise, that I have
had little time besides except for eating and sleeping.   I left
Chamounix with Powles and his wife on Monday morning, my
travelling friend not being well and riding to Martigny.   We
were only together for an ascent of about an hour and a half to
Montanvert, where you get upon the Mer de Glace.   Here I was
again fortunate in meeting a party going upon the same expedition as myself to the Jardin, and they kindly allowed me to
accompany them.   They turned out to be Captain Fowke, the
architect of the late Exhibition Building, *alias* the Brompton
Boilers, Dr. Lyon Playfair, and a friend.   Our walk was over a
rather difficult moraine (as the loose earth and stones which the
glaciers throw up are called); then over the Mer de Glace, an
immense glacier from Mont Blanc, very interesting to me as my
first expedition upon a glacier; then up a steep and rocky path
over an intervening mountain, and then across another glacier,
the Glacier de Talc.   The interest of this expedition is that it
takes you into the very heart of Mont Blanc, among very wild and
arctic scenery, ice and rocks and snow on every side.   It took

me about nine or ten hours from Montanvert, spending about an hour at the Jardin, which is a sort of oasis of verdure in the midst of the ice. I slept at Montanvert that night, started off at 6.30 the next morning, again crossed the Mer de Glace, and on by a passage called the Mauvais Pas—steps cut in a perpendicular rock, though now made safe enough by a cord ; and on to Martigny, by a very beautiful pass called the Tête Noire, which carried me through some splendid mountain and valley scenery, and at last by a very long and steep descent upon Martigny. There I again met my friend, who was now quite ready for work, and we started the next morning for Sierre in the valley of the Rhône. Thence we started on foot for a mountain expedition, first into the Valley of Ananviers, sleeping at a little village in the mountains, called St. Luc. The next morning we started before six, up a very beautiful mountain called Bella Tola, whence we had a magnificent view ; they say you can see two hundred peaks which are very clear, Monte Rosa, Matterhorn, Mont Blanc, and many other giant peaks covered with snow. We descended by the Pas du Bœuf, a wild pass, and our guide not knowing his way, we had a very difficult and fatiguing walk, skirting the sides of the mountain and crossing snow, into the Valley of Tournant, where we again slept in a little inn. Off again the next morning early into the mountains, and by a fine pass into the valley of the Visp. The next day, Saturday, we got to Zermatt, a short walk of about five hours, but, after all our walking before, and in the sun, rather fatiguing. Zermatt is beautifully situated just under the Matterhorn or Mont Cervin, a very rugged peak, rising abruptly and majestically like the ridge of a house. It has never yet been ascended, as the top is a sheer precipice, and it never can be ascended until steps are cut in it. We were very glad that Sunday brought us a day's rest ; unfortunately it did not bring me my Sunday clothes, as my bag did not arrive until Sunday evening, when I did not care about it. We met the Bishop of Oxford at Zermatt, and he preached and celebrated. Monday we started about five, and ascended a steep mountain, the Riffel, getting our breakfast at the top and continuing our walk afterwards to the Görner Grat and Görner glaciers, where beautiful views of Monte Rosa are obtained. . . . Other parties came into the little inn in a severe thunderstorm, drenched, some from one expedition and some from another. It was alto gether an amusing scene . . . ladies drenched, others disputing about beds, of which there were far from enough to accommodate the party, so some had to make up their minds to a shake-down in the *salon.* . . . Then the party was so large that many could not find places in the only sitting-room ; then a part sat round, looking on while the rest took their meal, we in our own turns making room for their tea. . . . Next morning we started about five, and took our breakfast at Zermatt. On our way down we met a man who missed his way up in the evening and was obliged to sleep in the wood. After breakfast we started for Visp, along the same valley by which we reached Zermatt, but from St. Nicholas to Visp was new to us. We reached Visp about 7 p.m., and took the diligence about 10.15 to Brieg. Next day (Wednesday), we drove to Visch, and ascended the Eggischorn as far as the hotel, but were not able to get farther that evening, and the next day there was such a severe snowstorm that we were obliged to make our way through it down into the valley, where it was pretty clear. We then walked on through the Rhône Valley by a very picturesque road to Oberwald, and thence attempted to find our way to the hotel of the Rhône glacier. We had quite lost our way in the dark and rainy evening in the wood, when we fortunately hit upon a hut full of workmen engaged in making a new road. They were a very picturesque party, though very like brigands. However, one of them kindly guided us into the right path, and after another hour's toilsome ascent in the dark, and fearing we might still miss our path and find ourselves among the snows of the mountain, we hit upon the cheering lights of the hotel, where I was glad to find a bed and get into it. The next morning, Friday, we started with two companions . . . over the Grimsel Pass. The snow was falling very heavily (this on August

21st) and the path was quite covered, and, more than that, our guide was obliged to avoid it, as it was deeper than in other parts. We ascended with some difficulty, but when near the top, came to a dangerous slope so covered with snow that the guide thought of turning back; indeed, he probably would have done so, had not a party of Germans with another guide come up, and the two guides set to work to make a path for us in the snow up to their middles. They also told us to beware of an avalanche, which was already forming over our path; indeed, one had slipped under us. In the midst of this, the wind blew off my hat, and as I called to my friend to stop it, he thought I was warning him of the avalanche, and so nearly fell down in his hurry to escape. Luckily I recovered it, as it would not have been at all pleasant to brave the storm on the other side without my hat, for it was very severe and cold. However, we got to the Hospice safely, and having taken breath for half an hour, proceeded through the snow, which became softer and softer as we descended. Below, we saw some very beautiful falls, which the rain and melted snow improved, and got on through almost continuous rain to Reichenbach near Meiringen, after a long and tiresome day's journey. A warm bath was very acceptable and succeeded in keeping off cold. Yesterday we drove down to Brienz, and came on by the steamer to Interlaken, where we are very much delighted to have quiet rooms in the old monastery, which is made a sort of *dépendance* of our hotel, a nice garden, and a beautiful view of the Jungfrau, the great charm of Interlaken. It is certainly a very enjoyable place, and I could gladly stay here some time, but I want to see a little more of the beautiful mountains of the Oberland. . . . This last fortnight has been very enjoyable, as we have seen a good deal of the mountains of Switzerland as well as the valleys, and met with sufficient adventures to keep us amused. I am glad to get a day's rest to-day (Sunday), and we had an early Communion here, at which the Bishop of Oxford celebrated. It is delightful to write this letter in sight of one of the most beautiful mountains in Switzerland.

I am afraid the service this evening, for which the bell is going, will prevent me from seeing the sun set upon it.

Want of clerical help began to tell seriously on his health, and in the spring of 1864 he became so ill that the usual festival in April was omitted, and he went abroad early in June, accompanied by his sister Susan. Of this journey she wrote—

I had a delightful tour with Charles, and made my first acquaintance with Switzerland. He was far from well, so at first, instead of rushing about, we spent a fortnight at Seelisberg, above the Lake of Uri, and enjoyed it immensely. Charles is a delightful travelling companion, arranges all for you without fuss, and is always a welcome addition to a party, full of spirit, genial, amusing, and unselfish, thoroughly enjoying the fresh air and bright sun, and gathering flowers with as much pleasure as a child.

To his mother he writes of "enjoying amazingly sitting out in the woods" and bathing. A few days later he says—

I found myself the first out in the morning (at the Righi), as from the window of my bedroom I saw the stars beginning to pale, and the clouds in the east catching a lighter tint by degrees.

After the sound of the horn, the whole company of young and old turned out, and the sight was certainly worth the labour. A heavy bank of clouds floated just over the tops .of the mountains, leaving, however, the summit exposed ; heavy mists hung over the lakes below, and the whole circle of the horizon was traced with snowy peaks, catching the sun's earliest rays ; and then at last the sun itself appeared gradually from behind a high mountain peak. I remember some finer effects in a sunrise from Cader Idris, but of course nothing like so grand a prospect of lake and mountain scenery.

. . . I feel quite set up by the change, and Mrs. —— said she never saw me looking so well; I hope I shall be able to get on well through the winter, till I can get down to Frome. I should like very much to have been able to have spent a few days now at Frome, but I suppose I must relieve Kane, who is not very strong, and will want some rest himself. I have brought you home an inkstand of Swiss carving, which I thought very spirited, and I intend it as a present to the house, thinking it would be more acceptable than a number of smaller presents to each of the party. I hope you will all like it as an ornament for the drawing-room. I will send it down the first opportunity. . . .

His sister returned home in about a month, and he travelled about for a time, going by St. Gervais and Servoz to Sixt. From thence he wrote—

We started about 4.30 a.m., following a new and pleasant route from Sixt to Chamounix for half an hour to the Châlets des Fonds, where Mr. Wills has built himself a beautiful châlet, on the top of a gorge overlooking a lonely valley, which he calls "The Eagle's Nest." Thence we struck up a very steep path for about an hour, and sat down for our luncheon at 8 a.m. We then started again, and worked up another stiff slope of half an hour on slippery turf; thence we soon got on to the shaly *débris* of the mountain, and for two hours were working up very steep sides of shale and snow, until we reached the summit, which is quite covered with snow. The view was magnificent, for though rather hazy towards Geneva, we saw the whole of Mont Blanc range beautifully, tracing the range by the Weisshorn down to the Matterhorn and Monte Rosa, with the surrounding mountains, and again, further east, the Jungfrau and all our old friends of the Bernese Alps, of which I had lost sight since we left the Col de Balme. We made our descent pretty rapidly, and got down to Sixt by 4.30 p.m., having been out twelve hours, including two or three hours' rest. It was certainly the finest ascent I had ever made. On Saturday we started back to St. Gervais by the Lac de Gers, a steep ascent of half an hour; there is a bit of shady forest and plain towards the lake, which we ought to have passed, but were misdirected; then up again for twenty minutes, skirting the sides of a ridge, partly on one side and then on another; and then, commencing our descent, we came down on a very nice little bit of water, where I had the most charming bathe I have had at all; still descending gradually over pleasant turfy slopes, till we came to a Col overlooking the Geneva road, near Maglan. Thence our descent was very steep, by a coal-mine cut into the sides of the rocks; then by a shady bit, with abundance of strawberries and a few raspberries, and some beautiful sweet-smelling pink cyclamens, which brought us down to the Geneva road at Bellegarde.

He returned to St. Gervais, from whence he writes to his sister on August 8th :—

I found Captain —— and his wife very pleasant friends, and am sorry to leave them behind here.

I gave them three services on Sunday; we had fourteen or fifteen communicants at nine, and twenty-seven or thirty at the morning service at eleven. We sang " Jerusalem the Golden," in spite of Lady ——, who said she hated it, and wanted " Rock of Ages " to " Rousseau's Dream." Our hymns went off very well, but we could not manage any chanting. I preached in the morning, but did not feel up to a sermon in the afternoon; it was so hot that I was melting. My aristocratic congregation expressed themselves much obliged for the services I had given them, and I was quite sorry to leave them without any priest on Sunday. At our two offertories we collected thirty francs for the poor of the parish, the amount of which I shall take to the *curé* to-day.

I feel very well again, and hope to enjoy my present trip very much.

On the afternoon of August 8th he started with a young companion on a tour in the Courmayeur district, and went from thence to Aosta.

I was particularly pleased with the cloisters of the Collegiate Church (at Aosta), and with the capitals of the piers, most quaintly carved, as far as I could examine it, with early Scripture history subjects—the history of Jacob, such as his meeting with Esau, and wrestling with the angel. The flocks and herds and camels were very good, but quaint. There were also carvings of the Prophets, with some remarkable verse from their prophecy. The carvings of the stalls were also good ; over each an article of the Creed, alternating with a text on the subject of the article. The Val d'Aosta, in approaching it from Courmayeur, though beautiful and dotted with the ruins of feudal castles, is not so striking as the descent from Mont St. Bernard. We drove on through the valley to Chatillon, remarkably situated over a deep gorge. Next morning we went up the Val Tournanche, a very delightful walk to Breuil. It was quite a beautiful specimen of a Swiss-Italian valley. Our walk lay in the shade, by the side of a mountain torrent, noble mountains of Savoy behind us, and after about two hours the Matterhorn in our front, its cold summit rising above the mountains in the foreground. The Matterhorn is a very grand and rugged mountain, its highest peak as yet inaccessible, though many attempts have been made upon it.

We got to Breuil about 2 p.m., and I spent part of the evening enjoying the glorious view of the mountain over us, and seeing the avalanches which came down from its sides. It was quite cold, from the height at which we were and our nearness to the glacier and snow, so that in the evening a good party assembled very happily round the fire. The next day we started about 5.30 for the Col St. Théodule ; we reached the snow about 6.30, and the top of the Col in an hour after. The ascent was very easy, as the snow was hard, but the view from the top is grand. You find a hut at the top, inhabited by a man, who is called the " Man of

P

the Mountain," and it is said to be the highest inhabited dwelling in Switzerland. He provides hot wine or water; of course the snow and height make it very cold. We stayed here about twenty minutes, and then commenced our descent, still on the glacier, which was well covered with hard snow and with few crevasses, so that we got on very easily for an hour or two, till quite the last part, which began to be a little soft, as it was now nearly 10 a.m. You have a view of Monte Rosa and the whole chain connected with it. In the descent Monte Rosa seems comparatively low, from the height from which you see it and your nearness to it, but it is at all times a grand view. After getting off the ice, and a short rest, we commenced our descent upon Zermatt, which we reached about 11.45, having crossed from Breuil in six hours and twenty minutes, a good passage.

From Zermatt he made the ascent of the Weisshorn, coming down upon Macugnaga and the Val Ansasca, and so to Stresa, returning, after some wanderings amongst the Italian lakes, by the St. Gothard Pass, and home through Strasbourg and Rheims.

On St. Peter's Day, 1865, the first stone of the church in Old Gravel Lane was laid, £4000 having been promised or given. The foundations of any building in this locality are extremely expensive, as the upper surface of the ground rests upon a bog, and the whole district is subject to inundations from the river.* Mr. Lowder writes at the time, of being obliged for want of funds to raise a temporary west front, leaving the building of the tower and spire for the future, as well as that of the schools and Clergy House, which, he says, "we may hope will soon

---

* It is necessary to lay the foundations of the Clergy House, which it is hoped may soon be begun, upon piles.

follow ; " adding, " Then a block of ecclesiastical buildings would be handed down to our successors as a lasting memorial of the Mission work here commenced."

Alas ! he was never to see the completion of what he hoped to leave ready for those who came after him. May we not hope that, now, hearts may be stirred to finish his material work, in memory of him who gave all he had—the treasures which silver and gold cannot purchase ? He wrote himself in 1864 :—

Is it too much in the present day, when the very spire of the church will rise amidst the crowded masts of our shipping and the gigantic warehouses which bear witness to the vastness of our commercial wealth, to trust that those to whom much of this wealth has been intrusted may be aroused, by the generous examples of those who have already promised large contributions, to complete what has been so auspiciously begun ? . . . Having been enabled, by God's grace, to stand our ground for nine years, amid the many difficulties which have surrounded us in this peculiarly trying parish ; having turned what at one time seemed a defeat of Catholic faith and practice in the parish church into their virtual triumph, because never have they been so firmly fixed as at present ; having seen the principles on which this Mission was founded now recognized, and more or less adopted and successfully carried out, in no less than seventeen neighbouring parishes or Mission districts of the East of London, we surely may claim the sympathy and support of all members of the Church in carrying out this work to the conclusion which we have long desired, and which now seems nearer than ever to its fulfilment.

Still he was often cheered by generous gifts to the Mission ; and a note written at this time mentions a thoughtful kindness towards himself :—

Mission House, Wellclose Square, E., July 6, 1865.

MY DEAR FATHER,

Yesterday I received, through Mr. Liddell, £100 from an anonymous benefactor for my own personal use. I have often wished that I could do something for you and my mother, which I did not feel justified in doing out of the Mission funds. I can, however, use this as I please. I hope, therefore, that you will allow me to send £50 for the use of yourself and my mother as you may like best to use it.

In the autumn of 1865 he travelled with Dr. Littledale and Mr. Nicholson, visiting Berlin, Dresden, Vienna, Belgrade, Venice, and Rome. From Belgrade he wrote :—

Immediately on our arrival, we set out to pay our respects to the Archbishop of Belgrade. Strange to say, we were directed to the German evangelical missionary, who kindly came out and took us to the palace, and acted as our interpreter. The Archbishop not speaking German or French, we had a long interview with him, delivering our letters of introduction from the Bishop of London, and Littledale brought some books from Dr. Neale and himself. We then asked him to admit us to communion, as Denton had been admitted at the monastery of Studentza lately. He said, however, that this had been done by mistake, and that the priest who admitted him did so without authority of his Bishop, and that, though a desire for intercommunion had been expressed, it was yet too early to sanction such an outward seal to it as this. We then asked if we might be allowed to celebrate after our own rite in a Greek church, but that was also refused; so eventually we gained permission to celebrate in a portion of his chapel, which we accordingly did on Sunday morning. Littledale sung the Litany, and afterwards I celebrated, with L. as deacon and Nicholson as sub-deacon, making it as choral as we could, and using incense which the priest present supplied. The Archbishop was not there himself, but an archimandrite provided us with all necessaries, such as paten, and chalice, and veils, and bread, etc., and some other priests were present during a portion of the time in the chapel. After our own service, we were taken into the cathedral, where the Liturgy was that for a high festival, as they are keeping the Feast of the Assumption, their calculation being twelve days behind ours. The service was in Sclavonian, so I could not understand it; but the ceremonies are more elaborate and numerous by far than a Roman High Mass. The singing was not very pleasing, being without any instrumental accompaniment. After the Liturgy, a good many communicated, even children; but this was not so reverential as with us, as they merely came up to the gates of the Iconostasis— a large screen, highly ornamented, which divides the nave and choir from the sanctuary—and received both species standing from a spoon which the priest put in their mouth, the deacon wiping their mouths afterwards with a napkin. The Iconostasis, I should say, is beautifully painted, and has many pictures of our Blessed Lord and St. Mary on it. There are also Eicons, or framed pictures, placed before it, which they kiss, and during the service many were engaged in kissing an Eicon in the church, while the priest crossed their foreheads. We were then taken into the Bishop's palace, where first a little cup of citron preserve was handed to us, and then a small cup of coffee.

He took a longer holiday than usual this autumn, remaining abroad for two months, and returned to his work in the Calvert Street district early in October.

CHAPTER XIV.

ST. PETER'S CHURCH—THE CHOLERA IN EAST LONDON.

1866.

"By objects, which might force the soul to abate
Her feeling, rendered more compassionate."

"I WAS in Oxford last week (Charles Lowder wrote, March 15, 1866), and got on pretty well with promises of help and collections in various colleges. The Vice-Chancellor was very kind."

April 14, 1866.

Our church is getting on nicely, but we shall have to stop the works soon unless we get some more money, otherwise it might be consecrated in the summer. I was very glad to be at Mr. Keble's funeral, as it was a day not to be forgotten, nor a scene either, to see Dr. Pusey at the grave of one he and we all loved so much.

St. Peter's Church was sufficiently completed to be consecrated on June 30th of this year ; but first, on St. John Baptist's Day, a farewell service was held in the iron chapel, endeared to the whole congregation as the place where most of them had received their first religious impressions, and where they had been taught and fed for ten years. Some of them said, with tears in their eyes, that even after the consecration they could never quite feel the same for St. Peter's as for their first spiritual home, the Chapel of the Good Shepherd.

The day of consecration was, of course, a festive one in the whole district. Old Gravel Lane was decked with streamers and gay with flags, and the school-children lined the way as the clergy received the Bishop at the school-room, in which he robed, and then followed the long procession, chanting the *Veni Creator* up the nave into the chancel. In Mr. Lowder's words—

It was a day ever to be remembered in the history of the Mission, whether for the fulfilment of long-indulged anticipations in the sight of a duly consecrated church, the beauty and solemn character of St. Peter's, the full attendance of clergy and friends, or, above all, for the hearty sympathy of the Bishop in the work of the Mission, and the warm applause which his encouraging words elicited from the large gathering of friends (about three hundred) at the luncheon.

The Bishop said in his speech that none could think of the self-denying labours of the Sisters without taking shame to themselves in their comparative ease and luxury. In the afternoon there was a flower-show in the school-room, opened by the late Lord Lyttelton, with prizes for plants, and a hearty Evensong in the newly dedicated church. The festival was kept up through the Octave, friends coming to preach each day, amongst others Canon Butler.

A district had been assigned to the church by the Ecclesiastical Commission, taken out of the parish of St. George's and St. Paul's, Shadwell. Mr. Lowder, having been nominated by the trustees, was licensed as Perpetual

Curate, and, on the resignation of the Rector of St. George's, became first Vicar of the new parish of St. Peter's-in-the-East. He described the church himself at this time as—

in the style of the later First Pointed Gothic, being faced externally with yellow stock bricks, relieved with stone dressings, and internally with red bricks, having bands and patterns of black bricks. The columns of the main arches are of blue Pennant stone. The plan consists of a lofty nave, sixty-eight feet by twenty-seven feet, with clerestory lights. It is at present four bays in length ; the three western have north and south aisles ten feet wide. The west walls are temporary, with provision for an extension, and for a north-west tower and slated spire. Eastward of the nave are transepts, north and south, connected with it by lofty arches piercing the clerestory. The chancel is thirty-five feet long by twenty-two feet wide, with two trefoiled windows in the east end, surmounted by a shafted wheel window about seventeen feet in diameter.

On the south side of the chancel is a chapel much beloved by the people, called after the iron church, the Chapel of the Good Shepherd. It is thirty-five feet long by sixteen feet. Here the daily Eucharist is celebrated.

The Octave services after the consecration of St. Peter's were scarcely over, when the first alarm arose of the approach of cholera. The clergy and Sisters had just begun to look forward to a little rest after the necessarily hard work and anxiety of preparing for the consecration, but now everything had to be put aside, and the Mission forces were obliged to gird themselves hastily for the hand-to-hand struggle of the next few weeks against deadly disease and death. A slight case occurred on July 16th, from which the patient recovered, so that Mr. Lowder saw no necessity for giving up attending a Retreat for clergy at Cuddesdon ; " little anticipating," as he wrote soon after, " for what scenes he was really preparing himself by those quiet meditations in the Bishop's Chapel."

He had no sooner reached home than he heard that one of the communicants of St. Peter's had died very suddenly the day before, and he was at once in the thick of a most fearful visitation, and of all the horrors which it involved in such a district as theirs. The night of his return he was called to the London Hospital by one of his men, who, with his wife, had lately been confirmed and received his first Communion. She had gone to the hospital that morning for medicine, was advised to remain, and grew rapidly worse. But Mr. Lowder's own words will best tell the story of this cholera time :—

When we arrived at the cholera ward we found her in severe paroxysms of cramp and sickness, and yet in the intervals of pain very thankful for such spiritual ministrations and prayers as we were able to afford her. Though tenderly nursed, she grew weaker, fell into collapse, and died early in the morning. But it was not merely this case which opened our eyes to the power of the visitation; the ward was full of cholera patients suffering terribly from the first fresh energy of the awful scourge. When once it was known that a clergyman was in the ward, one request after another was made to him to minister to some distressing case. Men, a few hours before hale and hearty, lay struck down for death ; women, young and old, groaning piteously in the agony of their cramps. On one bed lay a nurse, whose mother and children lived in St. Saviour's district, and who had been attacked while on duty in the hospital, and died in a few days. Others were sailors just returned from sea ; some Germans, either sailors or labourers in the sugar-bakeries, or their wives ; another was a Jewess, who, alas ! could receive no Christian comfort.

In ordinary circumstances it was not for a stranger to minister indiscriminately to the sick in the hospital, for whom a chaplain is provided; therefore the first course was to inquire for our own parishioners, or at the most for those of St. George's parish.

But now it was impossible to continue this distinction. For ministering to one sufferer we were immediately appealed to by a neighbour, or a nurse or friend in his behalf; and thus Sunday morning overtook us in the midst of scenes little realized by those who were enjoying their rest and sleep at a distance in health and safety.

At first, before the disease fell so heavily upon the Mission districts, the Mission clergy were glad to offer the Chaplain of the London Hospital what little help they could, overburdened as he was by this distressing addition to his ordinarily excessive labours; and very interesting indeed were many of the hours, especially in the night, spent in these cholera wards, when hearts were opened and tears shed, and, we may hope, repentance accepted from those who had been too little touched in the time of health and strength. But the overpowering calls of our own district soon made it impossible to withdraw any time from our immediate charge.

It can be no wonder that in such districts as ours, where there is at all times so much poverty and distress ; where the drainage was as yet untouched by the improvements made in other parts; where our poor are so crowded from want of house-room (an evil, alas ! increasing instead of diminishing) ; where the alleys are so close, and the sanitary arrangements very defective (for where landlords can always get tenants it is very difficult to induce them to lay out money on improvements) ; where, during the hottest part of the season, we had fermenting amongst us a large manure manufactory, in which was collected, in a very mountain of impurity, hundreds of tons of the very refuse of the streets, the stinking sweepings of the market, rotten fish, oranges, etc., to be mixed up and then carted off to barges in the river,—it can, I say, be no wonder that when the cholera once broke out amongst us it should have proved most fatal ; in fact, that the death-rate, in proportion to the population, should have been higher than in any other part of London. . . . From a close court situated in the district, a woman had been removed to the workhouse infirmary for her confinement, leaving at home her husband and six children. The youngest, a little boy, sickened, and though her husband did his best as a nurse, yet he fretted over the care of a large shiftless family (for they were Irish) and himself fell ill. The little boy died, and one Sunday evening, after service, we were called to see the father, that he might be removed to the cholera ward. In a wretched room upstairs the poor fellow lay on a bed, unable to help himself, and almost too ill to allow others to do so, the children clinging to him, and crying at his being taken from them. With difficulty he was supported through the court to the stretcher-bed ; while another child, who was also suffering, was taken with him to the temporary hospital. Thus the poor man lay in agony on the next bed to his child and died. The wife, hearing that he was in the infirmary, but not knowing that he was dead, resolved to come out of the workhouse, though still weak after her confinement, in which she had lost her baby. No inducements would prevail to keep her, though it was naturally feared that in her state of health the return to an infected house would be dangerous to herself, and it was desired to take her children out of it into the workhouse. While the medical man was drawing up a certificate, which might have the effect of retaining her, she made her escape, and was soon home, surrounded by her children and a large assembly of neighbours. The only resource was to induce her to leave this house for another, which, after an interval of two or three days, was done ; and though two more of her children were taken ill, with a girl who was helping to wash for her, yet they eventually recovered, and the rest escaped.

The disease, however, had laid hold upon the court. Another man, a strong hearty fellow, died ; two of his sons were taken ill, one very seriously, and his daughter was attacked so violently that it was necessary to remove her to the cholera ward. A young man next door followed, and while he was being got ready his wife felt so ill that, rather than leave her husband, she determined to go also, and both lay for a long time dangerously ill, the husband, indeed, at death's door. These, however, recovered, and were afterwards sent down to Seaford, where they regained their health, and returned to their homes and work. Others were dangerously ill in the same court ; one an unbaptized man, who professed infidel opinions even on his death-bed, though afterwards, through argument and prayer, he appeared to give them up ; yet, like so many sick-bed impressions, his better feelings seem to have passed away, and he has returned to drunken habits.

Among the many sad scenes of this time, one of the saddest was that of a poor woman whose child was just taken ill, and laid on a little bed on some chairs in a wretched room at the top of the house. She nursed the child as long as she could, and then fell ill herself, lying in the agony of the cramps on the floor with scarce anything to cover her, entreating the nurse, who had been sent by the Sisters for the child, to ease her pain by rubbing her legs, while the husband in his affliction was pacing up and down the room, or getting away from the sad scene into the street, until the ambulance-bed came from the workhouse to remove her to the cholera ward, where she died, the child not long surviving.

The cholera wards of which we have spoken were the casual wards of the workhouse, temporarily adapted by the guardians, in obedience to the Orders in Council, for cholera patients. They were not, indeed, all that could be desired, and yet the best provision that could be extemporized under the circumstances. There were two large wards—one for men, another for women—and a smaller one, afterwards used for convalescents. Hither the sick were brought from all parts of the parish ; all who could not be well tended at home, or where there was danger in close houses and large families of the disease spreading, were received at once, day and night. Happily the workhouse authorities, in the imminent urgency of the circumstances, having had sad experience of the inefficiency of pauper nurses, themselves applied to the Sisters of St. John's Home for Nursing Sisters, who were at once sent down, and devoted themselves most lovingly to the poor sufferers entrusted to them. It was indeed quite touching to witness the tenderness and yet fearlessness with which each Sister in turn gave herself to this work. One Sister, with a trained nurse and others specially employed for that purpose, was always in the hospital, taking the day and night duty by turns.

The patients were no sooner brought in than they were at once attended to, their beds prepared, and all that loving ministry could do was certainly done for them. It was sad to see how little even this could avail for their recovery; medical remedies, the most assiduous nursing and care, were all baffled by the virulence of the disease; one remedy after another, one system of treatment after another, one theory after another, was tried, but without any apparent effect. Still the Sister's love and perseverance never failed : and though there were days and nights of most trying discouragement, when one body after another was carried out to the dead-house, only that its place might be taken by another living yet already doomed sufferer; when we used to look round in the morning and see bed after bed filled with fresh patients, knowing too well that the former tenant was in a rough coffin,—though the Sister who was throwing herself heart and soul into this work of mercy, was often tempted in the silence and loneliness of her night watch to sit down and cry over the sad scene which lay before her, yet bravely and nobly she bore up, and never left her post as long as her presence was needed.

There was something very touching, too, in the early morning Communion at St. Peter's—when we all felt our great need of Divine help, the clergy for their spiritual work, the Sisters for their bodily and yet also spiritual ministries; when our own Sisters were preparing for their labours in the district, not knowing what the day would bring forth,—to see their little band at the altar joined by the Sister of St. John's, who had been taking her night duty in the cholera ward close by, under the very "shadow of

St. Peter," her very dress tainted by the smell of the disinfectant used in the hospital,—bringing their sorrows, and the sorrows of their suffering charges, to lay them at their Saviour's feet, and ask for grace and mercy for themselves and them.   It was a touching thought to feel at that moment how safely we were all gathered together under those loving wings ; how mercifully we were being fed with that Bread of Life which could best sustain us ; how the Precious Blood which touched our lips was cleansing us and them, and the Communion which was knitting us together in the bundle of life was joining us closely to Him Whom we could thus recognize as walking with us in the midst of this fiery furnace, so that not even the smell of fire passed on us, not one among ourselves was touched by the power of the plague. . . .

In the morning, when the clergy, after the services in St. Peter's, were going forth to their daily rounds, while some would take the pressing or dangerous cases which remained from the day before, another would find out from the relieving officer's list at the workhouse, and the Sisters' list at the Mission House, the new cases which needed attention.   We had also some laymen engaged in a house-to-house visitation—one with a special view to the sanitary state of the houses, that deficient drainage or water supply upstairs and nuisances might be reported at once to the parochial officer ; the others attending chiefly to cases of urgent distress, that the funds, which were so liberally contributed at this time, might be well and judiciously dispensed.   But with every effort to organize our staff and systematize our work (and certainly most thankful we have been that this heavy visitation found our community of clergy and lay helpers, as well as our Sisterhood, thus prepared), it was difficult to cope with the strain and pressure of the need.   The suddenness of the attack, the awful rapidity with which it spread, and the speedy issue of each seizure, requiring immediate attention both for spiritual and physical relief, continually baffled our most earnest endeavours to provide it.   We were continually impressed with the great truth that all was in God's hands ; that we were but instruments to be used as He might choose; that our spiritual ministrations were of no avail without His blessing. It seemed as if all had to be done in a moment. For the soul, it was required that the very first moments of illness should be seized and improved in fulfilling the whole work of the priest—exhortation, prayer, self-examination, confession, absolution, comfort; preparation for the last struggle must be now or never; collapse so soon followed the first symptoms that there was not a moment to lose. And yet for the body these moments were also most precious. Medical attention, the best preventive measures, violent friction, hot applications, the most careful watching and nursing, were demanded at the very moment when we should have been glad to have kept the patient perfectly quiet for the preparation of his soul for death. Then, alas! the perpetual vomiting made the reception of the Blessed Viaticum in the great majority of cases physically impossible, so that all that could be done was to exhort to a spiritual Communion, and, most frequently, shortly after it to commend the soul into the hands of a merciful God and Saviour.

By the end of August the plague had lessened. One of Mr. Lowder's sisters had come to stay with the Sisters and help them. She wrote on August 18th :—

I am glad to say the cholera seems much less than it was. My district is in Wapping. I carry little bottles of camphor and give them where they are wanted. We are all very well here, and everybody very busy, but we are not at all a melancholy party, everybody in very good spirits. I generally see Charles some time every day, and he is quite well. Sister Louisa has had, and still has, a great many cases in her district; she visits all the morning, and sits in the hall in the afternoon to give relief to all who come, several dozen of small bottles of camphor before her. The bell goes incessantly, and some one sits in the hall all day long till quite late in the evening. They give good dinners away daily, of meat and rice, to those who are half starved to keep off the cholera, and besides this, beef tea, wine, and all sorts of things to the sick. Boxes of clothes are coming in almost every day, but the demand is so great for them that I dare say they will soon go. I think there are about fifty children in the house to be clothed. The Bishop of London is going to preach to-morrow evening at St. Peter's, and many of those who have recovered are going to return thanks for their recovery.

The Bishop had kindly written to Mr. Lowder, inquiring about his own health and the state of the district; adding, "You will not fail to command my services if I can be of any use." Mr. Lowder replied that a visit from him and a sermon in the church which stood in the midst of the infected district would be most useful. The Bishop granted his wish, and came to St. Peter's with Mrs. Tait on Sunday, August 19th. He first visited the workhouse cholera wards close to the church, speaking a few kind words to the patients, praying for them and the parish, and giving them his blessing; then, after a visit to the Wapping Cholera Hospital, and the Sisterhood in Calvert Street, he went to the church, where a congregation of nine hundred had assembled. The service consisted of hymns and the Litany, with a sermon from the Bishop. It was a great gratification to Mr. Lowder that, so soon after the consecration of St. Peter's, his Bishop should come into the district, and prove his value for the blessings which it brought to the district.

The public, too, had given him all the help that money could give. As his district was one of the first attacked, a letter written by him in the *Times* was amongst the first which appeared asking for help, and within a week £1000 had been sent to him. Two thousand pounds had been sent before long, so that the clergy and Sisters were able to meet all the wants which pressed upon them. Medicines, nurses, food, and blankets were dispensed largely night and day; families weakened by insufficient food, and others specially open to attacks of the disease, were fed and strengthened by warm, wholesome dinners, daily sent from the Sisters' kitchen; comforts of every kind were supplied to the sick and dying, and yet there was a surplus left from the generous gifts sent to St. Peter's. It was given for the support of a Convalescent Home, which Mr. Lowder had opened at Seaford for the cholera patients. Of this Home he wrote at the time :—

Two well-situated houses were found at Seaford, in Sussex, commanding a fine view of the sea, and open to the fresh air and beautiful neighbourhood of the Downs. The houses were no sooner secured than the Mother Superior, with one of the Sisters, arranged the furniture; and though empty on the Tuesday, they were ready to receive the guests on the Friday of the same week. A party of nearly thirty, including some children and orphans, arrived on that afternoon, and were soon tempted out on the beach and cliffs. The thorough enjoyment of those who had never seen the sea before, at their release from their close and pestilential homes, and the happy exchange of them for the pure and healthy climate, was an exhilarating spectacle. The party consisted of a coalheaver, a dustman and his wife and child, a labourer in a bone charcoal manufactory, a boy whose young sister died and who himself worked at a soap manufactory, with other men and women, some of whom had been amongst our worst cases, but by God's mercy had recovered. All settled down in their places; those who were well enough assisted in the work of the house very cheerfully, and soon found out the neighbouring attractions by sea and land.

On the first Sunday, after attending the early celebration of the Holy Eucharist at the parish church, we were told that some inhabitants were alarmed at the idea of convalescents from cholera coming to church, though every precaution had been taken to prevent infection. Every one had a bath and an entire change of clothes the last thing before leaving London, and everything in the house was new, so there was no ground for alarm, though it was naturally excited. In consequence it was proposed, being a fine morning, to have an open-air service, which was joyfully agreed to ; and priest and congregation, men, women, and children, betook themselves to a lovely spot on the cliffs, under an old Roman encampment, commanding a rare view of the sea and coast towards Beachy Head on one side, and Brighton on the other. Here we sang Matins, the men on one side, and the women and girls on the other, while the Gospel of the day, " Consider the lilies of the field," naturally furnished a most appropriate text. It was a delightful service, to which even that noble philanthropist, who said he would "rather worship with Lydia by the river side than in the rich shrine of St. Barnabas'," could hardly have objected ; and yet even to this retired spot we were tracked by a jealous Protestant distributor of anti-ritual and anti-sacramental tracts.

The service over, our party, with the exception of a few of the weaker ones, made their way to the flagstaff, whence a more extensive view was obtained ; and then all returned happily to dinner. In the evening our church quarantine was taken off ; and though occasionally a few expressions of fear were heard in the town, yet it was found that there was no real danger to be apprehended from the cholera convalescents. The sea-air, bathing, walks, and excursions over the cliffs and into the neighbouring country soon made a wonderful change in the appearance and strength of our patients, until at last a party of the men were able to accomplish a walk of nine miles along the cliffs from Eastbourne, whither they had been taken by railway. In the evening they assembled in their sitting-room, and related their several adventures during the day, read or listened to some amusing or instructive reading from others, and joined in the games provided for them. Before supper they met for prayer in the little oratory, when a short service was held, with a few words of instruction.

The greater portion of the first party, being restored to health in the course of three weeks or a month, returned home, and was succeeded by a fresh detachment, and thus we were enabled to extend the benefits of our Home to seventy or eighty convalescents.

The cholera visitation marked an important era in the history of the Mission. For it broke down the last barriers remaining between " Father Lowder," as he was henceforth universally called, and the confidence of his people. " We had never any trouble after the cholera," was said to the writer by one of the Sisters who has worked at St. Peter's for twenty-one years. Mr. Linklater, who joined the Mission in 1869, gives the following account of the impression made :—

It would require a whole book to tell all the brave acts of heroism and self-sacrifice of Mr. Lowder and the Sisters. The poor people have never forgotten the lesson they learnt during this fearful time. Hearts that had hardened themselves against the Gospel message in health were crushed with shame and sorrow when, in the agonies of sickness, they experienced the tenderness and love of true Christian charity. The dens of poverty and vice seemed more grim and ghastly to those who witnessed the solemn ministrations of grace amidst their horrible surroundings. Walls that had for years resounded with the blasphemies of seemingly hopeless reprobates now echoed with the sobs and prayers of hearts touched with penitence. Night and day the clergy and Sisters toiled as hearts can only toil that toil for the love of God. The sights and smells they had to endure are past all telling. As usual the public were most generous, and money came plentifully in. A Convalescent Home for the patients

.was opened at Seaford, and to this day people in the parish talk of the kindness they there experienced, and the good there received. In a word, such a bond of confidence and love was created between Mr. Lowder and his people, that even in the severe strain of the secession period it held good, and against all the false accusations and malicious triumphs of the enemy they stuck true to the man whose truth and constancy they had proved in their great hour of need.

It was a time which also did much to break down popular and official prejudices against the work of Sisterhoods in the English Church. Seven communities of Sisters worked in the East of London during the prevalence of cholera, in hospitals or districts. One of the doctors at the London Hospital expressed his opinion "that the presence of the All Saints' Sisters in that hospital was, under God, the means of allaying a panic among the nurses, which, if not checked in time, might have disorganized the whole discipline of the hospital."

Still, however ready and efficient was the help of both Sisters and doctors, it was to "the Father" that his people turned chiefly, with absolute and childlike trust, even for their bodily needs. He was frequently first sent for ; his influence was invoked to induce the sick to go into hospital, and more than once his own arms carried sick children through the streets, wrapped in a blanket, to give them into the Sisters' charge in the cholera ward. His devotion to them was never forgotten by his poor stricken flock ; he had won "the golden tribute of a people's love," and he kept it to the end.

CHAPTER XV.

1866–1869.

"God doth not need
Either man's work or His own gifts ; who best
Bear His mild yoke, they serve Him best."

AFTER the strain of the cholera time was over, Mr. Lowder took a short holiday. He wrote from Alne on October 18, 1866 :—

I have been moving about for nearly three weeks, not quite idly. I came up from Seaford to spend Michaelmas Day in London, and left this afternoon for Sheffield, where I preached twice at St. Luke's on Sunday, having also preached at another church, St. Jude's, in the evening of Michaelmas Day. I made my way to Lincoln on this day, where I was delighted with the Cathedral. Chancellor Massingberd kindly entertained me at luncheon.

He attended the York Congress, and assisted at a Mission in his brother's parish at Wolverhampton before returning home.

The year 1867 was one of peace and comparative rest, since he had now much more clerical help. Mr. Akers had joined the Mission in 1865, and was in charge at Wellclose

Square. It was a severe winter, and on January 2nd
Mr. Lowder writes from Hendon :—

Here I am so snowed in that I could not get off to marry an
unfortunate couple, who chose an unfortunate day. This morning,
in jumping out of bed in the dark, I came with my bare feet into
a snowdrift which had formed under the door to about five inches,
and is now trying to form again.

At Easter he wrote to his mother :—

Many thanks for your letters. I have been so engaged lately
that I have had no time for answering. I was sorry not to write
to you on Mid-Lent Sunday, but I am glad you liked the volumes
of Moultrie's poems. We have had a very happy Easter—far more
communicants than I at all anticipated ; 180 at St. Peter's at the
two early celebrations, and two at midday, and very good congregations. The altar was beautiful—a new frontal worked by the
Sisters, and vestments for the clergy given by the communicants.
There were eighty communicants at St. Saviour's, making altogether
260 against 160 last year. I hope my father is better. I did not
like his feeble writing in his last letter. All Easter happiness to
you all.

Your dutiful and affectionate son,

CHARLES.

Father Lowder's annual holiday was taken this year in
Scotland, touring amongst the lakes, with a week's quiet
and rest at Cumbrae College, a visit which he greatly
enjoyed, as well as his trip afterwards to Staffa and
Iona.

. He returned in September to five months of hopeful
and happy work ; for his long-cherished desire of forming a
separate district round Wellclose Square seemed near its

fulfilment. Mr. Akers, the curate in charge of the district, possessed good means, and had offered a contribution of £4000 for building a church. If a site could have been procured earlier, this sum would have been secured. But now, in February, 1868, a crushing blow fell upon the Mission and upon its devoted chief. The details will be best told in the narrative supplied by Mr. Linklater :—

The good bark of St. Peter's had been duly launched on her voyage, with many prayers, much interest of kind friends, and careful observation of the outside world to watch her seaworthiness. For a time all went on well. Mr. Lowder was backed up by a staff of four zealous curates, and the parish was thoroughly worked, the services were well attended, and a great many parishioners were prepared for Confirmation and Holy Communion.

Then, at the very height of prosperity, came a blow that well-nigh wrecked the ship. Three of the curates deserted and joined the Church of Rome. The secession took place before Easter, 1868.

I have before me an account of this unhappy event, written by a gentleman who was living with the curates at that time in the Mission House at Wellclose Square.

They gave no warning or indication of their intention. One (Mr. Wyndham) was supposed to have gone to Kensington to visit a sick relative; he did not return to the midday dinner, and in the afternoon it was known that he had been " received." The next day he reappeared at dinner : after dinner he went up into Mr. Akers' room; in about an hour they both went out, and Mr. Akers was " received." The day after Mr. Lowder heard of it (he lived at the Clergy House in Calvert Street, at the other end of the parish). He came at once to Wellclose Square, and asked the schoolmasters, who were at dinner, where Mr. Akers was. They did not know. Mr. Lowder at once sent for Mr. Shapcote, who was away on his holiday, to return immediately to the desolate parish. Mr. Wyndham and Mr. Akers met him at the Junction, and in the waiting-room he decided to follow their example.

All this happened in the inside of a week, not only without any notice, but just after the people had been agreeably surprised by a sermon preached in the church in Wellclose Square, the previous Sunday, by Mr. Akers, in which they were told that they ought to be grateful to God that they were members of the Church of England, and could read their Bibles without fear of the Inquisition, and that our age and Church contrasted favourably with that of the Middle Ages.

This sermon was preached on the Sunday evening; two days afterwards, the preacher had made his submission to the Church of Rome.

The blow was indeed a most terrible one for the Mission. It nearly killed Mr. Lowder. He had to go away for a time, and Father Benson, Superior of the Cowley Fathers, with Mr. Statham, worked the parish for him. A half, and the most important half, of the St. George's Mission district was lost; for Mr. Akers had arranged to build a new church in Wellclose Square, of which he was to have been the Vicar, and now it passed into other hands, and the people were shaken in their confidence—not that any of them, or very few, followed the seceders, although Mr. Akers came back into the neighbourhood.

But it will be said, how came Mr. Lowder to have such curates? To answer this I have to acknowledge what I consider to be his greatest defect, almost his only one. He had absolutely no discrimination of character. He was always being taken in. He was so transparently simple and true himself that he expected to find others as sincere and real.

It was not the first time he had been so betrayed. Ten years before a similar blow had fallen on the Mission. At that time the party in the Mission House in Wellclose Square consisted of four persons, two priests and two laymen, of whom I was the youngest. A scare took place, and I was the only one left.

Mr. Lowder's letter to "the Friends and Subscribers of St. George's Mission," dated "All Saints', 1868," has the most melancholy ring about it. He never cared to show his deepest feeling either in speaking or writing, and consequently to those who did not know him he may have sometimes appeared stiff; but in this particular letter, in which he speaks of his broken health (and it must have been broken to make him say so), he continually harps upon the sad blow this secession was to the work, and the disappointment it was to him to have to give up the Wellclose Square district.

I believe he never forgot it to his dying day, and that it was written on his heart.

There are no letters of Mr. Lowder's about this trouble. He seems to have been too overwhelmed to be capable of writing. Letters of sympathy poured in, and, far better, offers of real help, as the following letter will show :—

28, Hans Place, February 21, 1868.

MY DEAR LOWDER,

To assure you of my sympathy in this most distressing trouble which it has pleased God to send upon you would be nothing.

I want to know if I can be of any service to you in act.

I must go back to Frome to-night, and settle matters for Ash Wednesday and Lent. But I could come up to you after Wednesday. I could remain with you and assist you in your labours through Lent—I mean reside with you and take what share of work you could allot me.

Perhaps one of a certain age, and one who has been tried might be a guarantee to the people, the Bishop, and the Church, that we are, though sorely wounded, yet able to continue on our ground, trusting to Him Who alone can give us deliverance.

I am therefore at your service after Ash Wednesday, and may God comfort and direct you.

Yours affectionately in our blessed Lord,

WM. J. E. BENNETT.

Mr. Bennett's generous offer was accepted, and on February 29 he went to Wellclose Square, working at the Mission for three weeks of Lent. But Mr. Lowder's health was so much shattered by the grief of losing those he had greatly trusted, that he was obliged to go away for four months to recruit his strength, accompanied by one of his sisters.

They went by Antwerp and Cologne to his old quarters at Seelisberg, and after a time over the Splügen to Bellagio and Chiavenna, returning by St. Moritz and Méran. His sister wrote on June 16th :—

Charles feels the heat very much, and it makes him weak. He is better, I hope, but his digestion is far from strong, and he is very careful of what he eats. We had some nice fresh trout for dinner yesterday, which he enjoyed, and it was a change.

This is the first notice of that kind of suffering which for the rest of his life was to be a continual trouble and drawback to his power of working. He had overtaxed even his strength by carelessness as to food, as may easily be imagined from the following account by Mr. Linklater of the Mission House commissariat :—

In the days when I first knew St. Peter's, the Clergy House dinners were proverbial. Mr. Lowder literally never noticed what he ate. His whole life had been one of the most ascetic self-denial ; in consequence at last he utterly ruined his excellent digestion. To us poor weaker ones, certain dinners meant sick headaches and agonies untold. Any one was good enough to be our cook; and—I shudder as I think of all we suffered in this respect. On one occasion I sent down my cup of cocoa to the cook with my compliments, and the remark that *cockroaches* were not the necessary ingredients of cocoa. The good woman thought I was very dainty, and I believe said as much, but took occasion to search the boiler, from which, and not from the kettle, she had drawn the water, and recovered more than one hundred specimens of the *Blatta orientalis !*

We managed our domestic arrangements at the Clergy House on the club-house principle, dividing the total cost each month and paying each our several share. Sometimes Mr. Lowder was caterer, and sometimes one of the curates. He would treat us to poultry on great occasions, and I am afraid he must have been well known in Leadenhall Market amongst those dealers in antiquities, for he always brought back the toughest and most ancient hen he could pick out. But it never ruffled his temper, and he would go to the same stall, time after time, with the most forgiving trust and simplicity. I am not sure that he ever noticed it, and I am quite sure we dared not call his attention to it.

On one occasion I had charge of the home department, and as I had just returned from a delightful holiday with some friends in Normandy, entirely set up in health, I proposed to my assenting brother curates to introduce the French mode of living, which had been such a sovereign cure to me. So that instead of dinner at one and tea at five, we had *déjeuner* at one and *dîner* at five. Mr. Lowder returned some days after the new order of things had been inaugurated, and was therefore unconscious of the change. It was near his tea time, which was our dinner. He evidently had a good appetite, and was looking forward to his cup of tea. We stole furtive glances at him when instead of the teapot came in the soup tureen. He said nothing, but helped us, expecting that the *next* arrival would be the teapot, etc.; but no, the *rôti* came next. Then the threatening storm burst upon us; the ministry was dissolved, I was degraded from my place in the home department, and we went back to the old conservative state of meals and hours.

And, writing this, I see more clearly than ever before how much of the comforts of life Mr. Lowder gave up for the sake of work —if it be not absurd to speak of *comforts* in connection with one who lived in such a place, and who never indulged himself, but endured hardness as a good soldier of Jesus Christ. It was a necessity that he should have a quiet home to rest in after the fatigues of work, and yet he gave up his Vicarage to a pack of curates, and allowed the place to be overrun by the lads and men who came to our Confirmation or communicants' classes. At one time even the choir used to practise in the dining-room. Ah well! *in cœlo quies.*

I am sure, now, that he suffered greatly from all this, and yet he bore it all without a murmur of complaint.

He writes to his mother from St. Moritz in July:—

I think I am getting on. The worst is I cannot walk much. I am hoping, however, to get a horse. The advantage of the place is that there are so many easy walks and places within easy distance to which you can drive, Samarden, Pontresina, Silva Plana, etc.

August 7.

I think of leaving this and starting for the Finstermünz, where I hope I may meet the Mother Superior and Miss Oldham; if so, I may go with them a little way towards Méran, and then branch off to the Stelvio. I want to hear how things are going on at home, and if satisfied, I may get on to Salzburg and Styria. . . . I think the air and waters here have done me good, and it has been a great thing to escape hitherto the heat which has been so intense everywhere. . . .

Méran, August 19.

Yesterday, Tuesday, I started with two Englishmen from Bormio to walk over the whole of the Stelvio Pass. It is a very grand undertaking, the highest carriage pass in Europe. . . . We unfortunately had a bad day for the view, and so did not see the Oetler and its glaciers well, though what we saw was extremely grand. . . . I hope to be at Ischl, Austria, about the 26th, and to meet the Mother Superior. I am anxious to see her because I now feel nearly well enough to come home, and unless she strongly advises me not to do so, I think of bending my steps homewards. However, I should feel more satisfied in trusting to some judgment besides my own.

Your very affectionate brother,

CHARLES.

He returned to his work on October 17, "after a four months' absence," his sister wrote, "looking better than we have seen him for years."

Out-of-door ·preaching had always been used as a Mission agency by Father Lowder, especially if any fatal accident happened, when handbills were quickly printed and dispersed, announcing a sermon in the open air. On one occasion two men were killed in a sewer near Calvert Street by foul air. On the Sunday after, notice having been given of a sermon, a large number of people was collected. The congregation was too large for the spot itself where the accident took place; and so, after singing some hymns through the streets, the *Dies Iræ*, and a portion of the Litany, the sermon was preached just outside the Mission chapel, and a number followed into the chapel afterwards and joined in prayer.

Sermons in the open air had often been given on Good Friday, and in 1869 the first "Way of the Cross" was sung and preached through the streets in St. Peter's parish. A full account of it was published in the *Times*, "with a

leading article commenting on the folly of such an attempt, and conjecturing that the author of it must have
been driven to despair by not being able to induce his
parishioners to enter the church."

The following account of the scene and of the service
appeared in the *Guardian:*—

Shortly after the conclusion of the Three Hours, the writer
turned his steps towards the east end of the town, where the
stations of the Cross were to be preached by Mr. Lowder,
of St. Peter's, London Docks. Leaving behind the Tower of
London, standing out against the dull grey sky, with its memories
of past days, when its now quiet courtyard was full of life
and bustle, we passed on through the narrow streets leading
to the Docks, amid many a strange sight of half-clad women
and rough seamen, an occasional swarthy negro looking up from
the sunken doorway of one of the low and ill-kept boarding-
houses with which the place abounds. Reaching the Dock wall,
and passing over one of its bridges, we turned down Old Gravel
Lane ; and here a new and unwonted stir was visible among the
people, caused, as it proved, by the starting of the procession
from the church. Headed by a stalwart cross-bearer, came
forth the choir of St. Peter's in their cassocks, followed by the
clergy in cassocks, cloaks and birettas, singing Faber's hymn,
" O come and mourn with me," and followed by a company
consisting partly of clergymen and friends from a distance, and
partly of the inhabitants of the district. On reaching Worcester
Street the Vicar removed his cloak and biretta, and standing on
a chair proceeded to address the people on the first station, the
choir first singing the words, " Is it nothing to you, all ye that
pass by?" which were repeated at each station. In touching
words did the preacher tell his hearers of the causes that had
brought that dear Child of Bethlehem, that dear Son on whom
the Spirit of God had descended like a dove, as a prisoner before

the judgment seat; and earnestly did he remind them of their need of preparation for His second coming. "Then," he said, "we shall be condemned unless we now judge ourselves, and lay our sins in true confession before Him. Oh, come then to-day and make your peace, or at least resolve that you will never more say the unclean word or do the unclean deed which keeps you from Him." Another hymn, "Jesus, Refuge of the weary," was then sung until the procession reached the school-house, where the second station, "Jesus receiving the Cross," was kept. Telling them of what the reception of that Cross involved, the preacher pointed to the causes why the Saviour not only received it, but received it willingly, and showed how in their daily lives, in their afflictions at home and among their friends, and in their own hearts, they were to follow in His steps. Speaking of the power of the Cross, he pointed with striking effect to the figure of the Good Shepherd in a niche over the schools, and begged his hearers never to pass it without looking up and remembering that the Cross of Christ is the true Shepherd's crook, which leads and guides us from earth to heaven. Then the procession advanced again, gathering strength as it went, young and old alike falling in, and striving with evident anxiety to walk near the "Father" and the "brothers," as we heard an old man affectionately describe the clergy. And as they sang the hymns, all lifting their hats at the oft-repeated mention of the Holy Name, the scene became more intensely striking. The windows of the houses, many of which were garnished with the plants whose growth has been encouraged by prizes at the flower shows, forming one of the numerous social agencies of the Mission, were filled with people, while some were to be seen on the roofs endeavouring to gain a good view of the strange sight. The next halt was near the Dock gate, where a fine merchantman, with flag flying at her masthead, was lying to, thus forming an effective background to the picture. On the third station, "Jesus falls beneath the weight of His Cross," the preacher showed that it was as God made man that the Saviour thus fell, in order to tell poor suffering men and women that He knows how to feel for them.   An earnest exhortation never to omit morning or evening prayer followed.   At five o'clock, opposite the church of St. John of Wapping, the fourth station, "Simon of Cyrene compelled to bear the Cross," formed the subject of an address on the marvellous power which a voluntary submission to the Cross exerts over our lives.   The fifth station was kept in Old Gravel Lane, which had been again . reached in the lengthened circuit, and here "the Women of Jerusalem mourning for Jesus" suggested some touching remarks on the tender kindness of the Saviour, as He bade them "Weep not for Me."   A few words on the right use of Good Friday were connected with an invitation to join in the service shortly to be held in the church, which has always been found an important means of deepening the effect of this open-air preaching.   And now the rain began to fall, the bitterly cold east wind blowing harder up the narrow street, but apparently having little power over the preacher, who still stood bravely bareheaded on his stool. A more suitable spot, a square plot of vacant ground called the Ruins, was chosen for the sixth station, "Jesus stripped of His Garments," conveying lessons which, it need scarcely be said, were peculiarly applicable in such a district, where many a half-dressed woman and child was listening intently.   "There will be no clothes in the kingdom of heaven," said Mr. Lowder, who, like a second Wesley, appealed to his hearers to dress the soul rather than the body, and never to be absent from church because of shabby clothes.   The seventh station, "Jesus nailed to the Cross," led to a pointed warning to those who hit the angry blow or say the angry word, to remember that they were hurting their Saviour by every such act.   The next station was kept in that portion of the parish which has been the scene of the loving labours of the Rev. R. Linklater, and here consequently many additions were made to the already vast procession.   The eighth station, at Wapping Wall, "Jesus dies on the Cross," was the subject of an eloquent address on the loving and forgiving spirit of the Saviour. At the ninth station, "Jesus taken down from the Cross," the preacher drew a graphic picture of the sorrowing mother receiving the Body of her Son, and pleaded with the people to emulate her love. The long stage before the last station was occupied by the singing of three hymns, " Soul of Jesus," " Rock of Ages," and " O Paradise," the last of which is so well known to all in St. Peter's parish, that it was heartily taken up even by the poor little ones, who literally swarmed round the prócession. After a most impassioned address on the tenth station, " Jesus laid in the Grave," exhorting all to prepare their hearts to receive Him in His risen glory on Easter Day, the Vicar concluded by inviting his hearers to church, and by wishing all "a happy Easter." Many of the poor people entered the church for Evensong, and listened attentively to Mr. Linklater's sermon, which is always looked for as Good Friday comes round at St. Peter's. The service of *Tenebræ* followed immediately after Evensong.

The Church Association tried in vain for eight months during this year to discover and utilize an "aggrieved parishioner." Possibly the insurmountable difficulty of the attempt may have been enhanced by the dangers to which the aggrieved one would have been exposed. It would not have been an enviable office amongst people who plainly said that any folk who came down there to worry " the Father " would be thrown into the river by the men, and have their eyes scratched out by the women. " Let them come on, we're ready for them," a sturdy farrier was heard to say, baring a formidable arm. " I took my pattens to church," an old woman said to the Sisters, "and kept them in my lap, ready to heave at them, if they came near him."

Mr. Linklater gives the following account of the matter :—

Many an attempt was made by the Church Association to attack such an important stronghold, but with no success. Their

R

agents had been down frequently to stir up strife and try to get some of the parishioners to lend their names to the proceedings against Mr. Lowder. But for a long time it seemed hopeless. It was commonly said in the parish that money was offered for the accommodation. At last three persons, none of whom ever attended the church, and two of whom were Dissenters, one being a preacher in the next parish, were pressed into the service. Mr. Lowder told me, shortly before his death, with the most charming glee, that he had made friends with the two persons who were most bitter enemies in this matter.

Bishop Jackson came to the see of London in 1869, and one of the first communications of the kind which he made to his clergy was received by Mr. Lowder (February 9), on the subject of the decision of the Committee of Privy Council in the case of Mr. Mackonochie. " I infer," wrote the Bishop, " from the newspapers, which however may be mistaken, that you feel conscientious difficulties in complying with it." He invited him to an interview, and expressed his own great repugnance to dealing in such matters with his clergy, especially those whose worth and earnestness he had learnt to respect, merely as their ordinary, and not rather as their fellow labourer, and, if they would allow him, their adviser. Ten days later, however, Mr. Lowder received a formal copy of the monition served on Mr. Mackonochie, with a kind expression of the Bishop's appreciation of the difficulties which had withheld him hitherto from acting in accordance with it, but with an express " request, as ordinary, that henceforth the services of his church shall be conducted in accordance with the ruling of the court."

On July 6, 1869, Bishop Jackson wrote to Mr. Lowder :

"At last I have received a formal complaint from a parishioner, and an application from him to institute legal proceedings." He expressed his willingness to issue a monition if he could receive the least hope of its being complied with. "But if not," the Bishop continued, "it would be only adding needlessly to the expense ; and it will be better to proceed at once, under the Clergy Discipline Act."

It was soon made plain to the Bishop that this "parishioner" had no *locus standi* to enable him justly to make complaints. And no fresh "presentment" seems to have been found possible till January 8, 1878, when the Bishop announces one, at the instance of "three parishioners," accompanied by testimonials as to their character. He explains that, on this occasion, in 1869, the petition is not as on the last for the commencement of legal proceedings, but for the exercise of his own "episcopal and fatherly influence."

Mr. Lowder was accordingly invited to a conference at London House ; but being at the time abroad and very much out of health, the consideration of the case was postponed. He wrote to consult Mr. Prideaux, and received the following answer :—

4, Brick Court, Temple, July 10, 1869.

REV. AND DEAR SIR,

   I am very sorry to find that you have been singled out as one of the victims of the Puritan prosecutions. I think the fact that the complainant is a non-communicating schismatic would justify the Bishop in refusing to allow him to promote his office. But if the Bishop thinks fit to allow him to do so, I am afraid it could not be successfully contended that he has not *legal* standing.

Yours very truly,
C. G. PRIDEAUX.

The result may be told in Mr. Linklater's words.

Two spies of the Church Association appeared one day in the front seats and began taking notes, and I am sorry to say that our churchwarden, who is a most respected lighterman, walked up quietly to these gentlemen and whispered, "If you go on with this 'ere, there's half a dozen men behind you will crack your heads." The note-books were put up at once.

It was most wrong of him, and I told him so afterwards. But you cannot get these working-men to be as gentle as lambs all in a minute.

I could not have believed, if I had not myself been in the thick of it, the extraordinary interest the working-men took in the Hatcham riots—the intense sympathy they had for Mr. Tooth. To be sure, they were on the spot and knew the whole history of the agitation, that the Deptford roughs were regularly hired every Sunday for their dirty job. Of their own kind thought, and without reward, a strong band used to go every Sunday morning to protect Mr. Tooth. One great strong giant said, "Oh dear! I hope nobody won't strike me, for I've had no sleep all night, and I'm afraid I'd hurt him." But they behaved splendidly, with firmness and self-control.

A visit from the Deptford mob to St. Peter's had been threatened, to avenge the protection given by our people to Mr. Tooth. There was the greatest excitement in our parish, and each Sunday the church was crammed with our own men, determined to protect the sanctity of the house of God. The rioters never dared to come.

On one of the saints' days an agitator appeared at the children's service, and when it was over he shouted out in church, "What would Ridley think of this?" The children were much astonished, and did not understand the allusion, so after church they followed the gentleman up the street, singing, "I'm old Bob Ridley O," the only Ridley they had ever heard of. He never came again.

I must tell just one story, which illustrates Mr. Lowder's temper of mind. When the Bishop of London wrote to him, summoning him to appear and answer the charges of the aggrieved, I wrote to the Bishop telling him that Mr. Lowder was in Italy, unwell, and that it would be a pity to disturb his holiday for the sake of such a trifling matter. The Bishop had written as though our parish was distracted by these ritual innovations. I begged to assure his lordship that we were in perfect peace and unanimity, which he might learn from the fact that the Church Association had been unable to get another aggrieved parishioner in the place of the one who for a time had withdrawn. The Bishop very kindly answered that the matter might stand over until Mr. Lowder's return. As I had sent on to Mr. Lowder the Bishop's summons the day I had received it, I was afraid that he would start on his return home before a letter could reach him, and so I determined to telegraph, thinking it was an act of charity to put him out of his misery as soon as possible. In a few days Mr. Lowder's answer came. I thought, as I broke the seal, "Now he will praise my management of the affair, and thank me for my telegram." But, on the contrary, it was quite a sharp little note, saying, "Don't do that again. Your telegram arrived in the middle of the night and disturbed the whole house. A letter would have done quite well." I was so amused at his coolness, and a little bit annoyed, that I had half a mind to go on telegraphing in the same way, and at the same hour, every night for a week.

Nothing came of the prosecution after all; it was transferred to the Archbishop of Canterbury, as the Bishop of London had a remote interest in St. Peter's, being eventually patron, and the Archbishop had the courage to quash it.

The dark storm-clouds of the Romanizing troubles cleared away; the gale had spent its fury, and we had breathing time to clear away the wreck and repair the damage. I say " we," for it was my privilege to join the Mission at this juncture, in 1869. There were 206 communicants on Easter Day, 1869, as against

180 in 1868. In 1880 there were 400 communicants at Easter, and the names on the communicant roll numbered 500. These were all won by the hardest labour from the parish and congregation : when Mr. Lowder first began the Mission, there were not half a dozen communicants in the whole parish of St. Peter's. The "Twelve Days' Mission" of 1869 helped onward the influence of the church.

Up to this time, 1869, there had not been any proper school buildings in the parish. The boys' school was held in Mr. John Knight's schoolroom in Old Gravel Lane—a convenient locality, but the room too small for the number of boys we had—and the girls were taught in the Iron Mission Room in Calvert Street. Mr. Lowder had constantly asked for money to enable him to build suitable school premises, and now the crisis had come. Unless the application for a grant were made to the Privy Council at once (1870), it would be too late. Spurred on by the emergency, he made a vigorous effort to collect the £3900 required for the buildings and fittings. He was so far successful that in 1871 the foundation stone was laid by Lord Powis, and in the next year large and convenient premises, capable of holding six hundred children, were opened for the use of the parish.

These are dry details, which will be hardly interesting to the general reader, but they are of the utmost moment to the people of St. Peter's, and they are part of the usefulness of Mr. Lowder's work.

CHAPTER XVI.

ST. AGATHA'S MISSION.

1869.

> " Ragged children with bare feet,
> Whom the angels, in white raiment,
> Know the names of, to repeat,
> When they come on you for payment."

IN the summer of 1869 Mr. Lowder returned for a short time to the Tyrol, whither his heart seemed always drawn. From Landeck he wrote : " It was delightful to get back into the mountain air of the Tyrol. To-day we are getting on into the Oetzthal, and shall probably stay a little among the mountains and make some glacier excursions, and so on to Innspruck." Soon after he made with much enjoyment an expedition over the Hoch Joch, coming down upon a place called Unsere Liebe Frau. A German inscription on a house in the Oetzthal took his fancy, and he translated it thus :—

> " The angels from their thrones on high
> Look down on us with wondering eye ;
> That where we are but passing guests
> We build such strong and solid nests :

But where we think to dwell for aye
We scarce take heed a stone to lay." *

A new Mission room was this year opened in the Shadwell part of the parish, through the efforts of Mr. Linklater, who began the work when chaplain to Mr. Peter Hoare, at Beckenham. The night-school for men and lads which was carried on there was at once filled by about a hundred of the very roughest of that rough district. It was the beginning of " St. Agatha's Mission," which has now been incorporated with the parochial work of St. Peter's.

Of the "Twelve Days' Mission" in Advent Father Lowder said, " It bore sensible fruit, though from the simple fact that Mission work had been so long carried on in the district, the attempt was not accompanied with the same excitement as that produced by its novelty in other parishes."

The increasing number of the Sisters obliged them, early in 1870, to form a mother house at Walworth, as they had failed in obtaining a site for building in St. Peter's parish. Three Sisters were left in the old house in Calvert Street to work in the district, but the House of Mercy at Hendon was given up, and the inmates removed to Walworth. One of the Sisters says, " Father Lowder was very tender and gentle to the girls at the House of Mercy at Hendon, and when that was given up he felt it terribly."

* Die Engeln in den Himmelreich
Berwundern sich alle zu gleich;
Daß wir hier bauen Häuser fest
In dem wir sind nur fremde Gäst;
Und wo wir sollen ewig sein
Dort bauen wir gar wenig drein.

His work seems, as it went on, to have become more concentrated and entirely parochial, partly from the want of funds to enable him to branch out in other directions. He writes at this time of being "surrounded by an amount of destitution and sickness with which it seems hopeless to contend." Begging was his hardest work. On this subject Mr. Linklater writes :—

I cannot tell how greatly crippled and disheartened he was at the difficulty, the impossibility, of getting the necessary funds to carry on the schools and parish work.

It was quite distressing to see how this black care sat upon him and crushed his spirits. It was a small matter that sometimes he could not pay the curates, but it became a very painful difficulty that he often was not able to pay even the school teachers.

But dark periods of money trouble only served as contrast to the light which sometimes came. For instance, one year Mr. Lowder received a cheque for £500 from a clergyman at Winchester, to enable him to clear off the liabilities of the Mission. Yet on the whole his life was saddened by the increasing difficulty in raising the necessary supplies, and this when money was most wanted, and when all the agencies he had so painfully planted were beginning to bring forth abundant fruit.

At one time he felt this so much that he seriously contemplated resigning the living. It was only at the urgent remonstrance of his curates that he yielded, and again submitted his stout shoulders and brave heart to the continual and overwhelming burden. And yet, with all these money troubles, I am sure that his heart rejoiced at the wonderful prosperity of the work, and the blessing of God as manifested in the changed lives of the people.

It is a great comfort to think that before he was taken from us, he knew that the ship was manned with a crew that he could trust, and who could trust him.

No account of Father Lowder's work would be complete without the story of St. Agatha's Mission. But here again we must turn to Mr. Linklater, its founder, for information, and let him tell, in his own words, the story of its origin, which he has been kind enough to write for this memoir :—

Some eleven or twelve years ago (in 1869), I was an idle man, living in the kindest and pleasantest society, my only duty being to say the Daily Office of the Church in the loveliest little private chapel in England, and having no cure of souls except the members of my patron's household and the people who lived at the different lodges of the park. Besides, I had charge of some twelve boys who formed our choir. But as these lived in a separate Choir Home, under the care of a schoolmaster and matron, the duties thus imposed on me were of the lightest.

There are few sweeter spots in England than the wild romantic park in which the Chapel of Saint Agatha stands. The ever-changing glory of the woods ; the weird mysterious silence of the lake, the then tangled wilderness of trees and underwood abandoned to nature's skill ; and the deeply touching story of the stricken life that sheltered in this old-world home—all these, and ten thousand other charms of nature and of life, made one's existence an unbroken round of ease and pleasure.

But while one had strength and the heart for work, and with so much doing and still to be done for God, it was impossible to live such an easy life within sound of the battle's din, and almost within hearing of the roar of our great London.

It was my kind patron who suggested that instead of resigning my chaplaincy, as I intended, I should add to it voluntary Mission work in some poor East End parish.

Alas ! my lips are closed with regard to these kind friends, whose priest and Levite for many years I was. It is a pity, for it would illustrate the wonderful power of our Church of England amidst all grades and classes of our national life ; the value set upon her ministrations in the hour of need; the penetrating influences of the religious revival in our land, which has reached every rank and age and disposition.

One little picture I must be allowed to paint. We had considerable difficulty in getting permission from the Rector of the parish for celebrations of the Holy Communion in the chapel. The parish was then the stronghold of the strictest Puritanism, and, consistently enough, the Rector flatly refused to grant his licence for our service. In our strait we appealed to the Archbishop, and his Grace kindly appointed an interview to hear our story. My patron drove up to Lambeth by himself; I had to meet him there with his son, who picked me up in town. This son, my kindest and most generous friend, had two great passions —horses and the Church; and, to use a Yankee phrase, *he ran them both*. To the Puritans of our locality this seemed incongruous. Knowing, as I knew, that he had the kindest, truest heart that ever beat, there seemed to me no inconsistency between his coachman's coat when tooling his four-in-hand, and his surplice when singing reverently in the choir. Both were true and real. Certainly it brought to one's care a class of life which has been greatly neglected by the ministrations of the Church, grooms and stable-helpers, and which consequently is not much conversant in Church affairs. Thus his new head groom, in looking over the chapel, which was then not finished, noticed the raised dais for the altar before the altar was placed, and, saluting with raised finger, inquired, " The family pew, sir ? " But it is a great thing to get an English gentleman of these tastes to take a real living interest in the services of the Church, and to have his· hearty co-operation in all efforts to help and encourage his servants to do their duty in their state of life.

But I must get on to the interview. I had to meet my friend at Tattersall's, and I noticed that he had not changed his dress, for he still donned the coachman's coat. I thought this was hardly the costume for an ecclesiastical audience in an Archbishop's palace, but it wasn't my business to speak. The Archbishop, I could see, was much impressed with his visitors. He kept his eyes intently fixed on the handsome, spiritualized, sorrow-stricken face of the father. He, dear old man, was away in heart and memory to the days when he was a boy at school, for he had seen in the ante-room a bureau exactly like those used in his time at Westminster. However, we got to business. The son did most of the talking, the old father's face lighting up with love and interest as he began to speak. The Archbishop summed up, "I understand that you want my licence for your chapel." Yes, we assured his Grace. "With the consent of the Rector of the parish," continued the Archbishop—at this our hopes fell—"if you can get it"—still no light—"without it if you cannot." "Precisely so, your Grace," was our delighted answer.

And now in that parish, where alone, for three years and more, we upheld the standard of the Church's ritual and taught the Church's faith, there are three churches, besides the chapel, where there is a daily celebration and where the Eucharistic vestments are worn.

Before the chapel was built, my patron used to drive up each day to town, twelve miles, starting at five o'clock in the morning, to be present at the daily celebration in a City church. It was the only comfort of his life, nay, the only power of living, in his sorrow and bereavement, thus to shelter in the love of Jesus.

At first, because he dressed so carelessly, the people at this church took him for a pious beggar, and the verger used to pass him over when he collected the alms. But the Vicar rebuked the verger, saying that even poor men had their mite to give; so the next time he took the bag to our friend, and seeing him put in a bit of paper had the curiosity to look at it before presenting the bag to the priest. It was a bank note for a large amount.

These were the friends who suggested the idea of St. Agatha's Mission, who encouraged me and helped me in every way through the work.

And also many of the residents, who gradually found their way to the chapel services and worshipped at its altar, gave both money and personal aid most liberally. Even those who were not able to sympathize with Catholic teaching and ritual felt that they could cordially co-operate with Mission work in the slums of London. Thus did not only our chapel services become more real by having this outcome of practical charity, but also the faith itself was recommended to those whose hearts were at first shut against it, and many of their prejudices in time were swept away.

I offered my services and the possibilities of St. Agatha's Mission to Mr. Lowder, and he gladly welcomed me. I had had some previous experience of the parish, some ten or eleven years before, having lived a year in the Mission House before I was ordained. Then my principal work was to organize a night school—in such a neighbourhood the most ungrateful, exhausting, killing work that one can do. I must ever remember the first night. We had hired an old house in a convenient street. As there was no gas in the house we had to improvise lights by sticking tallow candles in the desks. It took all my strength to keep out the tide of young men who tried to swarm in after the room was full. At last the door was closed. There were a large number in the school, young men of about twenty years of age, and they worked away pretty well during the time of instruction ; but as soon as the command was given, " Close your books," as if by a preconcerted signal all the "dips" were blown out, and in the helpless darkness whack they came at my devoted head, at every possible angle and from every corner of the room.

The next night I was on the alert, and caught the ringleader in the very act of giving the signal. I boxed his ears as hard as I could. He coolly began to take off his coat and necktie, and some of my friends hallooed, " Mind what you're at, sir ; that's Bill ——, the Wapping Pet." I had got hold of a prizefighter. I answered, " I don't care who he is ; if he comes here he must behave himself." Luckily my man took it good naturedly and did not hit me. He could have smashed me to atoms if he had chosen. There is a great deal of genuine good nature amongst these fellows, if they know that you are trying to do them good, and if you are not afraid to look them straight in the face.

Another duty was to catch the very ingenious rascals who disturbed our services in the Iron Church by rolling stones down the roof. They found out that this made a noise like thunder inside. I caught one fellow in the very act and shook him heartily. I fancy he was a costermonger, for he jerked out as well as his breath would let him, "What do you shake me for as if I was a —— cauliflower!"

And now, after so many years, the world had so turned round that I found myself at my old work again, and in the same old place. This time we were able to start with greater pretensions. We rented a large warehouse, and my dear friend the Rev. Sydney Brooke Lobb became our partner and counsellor. A large staff of gentlemen came with me each night from the country, who used to be escorted down the Wapping Street by an admiring crowd of lads shouting " Halloo, teacher!" I don't know what these friends thought of Wapping, and of the dark mysteries of the streets, for they never saw them in daylight. We used to cross the river in the ferry (this was before the Tunnel Railway was made), shooting out into the dark tide, seeing the awful "port and starboard" lights of steamers glaring upon us; hear the gruff roaring of the pilots and look-out men, with a sense that the fierce tide was bearing us down and down—Charles Dickens only knew where; and at last hear the keel grate on the gravel shore as we touched land, and jumping out, tendered our penny to poor one-legged Jack. I treated my friends well, for I introduced them to a greater delicacy than Sybarite e'er dreamt of—roast potato " all hot," eaten in the street with pepper and salt.

The night school from the first became a great success. It seemed born in full vigour. The very first night we had forty or fifty stalwart fellows, and soon the average number of one hundred was reached. . . . I really have never seen such a sight in my life as this large number of young men gathered from the streets, hard at work all the evening, as quiet and orderly as possible;

some learning their letters; others, with distended tongue and with sprawling arms, going through the travail of a "copy," and now and then some extraordinary genius turning up—as, for instance, one young man who set himself a copy, *Maxima debetur pueris reverentia*, which, when I asked him if he understood it, he translated word by word, and who, when I was fascinating my class with an account of the battle of Pultowa, showed himself quite intimately acquainted with every detail and consequence of it. I at once raised him to the rank of teacher, at some trifling payment each night.

The every night scene was varied now and then by some striking incident. One night, in the middle of school-time, a knock came to the door; and having opened it, there stood revealed the ominous figures of two policemen. I went to them to learn their pleasure; they had come after one of my promising pupils. When I expostulated with them for choosing such a time and occasion, they said it was their only chance. The lad baffled pursuit during daytime; but his thirst for knowledge was so great, that he ran the risk of capture, because he could not resist the attraction of the night school. The charge was that, being very hungry, he had stolen a piece of meat. I went back to my boys to consult as to what was to be done. There was no escape (the chimneys were out of the question, and the river barred egress on the other side), so I advised the poor lad to give himself up. I never can forget the unnatural hush of the large, excited crowd of boys, the stilled silence of their suspended breaths, whilst he was making up his mind; then with a stage-struck air he posed himself in the middle of the room, and said, " Comrades, farewell !"

Another night we had an internal commotion. A huge, cowardly, hulking, savage lad had made himself particularly objectionable for many nights, both to myself and to the general mass of boys. I had to threaten condign punishment. The monster could have pitched me out of the window; but unexpected success was at hand. One night a new face appeared, a quiet, mild young man, who retired into a corner of the room, applied himself diligently and, as I thought, with absorbed attention to the business of the school. He was only biding his time. My friend the bully began his tricks, when the new-comer sprang like a lion over the desk, and gave him one! two! before he knew where he was. At once space was cleared for a fight. I did not choose to interfere till I thought the bully had had enough, and then I separated them. It was the reformation of that young man. He wiped the blood off his bruised face, and sat down like a lamb to his copy-book. Out of pity to the vanquished, I paid him some attention, when bye-and-bye he said, " Did you see, sir, how that fellow struck me?"

On Tuesday and Thursday evenings we had a Bible class— by which name is not to be understood a nice orderly assembly of quiet, decent men, sitting all round with Bibles in their hands, and looking out their references. No; my Bible class was a surging mob of noisy and blaspheming roughs, whom one had to quell by psychic force, as one would quell wild beasts by a commanding eye. Yet this great roomful could often be held entranced and in rapt astonishment, especially when they were told of their mysterious, unknown benefactors. I remember trying to represent to them a picture that at the time was thrilling in my heart : a little child, daughter of a wealthy house, stealing down the stair-case into the hall to give me her tiny savings, saying, "These are for the poor Wappers." I had to go on my knee to stoop and kiss her little hand.

In teaching them, the ordinary style of sermon—text, heads, and application—would not go down at all. I may shock my readers if I confess that I once preached on such a text as this : "If you want to spend a happy day, go to Rosherville Gardens." They were all ears to this, and I don't know that one could have chosen a more touching subject than that ceaseless, never-satisfied craving of the heart for happiness, if only for one day, which yearning can find rest alone in the heart of Jesus. The night school is a very heavy drag upon energies and health. It would be labour enough even were the lads as quiet as lambs and eager for instruction; but it is fifty times worse when you have first of all to coax them to come in, then when inside to keep them in order, and to teach them, when perhaps all the time the opposition party outside are heaving bricks and paving-stones at the door, or chaffing their friends inside by shrieking the funniest things through the keyhole.

But yet I must be grateful to the night school; for our real Mission work has resulted from it. First of all, it brought us into close quarters with the most difficult portion of our population, the young lads and men; and it is always a good thing to have dealings with men, even if no immediate result follow. But one night, noticing that they were interested in some scripture prints I had placed about the room, which they were trying to explain to one another—it occurred to me to offer to explain these pictures one by one after night school. The thing took most wonderfully. The whole school stayed behind, and arranged themselves on the seats and desks tier above tier, I with my picture standing in the midst. If anything could inspire a man to be really eloquent, and to shake and grasp living hearts, it would be such a scene—the eager, entranced, upturned faces, the tear starting unbidden when the crisis came of some touching story of Joseph, of David, or of our Lord; the suspended breathing; the sigh of relief when all came right; the united cry of "Oh, please go on !" when we had finished for the night.

The history of our special Sunday evening service is full of most important lessons. At first we merely tried a class sitting round the fire. It was a motley group, all young faces—at least, all under twenty years of age—and all lads, no girls—such a gang of roughs ! Well, for months they resisted; the blasphemy and misbehaviour were enough to break one's heart.

We never dared to venture on a prayer, and often had to stop the hymn, because they were only mocking God. In rebuking them I used to tell them how different it might be; and once, to encourage them, I gave vent to what I then thought was an im-

s

possible fancy. I described a reverent service, the psalms and hymns sung, and they themselves the choristers. The idea took. They began to prepare; a choir class was formed, the conduct of the lads improved every week, and you could see in their faces that their lives were different; and actually, after some six months' training, and being sure that the improvement was real, on one St. Agatha's Day we inaugurated the new order of things. One friend gave a piece of carpet, another a curtain, and so we arranged the end of our room to look something like a church; cassocks and surplices were made, and a reverent choir offered a really hearty service of praise to God. By-and-by a cheap harmonium was furnished, and choral Sunday Evensong has from that time been the established thing.

St. Agatha's has always been fortunate in its teachers. Under the present devoted mistress, Miss Pitt, one hundred per cent. of the children have passed the Government inspection these last two years. Not only is she thus efficient in secular work, but she enters heart and soul into the missionary spirit of the place, and words are inadequate to tell all that a really faithful servant of Christ can do in such a neighbourhood to advance our Master's cause.

As year after year we prospered, so we had to enlarge, and alter, and finally rebuild our premises. At last it became necessary to build a new school chapel as well. Mr. Richard Foster, who is at the bottom of nearly all church extension in East London, literally drove us to this. Without his encouragement and help we never would have attempted such a venture, and just at the proper moment the boys of Winchester College gave us £41 towards this purpose.

At this time I had given up my chaplaincy, and had settled down as one of the resident staff of St. Peter's parish. But my old friends' interest in St. Agatha's did not flag. My patron's little daughter Agatha, who is also my godchild, laid the foundation stone of the new buildings, and she was supported by a bevy of children, the representatives of the many houses who had supplied us for so many years with the sinews of war.

I don't think any set of buildings can be better used, or more got out of them, than these of St. Agatha. They are occupied morning, noon, and night.

First of all, in the daytime, there is the regular day school with a babies' *crèche* in the old school. On Monday afternoons two ladies, who used to attend the services of St. Agatha's-in-the-country, hold a crowded mothers' meeting in St. Agatha's-in-the-town. I am afraid to say how many mothers attend (nearly all with babies), for fear of being accused of exaggerating. I know I have been with them in their country excursions, and have been fairly crushed with the responsibility. On two days in the week some other friends come from the West End and shed a few hours' sunshine on our murky courts. In good truth many a home of sorrow, many a sick bed, has been brightened by the kind words and kindly looks of these gentle ministrants. The most ungrateful and the most useful work they have attempted is to try and win the confidence and love of the big girls, and gradually get them away from our dreadful streets to decent service. God will reveal one day the good that has thus been done.

In the evening the men fill the new schoolroom, smoking, reading, playing bagatelle (there are two good tables) or skittles, or racing in the running ground outside. On Monday evenings the St. Agatha's Benefit Society meets to transact business. This is a sick club, managed entirely by the men themselves. On Wednesday evenings the desks are cleared, and the neighbours pour in for the weekly concert, which once a month resolves itself into a ball (I wish my readers could see how correctly and pleasantly the guests behave). The drum and fife band practises twice a week; the stringed instrument band also twice a week. In the winter there are all sorts of things going on—theatricals, nigger entertainments, *anything* to keep them out of the public-houses and out of the streets.

In the old buildings night school is held three nights a week. One year we presented sixty-two lads at the Government examination, another fifty, and so on. This means that so many completed the forty nights' attendance during the winter; and to get this number perhaps we had two hundred on the books. After the school is over, and on the other nights, the lads use the rooms for club purposes until ten o'clock at night; of course under the superintendence of a regular paid officer, who is known as the "chucker out." No boys' club in East London can possibly exist without such a functionary. I tried to do without him once, and put the lads on their honour, but I suppose the moral strain destroyed all the fun, for they insisted on his restoration. Monarchy, absolute monarchy, is the only real paternal government after all.

It tires one only to think of the life—boiling, mad-hot, overflowing life—that is exhibited in this lads' club; some of them performing daring feats on the trapeze, turning somersaults backward, playing single-stick, boxing with the gloves, playing bagatelle, and upstairs the quiet ones either playing bagatelle or dominoes, or discussing the politics of the neighbourhood. We used to have a famous boating club, but the accidents were so frequent and so serious that I was glad to dissolve it. In the summer the lads play cricket either in the playground or in Victoria Park (which is more than two miles away). A cricket madness has seized them, and their club is called the "Wellington," out of compliment to the boys of Wellington College, who support the club and the fife and drum band.

I am of course giving a picture of the state of things now that the clubs have gone through years of discipline, and things are in full swing. Those who have had to do with these sort of things will know something of the disappointments, rebellions, discouragements, ingratitude, and failures that have to be patiently borne with and triumphed over before a constitution can be settled.

Perseverance is really the secret of success in such work, of course under the blessing of God. "It's dogged that does it." On Sunday evenings, and on Thursday evenings, there is service in St. Agatha's Chapel—hearty encouraging service. The stringed band accompany the psalms and hymns. Miss Pitt plays the organ, which was presented by one of the daughters of my patron.

It is a hard thing in writing such an account as this to steer clear of names. The individuals, even if nameless, must be dragged in to give a true colour to the scene. For instance, it would be quite impossible to write a true account of St. Agatha's, without introducing the person of one gentleman in particular, a son-in-law of my patron, who has been our most stanch and generous supporter throughout, not only by his large subscriptions and gifts to the Mission, but by his personal interest and presence at committee meetings, night school suppers, and other occasions.

And then how am I to express the obligations we are under to the many gentlemen who have helped on the work of teaching in the night school and managing the club? It could best be done by detailing some of the results of their labours; but space will not permit. I must give one case—a lad who came to us, not even knowing his letters. He worked away, and got on in his business, until from earning three shillings a week he has risen to twenty-four; and he saves up his money (after helping the old folk at home) in order to take little holiday trips, sometimes in England, sometimes on the Continent. Last year he went to Paris; this year he has gone up the Rhine. If that is not "raising the masses," I don't know what is; and I have only spoken of the material improvement which is the least part of his cultivation and progress. I should like to pay a passing tribute of affection and respect to the conscientious and talented master who for so long a time conducted the St. Agatha's Day School, the late John Martin. Mrs. Craik has written his life in her charming book "A Legacy," and has given us some of his writings. It is for me to bear grateful witness to the wonderful influence for good he exerted on his pupils, the results of which can never be effaced.

Surely life is a mystery, and especially the sort of life that settles itself in such muddy holes and corners, when from the seeming refuse can be dredged such a brilliant intelligence as this gifted youth.

My opinion is that the best way of working a large East End parish is in this way, by opening Mission rooms and clubs in suitable localities, to get at the poor, teach them the Christian faith, and gradually lead them on to the altar of the parish church.

Two other branches of St. Agatha's Mission in conclusion must be spoken of—the Convalescent Home and the playground.

I was opening my letters one morning when out of one of them tumbled a cheque for £1000. Liberal friends had already formed within me the habit of receiving large sums of money with an even heart, but I confess this took away my breath. It was but the first instalment of a sum of £2000 which the late Mrs. Walter Morton gave for the purpose of founding a Convalescent Home for the poor of our parish. This Home has been in good working order for more than three years, and has been the greatest possible blessing to the poor. It is at Reigate in Surrey, and is under the effective management of Miss Challen, the honorary lady superintendent, who makes herself the personal friend and comforter of the invalids who are put under her care. Dr. Walter Smith is the honorary physician, and he spares neither time nor trouble to benefit his patients. Funds are desperately needed to complete the endowment, and thus perpetuate this noble work.

The playground was a more cold-blooded venture. A large plot of ground in our parish was to be sold for building purposes. It is not often that spare ground is to be had in the heart of London, and this was only vacant because the houses had been pulled down by the East London Railway. I thought it would be a good thing to secure it as a playground for the poor little children who have no place to play in, and who are hunted by the police if they play in the streets. The editor of the *Standard* inserted my appeal, and added kind words of recommendation ; *Punch* also took up the cause, and the money came in fast and furious—so fast that in a month's time I had to cry, "Hold ! enough !" Mr. Robert Loder, M.P., had offered to make up the deficiency.

The freehold was purchased and a wall built round it at a cost of about £1300. We had a grand opening. Mr. and Mrs. Loder came down to perform the ceremony, and many other subscribers were present. The gift to the children has been the greatest boon.

I have finished. I shall be more than repaid if what I have tried to say stirs up the heart of any reader to do something to help the work of Christ in East London. Many young curates in West End or suburban parishes have no poor to visit. Would it not be a grand thing for themselves, and for their congregations, were they during the week to meet our Lord in the person of His poor in this spiritual Galilee? The Bishop of Bedford could find them work to do.

CHAPTER XVII.

OBER-AMMERGAU AND THE AUSTRIAN TYROL.

1870, 1871.

"Some vague emotion of delight
In gazing up an Alpine height,
Some yearning toward the lamps of night."

IN 1870 Mrs. Lowder's health began to fail. It was but the beginning of the end, and the first warning of a bereavement which was deeply felt by Father Lowder during the rest of his life. All the tenderest feelings of a heart most constant in its affections had twined themselves around the mother who well deserved her son's love and duty. In July she was well enough to receive her youngest son and his bride on their wedding visit. "Whilst they were with us," her daughter wrote, "she was very bright and cheerful, and able to enjoy their society. After that her complaint showed dropsical symptoms. In October the doctor said nothing could be done except by way of alleviation. My mother was always patient and cheerful, and full of thankfulness." The following extracts from letters are almost all addressed to her; the first being written on his fiftieth birthday :—

Rectory, Chislehurst, June 23, 1870.

. . . . I came over here yesterday for a day in fresh air, but I go back this evening. It makes one feel very old to have passed one's fiftieth birthday, but I have great reason to be thankful for the many mercies and blessings I have had, and not the least of them is the gift of good parents. . . . I hope to meet Murray and some of his party at Ober-Ammergau, and probably Murray will do some walking with me and Body. '

He gave up this hoped-for excursion, however, and paid a visit instead to his friend, Mr. Wynne of Peniarth.

Aberamfra House, Barmouth, August 15, 1870.

MY DEAR MOTHER,

As I know you will be glad to hear of my progress, I take the earliest opportunity of writing. I had a pleasant ride to Shrewsbury, getting a good sight of Ludlow Church and Castle, which must command a very fine view from its high situation. The country between Ludlow and Shrewsbury is also well worth seeing ; there are some high ranges of hills immediately over the line. I met Mr. Wynne at Shrewsbury station, and we went on together to Chirk, about an hour's travelling from Shrewsbury. Lord Dungannon met us at the station, and we went with him to Brynkinalt, a very beautiful place about a mile from the station. Then we lunched, and then started for Valle Crucis Abbey on his car. We drove through the Vale of Llangollen to Llangollen and Valle Crucis. There was a large party of the Archæological Institute there; and as Lord Dungannon and Mr. Wynne have been chiefly concerned in clearing out the abbey, we saw it to great advantage. It was also a lovely afternoon, and this added to the charm of the scenery, which is very beautiful, the abbey being situated in the most romantic part of the Vale of Llangollen. There is a great deal of the church remaining, and in very good order. The west end is especially beautiful from a small rose window over the three lights. There are some remains of monuments of about the twelfth or thirteenth century, which have been put together. The abbey buildings, consisting of the abbot's house and what is supposed to be the refectory and dormitories, are also standing, and there is a very ancient Saxon cross of about the eighth or ninth century in a field near. I met Miss Lloyd of Rhagate, near Corwen, whom I have known for some time, and who has asked Mr. Wynne and myself to stay at Rhagate, which perhaps I may do on my way back, if I do not go by way of Monmouthshire. Mr. F. Baker and Mr. Scarth were also among the Archæological party. We returned to a late dinner, enjoying the rich sunset among the hills, and slept at Brynkinalt, which is a very fine house, well situated in a large and wooded park, in which I managed to take a short walk after breakfast yesterday. We also took a stroll in the grounds of Chirk Castle before the train started, and then met the coach at Llangollen Road Station, and had a beautiful drive through Llangollen, Corwen, and Bala, to Dolgelly, where Mr. Wynne's carriage met us, and brought us to Barmouth about eight. The day was very fine, though the highest peak of Cader Idris was tipped part of the time by mist. As Mr. Wynne knew every place and everybody, the drive was the more agreeable. To-day we are going to Harlech Castle, and as the weather is very fine I think we shall enjoy it. I got a bathe before breakfast among the rocks just under the house, and feel all the better for the sea air already. I am writing now with a fine view of the sea before me. My love to uncle and aunt, and believe me,

Your dutiful and affectionate son,

CHARLES.

Aberamfra House, Barmouth, August 16, 1870.

MY DEAR ANNIE,

The letter which I wrote yesterday to my mother will, I conclude, be sent to you, and give you an account of my journey hither from Hereford on Monday, and a very delightful excursion to Valle Crucis. I was not able to give any description of the pleasant place at which I was staying, for I had not time before the post to explore its beauties. The house is situated over the river Mather or Mawr, which runs into the sea at Barmouth, but commanding a beautiful view of the sea looking south-west. Yesterday we saw the extreme point of Cardigan Bay, and, we thought, St. David's Head from the road just under the house. The house itself is nothing particular, being only a large lodging-house improved and enlarged. It does not belong to Mr. Wynne; his own place is the other side of the river, called Peniarth, not far from the foot of Cader Idris, near Towyn, but it is now under-going repair. But the grounds behind the house are most lovely, consisting of large woods and plantations, covering the slope of the hill and descending almost to the water's edge; the walks winding up the sides, with views every now and then of Cader and its different peaks, and the other hills around it, until you come out at the top on some fine rugged rocks, which I have not yet explored, but which, I believe, command some lovely scenery. The flower and kitchen gardens are pretty enclosed spots among the woods, sheltered by the hills, so that altogether it is one of the most charming places of the kind I know. Yesterday we drove to Harlech Castle, about ten miles. The day was lovely; the Bay of Cardigan to the south, the Carnarvonshire hills to the north, with the Isle of Bardsey at the extreme point perfectly clear; Snowdon towering above the surrounding mountains, alternately misty and clear, the thin snowy drifts of cloud hiding one moment its highest peak, and then lifting off, and forming a bank of darker clouds above; beautiful wooded hills forming the sides of the bay up to Portmadoc, which divided us from the mountains. The castle, a fine specimen of a large and very strong Norman fortification, in good preservation, stands upon a high inland rock, separated by some salt marshes from the sea, which seems once, though not since the building of the castle, to have washed its foot. There are two round towers at the extremities, connected by a high cur-tained wall and battlements. The remains of the large hall to the west, looking out on the sea, of the chapel, north-west of the main building looking into the court, are well preserved. There is a beautiful view from the battlements, which we enjoyed thoroughly from the brightness of the day, and perhaps also the more from some excitement in climbing up dangerous places to obtain it. The road from here to Harlech by the line of coast has everywhere a fine prospect seaward, and in some places, besides the mountains, some wooded glens inland.

Yesterday we walked to a new house which Mr. Jelf, formerly tutor of Christ Church, has built, with a splendid view of the river and mountains beyond. To-day we have had a pleasant expedition to a house of Sir H. Bunbury, on the other side of the river; we rowed there and back, had a long walk among the woods and shore, and a bathe. To-morrow we hope to accomplish Cader Idris. Sunday I am to preach at the church, and we have in view an expedition to Bardsey Island, off the coast of Carnarvonshire. On Wednesday we shall probably go to Mr. Lloyd's at Rhagate, near Corwen, and spend a couple of days, which will bring me so far on my way back to London by Shrewsbury and Birmingham. I suppose my mother returns to-day. I had hoped to have heard from her, but conclude she had no time before she left Hereford. Give my duty to my father and her, and love to all the rest of the party. I feel all the better for the sea air and bathing, which I enjoy every day, to-day twice.

Your affectionate brother,

CHARLES.

Barmouth, August 20, 1870.

MY DEAR MOTHER,

I hope you received the letter which I sent on Wednesday to Hereford, giving you an account of my arrival here. On Friday we took a boat up the river to a very pretty place of a Sir Henry Bunbury, under the mountains and surrounded by very beautiful woods, returning by the shore. In the evening a sudden plan was formed of ascending Cader to see the sunrise, so at midnight Mr. Wynne, another gentleman, and myself, with a guide, started on our expedition. We crossed in a boat to the other side of the river, having to be carried some way on the boatman's shoulders to the dry sand; then we had a difficult walk through a bog, and then began to ascend. At first the walking was pretty easy through the lanes in a wood; then we struck into a road for a little way, but soon after crossing a field or two, began a very tough pull up the side of the mountain, which nearly finished one of the party. However, we had a capital guide and a very fine night, rather too warm. After this ascent of about a mile, we struck off by the side of the mountain over some more even ground. It was then pretty light, and we almost feared we should be late on the top; however, we rested to take some refreshment at a spring about a mile from the top, and then hastened on, and reached the summit at about twenty minutes to five. The rosy tinge was already on some of the clouds, and in about a quarter of an hour we caught sight of the top of the ball of fire bursting through the clouds; this gradually rose, melting the clouds into the most lovely ruby and golden colours; and at last we saw the whole circle above the clouds, and the tops of the hills first, and at last the valleys at our feet, began to receive its light and glow in the morning brightness. It was altogether a glorious prospect, to see the hills, which the day before were towering above us, now far below; to catch the distant mountains, Snowdon and its surrounding hills, on one side, Plinlimmon to the south-east, the sea to the south, Barmouth north, and then the beautiful valleys immediately below, was a rich reward for our exertions. I never saw anything like it before. A sunrise at sea is very grand, but you lose the hills and valleys which we saw glowing in the early rays. We remained at the top for about an hour and a half, and had some refreshment for the inner man in a little hut on the top, and about half-past six we started on the descent, and reached home about half-past nine. I took a good bath, made myself comfortable, and got breakfast, and then rested in an armchair for two or three hours, took a walk in the afternoon to an interesting old church on the sands, and we were none of us sorry when bed-time came.

St. Peter's Vicarage, September 13, 1870.

I got home last Saturday, feeling much better for my holiday, though it has not been the same change as that anticipated in the Tyrol. You have no doubt heard of me at Alvanley, where I was very glad to see Willy so happily settled ; for though it would not suit my idea while I have health and strength, yet I think he may find much to interest him in his parish, and he and Janie seem very happy together. I spent a day with an old friend at Tarporley, after leaving them, and then took the opportunity of a Retreat at Stoke, in Shropshire, where some friends of mine have commenced the Society of the Holy Spirit. The house is delightfully situated and wonderfully adapted for a brotherhood, and the work they contemplate, I think, promises to do great good. The few quiet days there have, I hope, braced me spiritually for my work, as my holiday did bodily.

In November Father Lowder preached a Mission at Plymouth and Devonport. He took the greater interest in it, because Plymouth was his mother's native place. He writes to her on November 25 : " I was very tired after all the work at Plymouth, but feel better now, and think we have every reason to be thankful for the Mission. The clergy were very thankful for it."

Years after, a Plymouth gentleman spoke of the lasting effects it had produced upon many. Of Father Lowder he says :—

I first saw him, I think, in November, 1870, when he came down to a Mission here in Plymouth. The Mission was held in five churches in Plymouth and Devonport. Most of the arrangements were made by him, and he invited most of the missioners. He conducted the Mission himself at St. Peter's Church, where the Rev. G. R. Prynne is Vicar. I was working as a lay helper at another church at some distance, and so did not see much of him during the Mission, but at its close a guild was formed for men, with simple rules, which was called the Society of the Good Shepherd. I think he suggested the name, and I know he took great interest in its formation and I saw him frequently about it, and afterwards he often asked me about its progress. What struck me then and often afterwards was the way in which he took apparently a special interest in whatever he was at the time attending to. He had a number of cares and anxieties at the time, I know, and many things to think about, but he gave his attention as fully to the formation of this guild as if he had nothing else in the world to care about. I noticed this often when I was with him in the Clergy House at London Docks. He would come in from the parish and sit down in his study, and talk with his whole mind given to the subject, and then, when called out, as he constantly was, to see some poor or rich persons, he would immediately give them his entire attention, and return to resume the conversation as if it had never been interrupted. I think it was this and his sweet serenity of temper that made the children so fond of him.

On the last night of the Mission most striking and joyous services were held at the different churches, at which a renewal of baptismal vows took place. . . . The fervour and determination with which the various questions were answered by both men and women augured well for the future loyalty to the crucified Lord of many a soul who had paid allegiance for so long to the Prince of Darkness. . . . Many who had never entered God's house since their childhood were to be seen, night after night, joining with all their hearts in the prayers and hymns, and listening intently to the earnest words of the missioner.

Father Lowder became very ill after his work at Plymouth—it was thought to be from blood-poisoning—and did not recover for some time. His father was also very ill at this time, and his beloved mother's end was plainly drawing near. He writes to her on December 14, 1870 :—

I fear you must suffer a good deal in the night, but you remember One who came to His disciples by night, walking upon

the sea, and I doubt not He is with you, comforting and supporting you. It is a great blessing to think how little serious
illness you have had, and I pray sincerely that you may be spared
a lingering illness, but all is in God's hands, and He will direct
everything best. West has just lost his mother,* who was a great
friend of mine at St. Barnabas', and one of my district visitors.
She had only a month's illness. I had a note from him yesterday,
in reply to one of sympathy I sent him, and he spoke of the
comfort they had in knowing how long she had been watching.
He mentioned you very kindly in the note. You may be sure
you have a great many praying for you. I am looking forward
very anxiously to spend one more birthday with you ; the rest is
known to God. . . .

To his sister he writes :—

Vigil of St. Thomas, 1870.

I will tell you my engagements and then put myself in your
hands. All the rest of this week I shall be engaged hearing
the confessions for Christmas ; next week we have our children's
treats and the communicants' supper, the latter on Wednesday,
St. John's Day. Of course I should be sorry to be away New
Year's Eve, or New Year's Day, or indeed Epiphany, if I can
avoid it ; but still I depend upon your writing or telegraphing to
me at once, in case of need. . . . I hope my mother received my
note the other day ; she need not doubt that she has many
prayers to support her. I asked Mackonochie to-day to remember
her . . . and he is now a confessor for the faith. She will, I am
sure, have the prayers of all our people here ; and tell her my
sincere prayer is that she may have abundant consolations of the
Holy Spirit, and that she may rest calmly and sweetly in the arms
of Jesus. Tell her I will come at any moment she wishes.

On Christmas Eve Mrs. Lowder's weakness and suffering became so great that a telegram was sent to her son at

* Lady Maria West.

St. Peter's. He received it in the vestry while preparing
to celebrate on Christmas morning. He celebrated at six,
and then travelled down at once to Frome. When his
mother heard he was come, his sister writes, " her face
beamed with joy."

Ten days of great suffering followed, Mrs. Lowder being
unable to stay long in bed or in the same position. Two
of her children sat on each side of her chair, and she
rested her head on one or the other as she could.

There was a radiant beauty in her face (her daughter wrote),
and it was a beautiful picture when Charles was supporting her,
and her head was on his shoulder. . . . Charles has been an inex-
pressible comfort to us all ; I do not know how we should have got
through it without him. The devotion and tenderness of mother
and son was touching, and she valued greatly the nightly prayers
and blessings from her two sons. It is not every mother who could
have such spiritual aid as she was afforded, and almost to the last
she was sensible and joined in the prayers. The last words we
heard were, " Lord Jesus, release me." My father is very weak
and shaken. . . . Charles' kindness and tenderness to him and to
us all is most refreshing.

On New Year's Eve Father Lowder sent the following
letter to his people at St. Peter's ; his mother had noticed
the bells ringing out the old year, and said, "I wish a
happy New Year to those who are left in it."

My dear Brethren and Sisters in Jesus Christ,
You may be sure that it is a great source of sorrow and
regret to me that I am not able to join to-night in your New Year's
Eve service, and to speak to you as usual of the warnings of the
past and the hopes of the coming year. It is the first time during
fourteen years that this privilege has been denied to me, and now
it is only the duty of comforting a dying mother in her last hours

T

that keeps me from you. When, however, a parent needs my presence in her last great need, to whose lessons and example of holiness I owe so much, whose prayers and encouragement have sustained me during many trials, especially in my work amongst you, and whose calmness and resignation in these hours of her own suffering are a source of edification to all who are permitted to witness them, I am sure that you will allow that I am rightly absent from St. Peter's this evening. . . .

Standing, as I do at this moment, in the presence of one so dear, whose span of life is nearly closed, I can the more urgently impress upon you the duty of remembering how short your own life is, and the necessity of preparing for that time when God may see fit to call you. May He grant that the same assurance of His abiding love, the same consolation of the Holy Spirit, the same absolution of the priest, the same Blessed Sacrament of His Body and Blood, may sustain us in our last moments in the valley of the shadow of death !

But a happy and peaceful death is the crown and completion of a holy life ; such calmness and submission to God's will are not to be attained in a moment, but are God's gifts, most precious gifts to those who have cultivated them in their time of probation. May the solemn thoughts which press upon us now help us in such resolutions for the coming year, so as to lead us all to seek more earnestly for that grace which can at once enable us both to live and die in the presence of God, and in the love of our Lord and Saviour Jesus Christ.

I ask your prayers that He who loved His own that abide in this world, may love her unto the end, and that we who survive may be comforted and blessed in this our earthly pilgrimage, and in our day be found watching. I wish you all a truly " happy New Year," and I pray that the blessing of the Holy Trinity, Father, Son, and Holy Ghost, may rest abundantly upon the clergy, the Sisters, the faithful, the children, and the whole parish of St. Peter's.

Yours affectionately in our Lord Jesus Christ,

C. F. LOWDER.

Frome, New Year's Eve, 1870.

Mrs. Lowder entered into rest on January 4, 1871 ; her eldest son remained at Frome for her funeral, and returned to his work on the 12th. One who knew him best in his life of labour said, "He never seemed the same after his mother's death." To his father he writes :—

St. Peter's, January 20, 1871.

MY DEAREST FATHER,

You must not think, because I did not write to you yesterday, that I was not thinking much about you and my dear mother, but I felt I was really doing my duty better in fulfilling your wishes than in staying at home.

First and best, I have been celebrating the Holy Eucharist for my dear mother's soul ; and many of our communicants, to whom I mentioned it in the class last night, assisted at the blessed sacrifice and joined with me.

It is indeed a continual growing comfort to feel thus able to hold communion with her in her happy state of rest and peace, and to be permitted to do that here which may bring light and refreshment to her dwelling in paradise.

I cannot help thinking how happy you are in being able thus to realize her happiness, and to know how much better it is for you that she is gone first, where you may so soon meet her again, never more to be separated. Ever since my communion on the day after her death, I have been able to think and speak of her without any breaking down, for it seems selfish to mourn for her great happiness.

I know it is more difficult for you, for you have not the same active work to distract your mind, but I thank God that you have been so wonderfully supported, and I pray that the same merciful Arm will be with you still.

And now, my dear father, let me wish you many happy returns of the 23rd. I pray sincerely that God may long spare you to us, and that we may be able to comfort your widowed old age.

I wish I was more able to do so, and that I could offer you

a home here, but that is an idle thought at present. Be sure it will be your children's great comfort to see you happy, and I trust that when we must lose you, we may have the truest assurance of being all re-united in a better world.

Your dutiful and affectionate son,

CHARLES.

In August of this year Father Lowder went abroad with Mr. Body, going over the battlefields of the Franco-German war, and from Metz to the Tyrol. The following letter contains his first impressions of the "Passions-Spiel" :—

Ober-Ammergau, August 14, 1871.

It is very difficult for me to write just after coming from the Passion Play, for it is like coming out of a Retreat, with one's feelings worked up to the very highest pitch, and so very difficult to return to one's ordinary state. I will therefore defer saying anything more about it now than that I was more than delighted ; indeed, it far succeeded my anticipations, and I trust I shall always be better for having witnessed it.

From Ober-Ammergau he went over much of the country where he spent his last days ; first to Innspruck by Partenkirchen, and then to Hofgarten and Krimmel, where he writes of "greatly enjoying the waterfalls, which are considered the finest in Europe." From thence he wrote :—

We descended upon a curious old chapel and our resting-place for the night. It was a very poor inn, of the roughest and most peculiar character, whence we were quite ready to start at 6.30, making our way over some steep glaciers and some splendid mountain scenery of a very wild description to Preyratten. We sent Body with two guides by a rather easier road for part of the way, meeting again in the course of an hour or two. The flowers as we descended, were mostly lovely. At Preyratten Parker and myself had thought of ascending the Gross Venediger, a very beautiful snow mountain; but the weather was not propitious, so, after waiting till the afternoon we walked on to Windisch Matrei.

Father Lowder never forgot his wish of ascending the Gross Venediger; it was his having missed it this year that made him so bent upon accomplishing it in 1880 that he attempted it when unfit for the fatigue. He writes to his sister :—

Heiligenblut, August 27, 1871.

We found a capital inn at Windisch Matrei, but left it about 10.30 for a beautiful mountain walk to Kals, where we arrived about three, having come in view of the great object of my ambition, *i.e.* the Gross Glockner. It is a splendid mountain, not quite so high as the Orteler, yet next to that the highest in Austria. We got our dinner at Kals, arranged with guides for Parker and myself, as well as for Body, who went the next day by the ordinary route to Heiligenblut. P. and I had three guides, and about 5 p.m. we started for our night's quarters, some huts about four or five hours' walk up the mountain. . . . As a good remedy for my weakness of ankles, which I have found very efficacious, I bathed them in a snow bath, making a hole in the snow, and covering them over as long as I could bear it.

Then follows an account of the ascent :—

Near the summit we had to be drawn up a great part of the way by the guides. At every stage we caught sight of the tints of the horizon deepening and lighting up the range of mountains which lay at our feet, and giving us a foretaste of the glorious view which awaited us. We reached the summit at six, when the sun was already above the horizon, and displaying clearly the most distant peaks. It was indeed a sight never to be forgotten.

One neighbouring range, the Gross Venediger, lay in all its snow-white beauty close beneath us; others at great distances. The Adamello, the Bernina, the Orteler, grand ranges in themselves, all clear and distinct. We could not have had a more glorious view.

From Heiligenblut he writes :—

We have enjoyed ourselves much in this beautiful place, and the more that our room is in full view of the Gross Glockner, so that we can watch all the various lights and shadows on the peak. Strictly speaking, there are two peaks : one, the higher, which is black and jagged ; the other, the lower, covered with snow. This stands in front of the higher one in our view, and the two seem but one peak. It is the passage between the two peaks which constitutes the chief difficulty of the ascent, as there is a very narrow ridge between them.

A delightful time of wandering among the Glockner glaciers followed, in company with Mr. Body and Mr. Parker, Curate of Chislehurst. Father Lowder wrote a glowing account of ascending three peaks in one day, the Bärenkopf, the Glöckerin, and the Wiesbachhorn, all over eleven thousand feet high.

The ascents and descents were very steep, almost entirely on snow. We had very good guides, but without our ice crampons and the ropes we could not have done it. In descending each step had to be dug in carefully, but the views repaid our labours, for they gave us a beautiful idea of the extent of the snow and ice regions around the Glockner, one peak rising close to the other, and glacier meeting glacier. . . . It was a hard day's work, for we did not get off the ice till 4 p.m., having been thirteen hours on snow without taking off our crampons except for the last hour, and being roped all day. We returned to the hut about 5 p.m., and were very glad to get some tea and an hour or more rest before we started back for Heiligenblut. . . . Of course I feel rather tired to-day, but I shall get a rest till Monday, when we are off to Cortina.

The last part of his holiday, until the middle of September, was spent in wanderings among the Dolomite mountains—"the grandest, the most fantastic, and yet most awful forms." Descending into the Grödner Thal, he writes, "we were overtaken by a grand thunderstorm. At one point there was a double rainbow, spanning the mountains and descending on one side to some fir slopes, which was the grandest sight of its kind I ever saw."

CHAPTER XVIII.

THE MISSIONER'S DAILY LIFE.

1872, 1873.

> " To keep unsteady Nature to her Law,
> And the low world in measured motion draw
> After the heavenly tune which none can hear
> Of human mould, with gross unpurgèd ear."

THE chief events of Father Lowder's Mission in 1872 were the opening of the new school buildings by the Bishop in January ; a parish Mission held before Lent by the Rev. R. A. J. Suckling and the Rev. A. W. Mills ; and the opening of a little hostel in Calvert Street for old people who had no other refuge but the workhouse.

The following reminiscences of the parish Mission are from a layman who took part in it :—

I remember one night we went out with the choir to sing hymns in procession and preach at the corners of the streets, before the eight o'clock Mission service. I was walking next to one of the choirmen. We went through one street, I do not know its name. There were a good many people standing about on the pavement and looking out of the windows, but we passed through singing without any disturbance. When we got through, the choirman said to me, " If we had attempted that ten years ago, we should half of us have had our heads broken, and as likely as not some of us would have been killed." . . . One night, when the service was nearly over, I went in, and seeing a very rough looking working-man in his working-clothes, just as he had come from his late work, sitting on a bench near the door, I went and sat beside him, intending tq try to get him to come to the after meeting in the room opposite, where Mr. Mills was to give an address, thinking that we might try to convert him. But when the sermon was over, to my astonishment my friend dropped down on his knees on the floor beside me, and began to sing the Litany in a style which showed me it was not the first time he had sung it. I had a talk with him afterwards, and found he was a regular communicant at the church, and was soon satisfied that I was much more likely to learn from him than to teach him.

His sister K——, who possessed much of his own missionary spirit, had a slight paralytic seizure on April 10. She had overtaxed her strength, which she thought equal to any exertion. The fatigue of nursing during her mother's illness had told on her, combined with the wear of daily teaching; but, besides her home duties, she spent time and strength on the rough factory girls at Frome, over whom she had a wonderful influence, teaching them both on Sundays and week days, preparing them for Confirmation, and working in the district.

Her brother writes to her on hearing of her illness :—

St. Peter's Vicarage, April 17, 1872.

I am very sorry indeed to hear of the serious attack which you have had, but I sincerely hope that by God's help you may recover from it and get strong again. You must, however, take entire rest of mind and body, which I hope you will be able to do.

Such an attack must be a warning to us all, for I quite feel I might be taken in the same way. Let us pray together that we may be ready whenever and however we may be summoned, and if we have done our work, though we must be sensible how imperfectly, yet done our poor best, we need not fear if we are found in Him.

I ought to have written before to have thanked you for your Easter letter, but I have not yet recovered from my work in Lent, and must try to get a week's rest.

Yesterday and the day before I was engaged on a committee for six or seven hours at a stretch.

Your very affectionate brother,
CHARLES.

He spent part of his August holiday at Tenby with this sister, and made a short visit with his sister Mary to the Lakes of Killarney and Glengariff, going and returning by Milford Haven and Cork. They took charge of a little stranger girl on their return journey, and Miss Lowder writes of Charles' tender care for the child, who was very ill ; nursing her, and attending to her in every way, until he gave her up to her friends.

In the end of 1872 Father Lowder had the sorrow of losing, after a sharp, sudden illness, his faithful friend and curate, the Rev. F. K. Statham. He had worked at St. Peter's for five years, and was the only one who had stood firm when, in 1868, the other curates had Romanized. His place was filled by the Rev. J. W. Biscoe, though not for long, as in the end of 1873 the latter joined the Evangelist Fathers at Cowley, and left England for the Bombay Mission. In the summer of 1873 Mr. Biscoe was Father Lowder's companion during a tour in the Chamounix district and at the Italian lakes. On his way home in September Father Lowder attended the Old Catholic Congress. " I was much interested," he wrote to his sister, " by all I saw and heard, though not in all things favourably impressed."

" St. George's Mission " had now, as we have seen, grown into St. Peter's parish.   Father Lowder's letters are dated, for the last ten years of his life, from " St. Peter's Vicarage." But the " Vicarage " was the only necessary parochial institution which had been neglected.   It was, and still remains, the old Mission House in Calvert Street, taken by Mr. King in 1856.

What his daily life was henceforth will best be gathered from Mr. Linklater's graphic narrative :—

Let us take a Sunday first.   The first celebration is at seven o'clock.   A number of communicants, principally men, will be found kneeling reverently in the little side chapel.   The solemnity of the service ; the silent grandeur of the church, as on a dark winter's morning its beautiful proportions seem magnified in the uncertain glimmer of the altar tapers ; the little group of worshippers kneeling, with quickened hearts, before the Lord ; the reverent gestures of the priest, pleading before God the merits of the all-atoning sacrifice of Christ, were the more touching when we knew that all around, for miles and miles, poor degraded souls were sleeping off the debauchery of sin.

There is a second celebration at eight, which Mr. Lowder generally took, and at which the body of the church is fairly filled, and a third at nine.   The clergy then get some breakfast, and at a quarter past ten Matins is sung.   The. High Celebration follows immediately after Matins, at eleven o'clock.

This is the great service of the day, and the people come pouring in.   When clergy complain that they can't get congregations in East London churches, I answer, let them give the people something to come for, and have faith in our Lord's promise, even in its secondary sense : " I, if I be lifted up from the earth, will draw all men unto Me."   The people come to St. Peter's, not because the ritual is beautiful and the singing most soul-stirring, but that they may assist in the great priestly act of the Church, the " lifting up " of Christ to the Father, the " showing forth His death " until He comes.

I shall not attempt any description of the majestic beauty of this service. I really do not think there is a more beautiful or more reverent service in Christendom. The charm to me has always been that it is real. The boys are our own boys, the men are our own men; they all come for love, and not for money. It always stirred my heart to look down the ranks of noble and serious-faced men who sing before the Lord in the choir of St. Peter's. We knew that the words came really from their hearts, and that their daily lives were in harmony with their sacred office. It makes all the difference in the spiritual life of a parish when the choir, who stand nearest the Lord's altar-throne, and speak to Him the devotions of the congregation, are worthy to be the body-guard of Christ, and are as pure in heart as the white surplice they assume.

Mr. Lowder was a thorough Church of England man. He was not a Ritualist at all in the modern sense of the word, after the gushing, effeminate, sentimental manner of young shop-boys, or those who simply ape the ways of Rome. He had glorious ritual in his church because he thought the service of God could not be too magnifical. He considered that it was as much his duty as parish priest to put before the eyes of his people the pattern of the worship in Heaven, as it was his duty to preach the Gospel. He felt that he had no more right to alter the features of the heavenly worship, as represented in the earthly service, than he had to alter the faith once delivered to the saints. He understood that those features are made known to us by our Lord's command, " Do this," by the revelation of heavenly worship to St. John, and by the testimony of the unbroken custom of the Christian Church. In a word, he believed that the Holy Eucharist is the divinely appointed act of worship which we are commanded to *do* on earth as it is done by our High Priest in heaven, pleading before God the merits of the all-sufficient sacrifice of Christ.

And in bringing back the Holy Eucharist to its lost position, as the fount and centre of all the Church's worship, and in restoring the old Christian mode of celebrating the most holy mysteries, Mr. Lowder, as I have said before, was acting within the then acknowledged liberties of the Church of England, and according to the express order of the Prayer-book, as at that time interpreted even by the Privy Council.

After the midday service we, the clergy, have an hour's rest for dinner. Not always an hour's rest, for very often in the spring-time one or other of us (mostly one) has to rush off with Confirmation candidates to the particular church in London where, on that Sunday, the Confirmation is held. Then, as we are still sitting at the table, a rush and scampering of feet is heard up the steps, the hall door is burst open, and the noisy tide passes (as they think quietly) into the room on the floor above. This is the big lads' Sunday class, and the race is to get the most comfortable seats either side of the fire.

It was my privilege and happiness to teach them, and the class was held in my room—one's only room for day and night—which I had made as pretty and attractive as possible with pictures and books and curiosities. A friend had given me a pair of splendid Indian idols, which I stuck up in suitable positions, and which, to my mind, were quite in keeping with the other oddities gathered from all corners of the world. But these idols produced a painful impression on my lads' minds; the first time they saw them they asked me straight out if I had changed my religion.

I found I had to be on the spot as soon almost as the first arrival, for although they were as honest as daylight, and I could trust them with any valuables, yet they developed an unexpected taste for medicine. My physic-bottles and pill-boxes were emptied. At last I made them share and share alike, and as they sat in a great circle with opened mouths, I had the pleasure of shying my poor pills down their throats one by one. I never heard that they were the better or the worse for them. This taste for medicine is not general in the parish, for I came across a man who had never taken physic in his life. Once he was very ill and near to die, and, urged by anxious friends, had actually consulted a doctor. But when it came to swallowing the stuff his heart failed him, so he made his wife take it (that it shouldn't be wasted), and he recovered.

It was really the most delightful and encouraging work to teach this class of big lads. Their ages ran from fourteen to twenty-two. The result of religious teaching and humanizing influence could almost be seen week by week. Very often a dear friend of Mr. Lowder's and mine, an Arab prince, the lineal descendant of Mahomet, and the first of his race to be a Christian, used to be present at this instruction. He excited the deepest interest in the boys. Their knowledge of modern dynasties was vague, and they generally spoke of him as the "young *H*emperor," but if they fancied that I was deficient in the respect and consideration due to him they used to be very angry and lecture me most seriously afterwards.

Well, it was a lovely sight, these poor boys and the rich Eastern, all kneeling humbly, side by side, saying the collect of the Holy Spirit, " Prevent us, O Lord."

During lesson time my boys were most orderly and serious. It was my compact with them that if they were good and attentive at lessons I would afterwards tell them a story, or show them pictures; the bribe was hardly necessary, for I never had a more interesting or appreciative audience. Having once seen the lighting up of the soul in their rapt gaze and expressive faces, it makes one rather exacting in addressing indifferent or matter-of-fact congregations elsewhere.

Ah! those were dear and happy times. It made up for all the trials of one's life and the dreary disappointing work around, to feel the glow of these generous young hearts, as they sheltered round one and supported one by their enthusiastic love. The boys used to call my room their "haven," and often through the week have they counted the hours till Sunday should come round again.

The story-telling was very exacting work, and required careful preparation. Old stories had to be hunted out and furnished with a new dress. The story had to be told, not read. They were delighted with my version of "Les Misérables," especially with the character of the grand old Bishop. They got perfectly frantic, I remember, as I dilated on the confused mind of the poor peasant, who was so much like the convict that he was taken for him, and who could only reiterate over and over again his name and small possessions as a proof of his identity. They begged and implored me to stop: "Oh, do stop, sir; I feel just like that." But I was most astonished at what I considered a daring experiment, the reading to them "Sintram." It made the most wonderful impression on them. They wrought it into their own lives. They called the different localities of the parish by the names in the book. They literally hungered for the next week's portion. I believe that nothing I have ever read or said to them has affected them so lastingly as this.

I must be forgiven for speaking so much of my own share of the work. It seems easier in this way to describe what an East End Sunday class is like. The same sort of thing was going on in many other classes at the same time. These other classes were, however, held in the school; mine was held in the Clergy House to save the pride of these "young men."

At half-past three we all troop off to church for the public catechizing. It is a glorious sight to see St. Peter's crammed with children, the girls on one side, the boys on the other—wonderfully interesting and intelligent children, even the smallest dots looking up with a beaming trusting smile as Mr. Lowder, or the clergy, or the teachers pass by. Mr. Lowder always catechized, and often elicited most original answers. On great festivals the children marched in procession round the church, singing hymns; each school headed with its banner.

After this service the various guild meetings are held—either the Guild of the Holy Child for lads, or the Guild of St. Katherine for young women, or the Guild of St. Agatha's, one section of which assembled every Sunday.

At half-past five we got some tea, six of the choir-boys by

turns honouring us with their presence. They, poor children, consider this to be a great treat, and after tea they have a romp in the room or in the yard.

At half-past six the Mission service at St. Agatha's began, and at seven Evensong is sung at St. Peter's. The church is generally quite full at this·hour, sometimes literally crammed. The service is very bright and hearty, and all the fittings of the chancel and sanctuary are good and beautiful, and give an air of comfort and dignity, which is not the least important lesson for the poor people to take back to their squalid homes. Mr. Lowder always preached at this service. It was very beautiful to see this large congregation listening most intently to his teaching.

After service there was very often a Bible class, for which the greater part of the congregation stayed behind. Sometimes we gave them no chance to get away, but the class was begun as soon as the service was over, and thus we were able to drive well home different lessons of Christian faith or practice. Last summer, after service, we had outdoor preaching in the children's playground, which was given to the parish by Mr. Robert Loder and the readers of the *Standard* newspaper at a cost of £1300.

And now my readers will say, " Well, at any rate the day's work is done at last ! " No, we have not done yet. Up in my room there is another gang of great big fellows—quite a different class—keeping the fire warm, as they say, and they expect me to speak to them as freshly as if one were only beginning the day and had not been talking almost incessantly since 7 a.m. The compliment of their coming, and the great opportunity it is, enables one to dash away, and when it is getting on to eleven I tell them that really I am sorry to disturb them, but I must point out a curious architectural feature of my room which they have not noticed—*the door*, and at once they depart. The sofa is then turned into a bed, and all things made shipshape for the night.

Now, just consider what wear and tear on body and mind such high-pressure work as this is, and how it must have told on Mr. Lowder after twenty-three years of it. He was fairly worn out.

For a long time he had to live in the country, only coming up for Sundays and special days. He was on the stretch from seven in the morning until ten at night, and had to put as much heart into the last half-hour's work as at the start. Indeed, he could not help it, it was so real and exciting. And week-day work was harder and later than even Sunday.

The atmosphere also was most trying. One got up in the morning more tired than when one went to bed. The normal condition of the air during the winter months was pea-soup fog. The same constant gloom and depression crushed down gradually the most buoyant spirits. At least, I only knew one person who was able to rise, Mark Tapley like, superior to it. In front of our house, on the other side of the street, was a large candle and soap factory, and if the air didn't blow that way it blew the other, and brought to us the sickening odours of burnt bones from the charcoal factory lower down. Behind us was a large marine store yard, principally convenient for airing salvage goods, and also for airing the foulest language. I have had to expostulate with the men from my window.

I can see Mr. Lowder in his room below, sitting wearily, in the midst of all these discomforts and vexations, waiting and waiting for the end. I have often been startled with this look of *waiting*, weary waiting, on his face, when I have entered his room to speak to him.

It will not be necessary to go very much into the details of a week-day's work. The services began a quarter of an hour earlier than on Sunday. The first celebration was at 6.45, Matins at 7.30, the second celebration at 8. We, the clergy, then had breakfast, and at half-past nine were all distributed in the various schools. Mr. Lowder was most particular about school-work; and our presence at prayers, and regular religious instruction afterwards, helped very much to promote punctuality of attendance, and to give a high tone to the children. I used to enjoy my class very much—the first class of the boys' school, bright charming little boys, grateful for our care, and so affectionate.

U

After morning school we tried to get a couple of hours for private reading. But this was most difficult to manage, for people used to call all through the morning for all sorts of things. I fancy Mr. Lowder stuck to this quiet time better than any of us. But that is not saying much, for in the exciting times in which he lived, if there was not some special distraction in the parish, he found it often in the duties of the various religious societies of which he was an active member.

At one o'clock we dined. In winter time we used to give dinners to about 150 poor children two or three times a week. A number of gentlemen in the West End subscribed amongst themselves for this most useful charity, and many parishes in the east of London are each winter the recipients of their bounty. It was indeed a touching sight, these poor children, many of them so barely clad, some of them shoeless, and looking, oh, so hungry, ranged at long tables in our iron schoolroom, Father Lowder carrying in great cans of steaming stew, and going from seat to seat, with his grand beaming benevolent face, helping the little ones.

The afternoon was spent in visiting. Of late years Mr. Lowder's health was so shattered that he did not take a regular district, and we suspect and hope that he often had a quiet nap after dinner, reserving himself for evening work, which in all such neighbourhoods is of most importance.

District visiting is dreadful work until one's blood gets hot. It requires an immense effort to make the start, and with a heart heavy with responsibility one knocks at the first door. But the work is so important and so real, that soon one is entirely absorbed by it. It is astonishing how much can be done by good, honest, thorough visiting. As it is the fashion nowadays amongst a certain clique of the younger clergy to disparage visiting, and to say that the people must come to them, and that the priest's place is in the church and not in the parish, I am the more anxious to give my testimony as to the value of house-to-house visiting in such a district as St. Peter's. Our work was entirely done by visiting. We made friends with the people in their own homes, and thus got them to attend the services of the Church : if we had worked on the other principle, St. George's Mission might just as well have remained at the West End. I have no patience with those who make a ridiculous theory the cloak for their own incompetence or laziness. Our Blessed Lord chose not angels, but men as His ministers, in spite of their imperfections and unworthiness, that by means of human sympathy men might win an entrance into sinners' hearts for the Divine love. Besides, His own example is our best pattern in all true missionary work.

There was no difficulty in effecting an entrance into houses—the people were only too glad to see us. Indeed, the complaint was the other way ; and I have been seriously taken to task, to my face, for having been negligent in this respect. I answered my complainant, "Well, if you don't like it, go and live in Mr. ——'s district" (one of my brother curates) ; "he'll call upon you three times a day." The woman answered she thought that would be too much, and she'd stay where she was.

We had thus an opportunity of getting at the people one by one. I am sure that we have wrestled with them, and pleaded a thousand times more eloquently, thus in their ruined dens and heart to heart, than ever one could speak to a congregation in church. An afternoon's visiting was no idle work, and we came back at half-past five, thoroughly exhausted. But now the day begins. After our hurried tea the Confirmation classes arrive. These are held all the year round : many of our candidates have been for years under careful training. As soon as the classes are over we disperse either to the night school in winter time, or to the men's club, or to the stringed-band practice, or to the lads' club, or to the drum and fife band practice, or to the countless other duties which crowd in upon us.

Evensong is sung at St. Peter's at eight, and afterwards we have classes again in our respective rooms until past ten at night.

To bed, but not, alas ! to sleep. Terrors by night disturb the broken slumbers of the weary priest. Sometimes he is able to catch these terrors and sometimes not. And when at last he is falling wearily to rest, all chance of sleep is banished by the horrible yells and shrieks of gangs of tipsy revellers who "won't go home till morning." The public-houses are closing, and a popula- tion of drunken madmen and mad women turn our streets into Pandemonium.

About a third of the population of St. Peter's parish are Irish, over whom we have no control. There is no mistaking the brogue one hears in these midnight revels. It is astonishing that these people cannot either smother their grievances in their own breast, or, if they must quarrel, quarrel within doors. But no ! the first impulse is to rush out into the street, and awaken all the echoes of the night with the most passionate invectives, the fiercest denunci- ations of the wrong. Where they get the variety of epithets from, the selections of abuse, is a wonder. They can go on for hours. I fell asleep one night in the midst of an angry woman's declamation in a court near our house, leaving her mistress of the night : I awoke in a couple of hours, and she was still as fresh and loud and eloquent as ever.

I once had the satisfaction of quieting one of these viragoes. I went up to her through the crowd, and quietly asked her why she was content to amuse these people and not charge them any- thing. She answered, "I am not amusing them." "Yes," I answered, "you are : just look at their faces." It was lovely to see her look of astonishment when her eye swept the crowd, and she saw a broad grin on all their faces. She was crushed, and went away quietly.

But I did this once too often. I went up to a woman in my district who was haranguing a crowd from her doorstep : I need not say she was Irish. I begged her to go indoors. She struck me as hard as she could all down my face. I was so astonished that I did not know what to do : I had never been struck before in all the many fights I had stopped ; besides, what could one do to a woman ? So I stayed there, and she struck me again. Then some of my own people dragged me away. The next morning I was going to communicate a sick person in that same street, when a man passed me who had seen the fracas, and taking his pipe out of his mouth he scanned my face and said, " Why, you haven't got a black eye, after all."

I have interwoven the curates' work in this account of Mr. Lowder's ordinary daily duty, because it was really part of his. He organized all, and took an interest in everybody and everything. And never had curates a more indulgent or trusting Vicar, and never had Vicar (although I say it who shouldn't) a more loyal and hard-working set of curates than the four who, for many a year, formed the staff at St. Peter's, London Docks.

There are many picturesque groupings in which we might portray him, especially in his dealings with the young. I have often seen him rowing " stroke " to a crew of rough lads in a boat that at one time belonged to the St. Agatha's Mission. And from all parts of the river, as we went upwards on the flood, would be heard across the tide, " *Hulloa, Father Lowder.*" Not chaff, but good-natured, honest greeting. Or I have seen his tall figure in the playground, stormed by wee children, who were clustering round him for skipping-ropes or balls.

But Father Lowder was greatest at an " excursion," and the untiring activity, unfailing good temper, and buoyant heart which sustained him through the day were wonderful. Excursions are delightful things for the children and the poor people whose one annual holiday it is ; but an excursion is no joke to those who have to manage the details and arrangements of it—trains, food, weather, and *counting*. I have heard of a large school in Belgium where they counted the boys before bathing them in the sea, and they counted them when they came out, and there were only *four* missing. It was a far more serious matter to lose children, as we always did on these excursions, for we had to face the angry mothers on our return home. Their first cry when we emerge from the Tunnel Station is, " How many missing ? " and if we truthfully say *three*, or whatever number it may be, the number becomes *thirty* before it is passed half up the street. Just think what it is to run the gauntlet of a population of angry mothers under such circumstances. All the return we get for our hard day's work and anxious labour is that we are looked upon as kidnapping and blood-thirsty monsters. It may be as well to state that the missing children generally turn up the next day. The little rascals lose themselves on purpose. Home is so awful to them and the streets so glum, that when they see the free woods, and the lovely wild flowers, and the green fields, their little hearts break out with an intense impulse and longing for freedom to run away and away, anywhere but back to the smells and horrors and unkindness of home.

In the summer time, as a reward for good conduct, I used to take them to Greenwich Park on the Saturday holiday now and then—a day of the purest joy and fairy enchantment to these poor children. The river steamboat takes us to Greenwich in half an hour, and the children's fare is only twopence. The great attraction of the picnic is the presence of my big St. Bernard dog, whom they have known from puppyhood, and who knows and loves them well. Bernard is wild with delight at the thought of a scamper on the green grass. It takes six or eight boys to hold his chain, and even these he whisks down the street and round corners at an alarming rate. He is well known on the steamboat pier, and greets the officials in a patronizing way, with proud distended tail and out-lapping tongue, marching about majestically, showing off his beautiful white breast. If the up-river boat comes first, it is as much as we can do to prevent him taking his passage in her. At last he is persuaded, and in due time our boat is discovered skimming round the bend of the river. The boys rush on board, headed of course by Bernard. Having arrived at Greenwich, we make straight for the park, and settle down to games. Bernard likes races best, although he takes interest in football, having just stopped a football match and demoralized the combatants—young naval cadets—by bounding after their ball, scurrying it up and down, and daring anybody to take it from him.

Greenwich Hill is a famous place for races; the boys once

started *must* go right down to the bottom, whether they like it or no. The difficulty is to find a winning-post. On one occasion I pressed into this service, without consulting him, an elderly gentleman with an umbrella who happened to be passing at the bottom of the hill. It was some time before he became aware of his interest in the event. But when at last he awoke to the fact that this human avalanche was making for him as fast as their little feet could carry them, and found that he could not dodge them, he turned at bay, and, brandishing his umbrella, prepared to receive cavalry. It was no use : the prize was the first who *touched* him, and touch him they did. I don't know what version of the affair he gave to his family afterwards, but I am afraid he did not see the joke, and I took care not to go near enough to him to explain it.

The clergy used to divide the labour of the expeditions. Sometimes Mr. Lowder took the first class of the girls' school to Victoria Park, or to Southwark Park, and spent a " good time " with them, amusing them with all sorts of games in which he joined. Sometimes the other clergy took the choir-boys or guilds. But of course the occasions were rare, and were understood to be rewards for good conduct. I am quite sure that these little outings did great good in enabling us to win the confidence and love of the children, and also in giving them a few hours' pure enjoyment, and healthy exercise, and fresh air. Now that we have our playground these excursions are no longer necessary.

The passengers on the steamboat used to look with astonishment at the poor little toes peeping out of the broken boots, and the ragged garments in which many of these merry-hearted children are arrayed.

The girls, too, we sometimes treated. I remember a poor child exclaiming, " Lawks, Sarah, here's a flower just the colour of my Sunday ribbon."

Mr. Lowder was also great at a " feed "—the annual gathering of our poor communicants, or a parish " tea." It was beautiful to see him going round the tables, with his pleasant smile and kindly greeting cheering up the poorest hearts who form the rank and file of our Church militant, and who in their different vocations in life bear the real brunt of the attack.

Like other low-lying districts on the banks of the Thames, our parish was liable to be inundated whenever the tide of the river exceeded its usual height. This was a terrible calamity for the poor people. Sometimes at the dead of night the cry would be heard, " The tide is rising," and the poor things had to move their children and household stuff into some neighbour's room upstairs as soon as possible. On one occasion the people suffered so much that a public subscription was opened for them at the Mansion House. I was the almoner for my own district, and I took great pains in going round to each house to see with my own eyes the damage done by the water. I then asked each proprietor to name the sum at which he computed the loss. Poor things ! they were most moderate—to be sure, they had nothing much to spoil—but five shillings and seven and sixpence were about the sums claimed. Now I thought by this means, and taking their own estimate, I had effectually barred any chance of a row, even in the Irish quarters ; but when I distributed the relief there was quite a " ruction "—they were all discontented. I said to one of the complainers, " My good woman, you only asked for *five shillings*, and I have given you what you asked for." " Well," she answered, " when I said five shillings I didn't know that Mrs. Mullooney, next door, was going to claim ' sivin and six.' "

Since I wrote this there has been another serious flood, and the curates had to wade through the water to take food to the school children, who were imprisoned by the tide in the schools all day.

I will finish my necessarily imperfect sketch of Father Lowder's work by giving a short account of certain special services which characterize St. Peter's—the " Way of the Cross " on Good Friday, the Rogation procession on Rogation Tuesday, and the midnight service on New Year's Eve.

The Rogation procession was purely a devotional service. There was no attempt made to gather a congregation, and there were no addresses. It was just a grand solemn act of prayer through the streets of the parish, supplicating God's blessing on the people and the industries of the place.

We left the church at five in the morning, the choir and clergy in surplices, the communicants and children following behind, and then sang as we marched along first the Church Litany, and then suitable hymns and litanies. The white-robed procession wending its way through the narrow streets was a striking sight to see, the bright banners standing out in bold contrast against the quaint smoke-stained gables of the houses, and the plaintive strains of the Litany, now swelling, now dying away, as we passed along. The windows were peopled here and there with occupants in the oddest *déshabille.* At certain points suitable prayers were said— for instance, on the Dock Bridge, where we prayed God to bless the shipping and sailors. The service ended with the Celebration in church.

The Good Friday procession went over the same ground, but was of an entirely different character. Here there were no surplices or banners, and the distinct motive was to gain the attention of the people, and bring before them the story of the Cross, and in any way—by pictures, by hymns, by earnest appeals—to gain the hearts of those for whom Christ died, and to reach those who never came to church.

To look at that pale earnest face of Father Lowder was in itself a powerful appeal. Year after year they had heard his invitation, and year after year they had seen him age, until on the last Good Friday we went round the parish they saw him a broken-down old man—but still young in heart, young in his love to Jesus, young in the intense vigour of his pathetic appeal.

One can hardly believe that hearts could resist such faithful waiting love as his. Ah, they resisted a higher Love, and it all flashed upon them when too late—when his dead body waited on that same bridge where he had so often spoken, and the long line of clergy and choristers conducted him for the last time, a lifeless corpse, to his church through the weeping crowds of mourning poor.

The fatigue of this outdoor preaching was very great, and yet Mr. Lowder had only just finished preaching for *three hours* in church when he started for the streets. He had also been present at the earlier services in church, and taken part in them. He never could be persuaded to save himself.

I may say for the sake of those who wish to try this experiment that we used some large coloured lithographs which we procured at Tattersall's in Southampton Row.

On the last night of each old year a special effort was made to gain those who hitherto had resisted every attempt to convert them. The service began at eleven, and consisted of prayers, hymns, and a stirring sermon. The people then knelt down, and Mr. Lowder read aloud questions for self-examination, and recited various acts of contrition and prayers for pardon. Just before midnight, a solemn silence was preserved; not a sound could be heard but the beating of the clock as it measured out the last few moments of the dying year. At midnight the bell was tolled, and then the people all sang the hymn for New Year's Day. After a short sermon, the service closed with the *Te Deum.*

I feel that my account has drifted into a narrative of Mr. Lowder's work, and is not sufficiently a picture of Mr. Lowder's self. But that is just the character of the man. He was retiring and modest, and lived only for his work. Therefore it is his best praise and monument that he is known by his work.

His life, as it was his, he lived for God. His real history is contained in his long private prayers, severe fasts, hard self-denying life, and in the conflicts of soul, when alone, deserted, and betrayed, he wrestled in bitterest agony of prayer with God, Who thus was hardening His soldier for continued warfare to the end, and preparing him for the grace of final perseverance.

But this, which is his true history, is written only in the Book of Life. We knew very little of his deepest feelings—we could only see the shine upon his face which told that he had been in the Mount with God.

CHAPTER XIX.

REST FROM WORK.

1874-1878.

" Qui sarai tu poco tempo silvano,
E sarai meco, senza fine, cive
Di quella Roma onde Cristo è Romano."

THERE is little to record of Father Lowder's work from this time, for in the eyes of men it was the same, year after year.

If the stories of souls could be told—of the rough men who from enemies became his stanchest friends—there would be abundance of variety and interest, but for obvious reasons this cannot be done. " I have been very tired, and unable to get through more than necessary work," is his own account to his father on January 2, 1874.

He took part, of course, in the general London Mission of that year ; Mr. Suckling coming a second time to St. Peter's, with Mr. Charles Gray as his colleague.

Much of Father Lowder's thoughts were taken up at this time with the sister who was slowly fading away, and in the midst of pressing work he wrote long letters of plans and arrangements for her comfort, and for moving her with as little fatigue as possible from Folkestone to

her home at Frome. To his father he wrote on Whitsun
Eve :—

We have been kept at work by the Archbishop's Bill. On
Tuesday I went with a deputation from the English Church Union
to Lambeth, and we tried to make some impression on the Archbishop, but I do not know that we succeeded ; however, he listened
very patiently to us.   Lords Devon, Nelson, Glasgow, and L.,
C. L. Wood, Shaw, Stewart, Majendie, with Carter, Medd, Butler,
White, and myself, were the deputation.   We also had a meeting
at St. Alban's and All Saint's.

In August he went to Switzerland with Mr. Body and
Mr. Gray, attempting less in the way of mountaineering
than in any previous excursions, but keeping to quiet
wanderings in the Bernese Oberland.   He parted with
his companions in about a fortnight, and made his way
alone to St. Moritz.   He wrote from thence :—

I am enjoying the perfect rest and quiet here, with little temptation to exert myself, as I feel my walking is over.   It is rather
lonely by myself, but I have plenty to amuse myself with in the
way of reading, and so I hope to come home fresh. . . . I have
heard nothing from St. Peter's, so I hope all has been going
on well ; but I dread plunging into all my work, not knowing what
is before me.

He returned in the middle of September, but by
January, 1875, was so broken in health that he was forced
to give in, and to go abroad again, making his way slowly
to Cannes, lingering at Dijon, Clermont, and Lyons.   At
Clermont he could not resist attempting an ascent in snow.

It was a lovely morning, but frosty, so I drove out to the foot
of the Puy de Dôme, and made an attempt to get to the top, but

though I nearly succeeded, I was stopped by the snow and ice, and having no one with me, I was obliged to give in; in fact, if I had not been somewhat used to snow mountains, I could not have gone so far, as it required a rope; and I had only an umbrella. However, I had a beautiful view, and though I had no gun, carried home a red partridge, which I found in the snow quite fresh. . . . It is something new to me to travel in winter abroad, and, among other things, I am learning to manage wood fires. . . . I got to Orange before 2 p.m., and was very glad I stopped there, as I enjoyed my first sight of the Roman remains of the *Midi*, amongst which I have been quite revelling this last week.

Hotel du Square Brougham, Cannes, February 7, 1875.

. . . This is a beautiful spot, and I hope I may be able to stay, but it is very full, and the room I am now in I shall be obliged to leave to-morrow. I hope I may get another room in this house, as it is quiet and in a good situation away from the town.

Though I have enjoyed my tour so much in the new objects of interest I have seen, yet I am very glad to get thus far, with the hope of being quiet for a little before I go on to Rome. I enjoyed amazingly to-day sitting out on the beach with the quiet ripple of the tideless Mediterranean, which I can now hear from my window. I wish Katey could be transported here, for I think the climate would give her new life. I can well understand how those who have once enjoyed a winter on this coast are tempted to come back.

Le Trayas près de Cannes, February 13, 1875.

MY DEAR KATEY,

You will all be surprised at my address and at the paper on which I am writing, but I am waiting for a train in a station·near Cannes, and as I have some time to wait I will employ myself in writing a letter to you. I have been thinking a great deal about you lately, and whether Cannes would suit you. . . .

To-day I have been to the top of one of the Esterel Mountains.

I intended to have walked back to Cannes, but I lost my way coming down, and so have come back to the station that I may return by the train. . . . I shall probably stay a week longer, and then go on to Nice and Mentone and so to Rome. I hear Eland has been here, but I missed him. We are a very quiet party in our *pension*—a clergyman named Woodhouse is here with his wife and niece, a Scotch lady and her daughter, and a few others. I hope Annie and Mary will be able to read this writing, but you must understand this is a little station on the seashore about six or seven miles from Cannes, perched by itself without a house near it, except one or two where the employés live. I am writing at the stationmaster's desk; in fact, they have made me a little coffee, and I am in charge of the booking-office while they are gone to supper, so I hope I have made a good use of my time. . . . Skinner and Mrs. Skinner are here in a *pension* close by. I called upon them to-day.

In March he went on by the Cornice to Genoa, spending a few days at the villages on the way, and sending a large box of palms from Bordighera to St. Peter's. He reached Rome by Holy Week—the first that he had spent away from his people since the Mission began. Here, on Easter Day, he received a telegram telling him that his sister had passed away on Easter Eve. He set out at once, and travelled three days and nights without stopping, arriving, his eldest sister's journal notes, on April 1, "very much knocked up and looking very ill." He celebrated early next morning, the day of the funeral. There are two or three entries in his sister's journal mentioning him at this time :—

St. Mark's Day, 1875.

Charles preached from the Epistle : " He gave some Apostles . . . for the *perfecting* of the saints."

"That is the object of all God's work for us. We are to set forth Christ's likeness in the world—are we doing it?"

April 29.

Charles left us. Now our loss makes itself more truly felt.

May 5.

Charles went to a lodging at Chislehurst—too unwell to continue at St. Peter's.

He had written to his father on April 30, "I have got through the Synod very well, and feel able to do my work, if I take it quietly." But in a few days he broke down, and was unable to return to live at St. Peter's for many months. Mr. Linklater says that

Even in the days of tolerable health he made a rule of sleeping out in the country one night in the week. The smells and vitiated atmosphere of his home were so poisonous, and the surroundings of his life so depressing, that a night in the fresh pure country air was a seventh-day need.

And what Mr. Lowder ordered for himself he ordered for his curates. Indeed, he went so far, at one time, as to provide a special room for them at Chislehurst. But I was the only obedient disciple. The others were too enamoured of their work to tear themselves away; they stuck to the ship morning, noon, and night, and so the plan fell through. This weekly run into the country served to prove how many sincere friends Mr. Lowder had who were always glad to receive him, and in how many pleasant country houses there was a "prophet's chamber" always ready for him.

But, alas! the time came when the one holiday became the one working day in the week. For a long time he was so broken in health that it was as much as he could do to drag through the duties of the Sunday. During this long period he lived at Chislehurst, which was of easy access, and the fine bracing air of which place suited him. It was a great comfort to him to have thus proof positive that he had so thoroughly established his work that it went on as easily and regularly in his absence as in his presence.

And thus he was able the more contentedly to obey the doctors and go abroad for several months in after years.

The spring of 1876 found him again in London.

St. Peter's Vicarage, March 7, 1876.

MY DEAR FATHER,

. . . I have been at St. Peter's for the last ten days, and of course full of Lent work. I hope I shall be able to get on pretty well. The East End is in excitement just now, as the Queen is, I suppose, at this moment in the London Hospital. The other clergy are gone to see her, as we had very good places offered to us, but I am keeping house quietly. I hear the preparations in Whitechapel are very grand.

1, Florence Villas, Chislehurst, Whitsun Tuesday, 1876.

. . . I will try to get over to Wilmington to-morrow. I was too tired to-day, as yesterday was spent in entertaining the choir over here. We had our head-quarters on the common, and we had a beautiful and very successful day. This is my first day of entire rest since I left Frome, as I was obliged to be in London every day last week, though I slept here several nights. I like my lodgings very much, and I have a spare room for the other clergy, all of whom have now been over to see me in turn. On Wednesday we had a large tea-meeting, at which they presented me with a very kindly expressed testimonial of congratulation at my return and sympathy with our bereavement, and £20, which I am going to devote to something in the church. . . .

I find plenty of friends here; so with the clergy coming over from St. Peter's I am far from dull. The people here are very pleasant and sociable, and my chief difficulty is to cut out my time for visiting them.

In December he wrote :—

We are making exchanges with Chislehurst this Advent; the clergy here are preaching for us, and I am preaching here on Thursdays.

The following letter from a clergyman in the Colonies may be given as a specimen of many others of the same kind which he received :—

July 5, 1875.

DEAR FATHER LOWDER,

I experienced a very pleasant surprise last week in the receipt of your "Letter to the Bishop of London on Sacramental Confession," endorsed with the author's kind regards. I don't know how you heard of my whereabouts, unless through our good Bishop, or my friend Mr. Lamborne of Bermondsey, who was to send me a copy. It brought back the remembrance of old times most vividly, when I used to make pilgrimages from Kensington to Calvert Street, and took my part in the St. George's riots! It is not likely that you remember my coming to you to make my first confession, and your putting me off for a week, doubtless to test my sincerity. Now, suppose you had contented yourself with giving me a little good advice, instead of giving me absolution, what would have been the consequence? Why, instead of being as I am (though so utterly unworthy) a priest of God, pronouncing His absolution to others, I might have been absorbed in the world or in some sect. I have never forgotten you, dear Father, through all these years : your latest photograph and the Scupoli* you gave me are before me now. I should have written to you, only that you told me when taking leave that, owing to your large correspondence, I need not expect an answer to a letter. I was not offended at this, but thought myself of too little consequence to occupy your attention.

How strangely events come about. Who would have thought

* "The Spiritual Combat," by Scupoli.

X

that the poor youth that heard you address the children one Good Friday at St. Barnabas', and who was afterwards advised by Mr. Crickmay to go over to the London Docks and encourage the Church there, should proceed to St. Augustine's and sail for the Colonies, there to proclaim the same blessed truths and propagate the Catholic faith. But so it has been ordained in God's good providence.

I have now fifteen churches under my care, all more or less adapted for decent ritual. Our new church of St. Peter at this place is very beautiful. The Bishop will consecrate it, if he is spared to return in safety. As we have no stained glass, I have decorated the walls with pictures of our Saviour, the Blessed Virgin, St. Peter, and St. John Baptist, besides a large crucifixion over the reredos. We have a surpliced choir of white, black, and mulatto men and boys, so you see we are following in the steps of our advanced friends at home as far as we can. If you see our Bishop again he will tell you about my work. The *Church Times* keeps me *au fait* to the various movements at home; they are of great interest to us, as the wave of progress reaches even to this distant diocese, and we reproduce in our humble way the grand ritual of the Church in England.

The following letter shows that by Easter Father Lowder had returned to his Calvert Street home.

St. Peter's Vicarage, London Docks, E., Easter Eve, 1876.

My dearest Father,

I write a few lines to wish you and my sisters all Easter blessings. I cannot but think of the cloud over our Easter joy last year; indeed, I have more than thought, for I spoke of it in my last address at the stations yesterday, on our Blessed Lord being laid in the grave. R.I.P. with our other loved ones, who are keeping a happier Easter in Paradise. May we be ready for our call. I am thankful to say that I have not felt so tired as usual after my Good Friday, which, on the whole, passed off very quietly, though the snow in the morning and the cold weather kept away many.

Most of the summer of 1876 was spent by Father Lowder at Chislehurst, where he lived in the Rectory, taking Mr. Murray's duty in his absence. He wrote to his sister on August 31th :—

I am afraid the Murrays will not be home till the end of next week, but I shall be glad now to be free. If I could do any good to the poor Servians or Bulgarians, I would gladly go out and help them ; perhaps I might by organizing a detachment of Sisters and nurses.

A little later than this, he made every arrangement to go to the seat of war, and went to East Grinstead with Lady Strangford's sister, to organize a band of Sisters who had promised to accompany him. But a telegram from Lady Strangford, saying that the religious prejudices of the Turks would be aroused by the Sisters' dress, prevented the plan from being carried out ; and, on November 12th, he wrote to his sister from Brighton :—

It was well for me that the Bulgarian scheme fell through, as I did not feel up to it. Dr. Drury prescribed for my complaint, and has given me some advice afterwards, but we did not go very deeply into it. He is a very clever homœopath. I am obliged to be very quiet at present.

He had felt deeply the death of his venerable father, to whom he had been summoned on September 5th, and who passed away on the 9th, at the age of eighty-three. The harvest festival at St. Mary's, Fromefield, was on the 11th, the eve of his funeral, and harmonized well with his children's feelings, for their father was indeed as a shock of wheat fully ripe gathered into the heavenly garner. The parents and the sister now slept in the same grave. There is a little notice of their next Christmas meeting in his eldest sister's journal :—

Christmas Day, 1876.

Dined with Charles in his room at the Clergy House, an event which we cannot remember since we left Tetbury. Drank tea with the Sisters, Charles joining us there, to their supreme delight.

A letter from the old friend who had given him a title for Holy Orders, Lord John Thynne, gave him much pleasure this Christmas.

Haynes Park, Bedford.

DEAR LOWDER,

In spite of seventy-eight years now completed, I am graciously permitted again to send you a little Christmas offering in behalf of your persevering and successful good works. I was pleased to hear of your visiting Arthur at Kilkhampton, where I hope he is doing some good, with encouragement.

Yours sincerely,
J. T.

P.S.—After writing as above, I received Report of St. George's Mission, pointing out the more wants, the more hopes, and the further extension of your good designs ; so I took out my cheque of £10 and put an o to it, for it is probable I may never again be permitted to strengthen the power of good deeds by my much-valued friend C. F. L., for whom my affection is unabated and my respect increased yearly.   J. T.

December 20, 1876.

His sisters went abroad early in 1877 ; he had now been working for twenty-one years in East London, and felt that he might take a long holiday, and devote himself for a time to cheering and helping them. He did not, however, join them until the autumn ; and the following extracts are from letters written to them before leaving England :—

Frome, Feast of St. John Baptist, 1877.

MY DEAR ANNIE,

Many thanks to you and Mary for your kind letters, which, though a day late, were none the less acceptable, for as I came into Frome I felt very dreary and desolate, considering that it was the first time I had come here for twenty-five years without having any of you to welcome me. Your letters helped to make up a little for that which can never be replaced, the love of my dear father and mother whenever I came home. The Vicar had been kind enough to let me celebrate at 6.30, and you may be sure I did not forget the departed ones ; indeed, my heart has been very full all day, and I was afraid once or twice of breaking down. While making my thanksgiving in the Lady Chapel, they were ringing a lovely peal, and the bells seemed like voices from heaven, saying, " Come home." I was able to finish (my thanksgiving), kneeling quietly at the grave while they were singing the *Kyrie.* I am sleeping at Mr. Penny's, and he and his wife are very attentive. Miss Maddox has made some beautiful wreaths (for the grave).

The gentians * are very lovely in colour, but have not come out much ; the other white flowers have revived very well. . . . The weather is lovely ; there were a great many communicants and a large congregation at Matins. I preached on Nehemiah vi. 15. I was in Oxfordshire on June 3rd ; St. Barnabas', Pimlico, on the eve of St. Barnabas, Lincolnshire the 11th, Bedford on the 19th, and have been much taken up with the unpleasant agitation about S. S. C. and a book written by Mr. Chambers (who was warden of the House of Charity), and dedicated it to us, but intended only for priests. One was stolen, and they have extracted a number

---

* Sent by his sisters from Champéri.

of questions from it, and represented that we ask them constantly in hearing confessions. There was a discussion in the House of Lords and questions in the House of Commons. The Bishops behaved shamefully. We were abused by name. We are going to some of them this week. I go back to-morrow. I expect my book out this week; I will send you one. . . .

I went to Chislehurst last Monday, and was in charming quarters with Parker the curate, in a new house built for him. Murray came back from the Holy Land the day I arrived. I hope to enjoy some more quiet here after our festival on Monday. Randall preached a fine sermon last night to a crowded congregation. . . . I go back to London at two, as I have a communicant class on Tuesday, and three meetings unfortunately, so that I cannot get back to Chislehurst till Tuesday night, and then I must be at St. Peter's every day this week, so that I envy your quiet at Champéri. I hope to call and see the old house.*

10.15 a.m.—This letter has been written by fits and starts. I have just had the comfort of kneeling in my father's and mother's old place; so though I do go back to London with a full heart, and with a great deal of very serious anxiety, for our conference with the Bishop is very serious, yet altogether it has been a great comfort being here. I have felt so much in the company of the departed that it has been refreshing. My best love to you both, and believe me,

Your very affectionate brother,

CHARLES.

St. Peter's Vicarage, September 18, 1877.

. . . I hope to start about the 12th, with one of Lord Nelson's sons as my companion. He will stay with us in Florence and Rome. My idea is to go over the Simplon, as it is almost the only pass that I do not know, and so down to Baveno. I think your best plan would be to go on to Milan when you are tired of Annecy, and take a lodging for a fortnight there, and then meet me at Baveno. . . .

* Ken House, where the family had lived for many years.

I shall be very glad to get off, for I am getting very tired, and though I have been away from home a good deal, I have not had a continued rest, and the year has been a very trying and anxious one. I do not know that I am quite safe yet from persecution, but I hope it will be so. I went to Exeter on September 3, preached at St. Sidwell's, and spent the next day at Exmouth and Powderham. It was my first visit to Exmouth since we were there together in 1823 or 1824. Charles Wood, who married Lady Agnes Courtenay, is staying at Powderham, and asked me over to stay with them, but I was only able to lunch and spend the afternoon, which I enjoyed much, as it was a lovely day and the views from the tower and the grounds beautiful. C. W. drove me to Exeter, and I had to speak at a meeting in the evening. The next day I went to a village near Okehampton, where John Knight and all his family were staying in a very lovely spot. They had hired the rectory of an old Exeter friend of mine, Archer. I slept there, and they drove me the next day to Dartmoor. I walked four or five miles to Princetown and saw the prison. I was there met by some friends, the Scobells, who drove me to Meavy. We had a beautiful view towards Plymouth, looking down upon the Tamar and seeing the breakwater. On the Friday I came home. I was very glad of the opportunity of seeing so much of Dartmoor. I am going next week to Cirencester on my way to Wakefield to preach for Chadwick. Last week we had our synod of S. S. C., which lasted two whole days, from 9 a.m. till after 7 p.m. It was very well attended, and I am thankful it went off so well. Body was up and Boddington.

. . . I should like much to see Annecy for St. Francis' sake, but I shall prefer getting more directly to the lakes. I wish, if you see anybody who knows, you would ask whether there is likely to be too much snow on the Simplon in the middle of October to prevent walking over, as I should prefer to walk if it is practicable. . . .

Yours very affectionately,

CHARLES.

His sister gives a few particulars of his time abroad :—

In October Charles came (with young Nelson) to the Italian lakes, walked over the Simplon, and joined us at Baveno. He had much wished to show us the Italian lakes, and we made several beautiful excursions with him.

He was with us for six weeks at Florence, and then we went on with him to Rome for six weeks. During our stay the King died suddenly, and by Charles's help we saw the lying in state.

He enjoyed taking long walks into the country about Rome. He used to sally forth with some lunch and his bag strapped to his shoulder, to search for marbles, of which he had a credence table made. Another great pleasure was picking flowers in the grounds of the surrounding villas—especially, I remember, at the Pamfili Doria.

He met many friends, and enjoyed sociable evenings with the Bishop of Bombay and Bishop Tozer, Dr. Nevins of the American Church, and other clergy.

From Rome we went to Castellamare, to a *pension* where, as we afterwards heard, his arrival was dreaded, but it was amusing to see how his brightness and geniality won his opponents. One evening he proposed that the company should be amused by certain gentlemen telling tales, and he led the way with a very humorous and curious story which he had heard in Cornwall, and which had tickled his fancy extremely.

Charles had intended to spend a month with us at Castellamare, but in consequence of the Pope's death he returned to Rome, and through the interest of Cardinal Manning, who was always very civil to him, he was admitted to the Sixtine Chapel for some of the funeral services. We remained at Castellamare, and did not see him again till we returned to England.

He returned home before the Easter of 1878. Mr. Linklater writes :—

It was this year when he only came back in time for Passion-tide, that he appropriated to the curates the Easter offering, which of course had before been always the Vicar's own.

I mention it to show how liberal and generous he was in money matters, and as the offertory generally came to about £40 (a wonderful sum for so poor a parish, and most eloquently testifying to the value the people set upon the Church's work), a fourth share of that sum (there were four curates) was a considerable addition to our net income of £50.

To his sister he wrote on his homeward journey, and after his return to England :—

Rome, February 18, 1878.

We started for Rome at six and reached it just before ten, but, alas ! too late for the lying in state or entombment. Yesterday, however, with great difficulty, I got into the Sixtine Chapel for the last of the requiem Masses, which was very impressive. The *Dies Iræ* was very touching. The choir, so long dispersed, were together again. An immense catafalque in the centre, with the Cardinals all present, ambassadors, Swiss guards, soldiers. All present in mourning, and the panegyric preached by a Cardinal. I afterwards saw the cells in which they are to be shut up to-day. The Mass of the Holy Spirit is, I suppose, just over in the Paoline Chapel, but it was quite private. This evening, if the rooms are ready, they will be shut up for the conclave, and then we shall be all on the *qui vive* to know the result. . . .

Cannes, Third Sunday in Lent, 1878.

. . . We spent two or three hours in Genoa, and came on late to Bordighera. I got my palms, which I hope to bring home with me, and arrived here about 4 p.m. Skinner is here, and I am just going to call upon him, and the Elands I have seen, who are also on their way to England.

July 3.

I am very glad that you have enjoyed yourselves so much and seen so many objects of interest. I was with Body at Cortina some years ago (1871), but we approached it from the other side, and did not remain there even to sleep, but went over the Tre Sassi to Andraz, and then to St. Marco and Ulrich for the Brenner line. If you go to Heiligenblut, remember me to Anton Granögger; he will remember my giving him a pair of mackintosh leggings. He went up with me and Parker to the Bärenkopf, the Glöckerei, and the Windelbachhorn in one day's long excursion in 1871. Parker and I went up the Gross Glockner before with Kals guides. Anton is a very good fellow; I send you a photograph which you may give him if you go, only perhaps he will not recognize me in a cassock, as I then wore a white flannel suit; but he would remember the year in which the Hoffman memorial was put up at the Johanneshöhe. . . .

The case arrived from Rome on the eve of St. Peter's Day, quite safe, and very handsome : it is much admired.*

. . . The Bishop of Bombay preached last night, and seemed well. I hope Dr. Medley, the Bishop of Fredericton, will come to us to-morrow. I do not think they will be able to do anything in Mackonochie's case for a long time, perhaps a year or two, as it will very likely go to the House of Lords, so that all prosecution will be stopped in the mean while.

. . . We had Lords Nelson, Glasgow, and Forbes here. . . .

I am going to write to the Lainsons about an excursion † at the end of this month.

Your very affectionate brother,

CHARLES.

P.S. Mackonochie has won his appeal. I hope we shall be quiet for the present.

Things are going on quite quietly in the parish. I hear nothing more of any attempt at prosecution. In fact, after the quietus which has been given to Lord Penzance, I do not think we shall have much persecution anywhere, though they seem to be attacking Mr. Dale.

* This was a credence table made of pieces of marble he picked up in Rome and the neighbourhood.

† Of five hundred school children.

St. Peter's Vicarage, July 26, 1878.

I was at East Grinstead on Tuesday, and a very storm of thunder and lightning began while we were dining in the tent. It cut the speeches short, beating through the canvas, and the lightning killed a man not far from the convent. Otherwise we had a nice day and a large gathering. . . . On my return from E. G., I stopped at Mr. Lainson's at Reigate to arrange about our school excursion there next Wednesday. The Lainsons have a beautiful place there, with very large grounds, so that if we have a fine day we shall enjoy ourselves much, I hope. Pickance took me over on Wednesday to an English Church Union meeting in a very pretty village near Godstone. I stayed a few days at the Randells', who are pretty well. The country is looking lovely; the early rains made everything so green, and now the bright sun has ripened the crops very rapidly.

. . . I was in the House of Lords the other night to hear Lord Beaconsfield's great speech on the Berlin Treaty, and I hope to be in the House of Commons next Monday for the debate on the question of the Treaty and the Convention. It was a very fine sight in the House of Lords—the Princess of Wales and many of the royal family, the House full, and the galleries crowded. I will send you the *Guardian* with the account of it.

. . . We have had some of the American and Colonial Bishops with us during the Lambeth Conference. The Bishop of Fredericton, a very nice old man, Dr. Medley, preached during the festival, and the Bishop of Bombay gave us a very interesting account of work in India. The Bishop of Albany, a son of old Bishop Doane, and Bishop Schereschewsky, a Pole, now a missionary Bishop in China . . . also preached for us, and Lord Beauchamp brought down the Bishop of Missouri; and the Bishop of Colorado, who was staying with the Dean of St. Paul's, came last Saturday. Some of them are very good Churchmen, and take great interest in the progress of things in England.

Your very affectionate brother,

CHARLES.

CHAPTER XX.

LAST DAYS IN ENGLAND.

1878–1880.

> "What are we set on earth for? Say to toil,
> Nor seek to leave thy tending of the vines,
> For all the heat o' the day—till it declines
> And Death's mild curfew shall from work assoil."

In October, 1878, Father Lowder paid a visit to the Paris Exhibition, and spent three weeks with his sisters at Folkestone.

He walked with them one day to Cæsar's Camp, and when not far from the summit ran to the top, to show them how little the steep ascent tried him. But he shrank from society, and seemed exhausted if he had to talk much or listen to conversation. An attempt had been made, while he was abroad, to get up an attack on St. Peter's. A few extracts from his reply to an address of his parishioners, expressing their confidence in him, are worth recording :—

Of the nearly seventeen hundred names attached to the memorial, I find that more than three hundred are communicants, between fifteen and sixteen hundred are parishioners, while of those not actually living within the bounds of the parish, the great majority are very near neighbours—either in Wapping or other parts of the parish of St. George's—and the others are communicants who come from a somewhat greater distance.

An anonymous writer, calling himself a Wapping Protestant, was kind enough to warn the Bishop against the memorial, and complain that many who signed it did not belong to the church. Now, though I am sorry that there are any in the parish who do not come to church—and they well know that I would do anything to bring them to it—yet I must say I derived a great deal of pleasure from seeing the names of many who do not come to church attached to the address. Because were I to feel that only those who are communicants or regular attendants at church were influenced by the work of the clergy, Sisters, or teachers, I should be very much disappointed; for then I should feel that we had failed in our duty to a large number of our parishioners. But I am encouraged by the thought that there are a great many who —though from various reasons, such as want of clothes, idle or bad habits, they do not come, or only come irregularly, to church, yet do not refuse the visits of the clergy and Sisters who strive to teach them—are thankful that they have a church where they may come whenever they will, that there are schools for their children, and who are influenced by the good example of neighbours who do value their church privileges; who, moreover, are convinced that the clergy are their true friends, and who know that in the day of sickness and the dying hour they can rely on their aiding them with their prayers, instructions, consolations, and warnings. And both those who come to church and those who do not are able to see how unjustifiable are the attacks of those who now put themselves forward as aggrieved parishioners, and how unfit they are to represent the feeling of sincere and consistent Churchmen in the parish. . . .

Now, I do not wish to attack or interfere with others. I am content to go on quietly and steadily doing my duty to God and to you, if they will kindly leave me alone. If I must go to prison for doing this duty and trying my best to save your souls, I shall give no trouble to the policeman, but go quietly, like my friend Mr. Tooth; but I had rather stay at my post in St. Peter's, and minister to you there, and in your own house when you need my visits.

But maintain the laws of the Church I will, for I vowed to do this when I was ordained thirty-five years ago, before the Privy Council or Lord Penzance had ever tampered with the Church's rubrics.

But the main object of this address is to impress upon you, my friends, the great duty of showing by your lives that you really value these Church privileges. That is, after all, the best answer to these complaints—the witness of our own lives and those of our people. Let those of you who are already communicants consider this festival a call to dedicate yourselves more strictly to God's service. Prepare to make a good communion, resolving to serve God more faithfully than ever. If you have been careless or lukewarm in your religious duties, remember that you are not only doing harm to your own souls, but also to the souls of others, who make your careless lives an excuse for going on themselves carelessly and without religion.

And to you who are not communicants, and some of whom, perhaps, seldom come to church, let me say this, that though I thank you very sincerely for your kind feelings to me in signing the address, yet I should be far more thankful—oh, how thankful to Almighty God !—if I might see you henceforth giving yourselves heartily and entirely to His service, loving the Church and religion yourselves, and bringing up your children to love God and their religious duties. Then I should indeed feel that this persecution was blessed to us. I would willingly go to prison—nay, even if it were needed to death itself—if I believed it were to lead to your salvation and sanctification.

June 22, 1878.

The real warm interest shown by Father Lowder to each individual parishioner with whom he had to do must have been one chief reason for the enthusiastic loyalty which they felt for him. In a letter to his parishioners he tells the story of one family, and it may well find its place here, as it is the only written record of his work in individual cases which he has left.

Benjamin —— was brought up as an agricultural labourer in Essex; he came up to London and worked as a carman, and then at coal work on the river. He married, but had little thought of God or of his soul, and lived the rough ungodly life of those with whom he worked and associated, drinking, swearing, and neglecting religion. Nay, so opposed was he to its duties, that he endeavoured to prevent his wife from attending the services in the Mission Chapel of the Good Shepherd; used such threats and actual violence towards her, when she persisted, that she was in bodily fear, even when kneeling at her prayers in the chapel. On one occasion he refused to allow me to visit her while ill and desiring my ministrations. This continued for many years, until, during the cholera of 1866, it pleased God to bring him low. He caught the disease, and while lying ill in his bed accepted the services of one of the Sisters. Her loving attention softened him, and by her persuasion he allowed me to visit him. Then, being sent with his wife, also recovering from cholera, to the Convalescent Home at Seaford, and moved by the care bestowed upon his body and soul by the chaplain and Sisters, he yielded to God's grace, repented truly of the past, and resolved, by His help, to lead a new life. He was prepared for Confirmation, and confirmed by Bishop Jenner in St. Peter's Church, which had been consecrated the year before, just before the outbreak of cholera, and then became a communicant. From this time he was most steadfast and regular in his duties, living happily at home, setting a good example to his children, as well as to his neighbours, of an honest and religious life. He was in the confraternity of St. Peter's, an active and useful member of the Church of England Working-Men's Society, and frequently assisted his fellow members in their defence of the clergy at St. James', Hatcham, was appointed a sidesman of St. Peter's Church, and, as you well know, was a bright example of what a hard-working man, albeit of the rough material of the working-men around us, might and should be in his religious life and duties. In all this he was helped by a good and loving wife, whose devout character, as well as industrious and tidy habits, tended to make his home happy and comfortable. They had three sons, the two eldest of whom were confirmed and became communicants, and the eldest was married, with one child.

A brother of ———, who had emigrated to Natal when he was quite a boy, had for some years invited him to come out, and at last, having had opportunities of consulting Bishop Macrorie and Dean Green when they were in England, he resolved to do so. Accordingly, in October of last year, after a solemn farewell service, at which a large body of communicants were present, and communicating together, the family started on their voyage, and arrived, after a good deal of bad weather, in Durban, the beginning of November. They made·their first communion in Durban, where they were delayed some time waiting for his brother's waggon to take them to Pieter-Maritzburg. They arrived there towards the end of November, and on the 27th, having with great difficulty secured a small cottage, he commenced working, but the climate was too much for him, and he was only able to continue his work for ten days. In a letter to me, written on the 8th of December, the first day that he gave up work, he complained of the heat and his consequent illness, but wrote with all love and affection to those whom he had left behind at St. Peter's. He tried to work again the next day, but was so ill that he was forced to give up and go home; and from that day, though tenderly nursed and cared for both in body and soul, he never got better. He received most kind visits from Canon Deedes, of St. Saviour's Cathedral, for whose loving ministrations, both to him and his son Benjamin (who soon followed his father to the grave), we have reason to be most thankful. Though this care was abundantly blessed to his soul, yet his body gradually sank under the painful disease. His mind, when sometimes wandering, returned to St. Peter's, and he often asked to see one of the clergy, and was unhappy that this wish could not be gratified, fancying he was at home. But his end was approaching. He made his last communion on Christmas Eve, at the hands of the same priest who had given him his first communion on landing in Durban, and who happened to be at Pieter-Maritzburg at the time. On St. John's Day he died very happily and peacefully, and was buried on the 29th.

But the poor widow's sorrows were not over. She had to resign not only her husband but her best-loved son; the son who had been her greatest comfort in England, the steadiest and most religious; who had most closely followed his father's example in his love for the Church, where he had served as a banner-bearer in the processions. It was to him that his father in his dying moments had committed the care of his widow, and now he was taken ill of dysentery also on the 3rd of January, and on the 9th was so ill that he was obliged to be removed to the hospital. There he lay for three weeks, nursed by his mother as well as the native attendants, and receiving the ministrations of the Church from Canon Deedes. His mother's account of the memory of his last moments, which she has tenderly treasured, was very touching. He could not believe that he was so near death until he learnt it from the priest, and then with great calmness and resignation he made his last confession and submitted himself to God's will. This was at night, and he desired to receive communion in the morning, but it was not so to be, as it pleased God to take his soul before the morning. Happily he had communicated two days previously.

Thus it pleased God to deprive the poor widow of husband and son, whose bodies she has left behind her in a distant colony, and yet with the comfort that the lessons which both carried away with them from home had borne good fruit, and that their souls were resting in peace. It happened most fortunately for her that a lady from Durban, returning with a child to England, engaged her as a nurse, and the captain taking her youngest son as a steward's boy, they returned in the same ship and arrived safely in England. This lad has just been confirmed and made his first communion, and I trust will follow in his father's steps.

I have given this sketch because I hope it may help to en-

Y

courage many of you, especially men living in the midst of so many trials and temptations, to see such fruits of God's grace in one of themselves, and the real comfort and stay which the blessings of religion and Church afford to those who are tried in the afflictions of this world. It proves also what I said at first, that the faithful who are taken from us are not a loss but a great gain, for they, by God's loving care, are brought safe home ; they are the ripe grain safely gathered into the heavenly garner. They are, moreover, as seals which it pleases Almighty God to set upon our work, assuring us that it is real and true and acceptable to Him.

The following letters to the emigrant and to his widow make us understand something of the affection which Father Lowder was able to inspire. There are few things that the poor value more than letters ; they know what is the truth, that a busy man must really care for them if he spends time in writing to them.

St. Peter's Vicarage, London Docks, January 11, 1879.
My DEAR ——,
I was very glad to receive your letter of December 8 yesterday. We had been much interested in the accounts we got from Algoa Bay, but were not sure until your last arrived what address would find you. I am sorry you have not yet found more suitable employment, but hope that you will soon be able to better yourself and that the boys will like their situations. No doubt the war must increase the price of provisions, but I hope by this time it is over, and that you will have peace and quiet. We have been going on very quietly here. The aggrieved parishioners presented me to the Archbishop, but things are so unsettled now in the ecclesiastical courts, that the Archbishop decided not to proceed; so it is put off, at least for some time. We have spent a happy Christmas, though the weather has been, and is, very severe, and we are expecting to have the Thames frozen over soon. We

had a good many communicants at Christmas, and, on the Sunday after, Father Biscoe got up some tableaux or living representations of the Nativity, in which many took part, with carols sung at each representation. The communicants' supper took place last Tuesday, and we had nearly two hundred at supper, with carols, songs, and speeches, as in former years. I am sorry to say Mr. Mabbitt is very ill ; I do not think he can last long, as he eats very little, and is very low.

I will send you an almanack or two, and see that you have the *Church Times*, and I will also send· you one of our last Reports, in which you will see I have mentioned you and your family. You do not say anything about your wife or Agnes ; I hope they are bearing the climate well. Give my kind regards to them, and say I hope they will keep their spirits up well, and comfort you and the boys when you get down-hearted about things. I am glad you are near the church, and have the opportunity of going, for that will be the most likely to give you real happiness in a strange country, and remind you that we are all one in the communion of saints, however distant we may be in body one from another. I am glad also you know better than to mind what the Wesleyans say to you. You have had to go through these sort of taunts before, and you have had grace to bear them, and so you will now find that good will come out of all this trouble. Keep steadfast to your communions, and tell the boys I hope they will do so too, and that George will be confirmed, for he wants the grace of God's Holy Spirit to keep him firm against temptation. It would be very good to have family prayers every night, to bind you all together. I will give your messages to all your friends, and I am sure, when I tell them, they will all return your kind remembrance of them. May God bless you all, and keep you in His holy faith and fear, and give you the blessings of a new year.

Yours very truly in our Lord Jesus Christ,

C. F. LOWDER.

St. Peter's Vicarage, London Docks, E., February 6, 1879.

MY DEAR DAUGHTER IN JESUS CHRIST,

You may be quite sure that we have all felt most deeply for you in your trouble, and that I have grieved not less than others, for after our long acquaintance, or rather, I should say, friendship for you and your dear husband for so many years, it is very sad to think that you should be left a widow in a foreign country, under such trying circumstances. I can understand, from his letter to me, that he was too much exposed to the heat, and that he suffered from it in the new climate. You will before this have received the letter I wrote to him in answer to his. The great comfort to us here is that he was so well prepared for his end, and that he had all the blessings and consolations of the Church to support him in his last hours. And what a comfort for you all to hear this, and that he valued the privileges which were offered him, and did not forget the instructions which he had received at St. Peter's. I am indeed grieved to think that I shall never see him again in this world, and yet the prospect of a happier meeting hereafter is quite sufficient to soften, if not to crush this grief. He is now amongst those ripe fruits of the harvest here, which it has pleased God should be already gathered in His garner. I am very glad that Canon Deedes was able to minister to him, as I knew him in Oxford, and hope that you will give him my kind regards, and say how thankful I am to him for his kindness. And now about yourself. Ben in his letter says that you think of coming home, and of course it is very natural that you should wish to do so; but do not be in a hurry, but ask the advice of Mr. Deedes and of the Bishop and Dean. We are making inquiries here, whether you can have some help on your voyage home, and I hope before the next mail I shall hear whether anything can be done in that way; and I hope that we shall hear from you soon, as to what your friends in Natal advise should be done. If there is no very pressing hurry, from the circumstances out in Natal, it would be better for you to give us time to see what help we can get you for your voyage. It seems remarkable that the news of your husband's death should have arrived on the day that Mr. Mabbitt died, and now I am writing this letter just before the funeral. He is to be buried in the same cemetery with his wife, and you remember going with us to Beckenham in April last. You did not then think how soon you would be a widow, but who will be next? We have just finished the service in church, and are going over directly to Beckenham. All here send their love, and pray sincerely that you may be comforted and strengthened in your affliction. My love to Joe and Agnes and the little one. Tell Agnes to be brave and of good courage, and a comfort to you. My love also to Ben and George, and I trust that God may sanctify their loss to them, and that they may all be watchful and ready.

Yours very truly in our Lord Jesus Christ,
C. F. Lowder.

He had taken a house for his sisters at Chislehurst from Midsummer, 1879; and here he generally slept one or two nights in each week, taking tender care for their comfort and welfare. He went for his holiday to his friend Mr. Wynne, who kindly asked his brother and sister-in-law to meet him. From Wales he wrote to his sister :—

Peniarth, August 28, 1879.

. . . Willie and I have had a very pleasant week together, though a great deal of rain has fallen, and the floods have done much damage in the valley, yet we have enjoyed some lovely days and made some pleasant excursions. The house here has been full, and we have had a pleasant party. They are now dispersing. Willie went to Barmouth yesterday to meet Jane and little Willie, and to find lodgings for them. I shall probably spend a day or two with them next week and come home by Chester.

I left Bethgelert on Monday and made an attempt on Snowdon, but after missing my way and getting at last into the right path, I was driven back by a hurricane which might have whirled me over a precipice if I had persevered. The rain came down in the latter part of the day and through the night in a deluge, so that the river at Capel Curig was swollen to a torrent and inundated the fields. It was a piteous sight to see the people up to their knees trying to save some of their hay. I got on to Penmanmawr, and called on the Bowens and slept at the hotel. . . . I go to Tarporley to-morrow, and expect to be at St. Peter's on Monday. I may come to you on Tuesday evening if I can.

His last " Report of St. George's Mission," dated November, 1879, is written brightly and cheerfully. He had been pleased by a few words in the " Dictionary of London," written by Mr. Dickens (son of the novelist), recommending his readers to pay a visit to St. Peter's Church, where, he says, " you will find in full work an agency which, if the people of the neighbourhood are to be believed, has had, in the marvellous transformation which has taken place, a more potent influence even than police or Parliament combined."

But, Father Lowder wrote, " it is very difficult for those who are engaged in a spiritual work like our own to measure its real advance. Physical improvements, cleaner streets and houses, healthier children, or even such outward improvement as is shown in a quieter and more orderly neighbourhood, we can more readily perceive. . . .

" Our work has gone on steadily and happily during the past year. Storms which threatened have apparently blown over ; aggrieved parishioners have made little or no sign, and we may hope for continued peace."

The encouragement which above all cheered him was the Bishop of Bedford's first visit to St. Peter's, on November 5, 1879. He first went to St. Agatha's night school, which was filled upstairs and downstairs. There he addressed the boys, and gave them his blessing. Then he went to the men's meeting at the Iron School, where between two or three hundred men were present; and nowhere in London could he have received a more enthusiastic welcome.

All through the winter and spring Father Lowder continued his habit of coming once or twice a week to sleep at Chislehurst. He was better than he had been five years before, but his sisters say that he looked very worn and weary—that he used to take a book or paper and fall asleep in his chair. He spent Christmas Day with them, coming to Chislehurst after the services at St. Peter's. His sister's journal notes :—

January 2, 1880.

Went to St. Peter's to see the tableaux of Bethlehem and Nazareth, only open to communicants. The idea is from the Passion Play. Scenery and tableaux very good, only too cramped for room. Charles represented the aged Simeon holding the Infant, a character which suited him admirably.

Mr. Lowder's last day in England, August 1, 1880, was spent in an excursion with the children of his flock to Walthamstow. There were nineteen large vans, crammed inside and outside, and "the Father" gave himself up to the children's pleasure, lying on his back on the grass when he had done all he could to amuse them, with little ones clustering about him, jumping over him and nestling in his arms. "I often think of it," says one who was there, "and can see him now, as I did on our return, sitting opposite to me in the van, bright and happy, though after a long wearisome day, a little child on each knee, and the children singing—

> 'We all love Father Lowder,
> Because he is so good,
> Because he is so kind,'

until the noise became so deafening that he appealed to me to stop the singing."

When they arrived at St. Peter's, they found the streets illuminated and decked as for a triumphal procession, banners flying, and the windows bright with coloured lights. A dense mass of people filled the streets, cheering and shouting, the parish band meeting the vans and playing before them. Every one who had not gone to Waltham-stow was in the streets, and a line was with difficulty cleared to allow of the children passing through. Nothing of the kind had ever been done before, though the school excursion was an annual event.

It was the last time Father Lowder entered his parish alive : six short weeks passed, and then the hearse containing his lifeless body passed slowly through those same streets and the same crowd, silent now, bringing back to them their Father and best friend.

CHAPTER XXI.

LAST JOURNEY.

1880.

" Patria splendida, terraque florida, libera spinis,
Danda fidelibus est ibi civibus, hic peregrinis."

On August 2nd Father Lowder celebrated as usual at
St. Peter's. He continued at work in his library until
about twenty minutes before he started for the Continent.
Then he ran upstairs, hastily packed, and left for the last
time the house to which he had come, twenty-four years
before, to begin the work which now was over. He met
his sister Rose and a friend next day at the station at
Brussels, and went on with them to Trèves, where he chose
the Maison Rouge to go to, as the oldest hotel in the town—
a quaint, weird-looking house. Early on the 4th they went
down the Moselle to Coblentz. Miss Lowder wrote to her
sister :—

Heidelberg, August 5th.

We had a most delicious day, and we all thoroughly enjoyed
ourselves, just gliding down the river and looking at lovely
scenery. . . . At Coblentz we landed and had some distance to
walk to the hotel, but Charles took as much luggage as he could
carry and walked on in front, going so quickly that we found it
difficult to keep up with him, the day's rest and quiet had so

refreshed him. . . . I went early this morning to the Cathedral at Coblentz, and met Charles there. The service was a children's Mass, and he was much taken by the hymns and Litany that they sang. As we returned together, he said, "I should like to get that music for the children at St. Peter's," and passing a book-seller's shop, we went in and found a copy of the Litany with the music, which he bought.

After breakfast we started for Burgen-brück, and on the boat he amused me with stories of the different castles we passed, and was bright and cheerful, getting amusement out of every little incident that occurred. We reached this place at nine this evening. Charles manages all for us, and I do not know what we shall do when he leaves us. Mrs. B—— is delighted, and thinks him a most capital manager, and we have no fuss or worry. Francis B. seems quite taken with Charles, and looks up to him with the greatest reverence. He is a particularly nice, gentlemanlike boy. . . . Charles much enjoyed the Moselle, and I think he is looking a little better and less tired.

From Heidelberg they went to Strasbourg, and next day, the 7th, to Constance. Of these last days with her brother Miss Lowder says—

We passed through part of the Black Forest. Charles was especially delighted with the scenery, which he had not seen before, and many times in the journey expressed his admiration. He was, however, very weary, I think, and once, on turning from the window, I was particularly struck, and indeed shocked, at his appearance. He was asleep, and looked so white and worn out that for the first time I felt anxious about him. He always managed to be bright and cheerful when in company with others, and one forgot sometimes that he certainly looked much paler and more worn than formerly. Before we reached Constance he had shaken off his weariness, and was as bright and energetic as ever.

August 8 (*Sunday*). We had delightful rooms at Constance, overlooking the lake; mine, I think, was the largest, and in it Charles celebrated the Holy Communion at eight, using the holy vessels he had brought with him in a little Communion case. Francis B. and I were the only ones present. I little thought then that it was the last time *he* would ever celebrate on earth. But so it was; for though he hoped to have done so at Ober-Ammergau the following Sunday, it could not be arranged, and the portmanteau containing the vessels he gave into my charge, and, through a mistake at the railway station at Munich, it never reached him again.

After breakfast we strolled out in different directions, but on my return I found Charles in his room, and he said Matins with me. The evening was cool and pleasant, and we took a walk by the lake; some few people we passed, and among them a mother and some children. One, a pretty little girl about four years old, on seeing Charles, ran up to him, and putting her hand in his, walked with him a little way in the most confiding manner.

The lad who, with his mother, was travelling with the Lowders said afterwards that he had been impressed by Father Lowder putting a stop to some disparaging remarks on a brother clergyman of a different way of thinking from himself, saying, " He cares for his poor," and by his different manner in speaking of another, professedly a High Churchman, who neglected them. " Once I asked him," young B—— added, " if he were not very lonely at St. Peter's, and why he had not a child to live with him or pets. He replied that the main inducement to be a celibate was the being able to devote one's self without distraction to God, and at the same time smiled and told me of the head of a confraternity who adopted a girl, and, when she grew up, to the consternation of the brotherhood, married her! He had never in his life had a pet, until a few weeks before our journey, when a friend gave him a little dog."

To his elder sister Father Lowder wrote:—

Zell-am-See, Austria, August 22 (Sunday).

. . . You know of our meeting at Brussels, our pleasant day on the Moselle, and visit to Heidelberg, and how much we enjoyed the Black Forest line of railway which brought us to Constance. . . . I parted with Rose on Monday on the quay, as we took different boats, she and her friends to Schaffhausen, I to Bregenz. On board my boat I fell in with a Mr. M'Caul, the Rector of St. Magnus (by London Bridge), and a young Ryder, and as we were all going to explore the Bregenzer Wald, we joined forces, took a carriage a little way out of Bregenz, and then commenced our walk. Though it rained part of the way, we had a very fine walk, and saw a most lovely sunset over the Lake of Constance. We slept at a country inn; walked for nine or ten hours the next day (Tuesday, 10th), to a high village, the Shrœcken, with splendid mountain views, marred by the clouds and mists. We started in rain the next morning (Wednesday, 11th); but it soon cleared, and we enjoyed the afternoon very much, coming down upon a beautiful village of Mittelberg, which reminded us of the situation of Cortina, and in the evening drove to Obertsdorf, a young girl of nineteen being our excellent charioteer.

Obertsdorf is the principal town of the Bregenzer Wald, which is an interesting country, mountains, rivers, and forests very Tyrolese, and the inhabitants well to do, in large comfortable houses—the young women very pretty, fair, and delicate. Here I met Mr. Carter and his two daughters, and left my companions in order to make for Ober-Ammergau.

On the Thursday I started with a guide over the mountains, had a beautiful walk over a high and difficult pass on which I was roped and pulled up, getting down about five into the Led Thal.

I started early the next morning, and got to Reuth about ten in pouring rain. Took another carriage on with a German (from Trèves), and arrived at Ober-Ammergau soon after Rose; found they had just secured rooms, and so we met again. She has told you of our enjoyment of the Passion Play. I suppose it is difficult to feel the second time what one felt at first, but I quite enjoyed it this time, though disposed to be more critical than at first.

He talked afterwards of the chronological sequence of some of the scenes; and in particular of the transposition of the Entry into Jerusalem with the Supper at Bethany, the former being chosen on account of the dramatic effect for the first scene of the play.

Here his companion-sister writes :—

August 9th.

There had been a great uncertainty about our rooms at Ober-Ammergau, and when Mrs. B., F., and I arrived there in pouring rain on Friday afternoon, we found that all the rooms at Sebastian Zwinck's were already engaged, and we were in some doubt what to do. Fortunately Mr. Sylvester, with whom we had travelled from Munich, was most kind, and managed to find two rooms near, which we thankfully engaged, and were just settling in, when, to our great relief, Charles arrived. Our accommodation was primitive, but everything was clean, and the people very civil and attentive. One room was to serve as a bedroom for the gentlemen and sitting-room for all; while a room above, to which the only means of access was a ladder and trap-door, was the sleeping-room for Mrs. B. and myself. We were fortunate in securing these, for many arrived on Saturday, and had the greatest difficulty in finding any rooms disengaged.

August 14. The day was very wet, but we managed to get out, and went with Charles to the theatre to settle about our places. Then we went to Joseph Maier's house, and Charles, who had lodged there in 1871, had a talk with the wife and children, and begged them all to write their names on a note he had received from Maier. The eldest little girl, he said, he remembered as an angel in one of the tableaux. They all seemed pleased to see and talk with him, and before leaving he asked Maier to write his name on a photograph I had bought of him in his character of the Christ. He met many friends at Ober-Ammergau, amongst others a Dr. Wood, and his sister-in-law, Miss Moorsom, who knew him very well.

August 15. This was the day on which I first saw the Passion Play. We did not get seats together, so I did not meet Charles till our midday meal. Afterwards, in talking over what we had seen, he remarked that the impression made on him was not quite the same as at the first time; *then* he felt as if he had been at a Retreat, *now* he was more disposed to be critical; but nevertheless he was much pleased and quite satisfied. When all was over his first feeling was to go at once to the church, and there I found him, and returned with him to our lodgings. After dinner he said the mental strain had been so great that he must take a walk to refresh himself, and we started together, first trying to find Dr. Wood's lodgings, which, after much difficulty, we succeeded in doing. Dr. Wood and Miss Moorsom joined us, and we walked through the village and down the road. It became so dark and dirty that I wished to return, but Charles said, " No, we must go a little further;" so after Dr. Wood had left us, we three went on, skirting some fields at the foot of a remarkable hill, which gives a peculiar character to the scenery around the village. Charles was very bright and amusing, joking about our late walk, and saying that perhaps we should meet the King of Bavaria, who always takes his walks at night.

As we returned he found a glow-worm, which he fastened on his hat as a lantern to guide us home.

That night Mr. Swallow called to settle with Charles about a walking tour they wished to make on leaving Ober-Ammergau, and then we had accounts to settle, so that it was late before we got to bed, and as we were to start early the next morning, we had to rise betimes.

By some mistake the carriage we had ordered never came for us, so Charles had to go into the village to see whether another could be procured. He stood at the door of the châlet waving his hand to us as we drove off, and this was my last sight of him.

He left Ober-Ammergau with Mr. Swallow at 3 p.m. on Monday, and walked to Partenkirchen. It was a very hot day, and at Ettal he spent some little time in devotion in the cool monastery church, then descended the hill and bathed in the Loisach, which runs at its foot, after plunging through some marshy ground to find a secluded corner. At most of the hotels at Partenkirchen they found all beds engaged by letter or telegram for returning pilgrims from Ammergau, but at last secured a comfortable room opposite the beautifully restored church, in a *dépendance* of the Hotel zum Rassen.

Next morning, August 17th, they started on an expedition to the Schlachten Alp, of which Mr. Swallow gives the following account :—

Our guide, a fine well-built fellow, had been wounded in the foot at Bazeilles, and knew Karl Hoffman well; upon which ensued much interesting conversation on the fortunes of the war, and later, on the king and his hunting-*schloss*, the goal of our expedition. Not far from this we turned aside to a rude châlet, where lived for the summer among their cattle a farmer, his wife, and two bright little children. With the latter we made friends as we frugally feasted on a bowl of creaming milk apiece and *schwarzes brod*. The little boy Franzl, as he trudged about with Father Lowder's stick, was complimented on being a true *bergsteiger*, while the little girl was at first nervous, clinging to her mother, who told us how they kept up their health in the warm weather on the mountain side, and attended to their lessons in the village in winter. Along the road we talked a little of parish matters, the friendliness of all the neighbouring clergy, with one exception, whom his Rector, Mr. Harry Jones, promptly dismissed in consequence; of the presently forthcoming paper at the Church Congress by the Bishop of Bedford, who had at first shrunk back from St. Peter's, in fear that if he came then to open the Mission, he would be held responsible for all that might be said and done, but afterwards, on being shown that this need not be, or that, as a logical consequence, he could not venture to enter the majority of the churches in the diocese, had given most kind assistance, holding at St. Peter's a special Confirmation. At last we reached a curtained royal summer-house on the edge of a small plateau, from which in the sunshine we had a glorious view—the Wetterstein range close on our left, and in front the Schneeferner and Zugspitze, with the Rainthal and its highly coloured lakelets, the Blanc Gumpen, between. Here we stayed for a couple of hours, Father Lowder retiring for his meditation, and then returning to enjoy the varying view as the clouds changed from peak to peak, or lifted entirely just before we came away. We gathered here our first Alpine roses. At last we reached the Partnachklamm, which we crossed and re-crossed by a couple of bridges, between which we met Jakob Rutz, whom we had seen on Sunday crowned, in a scarlet robe, as *Choragus* at Ammergau. A friend of Father Lowder's had lodged with him, and so he was ready, when accosted, to tell us how glad he was to rest and refresh himself with a holiday among changed scenes after all his exertions of voice and memory. The Klamm itself is very grand, as the frothing stream hurries, hundreds of feet beneath the bridge, through its narrow rock-hewn channel, with precipitous cliffs reaching to the pinewood far above. At the hotel we found Rumsey ready to join us at Evensong and supper.

The three friends left Partenkirchen after church and breakfast on Wednesday morning, August 18th, in an *einspänner* driven by the wife of the owner. She gave them much information about her family life, and was in return greatly complimented by Father Lowder on her powers as *kutcherin*. She was very anxious when they arrived at the end of the Walchensee that the party should make the rest of the journey by water, in order to spare her horse ; but as it was raining, she was held inexorably to her bargain to take them to the village of Walchen.

Here they slept, breakfasting next morning on delicate *forellen* from the lake, and crossed by water to Urfeld, at the north end, walking from thence to the Kochelsee, and amusing themselves by deciphering the old German inscriptions on tablets beside the road, which bore records of the troubled history of the district in earlier times. They crossed the lake to Kochel, and partly drove, partly walked to Tölz, where they slept. Next day, Friday, 20th, they crossed " Iser, rolling rapidly," and went by train to Schaftlach, where Father Lowder and Mr. Rumsey left the railroad to walk to Gmünd. They spent most of the day on the Tegernsee, and took the diligence through Wildbad-Kreuth to their night's quarters at Achenkirch.

On Saturday they made an early start (at 4.30 a.m.), reaching Jenbach to breakfast, and then going to Wörgl by rail. Here Father Lowder hoped to take up the luggage which he had entrusted to his sister to be sent from Munich to Wörgl, but, finding nothing, he made a weary and fruitless excursion to Kufstein and back, and followed Mr. Rumsey by the last train to Zell-am-See, thoroughly tired out. He could not celebrate next morning, as his Communion case was in his portmanteau, and although after church he rested quietly, the effects of his over fatigue

z

on the previous day began to be apparent. On Monday morning he was so unwell that he had to leave the village church before the service was ended, and was unable to stay with his friends till Matins, which he tried to say with them, were finished. He spent the rest of Monday, on which he was to have started for the Gross Venediger, in his room, oppressed by a dyspeptic attack. He had written to his sister the day before.* On Tuesday he was better, but still unfit to travel.

"During our stay at the Krone," Mr. Swallow wrote, "we were treated with great courtesy, and supplied with English papers by fellow travellers—the loan of the *Tablet* in particular—any salutes we received from villagers here or elsewhere being jocosely passed on by the Father as intended for my special benefit. He declared that any sacerdotal pretension on his own part was discounted by the grey suit and Panama hat which he wore, whilst Rumsey's beard quite spoilt the effect of his clothes."

On Wednesday, 25th, Father Lowder was quite bright again, ran off to the chemist's to get lint and ointment for a footsore companion, and declared himself fit to move on. They set out with two guides, taking the route up the Kapruner-Thal. Mr. Swallow gives the following account of the expedition :—

Passing through Kaprun, as we lunched at a wayside inn further up the valley, we found two German travellers, who gave us good hopes of a successful ascent next day. The two indefatigable bathers took an opportunity for a plunge in the rapid stream.

We had left all our baggage, except what was absolutely neces-

* See p. 332.

* See p. 332.

sary, at the Krone. The rest was shouldered by our guides, whom, as the valley grew narrower and the road more steep, we left further and further behind. Beside the stream we saw quantities of timber, which is drawn down over the ice in winter (so we were told), and not far from the road was a fine waterfall which has gradually worn away a deep passage through the rock. After some hours we came upon our quarters for the night, the Rainer-hütte. We made a hearty meal on such meat as was to be had, and then took a short rest lying on our beds. The air, at about five thousand feet, was rather keen, and we put on our macin-toshes. After our rest, I found " the Father " on a little eminence not far off, hoping (in vain) for a sight of the rose-coloured tints of the setting sun upon one of the snowy peaks. Two-thirds of our bedroom were filled by five beds, placed close side by side, cut off from one another by a curtain. Two wash-stands in the remaining third and two small window-sills completed its furni-ture. Arriving first, we had the choice of beds, the other two being filled by German travellers, a third, who came late in the evening, putting up with inferior accommodation upstairs. We turned in at nine, to prepare for an early start in the morning.

August 26, *Thursday.* Up at 3 a.m. Making a hurried break-fast, we set out at 3.45, our guides leading us on at a very rapid pace, in the hope of catching up the other party, which was better led, and had started a quarter of an hour earlier. Lighted by the now faint rays of the moon, we made our way over a rough and stony steep, till we saw them in the distance, and overtaking them, passed together by the Mooserboden, and soon our feet touched for the first time a moraine at the foot of the Karlinger Glacier. Pre-sently, as we ascended, the rays of the rising sun tinged with rose colour the snow on the heights to our right; and in the purple distance, miles away, but just as if it formed a sheer barrier at the foot of the valley, the Watzmann stood out in striking clearness as we looked back. A light refreshment followed during a brief halt, and still climbing upward we soon struck the snow, to find to our dismay that our guides had left their ropes behind, and had

nothing but a short piece of cord, by which we were tied together at a distance of less than two yards. The cord, instead of
being secured to our waists, was only long enough to be passed
once round the upper part of our left arms, in a running noose,
which, on the only occasion when a footing was difficult, grew
tighter till it threatened to cut the muscle in half. The other
party were better supplied, and in their wake we followed, more
slowly, it is true, because we were obliged to proceed with greater
caution over dangerous portions of the route. Fortunately these
were few—a couple of narrow bridges over a crevasse, and in
descending, where there was no bridge even of snow, an opening
over which we had to jump one by one, aided by our guide's
strong " stock." Our guides were trusting to the example of the
one belonging to the other party, who was a splendid specimen of
humanity *quâ* animal, and knew his business far better than ours.
To keep up with him our leader maintained a rapid pace, to
which at first we were able to respond ; but as the heavy work in
the snow told on his sixty years, Father Lowder was obliged to
ask to be eased. The coldness of the air had told upon him, and
almost taken away his appetite, so that he was physically weaker
from this cause. After a climb of some hours we reached through
the Riffel-Thor our highest point (almost ten thousand feet), where
we waited more than half an hour to take food, and turn to
account the splendid view of a grand mountain panorama, the
main features of which were, of course, the Gross Glockner and its
companions close at hand. The Father now was able to eat with
somewhat better appetite, but on the descent was still conscious
of failing powers in want of precision in striking amid the deep
snow the exact footprints of those who had gone before. At
length we left the snow, and over glacier and moraine trudged
on till the Hofmannshütte was in sight, at the foot of a slope,
where we were able to gather edelweiss. We reached the hut
about 2 p.m., and then the others rested, while I went on with
the guides to order dinner for four o'clock at the Neues Glocknerhaus, built for the use of mountaineers by the Austrian Alpine

Club. The situation of the house, opposite the Gross Glockner, the Father's "old love," and on the edge of the Pastergen Glacier, is unequalled; its accommodation supplies every necessary comfort in most cleanly fashion, and the food, even without hunger-sauce or the keen air, would be found appetizing at any altitude. We had some amusement in the delight of one of our friends at sleeping more than six thousand feet above the level of the sea; and found entries in the visitors' book, interesting or entertaining, one of which, written by an old friend, the Father determined to criticise in an expostulatory postcard. As may be imagined, after our long day's work we went "early to bed."

Of this expedition Mr. Lowder's other companion, Mr. Rumsey says :—

The walk of Thursday, 26th, was with much fatigue to Father Lowder. We started, I think, about 4 a.m., and walked fast at first, as our guides were not up to much, and were anxious to overtake two parties who started a quarter of an hour before us. Father Lowder felt this fast walking, and spoke of it as injudicious in the guides. When we came to the snow (perhaps about 7 a.m.), it appeared that our guides had forgotten their rope, and had borrowed a short and poor bit of box-cord from a place at which we had lunched on Wednesday. This negligence added to our fatigue by forcing us to be tied so close together as almost to tread on one another's heels. We kept up with the two other parties (six people in all) until we reached the top of the pass (about eleven o'clock?). Father Lowder here spoke of feeling painfully the rarity of the air, and henceforward we walked very slowly, allowing the others to go away much faster. At about three o'clock we reached a hut at which four of our late companions were already preparing to make a night, previous to some other ascent next day (two having pushed on). Here we were only one hour from our destination, so Mr. Swallow pushed on with one guide to secure beds for us, while Father

Lowder and I and the other guide waited for an hour or two's rest.

On Friday, while I walked with Swallow, who was leaving us to return to England, Father Lowder walked down to Heiligenblut, about three miles, and back. He had not been able to eat well on Thursday's walk, nor since; but on Saturday he and I went out for a stroll, and he much enjoyed a cold chicken we took with us, and seemed much better.

He wrote to his sister on Friday :—

Neues Glocknerhaus, Heiligenblut, August 27.

MY DEAR MARY,

You know my present standpoint two hours above Heiligenblut, which we reached yesterday. When I wrote from Zell-am-See on Sunday, I told Annie that I would tell you how I got to Zell-am-See. I left Ammergau with Swallow, a curate of Clewer, and walked to Partenkirchen. We had a beautiful walk the next day to the Schlachten Alp, where there is a châlet of the King of Bavaria, with a splendid view of the Wetterstein range. We were joined by Rumsey, Rector of Burnham, Berks, and drove to the Walchensee. Slept there, and next day by lake and road, boating, walking, driving, on by the Kochelsee to Tölz; slept there. By train to Schaftlach; walked to the Tegernsee, where we had two storms, one a grand thunderstorm while rowing on the lake. Then by Stellwagen to Wilbad-Kreut, and Postwagen to Achenkirch; slept there; up at 4 a.m. By Achensee in another storm to Jenbach, and so on to Wörgl; but not finding the portmanteau I had sent by Rose to Munich to forward, I went to Kufstein, but no portmanteau. Rumsey went to Zell-am-See; I followed by a later train. Swallow rejoined us on Sunday. I was not well, so did not start till Wednesday. Had a fine walk to the Rainerhütte in the Kapruner-Thal. Started at 3.45 a.m. over the Riffel-Thor, and a great deal of difficult snow to the Hoffmanshütte right through the heart of the Glockner Gruppe, making up the connection of an excursion I made in 1871, of which I found the record in the book of the Hoffmanshütte. We have had some storms on our way, but nothing to hurt or drive us back. I fear I may have lost my portmanteau with money, £16 or £17, and other things—the small Communion case, etc. Swallow leaves us here, and takes this to Zell-am-See (Krone) Thursday or Friday. I am here with a very small allowance of clothes, as they are in my portmanteau; only socks to change, so I doubt about getting far. I have had very pleasant companions; Rumsey and I remain together for another week.

I send this at once with all good wishes and prayers for your birthday. I have not been down to Heiligenblut for letters, and am going down soon. . . .

Yours very affectionately,
CHARLES.

P.S.—I am very well after very hard work yesterday. Edelweis I picked at Hoffmannshütte.

He was now in the very heart of the country which he had long loved well, and was about to accomplish the most cherished project of this his last tour. It was evident to his companions that "the mountains themselves, and anything connected with them, had grown to be very close to his heart. From Oberstdorf until this last ascent had become an accomplished fact, they formed a constant topic of conversation. At one time he would recur to the past, and detail his experiences of 'Ein und Siebenzig,' the ascent of the Gross Glockner, the climbing of 'drei Spitzen in Einem Tag' (the three peaks being the Bärenkopf, Glöckerin, and Gross Wiesbachhorn)—a feat which sometimes was recounted amid the raised eyebrows and doubting looks of some of our less venturesome guides; his connection with the inauguration of the Hofmannshütte and memorial of Karl Hofmann, a Bavarian soldier-mountaineer, whom he had himself known, and who had fallen at Sedan in 1870, and the courtesy of Herr Stüdl upon that occasion."

Mr. Rumsey notes that when, at Ober-Ammergau, he and Father Lowder planned to get some walking together in the Tyrol, " he specially had in view an ascent of the Gross Venediger from the first." Mr. Rumsey adds :—

On Saturday I walked with Father Lowder on the Upper Pfandl Gletscher, and in the evening we walked down to Heiligenblut. Our accommodation at Heiligenblut for Sunday was very rough, but Father Lowder enjoyed the place, and the church, and a procession of all the villagers. It was a wet afternoon, and a party in the house drinking were rather noisy. It was very striking to hear them suddenly sing the *Angelus*, and then continue their revelry.

On Monday (August 30) we were to have walked only to Kals, and the following day to Windisch Matrei, but it was owing to my evident anxiety to push on that Father Lowder took so long a walk, and then felt unequal to much exertion on Tuesday.

They walked to Windisch Matrei in bad weather on Monday, and on Tuesday Father Lowder rested, in preparation for the ascent next day. He wrote a note to his brother, the last in his own handwriting received by any of his family :—

Windisch Matrei, Austria, August 31.

My dear Willie,

I only got your letter of the 21st yesterday, just as I was leaving Heiligenblut for a nine hours' walk over here. I take advantage of a day's rest to write the enclosed, which you can forward if in time to do any good. Love to Janie. I hope to be home on September 13.

(No signature.)

He enclosed letters to three Charterhouse governors.

Father Lowder and Mr. Rumsey made part of the ascent towards the Gross Venediger on Wednesday, September 1, with one guide, taking luncheon at the Tauernhaus, passing through Gschlöss and sleeping at the Präger Hütte. "He seemed to be very comfortable on that walk," Mr. Rumsey said, "and to enjoy it very much. We bathed about midday (as we often did) in a clear stream." They started next morning at 2 a.m., and Mr. Rumsey notes that Father Lowder "seemed very well during the ascent, and walked briskly and strongly, and with great enjoyment of the morning."

Before sunrise he was on the summit, gazing upon the wonderful panoramic view which for nine years he had longed to see :—

"One crowded hour of glorious life,"

to him who was about to enter into the fulness of life and beauty. Mr. Rumsey writes that "the ascent was in perfect weather ; a sharp frost, and the snow beautifully hard. And the view from the summit was perfect ; the clouds all below in the valleys, but the peaks clear in every direction. We could not stay more than twenty minutes, because of the cold."

After they had gone down a little way, Mr. Rumsey proposed that they should go back, and look once more at the view from the summit. But Father Lowder said, "No, it is a κτῆμα ἐς ἀεί,*—I can never forget it." They reached the hut at 8 a.m., slept there for an hour, and then walked to Gschlöss on the way to Mittersill, bathing, and saying their English matin office in a little chapel.

* "A possession for ever."

Mr. Rumsey was obliged to push on that day to Mittersill, another seven hours' walk ; he persuaded Father Lowder not to attempt to accompany him, on account of the fatigue, and about half a mile from Tauernhaus the friends parted, the guide going on with Mr. Rumsey and carrying Father Lowder's bag, out of which he took bare necessaries for one night. He decided to sleep at Tauernhaus, a tolerable inn where they had dined on Wednesday, and two Austrians, with whom they had made the ascent, were also to sleep there that night, and come on with him to Mittersill next day. Mr. Rumsey afterwards wrote to his sister :—

I felt quite comfortable about him, having persuaded him to take the walk comfortably the next day instead of hurrying on with me. He spoke several times of getting thin with walking, and said that when I was obliged to go, he should go to some place with a good *table d'hôte* and feed up before his return. He was enthusiastically fond of that neighbourhood, and we were taking a course through it which brought him to some of his favourite places, yet in new combinations, so as generally to get over new ground. I quite hoped he had got over his illness, and would, after a little rest, return home refreshed and strengthened.

Of the next few days we know nothing. He must have gone to Mittersill and slept there on Friday, September 3, as he took up his bag and umbrella, which Mr. Rumsey had left there. The visitors' book at the Hotel Krone shows that he arrived at Zell-am-See on September 4,—the head waiter said, in heavy rain. Zell-am-See is four hours' drive from Mittersill, and two coaches run daily between them. The hotel being full, he was sent to the

dépendance close by, a little châlet. They said at the hotel
that on Sunday he came in for his meals and seemed well.
On Monday he remained in his room, and he never left
it ; he sent for the village doctor, who came again on
Tuesday. Then the doctor became ill, and on Wednesday
another doctor came, who told him to keep in bed, and
sent for a nurse. About 2 p.m., Mr. and Mrs. Ffoulkes
Taylor and their two daughters arrived from Salzburg,
intending to stay only one night at Zell. They spent the
afternoon on the lake and in sight-seeing, and their seven
o'clock meal was being prepared, when the head waiter
said he had a favour to ask of Mr. Taylor : would he go to
the châlet *dépendance* and see an English clergyman, who
was ill there, and wanted a letter written for him ? Mr.
Taylor immediately went to him, and he introduced himself as an English clergyman, named Lowder. " Oh, Father
Lowder," Mr. Taylor replied. " I have heard you preach
at Folkestone, and I know your sister Rose." He did not
think from appearances that there was much the matter
except a chill, as Mr. Lowder chatted cheerfully about his
ascent of the Venediger, and the great enjoyment he had
had. After a short visit, Mr. Taylor said he would go back
to the hotel for tea, and return afterwards. Between eight
and nine he came back to the châlet, and wrote from
Father Lowder's dictation the following letter :—

Hotel Krone, Zell-am-See, September 8, 1881.

MY DEAR ANNIE,

I am sorry to have to write by another hand, but I
have been laid up for a few days by a severe attack of colic, brought
on by overstrain in mountaineering, and especially by ascending
the Gross Venediger on Thursday. I have had to call in a doctor,

and I hope I have got some relief, but I shall not be able to get home by the time I had hoped, and may have to stay in Munich to look after my lost portmanteau, which may be stolen. I shall be at Belle Vue, Munich, but the rest must depend on my getting up some strength. Please to write to Mr. Wainwright and say how it is that I shall not be able to get to St. Peter's when I expected. I will write myself as soon as I am able. Mr. Ffoulkes Taylor, a friend of Rose's, is kind enough to write this note. With best love to all,

Your affectionate brother,

CHARLES.

On his return to the hotel Mr. Taylor looked grave, and told his family they must not leave Zell as soon as they had intended. He had left the nurse in attendance, desiring her to send for him if he should be wanted. Between 12 and 1 a.m. he was called up, and told that Mr. Lowder was worse and wished to see him. He went at once, taking his daughter with him, as he could not speak German. Outside the room they found the doctor and the priest, who had been sent for by the nurse, but had not as yet been in the sick room. Mr. Taylor went in alone to Father Lowder. The inflammation had increased, and the doctor thought that he could not live till morning. When Mr. Taylor told him this, he seemed amazed. At his request telegrams were sent to his brother and to his sister: "Charles Lowder is sick; come at once." Mr. Taylor then assisted him to put his signature to some papers of importance, which he told him where to find, and these he gave, with his watch and money, into Mr. Taylor's care. Then he dictated the following words : —

"I leave all my books to my brother, the Rev. W. H. Lowder.

"The little money I have, to my sisters.

"If in consecrated ground, here I wish to be buried; if not, at Chislehurst.

"I send my blessing to the Sisters and clergy in my parish."

Mr. Taylor took the papers and valuables at once to the hotel to be locked up, and his daughter took his place by Father Lowder. She asked him if he would like to see the priest, who was waiting outside, and as he consented, she brought in the priest. He went up to the bed and shook hands with Father Lowder; the nurse left the room. Miss Taylor has related what passed in the following words :—

The priest, a simple but kind man, asked me if he could be of use to confess him. I replied, "That I cannot say; he is a Catholic, but *not* a Roman Catholic." The priest did not seem to know what to do, and tried to explain: "Does he believe in the Pope?" "No," I replied, "not as you believe in him." Mr. Lowder had expressed a wish to be buried *here*, if in consecrated ground, so I asked the priest; but he said it was impossible, as he was not a Roman Catholic. Mr. Lowder being willing to see the priest, I went in with him to interpret (if need be), at my father's wish. He seemed quite able to speak, and in German said he was an Anglican priest, and asked if he could have the blessed Sacrament administered to him. This was not possible. Then Mr. Lowder asked the priest if he would give him his blessing. The priest put on a stole, and said something in Latin which I failed to follow. He then asked Mr. Lowder if he should come in the morning, which was acquiesced in, and as he went out Mr. Lowder turned to me and said in a clear voice, "You are witness that I die in the faith of the Anglican Church, for they may say that I died a *Roman* Catholic;" and I answered, "I am." My father then returned, and I mentioned this incident to him.

Father Lowder then thanked Mr. and Miss Taylor for coming, and shook hands with them. This was his farewell; after this he spoke no more to them, except to mention the prayers and psalms that he wished for. Miss Taylor asked him if he would like any reading or prayers, and he asked for the Penitential Psalms. Mr. Taylor began to read, but as his voice seemed to be too loud for the sick man's nerves, he gave the book to his daughter, and she read the remainder, Father Lowder telling her the number of each. He then wished for the "Prayer for a Happy Death," and a Confession of Sin from the "Vade Mecum." She knelt down, the nurse, who was weeping, holding the candle for her, and read the prayers, Father Lowder joining in the Lord's Prayer. The pain seemed to increase, and he asked for the Commendatory Prayer; they brought him fresh medicine just then, which he took, and then asked again for the prayer, saying "Amen" distinctly at its conclusion. "After that," Miss Taylor said, "he turned his face to the wall, and apparently left this world and its cares, and held communion with his God." He became so quiet that Mr. and Miss Taylor thought he was going to sleep, and left him in charge of the nurse, telling her to call them if there was any change for the worse.

They were summoned at half-past four in the morning, as he was much worse, and had been restless. When they arrived, he was sinking fast, but in perfect peace and rest.

The pain was gone, but mortification had begun, and at five in the morning of September 9, the anniversary of his father's death, he passed away,—so gently, that Miss Taylor could not believe that all was over, and begged a servant who was in the room to bring a looking-glass. But no dimness passed over it—the spirit had returned to God.

" The peasants belonging to the châlet were round the bed," Miss Taylor said, " reverently waiting and praying, and one of them sprinkled the bed with holy water." When the English friends returned, they found flowers all around him, a cross of asters on his breast, and a crucifix, which the priest had sent, in his hands—"his face," they said, " like one of the paintings of the saints of old."

The master of the hotel and all the servants had been kind and thoughtful, and the peasant nurse had been full of real tenderness. Her letter,* written some months afterwards to Father Lowder's sisters, is too beautiful and touching to be withheld from those for whom this record is chiefly written—his friends and mourning parishioners at St. Peter's-in-the-East.

MY DEAR FRIENDS,

I can no longer keep silence, for the thanks I owe you press heavily, though sweetly, on my heart. My dear friends, I thank you a thousand times for all your love and friendliness; you can never be forgotten by me. I can never think of you and of your departed brother, and of the sorrow which pressed so heavily on you in the past year, without many tears.

Yes, my dear sisters and brother in Christ, when I think over all the severe pain which your brother suffered, and his invincible patience, my heart breaks. I thank God that He so ordered it

* Written in German *patois.*

that I should have the honour of nursing so good a priest in his last sickness. When I was summoned to him, what joy it was for me to hear that he was a priest. I was at the time in church at my devotions. I quickly rose up and went to your brother. The doctor was then in the room with him; he gave his patient into my care, and told me how I ought to nurse him. The sick gentleman looked quite imploringly at me. I can well imagine the struggle there must have been in his heart, to feel himself surrounded by strangers, in a strange land. What a hard trial it was for him! I could only weep and pray for him, and offer his great sufferings to God. I spared no trouble, and he expressed his thankfulness to me, the greatest proof that he was satisfied with my services. But all was in vain! he became worse hour by hour; he had already the presentiment that he was going to die. Oh, how my heart trembled when I saw that all was in vain!

It was about eleven o'clock at night that your brother asked me, "Is the doctor gone to bed?" I said, "Yes, sir; shall I call him?" He answered, "Yes." I went for him directly, and he came quickly. Oh, what were my feelings when your brother asked the doctor, "What do you think, doctor? Do you really think there is any more hope? *I* think not. I think it will not last much longer. I must die."

The doctor spoke encouragingly, and tried another prescription, but all was in vain. About twelve o'clock he sent for the English; they arranged everything, and then they prayed, and your brother himself directed them what to pray.

I did for him all I saw he wished. I wiped from his brow the sweat of death, which now covered his face like dew, so that henceforth, O beloved in Christ, I could do nothing else than weep, so deeply did I feel, as I saw him with trembling hands signing his name, and the tears falling down over his face. Oh, how hard it is to die amongst strangers!

He often held me with both hands from the greatness of the pain, for he had very great difficulty in breathing. The English then went back to bed.

When I was again alone with him your brother took nothing but a little water. It was four in the morning, and the Angelus bell sounded loud in that room, and the sick man clasped his hands over his head and gave a deep sigh. Suddenly he turned himself towards me as though he would take hold of me; bowed his head; uttered a loud exclamation, and became unconscious. Then began the death struggle, which your brother victoriously sustained, and then gently fell asleep, and so went up to that place where there is no more grief or tears, to receive his eternal reward. Oh, my never-to-be-forgotten friends, I was convinced that your brother was a good man, for he asked me to place the crucifix at the foot of the bed, that he might see it better. Oh, what joy for me! I prayed to the Mother of God that she would aid him in the last conflict, for she is ever the Mother of the dying.

And after he had departed, I washed him and closed his mouth and eyes; and then we dressed him and laid him on the bed, and I decked him with fresh flowers, and I could not restrain my tears, so grieved I was that he should die in a foreign land. I could not leave him without sorrow, for your brother had so endeared himself to me during his last illness. God ordered it all.

My dear friends, I have a great favour to ask you, if it is possible. I ask for a photograph of your departed brother, or, if you have not one of him, I ask for one of yourself or of your sisters. Who knows if we may yet see each other once more? I am often in spirit in England, in the midst of you. Oh, what pleasure if you will send me a remembrance. Since your departure from Zell I have heard nothing of you. I thought you must either have quite forgotten me, which I cannot be offended at, or you have no suitable memento, which may easily be. I hope, however, to receive one from your kindness, when you have one, which would be dear to me all my life; therefore I pray you to send me something, if it is possible. I beg you earnestly to send me at least an answer quickly. And if you wish, I will send another photograph with my hat on, which I shall be much pleased to do.

2 A

Meanwhile I kiss your hand for your great kindness, and remain,

Your grateful and indebted friend,

MARIA NEUMAIER,

Sick nurse to your brother at Zell-am-See.

There is at Salzburg a convent of the Sisters of Charity, and they have a branch house at Zell-am-See. Here, until his bereaved ones could arrive, the Sisters received into their care all that was mortal of Charles Lowder. He had chosen hardness and toil as his portion in life, and had fought on, faint, yet pursuing ; for He whom he loved and followed is a Man of war. Now, at last, he slept in peace, reverently watched by the daughters of St. Vincent de Paul, the saint whose example had kindled in him that ardour for the battle which burned steadily and brightly to the end.

CHAPTER XXII.

BURIAL.

1880.

"Why march ye forth with hymn and chant,
Ye veteran soldiers jubilant,
As though ye went to lay to rest
Some warrior that had done his best?"

THEY said, who knew the truth, that when the tidings from Zell-am-See reached St. Peter's-in-the-East, and spread through court and alley, there were stricken hearts, in homes so poor and wretched that they might be thought beyond the sympathies of life, crouching over the few embers in the grate, too crushed to speak, almost too crushed to think, but trying to take in the meaning of the words, "Father Lowder's dead."

The telegram, sent at midnight on Wednesday, reached Chislehurst about eight on Thursday morning, September 9. The sisters left England by the first boat after receiving it, travelled three days and two nights without stopping, and arrived at Zell at nine on Saturday night. From Mr. Taylor they learned that their brother had departed before the telegram had reached them. He took them to "The Cloisters," as the Sisters' house is called, where in a mortuary room, with an altar in a recess at one end, the closed coffin lay. Mr. Taylor had caused a piece of glass to be inserted in the lid. Close to this room were the schoolrooms of children taught by the Sisters, beautifully clean, and nicely fitted up. " The view over the lake was lovely from the windows," his sister said, "and we thought how pleased he would have been to see the children so well cared for." The peasants had put a large wreath of flowers on the coffin ; it was brought to England and laid on the grave.

When it was rumoured in the parish that the remains would probably be interred in Austria, on account of the great expense of bringing them to England, the St. Peter's branch of the Church of England Working-Men's Society met, and at once subscribed £30, telegraphing to guarantee all further expenses, and to entreat that nothing might prevent the body of " the Father " from being brought home.

The strain and distress of the parishioners at St. Peter's, and especially of the clergy and Sisters, were greatly increased by the extreme difficulty of arranging for the funeral, as there was no time for anything but telegrams between London and Zell, while hundreds of inquiries were coming in from those, in all parts of England, who wished to attend. At length Friday, September 17, was fixed upon, as it was hoped that the precious burden would arrive on Thursday night. It was to lie all night in the little oratory of the Sisters' house, the first room where he had gathered a few together in the early days of the Calvert Street Mission. But at the last moment, late on Thursday night, a telegram arrived from the mourners at Zell, putting the funeral off till the following Tuesday, as they feared that the body could not arrive even on Friday.

It was impossible now to put off the great numbers of country clergy who were to arrive next morning ; besides, the poor people, at great personal sacrifice and loss, had arranged for a holiday, that they might follow their Vicar to the grave.

His brother had arrived at Zell on Monday, and was now returning to England ; his sisters were also on their way home, but no one knew where they were. So it was determined not to alter arrangements already made. The church was kept open all night, the clergy and people remaining there till near midnight : they had hoped once more to sing Evensong with all that remained of Father Lowder in the midst. The first celebration was at 3 a.m., and many more followed, hundreds of the people communicating. "It was the most solemn sight I ever saw," one said who spent the night at St. Peter's, "the crowds of people in the street that night waiting for news : all poor people, with blanched faces, and the sorrow of their hearts speaking through their eyes ; so quiet and resigned, and not murmuring at this cruel delay, and more cruel suspense ; just hanging about in groups as people do when struck down by a common sorrow. So the night passed, and in the morning we had a telegram from the railway people to say that the coffin would arrive at Holborn Viaduct early that morning."

Even this could not have been managed, but for the affectionate devotion of Mr. Robert Hunt, of the Working-Men's Society, who went to Queenborough on Thursday evening, and spent the night in efforts to arrange that the body should, if it arrived, be sent by the earliest train on Friday. Orders had been given that it should be forwarded by a later train, and it was with the greatest difficulty that Mr. Hunt obtained a reversal of the order. He waited at Queenborough till the vessel came in, and received the sacred charge. It had left Zell on the previous Tuesday, under the care of a trustworthy German.

At the Holborn Viaduct Station it was met by one of the curates of St. Peter's, and two of the Sisters, bringing a pall and flowers, which they laid over the coffin in the hearse, and then followed it to Old Gravel Lane. There, at the point where St. Peter's parish begins, it was received by a solemn procession from the church—his own sister, who had been prevented by illness from going to Zell, with the Sisters of Mercy, and a great white throng of choristers and clergy, led by the cross, passing up the lane through the crowds of weeping people to the dock-bridge, which bounds the parish. Once, during the St. George's riots, his friends had made a line across this bridge, and held it against the mob who had hunted him down, threatening to throw him into the docks; and now, in the streets where he had been pelted and ill-treated, the police were obliged to keep a line amidst the crowds of weeping men who pressed forwards to see and touch the pall beneath which their benefactor slept. The pall-bearers were:—

Rev. F. Benson.	Rev. G. Cosby White.
Rev. H. D. Nihill.	Rev. Bryan King.
Rev. A. H. Mackonochie.	Rev. F. W. Kingsford.
Rev. Harry Jones.	Rev. R. A. J. Suckling.

"Nearly twenty-five years ago," Mr. King writes, "I

received Mr. Lowder, and introduced him into his district amidst all but universal distrust and obloquy; on his funeral day it fell upon me as a pall-bearer to meet his body at the boundary of his parish, and to conduct it to the church between dense crowds of his people, all intently gazing upon his remains with feelings of deep emotion, many giving utterance to that emotion by unrestrained tears."

The coffin was lifted from the hearse and carried by some of the working-men on the bier to St. Peter's Church, followed by the mourners and the immense procession, chanting the funeral sentences, and Psalms xxiv., xxvii., xxxix., and xc. Admittance to the church was by ticket, but every seat had already long been filled. The altar and chancel were vested in white; Father Lowder's stall was covered with white linen, on which his surplice and stole were laid. When the bier was placed in the chancel, it was soon covered with offerings of flowers, handed to the Sisters, while the prayer of the introit arose: "Grant him eternal rest, O Lord, and let light perpetual shine upon him." Then followed the celebration, with the *Dies Iræ* as a sequence. At its close the Sisters took up the flowers from the coffin, and the procession formed once more, and passed out at the western door, singing, "Jerusalem, my happy home," and slowly up to Wapping Bridge, amidst the dense crowd, still singing the hymn. At the bridge, the procession divided and lined each side of the road, while the hearse, in which the coffin had once more been placed, passed slowly through the ranks on the road to Chislehurst, followed by the carriage containing Father Lowder's sister and cousin.

À train to carry six hundred had been engaged for the communicants of St. Peter's, but hundreds besides these set off for Chislehurst, those who were too poor to pay for a ticket on foot. Long before the hearse arrived the church at Chislehurst was crammed, and hundreds were waiting in the churchyard. The scene on Chislehurst Common, when the trains of mourners had arrived from London, was wonderful ; the men of Wapping and Shadwell, whom none will credit with extravagant religious weakness, gathered to manifest their gratitude and affection for the heroic priest who had laboured so long among them. It was computed that at least three thousand were present, including about two hundred clergy.

After a very long delay, the choir of St. Peter's were seen coming from the school-house, where they had vested, across the common to the church, preceding the body, with the same pall-bearers as before, mourners, Sisters, and four or five hundred of the congregation, members of various guilds, chanting the Litany of the Dead. They were met at the lych-gate by the choir and clergy of Chislehurst, and the choirs joined and led the way into church, singing, "Brief life is here our portion." During the hymn, as the coffin was brought into the chancel, the deep unspeakable grief of the people who had lost so good a shepherd broke out in uncontrollable sobs and tears from both men and women.

Once more the procession formed, singing "Light's abode, celestial Salem," on the way to the last resting-place, which is on the north side of the church, exactly on a line with the chancel. The sun was just setting, at the close of a lovely day, as the coffin, covered with flowers, was lowered into the moss-lined grave, the choirs singing, "Brother, now thy toils are over." Slowly and tearfully the multitude of men, women, and children passed round while the Rector of Chislehurst stood by the grave, to take a last look at the resting-place of him they loved.

No such funeral, it was truly said, has been seen in England in modern times. Thanksgiving and the voice of melody in the streets of East London on a working-day, the whole populace turning out, the church adorned in white and beautiful with flowers—all symbolized, not the sorrow of those without hope, but the last and best genuine earthly reward of a good man. But of all grand points in that funeral, certainly the most beautiful and touching was the little children, fringing the crowd, and weeping as if their hearts would break.

So, "with large tears of sorrow and of joy" he was borne, a victor, to his rest. "Of joy"—for though ten years were still lacking to make up the threescore and ten, his work might have filled the fourscore, if measured by the ordinary scale of good men's labour. And they who loved him best, remembering the bright promise of his boyhood and youth, and the worn weary face of later years, could not mourn that the patient, faithful soldier should now wear the crown, and hear his Master's gracious call: "Enter thou into the joy of thy Lord."

———————

There is no need to ask the way to Father Lowder's grave in Chislehurst churchyard; for a path leads to it, worn in the turf by many feet, and, while the grass is green round other graves, it is quite trodden away for a broad space

round the stone kerb which encloses his resting-place. And
though the mark which he has left upon the memories of
all who knew him, even of those who least agreed with his
opinions, is not likely to be soon effaced, the words spoken
about him from the pulpit, on the Sunday after his funeral,
by the Rev. Harry Jones, Rector of St. George's-in-the-East,
will not be thought unwelcome here :—

On divers occasions in the course of my ministry I have been
asked to preach what is called a funeral sermon. No such request
has been made to me now. But if I were to let this Sunday pass
without speaking to you of one who has been so prominently
known in St. George's as Mr. Lowder, I should not be doing what
you expect, and what certainly I desire. It is easy to speak of
him. In divers cases where a clergyman is asked to say something from the pulpit about one who is dead, he is embarrassed
by the thought that, if he did, he would be obliged to introduce
his name to the congregation, and tell them something about him,
before he ventured on such remarks as he could make. That is
needless now. I have no excuses to offer for the bringing in of
personal allusions and details, which, however familiar to the
friends of the dead man, and pathetic when told, have nevertheless to be told.

Mr. Lowder has been in these parts for the long period of
twenty-four years. You know the man and his communication.
He is now, certainly, in all your minds. . . . Sometimes when a
preacher ventures on so delicate a business as a funeral sermon
he has a latent and uncomfortable consciousness that, however
amiable, useful, and conspicuous the departed may have been, the
remembrance of him does not quite fit in with the mystic and
spiritual thoughts which press upon us when we reflect that one
whom we have known in this world has passed into another. It
is possible to deliver an heroic oration over a grave, and yet evade
allusion to that side of human character which shows an interest
in the unseen. But now, in speaking about him who is gone, no

such suspicion of incongruity presents itself. His memory suits
the atmosphere of the house of God. He led this life with the
thought of another ever in his mind. The mention of him meets
the most sacred moods of the soul. He was marked by continuous personal holiness. Those who knew and loved him best
will be able to talk freely of him, as if death did not sharply break
the real course of his life. . . .

Again, when we call to our mind him of whom I now speak,
we see something beside or along with personal holiness. We
see marks of a character which cheers honest souls wherever they
may be found, and which is highly prized in man himself, whoever
he may be; whether among the ministers or hearers of the Word,
whether among the priests or the people. He showed marks of
a character which we value in Churchman or Nonconformist, in
Protestant and Papist, in Christian or in Jew.

Mr. Lowder was perfectly fair. Whether he agreed with you
or not, he never descended to any stratagem. I have, in my
time, come across such a thing as ecclesiastical diplomacy,
whereby one opponent has sought to steal a march or spring
a mine upon another. But he always flew his colours. There
was no smack of theological cunning about him. He ever meant
what he said, and said what he meant. This enabled him
always to take a personally hearty tone with all. His heartiness
was not forced. It was not tainted with a suspicion on the part
of those who witnessed it, that he was affecting an air of cheery
proselytism. No after-taste of pious guile ever spoilt the flavour of
any communications with this man. All felt that he was open
and fair.

With this he combined an equally natural kindliness of tone
towards and about all from whom he differed, or who spoke evil
of him. I never heard him say a bitter word, even when he
might have had an excuse for being sore. Though keenly suscep-
tible, he was enabled to keep his temper in trying positions; and
always carry himself as a Christian and a gentleman. He and I
failed to look at some of the questions which exercise the Church

in the same light, and often found ourselves, so to speak, in different lobbies at gatherings of the clergy and others. We agreed to differ, not, I hope, ever in radical desire to promote the righteousness of God and the well-being of man, but in the way of looking at and using some of the great facts of Christianity. Indeed, there would be something questionable in the thought of perfect accord in opinions among men here. Individuality is one of our most precious possessions. He prized his and I prized mine. But we were always good friends, and I ever found him keeping good faith in controversy, and willing to think the best of those from whom he differed, and, be it added, those from whom he suffered most. He had, moreover, that wholesome sense of humour, even under the most provoking conditions, without which this world and Church would be unbearable.

It was not, however, for these things alone that he will be long remembered here. He was simply fearless. I do not now refer to theological matters, in which he certainly had the courage of his convictions, but to other things which test the mettle of the man. He showed the grit of true courage in times of special social difficulty and distress. Many of you can remember how he carried himself when the cholera came. . . . There are people who, as we say, rise to the occasion in great emergencies, and yet are unable to endure the dull, continuous tug of toilsome ordinary difficulties. It was not so with Mr. Lowder. He not only came to the front and stood to his guns when the enemy Disease suddenly opened fire on the whole parish, but throughout a long period of labour and trial he stayed at his post, and did its daily wearisome work. I am not going to speak ill of the surroundings of St. Peter's, where so many toil honestly to win their bread and do their duty throughout their lives. And yet it has never been so singled out as to be called a social paradise. But while divers of his brethren in the ministry moved from place to place, Mr. Lowder held to St. Peter's. . . . Any one during the last twenty-four years who came to St. Peter's, would have found Mr. Lowder on his thwart in the old boat, with the oar in his hand. And it was a heavy oar to pull.

Still, there he was. There he lived, there he worked, and we might almost say, there he died; for his arm was stretched out ready for the oar again when he was called out of *this* nave of Christ, and left the waves of a troublesome world. He held to his work, though—without incurring the least reproach—he might have found abundant occupation in some other place where the harness was not so heavy, and the circumstances of life were less exhaustive. . . . Much of his work was wearisomely commonplace and heavily uphill. Yet it was eminently missionary work which he did. It needed, and had spent on it, the genuine fire of a holy life, and it has made a mark upon St. Peter's which those who can remember what it once was, know full well.

. . . Moreover, the work in which our neighbour was engaged so long was done in a never-failing kindly spirit towards the neediest, roughest, or most sensitive of those amongst whom he lived. He did not do it doggedly, but heartily. There are people who hold to their posts with a sort of grim tenacity which is more striking than amiable. They grind steadily through their business without professing any love for it. Their work has to be done, and it is done. Much is to be said in praise of this dogged determination, but Mr. Lowder seemed to me to preserve a remarkable elasticity and heartiness in the discharge of what he set himself to do. He never lost his kindly interest for bodies and souls of men within or without the circles of those around him. I need not say he was beloved among the poor amongst whom he administered, and to whom, however ignorant of ecclesiastical nomenclature, he was always Father Lowder, ready to help them in their affliction. They mourn for him with sorrow deeply sincere, for they well know what a loving friend they have lost in him. Those present last Friday, when the body was brought to St. Peter's, on its way to Chislehurst, will never forget that day. It is well to see crowds respectful; it is rather uncommon to see so many men, women, and children in tears. Such a sight speaks not only for him who was mourned, but for those who mourned for him. They must have carried away in their hearts some better sense of self-sacrificing personal holiness. Twenty years ago he entered some of those very streets among the jeers of such as lived there. He has now left them amid their sobs—they laughed when he came, and wept when he left us. They did not sorrow as men without hope, for they felt he was taken away by God to be with Him for ever.

One word in conclusion, from the friend under whom Father Lowder first worked in London :—

"He has gone to his rest, and to the reward promised to the winner of souls. What a reward it will be we may imagine from St. Gregory's aphorism, that 'it is a greater miracle to convert a soul by the preaching of the Word and the consolations of prayer, than to raise a body from the dead.'"

AT ZELL-AM-SEE.
(*From a Sketch by Rev. William Lowder.*)

PRINTED BY
WILLIAM CLOWES AND SONS, LIMITED,
LONDON AND BECCLES.

A LIST OF

C. KEGAN PAUL AND CO.'S

PUBLICATIONS.

7.81.

A LIST OF
C. KEGAN PAUL AND CO.'S
PUBLICATIONS.

ADAMS (F. O.), F.R.G.S.

The History of Japan. From the Earliest Period to the Present Time. New Edition, revised. 2 volumes. With Maps and Plans. Demy 8vo. Cloth, price 21s. each.

ADAMS (W. D.).

Lyrics of Love, from Shakespeare to Tennyson. Selected and arranged by. Fcap. 8vo. Cloth extra, gilt edges, price 3s. 6d.

ADAMSON (H. T.), B.D.

The Truth as it is in Jesus. Crown 8vo. Cloth, price 8s. 6d.

The Three Sevens. Crown 8vo. Cloth, price 5s. 6d.

A. K. H. B.

From a Quiet Place. A New Volume of Sermons. Crown 8vo. Cloth, price 5s.

ALBERT (Mary).

Holland and her Heroes to the year 1585. An Adaptation from Motley's "Rise of the Dutch Republic." Small crown 8vo. Cloth, price, 4s. 6d.

ALLEN (Rev. R.), M.A.

Abraham ; his Life, Times, and Travels, 3,800 years ago. Second Edition. With Map. Post 8vo. Cloth, price 6s.

ALLEN (Grant), B.A.

Physiological Æsthetics. Large post 8vo. 9s.

ALLIES (T. W.), M.A.

Per Crucem ad Lucem. The Result of a Life. 2 vols. Demy 8vo. Cloth, price 25s.

A Life's Decision. Crown 8vo. Cloth, price 7s. 6d.

AMATEUR.

A Few Lyrics. Small crown 8vo. Cloth, price 2s.

ANDERSON (Col. R. P.).

Victories and Defeats. An Attempt to explain the Causes which have led to them. An Officer's Manual. Demy 8vo. Cloth, price 14s.

ANDERSON (R. C.), C.E.

Tables for Facilitating the Calculation of every Detail in connection with Earthen and Masonry Dams. Royal 8vo. Cloth, price £2 2s.

Antiope. A Tragedy. Large crown 8vo. Cloth, price 6s.

ARCHER (Thomas).

About my Father's Business. Work amidst the Sick, the Sad, and the Sorrowing. Crown 8vo. Cloth, price 2s. 6d.

ARMSTRONG (Richard A.), B.A.

Latter-Day Teachers. Six Lectures. Small crown 8vo. Cloth, price 2s. 6d.

Army of the North German Confederation.

A Brief Description of its Organization, of the Different Branches of the Service and their *rôle* in War, of its Mode of Fighting, &c. &c. Translated from the Corrected Edition, by permission of the Author, by Colonel Edward Newdigate. Demy 8vo. Cloth, price 5s.

ARNOLD (Arthur).

Social Politics. Demy 8vo. Cloth, price 14s.

Free Land. Crown 8vo. Cloth, price 6s.

AUBERTIN (J. J.).

Camoens' Lusiads. Portuguese Text, with Translation by. With Map and Portraits. 2 vols. Demy 8vo. Price 30s.

Seventy Sonnets of Camoens'. Portuguese text and translation, with some original poems. Dedicated to Captain Richard F. Burton. Printed on hand-made paper. Cloth, bevelled boards, gilt top, price 7s. 6d.

Aunt Mary's Bran Pie. By the author of "St. Olave's." Illustrated. Cloth, price 3s. 6d.

AVIA.

The Odyssey of Homer Done into English Verse. Fcap. 4to. Cloth, price 15s.

BADGER (George Perry), D.C.L.

An English-Arabic Lexicon. In which the equivalents for English words and idiomatic sentences are rendered into literary and colloquial Arabic. Royal 4to. Cloth, price £9 9s.

BAGEHOT (Walter).

Some Articles on the Depreciation of Silver, and Topics connected with it. Demy 8vo. Price 5s.

The English Constitution. A New Edition, Revised and Corrected, with an Introductory Dissertation on Recent Changes and Events. Crown 8vo. Cloth, price 7s. 6d.

Lombard Street. A Description of the Money Market. Seventh Edition. Crown 8vo. Cloth, price 7s. 6d.

BAGOT (Alan).

Accidents in Mines: their Causes and Prevention. Crown 8vo. Cloth, price 6s.

BAKER (Sir Sherston, Bart.).

Halleck's International Law; or Rules Regulating the Intercourse of States in Peace and War. A New Edition, Revised, with Notes and Cases. 2 vols. Demy 8vo. Cloth, price 38s.

BAKER (Sir Sherston, Bart.)— *continued.*

The Laws relating to Quarantine. Crown 8vo. Cloth, price 12s. 6d.

BALDWIN (Capt. J. H.), F.Z.S.

The Large and Small Game of Bengal and the North-Western Provinces of India. 4to. With numerous Illustrations. Second Edition. Cloth, price 21s.

BANKS (Mrs. G. L.).

God's Providence House. New Edition. Crown 8vo. Cloth, price 3s. 6d.

Ripples and Breakers. Poems. Square 8vo. Cloth, price 5s.

BARLEE (Ellen).

Locked Out: a Tale of the Strike. With a Frontispiece. Royal 16mo. Cloth, price 1s. 6d.

BARNES (William).

An Outline of English Speechcraft. Crown 8vo. Cloth, price 4s.

Poems of Rural Life, in the Dorset Dialect. New Edition, complete in 1 vol. Crown 8vo. Cloth, price 8s. 6d.

Outlines of Redecraft (Logic). With English Wording. Crown 8vo. Cloth, price 3s.

BARTLEY (George C. T.).

Domestic Economy: Thrift in Every Day Life. Taught in Dialogues suitable for Children of all ages. Small crown 8vo. Cloth, limp, 2s.

BAUR (Ferdinand), Dr. Ph.

A Philological Introduction to Greek and Latin for Students. Translated and adapted from the German of. By C. KEGAN PAUL, M.A. Oxon., and the Rev. E. D. STONE, M.A., late Fellow of King's College, Cambridge, and Assistant Master at Eton. Second and revised edition. Crown 8vo. Cloth, price 6s.

BAYNES (Rev. Canon R. H.).

At the Communion Time. A Manual for Holy Communion. With a preface by the Right Rev.

BAYNES (Rev. Canon R. H.)—
continued.
the Lord Bishop of Derry and
Raphoe. Cloth, price 1s. 6d.
*** Can also be had bound in
French morocco, price 2s. 6d.; Per-
sian morocco, price 3s.; Calf, or
Turkey morocco, price 3s. 6d.

BELLINGHAM (Henry), Barrister-at-Law.
Social Aspects of Catholi-
cism and Protestantism in their
Civil Bearing upon Nations.
Translated and adapted from the
French of M. le Baron de Haulle-
ville. With a Preface by His Eminence Cardinal Manning. Second
and cheaper edition. Crown 8vo.
Cloth, price 3s. 6d.

BENNETT (Dr. W. C.).
Narrative Poems & Ballads.
Fcap. 8vo. Sewed in Coloured Wrap-
per, price 1s.

Songs for Sailors. Dedicated
by Special Request to H. R. H. the
Duke of Edinburgh. With Steel
Portrait and Illustrations. Crown
8vo. Cloth, price 3s. 6d.
An Edition in Illustrated Paper
Covers, price 1s.

Songs of a Song Writer.
Crown 8vo. Cloth, price 6s.

BENT (J. Theodore).
Genoa. How the Republic
Rose and Fell. With 18 Illustra-
tions. Demy 8vo. Cloth, price 18s.

BETHAM - EDWARDS (Miss
M.).
Kitty. With a Frontispiece.
Crown 8vo. Cloth, price 6s.

BEVINGTON (L. S.).
Key Notes. Small crown
8vo. Cloth, price 5s.

Blue Roses; or, Helen Mali-
nofska's Marriage. By the Author
of "Véra." 2 vols. Fifth Edition.
Cloth, gilt tops, 12s.
*** Also a Cheaper Edition in 1
vol. With Frontispiece. Crown 8vo.
Cloth, price 6s.

BLUME (Major W.).
The Operations of the
German Armies in France, from
Sedan to the end of the war of 1870-

BLUME (Major W.)—continued.
71. With Map. From the Journals
of the Head-quarters Staff. Translated by the late E. M. Jones, Maj.
20th Foot, Prof. of Mil. Hist., Sand-
hurst. Demy 8vo. Cloth, price 9s.

BOGUSLAWSKI (Capt. A. von).
Tactical Deductions from
the War of 1870-71. Translated
by Colonel Sir Lumley Graham,
Bart., late 18th (Royal Irish) Regiment. Third Edition, Revised and
Corrected. Demy 8vo. Cloth, price
7s.

BONWICK (J.), F.R.G.S.
Egyptian Belief and Mo-
dern Thought. Large post 8vo.
Cloth, price 10s. 6d.
Pyramid Facts and Fan-
cies. Crown 8vo. Cloth, price 5s.
The Tasmanian Lily. With
Frontispiece. Crown 8vo. Cloth,
price 5s.
Mike Howe, the Bushranger
of Van Diemen's Land. With
Frontispiece. New and cheaper
edition. Crown 8vo. Cloth, price
3s. 6d.

BOWEN (H. C.), M. A.
English Grammar for Be-
ginners. Fcap. 8vo. Cloth, price 1s.
Studies in English, for the
use of Modern Schools. Small crown
8vo. Cloth, price 1s. 6d.
Simple English Poems.
English Literature for Junior Classes.
In Four Parts. Parts I. and II., price
6d. each, now ready.

BOWRING (Sir John).
Autobiographical Recollections.
With Memoir by Lewin B. Bowring.
Demy 8vo. Price 14s.

Brave Men's Footsteps.
By the Editor of "Men who have
Risen." A Book of Example and
Anecdote for Young People. With
Four Illustrations by C. Doyle.
Sixth Edition. Crown 8vo. Cloth,
price 3s. 6d.

BRIALMONT (Col. A.).
Hasty Intrenchments.
Translated by Lieut. Charles A.
Empson, R. A. With Nine Plates.
Demy 8vo. Cloth, price 6s.

BRIDGETT (Rev. J. E.).
History of the Holy Eucharist in Great Britain. 2 vols., demy 8vo. Cloth, price 18s.

BRODRICK (The Hon. G. C.).
Political Studies. Demy 8vo. Cloth, price 14s.

BROOKE (Rev. S. A.), M. A.
The Late Rev. F. W. Robertson, M.A., Life and Letters of. Edited by.
  I. Uniform with the Sermons. 2 vols. With Steel Portrait. Price 7s. 6d.
  II. Library Edition. 8vo. With Portrait. Price 12s.
  III. A Popular Edition, in 1 vol. 8vo. Price 6s.

The Spirit of the Christian Life. A New Volume of Sermons. Crown 8vo. Cloth, price 7s. 6d.

Theology in the English Poets. — COWPER, COLERIDGE, WORDSWORTH, and BURNS. Fourth and Cheaper Edition. Post 8vo. Cloth, price 5s.

Christ in Modern Life. Fifteenth and Cheaper Edition. Crown 8vo. Cloth, price 5s.

Sermons. First Series. Eleventh Edition. Crown 8vo. Cloth, price 6s.

Sermons. Second Series. Fourth Edition. Crown 8vo. Cloth, price 7s.

The Fight of Faith. Sermons preached on various occasions. Fifth Edition. Crown 8vo. Cloth, price 7s. 6d.

BROOKE (W. G.), M. A.
The Public Worship Regulation Act. With a Classified Statement of its Provisions, Notes, and Index. Third Edition, Revised and Corrected. Crown 8vo. Cloth, price 3s. 6d.

Six Privy Council Judgments—1850-1872. Annotated by. Third Edition. Crown 8vo. Cloth, price 9s.

BROUN (J. A.).
Magnetic Observations at Trevandrum and Augustia Malley. Vol. I. 4to. Cloth, price 63s.
  The Report from above, separately sewed, price 21s.

BROWN (Rev. J. Baldwin).
The Higher Life. Its Reality, Experience, and Destiny. Fifth and Cheaper Edition. Crown 8vo. Cloth, price 5s.

Doctrine of Annihilation in the Light of the Gospel of Love. Five Discourses. Third Edition. Crown 8vo. Cloth, price 2s. 6d.

The Christian Policy of Life. A Book for Young Men of Business. New and Cheaper Edition. Crown 8vo. Cloth, price 3s. 6d.

BROWN (J. Croumbie), LL.D.
Reboisement in France; or, Records of the Replanting of the Alps, the Cevennes, and the Pyrenees with Trees, Herbage, and Bush. Demy 8vo. Cloth, price 12s. 6d.

The Hydrology of Southern Africa. Demy 8vo. Cloth, price 10s. 6d.

BROWNE (W. R.).
The Inspiration of the New Testament. With a Preface by the Rev. J. P. NORRIS, D.D. Fcap. 8vo. Cloth, price 2s. 6d.

BRYANT (W. C.)
Poems. Red-line Edition. With 24 Illustrations and Portrait of the Author. Crown 8vo. Cloth extra, price 7s. 6d.
  A Cheaper Edition, with Frontispiece. Small crown 8vo. Cloth, price 3s. 6d.

BURCKHARDT (Jacob).
The Civilization of the Period of the Renaissance in Italy. Authorized translation, by S. G. C. Middlemore. 2 vols. Demy 8vo. Cloth, price 24s.

BURTON (Mrs. Richard).
The Inner Life of Syria, Palestine, and the Holy Land. With Maps, Photographs, and Coloured Plates. 2 vols. Second Edition. Demy 8vo. Cloth, price 24s.
  ₊ Also a Cheaper Edition in one volume. Large post 8vo. Cloth, price 10s. 6d.

BURTON (Capt. Richard F.).
The Gold Mines of Midian and the Ruined Midianite Cities. A Fortnight's Tour in

BURTON (Capt. Richard F.)— *continued.*

North Western Arabia. With numerous Illustrations. Second Edition. Demy 8vo. Cloth, price 18s.

The Land of Midian Revisited. With numerous illustrations on wood and by Chromolithography. 2 vols. Demy 8vo. Cloth, price 32s.

BUSBECQ (Ogier Ghiselin de). **His Life and Letters.** By Charles Thornton Forster, M.D. and F. H. Blackburne Daniell, M.D. 2 vols. With Frontispieces. Demy 8vo. Cloth, price 24s.

BUTLER (Alfred J.). **Amaranth and Asphodel.** Songs from the Greek Anthology.— I. Songs of the Love of Women. II. Songs of the Love of Nature. III. Songs of Death. IV. Songs of Hereafter. Small crown 8vo. Cloth, price 2s.

BYRNNE (E. Fairfax). **Milicent.** A Poem. Small crown 8vo. Cloth, price 6s.

CALDERON. **Calderon's Dramas:** The Wonder-Working Magician—Life is a Dream—The Purgatory of St. Patrick. Translated by Denis Florence MacCarthy. Post 8vo. Cloth, price 10s.

CANDLER (H.). **The Groundwork of Belief.** Crown 8vo. Cloth, price 7s.

CARPENTER (W. B.), M.D. **The Principles of Mental Physiology.** With their Applications to the Training and Discipline of the Mind, and the Study of its Morbid Conditions. Illustrated. Fifth Edition. 8vo. Cloth, price 12s.

CARPENTER (Dr. Philip P.). **His Life and Work.** Edited by his brother, Russell Lant Carpenter. With portrait and vignette. Second Edition. Crown 8vo. Cloth, price 7s. 6d.

CAVALRY OFFICER. **Notes on Cavalry Tactics, Organization,** &c. With Diagrams Demy 8vo. Cloth, price 12s.

CERVANTES. **The Ingenious Knight Don Quixote de la Mancha.** A New Translation from the Originals of 1605 and 1608. By A. J. Duffield. With Notes. 3 vols. demy 8vo. Cloth, price 42s.

CHAPMAN (Hon. Mrs. E. W.). **A Constant Heart.** A Story. 2 vols. Cloth, gilt tops, price 12s.

CHEYNE (Rev. T. K.). **The Prophecies of Isaiah.** Translated, with Critical Notes and Dissertations by. Two vols., demy 8vo. Cloth, price 25s.

Children's Toys, and some Elementary Lessons in General Knowledge which they teach. Illustrated. Crown 8vo. Cloth, price 5s.

Clairaut's Elements of Geometry. Translated by Dr. Kaines, with 145 figures. Crown 8vo. Cloth, price 4s. 6d

CLARKE (Mary Cowden). **Honey from the Weed.** Crown 8vo. Cloth, price 7s.

CLAYDEN (P. W.). **England under Lord Beaconsfield.** The Political History of the Last Six Years, from the end of 1873 to the beginning of 1880. Second Edition. With Index, and Continuation to March, 1880. Demy 8vo. Cloth, price 16s.

CLERY (C.), Lieut.-Col. **Minor Tactics.** With 26 Maps and Plans. Fifth and Revised Edition. Demy 8vo. Cloth, price 16s.

CLODD (Edward), F.R.A.S. **The Childhood of the World: a Simple Account of Man** in Early Times. Sixth Edition. Crown 8vo. Cloth, price 3s.
A Special Edition for Schools. Price 1s.

The Childhood of Religions. Including a Simple Account of the Birth and Growth of Myths and Legends. Third Thousand. Crown 8vo. Cloth, price 5s.
A Special Edition for Schools Price 1s. 6d.

CLODD (Edward), F.R.A.S.—
continued.
Jesus of Nazareth. With a
brief Sketch of Jewish History to
the Time of His Birth. Small
crown 8vo. Cloth, price 6s.

COGHLAN (J. Cole), D.D.
The Modern Pharisee and
other Sermons. Edited by the
Very Rev. A. H. Dickinson, D.D.,
Dean of Chapel Royal, Dublin. New
and cheaper edition. Crown 8vo.
Cloth, price 7s. 6d.

COLERIDGE (Sara).
Pretty Lessons in Verse
for Good Children, with some
Lessons in Latin, in Easy Rhyme.
A New Edition. Illustrated. Fcap.
8vo. Cloth, price 3s. 6d.

Phantasmion. A Fairy Tale.
With an Introductory Preface by the
Right Hon. Lord Coleridge, of
Ottery St. Mary. A New Edition.
Illustrated. Crown 8vo. Cloth,
price 7s. 6d.

Memoir and Letters of Sara
Coleridge. Edited by her Daughter.
Cheap Edition. With one Portrait.
Cloth, price 7s. 6d.

COLLINS (Mortimer).
The Secret of Long Life.
Small crown 8vo. Cloth, price 3s. 6d.
Inn of Strange Meetings,
and other Poems. Crown 8vo.
Cloth, price 5s.

COLOMB (Colonel).
The Cardinal Archbishop.
A Spanish Legend in twenty-nine
Cancions. Small crown 8vo. Cloth,
price 5s.

CONNELL (A. K.).
Discontent and Danger in
India. Small crown 8vo. Cloth,
price 3s. 6d.

CONWAY (Hugh).
A Life's Idylls. Small crown
8vo. Cloth, price 3s. 6d.

COOKE (Prof. J. P.)
Scientific Culture. Crown
8vo. Cloth, price 1s.

COOPER (H. J.).
The Art of Furnishing on
Rational and Æsthetic Prin-
ciples. New and Cheaper Edition.
Fcap. 8vo. Cloth, price 1s. 6d.

COPPÉE (François).
L'Exilée. Done into English
Verse with the sanction of the Author
by I. O. L. Crown 8vo. Vellum,
price 5s.

CORFIELD (Prof.), M.D.
Health. Crown 8vo. Cloth,
price 6s.

CORY (William).
A Guide to Modern Eng-
lish History. Part I. MDCCCXV.
—MDCCCXXX. Demy 8vo. Cloth,
price 9s.

COURTNEY (W. L.).
The Metaphysics of John
Stuart Mill. Crown 8vo. Cloth,
price 5s. 6d.

COWAN (Rev. William).
Poems : Chiefly Sacred, in-
cluding Translations from some
Ancient Latin Hymns. Fcap. 8vo.
Cloth, price 5s.

COX (Rev. Sir G. W.), Bart.
A History of Greece from
the Earliest Period to the end of the
Persian War. New Edition. 2 vols.
Demy 8vo. Cloth, price 36s.

The Mythology of the
Aryan Nations. New Edition. 2
vols. Demy 8vo. Cloth, price 28s.

A General History of Greece
from the Earliest Period to the Death
of Alexander the Great, with a sketch
of the subsequent History to the
present time. New Edition. Crown
8vo. Cloth, price 7s. 6d.

Tales of Ancient Greece.
New Edition. Small crown 8vo
Cloth, price 6s.

School History of Greece.
With Maps. New Edition. Fcap
8vo. Cloth, price 3s. 6d.

The Great Persian War
from the Histories of Herodotus.
New Edition. Fcap. 8vo. Cloth,
price 3s. 6d.

A Manual of Mythology
in the form of Question and Answer
New Edition. Fcap. 8vo. Cloth,
price 3s.

An Introduction to the
Science of Comparative Mythology and Folk-Lore. Large
crown 8vo. Cloth, price 9s.

COX (Rev. Sir G. W.), Bart., M.A., and EUSTACE HINTON JONES.

Popular Romances of the Middle Ages. Second Edition in one volume. Crown 8vo. Cloth, price 6s.

COX (Rev. Samuel).

A Commentary on the Book of Job. With a Translation. Demy 8vo. Cloth, price 15s.

Salvator Mundi ; or, Is Christ the Saviour of all Men? Sixth Edition. Crown 8vo. Cloth, price 5s.

The Genesis of Evil, and other Sermons, mainly Expository. Second Edition. Crown 8vo. Cloth, price 6s.

CRAUFURD (A. H.).

Seeking for Light : Sermons. Crown 8vo. Cloth, price 5s.

CRAVEN (Mrs.).

A Year's Meditations. Crown 8vo. Cloth, price 6s.

CRAWFURD (Oswald).

Portugal, Old and New. With Illustrations and Maps. Demy 8vo. Cloth, price 16s.

CRESSWELL (Mrs. G.).

The King's Banner. Drama in Four Acts. Five Illustrations. 4to. Cloth, price 10s. 6d.

CROZIER (John Beattie), M.B.

The Religion of the Future. Crown 8vo. Cloth, price 6s.

DALTON (John Neale), M.A., R.N.

Sermons to Naval Cadets. Preached on board H.M.S. "Britannia." Second Edition. Small crown 8vo. Cloth, price 3s. 6d.

D'ANVERS (N. R.).

Parted. A Tale of Clouds and Sunshine. With 4 Illustrations. Extra Fcap. 8vo. Cloth, price 3s. 6d.

Little Minnie's Troubles. An Every-day Chronicle. With Four Illustrations by W. H. Hughes. Fcap. Cloth, price 3s. 6d.

D'ANVERS (N. R)—*continued.*

Pixie's Adventures ; or, the Tale of a Terrier. With 21 Illustrations. 16mo. Cloth, price 4s. 6d.

Nanny's Adventures ; or, the Tale of a Goat. With 12 Illustrations. 16mo. Cloth, price 4s. 6d.

DAVIDSON (Rev. Samuel), D.D., LL.D.

The New Testament, translated from the Latest Greek Text of Tischendorf. A New and thoroughly Revised Edition. Post 8vo. Cloth, price 10s. 6d.

Canon of the Bible : Its Formation, History, and Fluctuations. Third Edition, revised and enlarged. Small crown 8vo. Cloth, price 5s.

DAVIES (G. Christopher).

Rambles and Adventures of Our School Field Club. With Four Illustrations. Crown 8vo. Cloth, price 5s.

DAVIES (Rev. J. L.), M.A.

Theology and Morality. Essays on Questions of Belief and Practice. Crown 8vo. Cloth, price 7s. 6d.

DAVIES (T. Hart.).

Catullus. Translated into English Verse. Crown 8vo. Cloth, price 6s.

DAWSON (George), M.A.

Prayers, with a Discourse on Prayer. Edited by his Wife. Fifth Edition. Crown 8vo. Price 6s.

Sermons on Disputed Points and Special Occasions. Edited by his Wife. Third Edition. Crown 8vo. Cloth, price 6s.

Sermons on Daily Life and Duty. Edited by his Wife. Second Edition. Crown 8vo. Cloth, price 6s.

DE L'HOSTE (Col. E. P.).

The Desert Pastor, Jean Jarousseau. Translated from the French of Eugène Pelletan. With a Frontispiece. New Edition. Fcap. 8vo. Cloth, price 3s. 6d.

DE REDCLIFFE (Viscount Stratford), P.C., K.G., G.C.B.
Why am I a Christian? Fifth Edition. Crown 8vo. Cloth, price 3s.

DESPREZ (Philip S.).
Daniel and John; or, the Apocalypse of the Old and that of the New Testament. Demy 8vo. Cloth, price 12s.

DE TOCQUEVILLE (A.).
Correspondence and Conversations of, with Nassau William Senior, from 1834 to 1859. Edited by M. C. M. Simpson. 2 vols. Post 8vo. Cloth, price 21s.

DE VERE (Aubrey).
Legends of the Saxon Saints. Small crown 8vo. Cloth, price 6s.

Alexander the Great. A Dramatic Poem. Small crown 8vo. Cloth, price 5s.

The Infant Bridal, and other Poems. A New and Enlarged Edition. Fcap. 8vo. Cloth, price 7s. 6d.

The Legends of St. Patrick, and other Poems. Small crown 8vo. Cloth, price 5s.

St. Thomas of Canterbury. A Dramatic Poem. Large fcap. 8vo. Cloth, price 5s.

Antar and Zara: an Eastern Romance. INISFAIL, and other Poems, Meditative and Lyrical. Fcap. 8vo. Price 6s.

The Fall of Rora, the Search after Proserpine, and other Poems, Meditative and Lyrical. Fcap. 8vo. Price 6s.

DOBELL (Mrs. Horace).
Ethelstone, Eveline, and other Poems. Crown 8vo. Cloth, price 6s.

DOBSON (Austin).
Vignettes in Rhyme and Vers de Société. Third Edition. Fcap. 8vo. Cloth, price 5s.

Proverbs in Porcelain. By the Author of "Vignettes in Rhyme." Second Edition. Crown 8vo. 6s.

Dorothy. A Country Story in Elegiac Verse. With Preface. Demy 8vo. Cloth, price 5s.

DOWDEN (Edward), LL.D.
Shakspere: a Critical Study of his Mind and Art. Fifth Edition. Large post 8vo. Cloth, price 12s.

Studies in Literature, 1789-1877. Large post 8vo. Cloth, price 12s.

Poems. Second Edition. Fcap. 8vo. Cloth, price 5s.

DOWNTON (Rev. H.), M.A.
Hymns and Verses. Original and Translated. Small crown 8vo. Cloth, price 3s. 6d.

DREWRY (G. O.), M.D.
The Common-Sense Management of the Stomach. Fifth Edition. Fcap. 8vo. Cloth, price 2s. 6d.

DREWRY (G. O.), M.D., and BARTLETT (H. C.), Ph.D., F.C.S.
Cup and Platter: or, Notes on Food and its Effects. New and cheaper Edition. Small 8vo. Cloth, price 1s. 6d.

DRUMMOND (Miss).
Tripps Buildings. A Study from Life, with Frontispiece. Small crown 8vo. Cloth, price 3s. 6d.

DUFFIELD (A. J.).
Don Quixote. His Critics and Commentators. With a Brief Account of the Minor Works of Miguel de Cervantes Saavedra, and a statement of the end and aim of the greatest of them all. A Handy Book for General Readers. Crown 8vo. Cloth, price 3s. 6d.

DU MONCEL (Count).
The Telephone, the Microphone, and the Phonograph. With 74 Illustrations. Small crown 8vo. Cloth, price 5s.

DUTT (Toru).
A Sheaf Gleaned in French Fields. New Edition, with Portrait. Demy 8vo. Cloth, price 10s. 6d.

A 2

DU VERNOIS (Col. von Verdy).

Studies in leading Troops.
An authorized and accurate Translation by Lieutenant H. J. T. Hildyard, 71st Foot. Parts I. and II. Demy 8vo. Cloth, price 7s.

EDEN (Frederick).

The Nile without a Dragoman. Second Edition. Crown 8vo. Cloth, price 7s. 6d.

EDGEWORTH (F. Y.).

Mathematical Psychics: an Essay on the Application of Mathematics to Social Science. Demy 8vo. Cloth, price 7s. 6d.

EDIS (Robert W.).

Decoration and Furniture of Town Houses. A series of Cantor Lectures delivered before the Society of Arts, 1880. Amplified and enlarged, with 29 full-page Illustrations and numerous sketches. Second Edition. Square 8vo. Cloth, price 12s. 6d.

EDMONDS (Herbert).

Well Spent Lives : a Series of Modern Biographies. Crown 8vo Price 5s.

Educational Code of the Prussian Nation, in its Present Form. In accordance with the Decisions of the Common Provincial Law, and with those of Recent Legislation. Crown 8vo. Cloth, price 2s. 6d.

EDWARDS (Rev. Basil).

Minor Chords; or, Songs for the Suffering: a Volume of Verse. Fcap. 8vo. Cloth, price 3s. 6d. ; paper, price 2s. 6d.

ELLIOT (Lady Charlotte).

Medusa and other Poems. Crown 8vo. Cloth, price 6s.

ELLIOTT (Ebenezer), The Corn Law Rhymer.

Poems. Edited by his Son, the Rev. Edwin Elliott, of St. John's, Antigua. 2 vols. Crown 8vo. Cloth, price 18s.

ELSDALE (Henry).

Studies in Tennyson's Idylls. Crown 8vo. Cloth, price 5s.

ELYOT (Sir Thomas).

The Boke named the Go- uernour. Edited from the First Edition of 1531 by Henry Herbert Stephen Croft, M.A., Barrister-at-Law. With Portraits of Sir Thomas and Lady Elyot, copied by permission of her Majesty from Holbein's Original Drawings at Windsor Castle. 2 vols. fcap. 4to. Cloth, price 50s.

Epic of Hades (The).
By the author of "Songs of Two Worlds." Twelfth Edition. Fcap. 8vo. Cloth, price 7s. 6d.
*** Also an Illustrated Edition with seventeen full-page designs in photomezzotint by GEORGE R. CHAPMAN. 4to. Cloth, extra gilt leaves, price 25s, and a Large Paper Edition, with portrait, price 10s. 6d.

EVANS (Anne).

Poems and Music. With Memorial Preface by Ann Thackeray Ritchie. Large crown 8vo. Cloth, price 7s. 6d.

EVANS (Mark).

The Gospel of Home Life. Crown 8vo. Cloth, price 4s. 6d.

The Story of our Father's Love, told to Children. Fourth and Cheaper Edition. With Four Illustrations. Fcap. 8vo. Cloth, price 1s. 6d.

A Book of Common Prayer and Worship for Household Use, compiled exclusively from the Holy Scriptures. New and Cheaper Edition. Fcap. 8vo. Cloth, price 1s.

The King's Story Book. In three parts. Fcap. 8vo. Cloth, price 1s. 6d. each.
*** Parts I. and II., with eight illustrations and two Picture Maps, now ready.

EX-CIVILIAN.

Life in the Mofussil; or, Civilian Life in Lower Bengal. 2 vols. Large post 8vo. Price 14s.

FARQUHARSON (M.).

I. Elsie Dinsmore. Crown 8vo. Cloth, price 3s. 6d.

FARQUHARSON (M.)—*continued.*

II. Elsie's Girlhood. Crown 8vo. Cloth, price 3s. 6d.

III. Elsie's Holidays at Roselands. Crown 8vo. Cloth, price 3s. 6d.

FELKIN (H. M.).
Technical Education in a Saxon Town. Published for the City and Guilds of London Institute for the Advancement of Technical Education. Demy 8vo. Cloth, price 2s.

FIELD (Horace), B.A. Lond.
The Ultimate Triumph of Christianity. Small crown 8vo. Cloth, price 3s. 6d.

FINN (the late James), M.R.A.S.
Stirring Times; or, Records from Jerusalem Consular Chronicles of 1853 to 1856. Edited and Compiled by his Widow. With a Preface by the Viscountess STRANGFORD. 2 vols. Demy 8vo. Price 30s.

FLOREDICE (W. H.).
A Month among the Mere Irish. Small crown 8vo. Cloth, price 5s.

Folkestone Ritual Case (The). The Argument, Proceedings Judgment, and Report, revised by the several Counsel engaged. Demy 8vo. Cloth, price 25s.

FORMBY (Rev. Henry).
Ancient Rome and its Connection with the Christian Religion : an Outline of the History of the City from its First Foundation down to the Erection of the Chair of St. Peter, A.D. 42-47. With numerous Illustrations of Ancient Monuments, Sculpture, and Coinage, and of the Antiquities of the Christian Catacombs. Royal 4to. Cloth extra, price 50s. Roxburgh, half-morocco, price 52s. 6d.

FOWLE (Rev. T. W.), M.A.
The Reconciliation of Religion and Science. Being Essays on Immortality, Inspiration, Miracles, and the Being of Christ. Demy 8vo. Cloth, price 10s. 6d.

The Divine Legation of Christ. Crown 8vo. Cloth, price 7s.

FRASER (Donald).
Exchange Tables of Sterling and Indian Rupee Currency, upon a new and extended system, embracing Values from One Farthing to One Hundred Thousand Pounds, and at Rates progressing, in Sixteenths of a Penny, from 1s. 9d. to 2s. 3d. per Rupee. Royal 8vo. Cloth, price 10s. 6d.

FRISWELL (J. Hain).
The Better Self. Essays for Home Life. Crown 8vo. Cloth, price 6s.

One of Two; or, A Left-Handed Bride. With a Frontispiece. Crown 8vo. Cloth, price 3s. 6d.

GARDINER (Samuel R.) and J. BASS MULLINGER, M.A.
Introduction to the Study of English History. Large crown 8vo. Cloth, price 9s.

GARDNER (J.), M.D.
Longevity: The Means of Prolonging Life after Middle Age. Fourth Edition, Revised and Enlarged. Small crown 8vo. Cloth, price 4s.

GARRETT (E.).
By Still Waters. A Story for Quiet Hours. With Seven Illustrations. Crown 8vo. Cloth, price 6s.

GEBLER (Karl Von).
Galileo Galilei and the Roman Curia, from Authentic Sources. Translated with the sanction of the Author, by Mrs. GEORGE STURGE. Demy 8vo. Cloth, price 12s.

GEDDES (James).
History of the Administration of John de Witt, Grand Pensionary of Holland. Vol. I. 1623—1654. Demy 8vo., with Portrait. Cloth, price 15s.

GEORGE (Henry).
Progress and Poverty. An Inquiry into the Cause of Industrial Depressions and of Increase of Want with Increase of Wealth. The Remedy. Post 8vo. Cloth, price 7s. 6d.

GILBERT (Mrs.).
Autobiography and other Memorials. Edited by Josiah

GILBERT (Mrs.)—*continued.*

Gilbert. Third Edition. With Portrait and several Wood Engravings. Crown 8vo. Cloth, price 7s. 6d.

GLOVER (F.), M.A.

Exempla Latina. A First Construing Book with Short Notes, Lexicon, and an Introduction to the Analysis of Sentences. Fcap. 8vo. Cloth, price 2s.

GODWIN (William).

William Godwin: His Friends and Contemporaries. With Portraits and Facsimiles of the handwriting of Godwin and his Wife. By C. Kegan Paul. 2 vols. Demy 8vo. Cloth, price 28s.

The Genius of Christianity Unveiled. Being Essays never before published. Edited, with a Preface, by C. Kegan Paul. Crown 8vo. Cloth, price 7s. 6d.

GOETZE (Capt. A. von).

Operations of the German Engineers during the War of 1870-1871. Published by Authority, and in accordance with Official Documents. Translated from the German by Colonel G. Graham, V.C., C.B., R.E. With 6 large Maps. Demy 8vo. Cloth, price 21s.

GOLDSMID (Sir Francis Henry).

Memoir of. With Portrait. Crown 8vo. Cloth, price 5s.

GOODENOUGH (Commodore J. G.), R.N., C.B., C.M.G.

Memoir of, with Extracts from his Letters and Journals. Edited by his Widow. With Steel Engraved Portrait. Square 8vo. Cloth, 5s. *** Also a Library Edition with Maps, Woodcuts, and Steel Engraved Portrait. Square post 8vo. Cloth, price 14s.

GOSSE (Edmund W.).

Studies in the Literature of Northern Europe. With a Frontispiece designed and etched by Alma Tadema. Large post 8vo. Cloth, price 12s.

New Poems. Crown 8vo. Cloth, price 7s. 6d.

GOULD (Rev. S. Baring), M.A.

Germany, Present and Past. 2 Vols. Demy 8vo. Cloth, price 21s.

The Vicar of Morwenstow: a Memoir of the Rev. R. S. Hawker. With Portrait. Third Edition, revised. Square post 8vo. Cloth, 10s. 6d.

GRAHAM (William), M.A.

The Creed of Science : Religious, Moral, and Social. Demy 8vo. Cloth, price 12s.

GREENOUGH (Mrs. Richard).

Mary Magdalene : A Poem. Large post 8vo. Parchment antique, price 6s.

GRIFFITH (Thomas), A.M.

The Gospel of the Divine Life. A Study of the Fourth Evangelist. Demy 8vo. Cloth, price 14s.

GRIMLEY (Rev. H. N.), M.A.

Tremadoc Sermons, chiefly on the SPIRITUAL BODY, the UNSEEN WORLD, and the DIVINE HUMANITY. Second Edition. Crown 8vo. Cloth, price 6s.

GRÜNER (M. L.).

Studies of Blast Furnace Phenomena. Translated by L. D. B. Gordon, F.R.S.E., F.G.S. Demy 8vo. Cloth, price 7s. 6d.

GURNEY (Rev. Archer).

Words of Faith and Cheer. A Mission of Instruction and Suggestion. Crown 8vo. Cloth, price 6s.

Gwen: A Drama in Monologue. By the Author of the "Epic of Hades." Second Edition. Fcap. 8vo. Cloth, price 5s.

HAECKEL (Prof. Ernst).

The History of Creation. Translation revised by Professor E. Ray Lankester, M.A., F.R.S. With Coloured Plates and Genealogical Trees of the various groups of both plants and animals. 2 vols. Second Edition. Post 8vo. Cloth, price 32s.

The History of the Evolution of Man. With numerous Illustrations. 2 vols. Large post 8vo. Cloth, price 32s.

Freedom in Science and Teaching. From the German of

HAECKEL (Prof. Ernst) — *continued*.

Ernst Haeckel, with a Prefatory Note by T. H. Huxley, F.R.S. Crown 8vo. Cloth, price 5s.

HALF-CROWN SERIES.

Sister Dora: a Biography. By Margaret Lonsdale.

True Words for Brave Men. A Book for Soldiers and Sailors. By the late Charles Kingsley.

An Inland Voyage. By R. L. Stevenson.

Travels with a Donkey. By R. L. Stevenson.

A Nook in the Apennines. By Leader Scott.

Notes of Travel. Being Extracts from the Journals of Count Von Moltke.

Letters from Russia. By Count Von Moltke.

English Sonnets. Collected and Arranged by J. Dennis.

Lyrics of Love from Shakespeare to Tennyson. Selected and Arranged by W. D. Adams.

London Lyrics. By Frederick Locker.

Home Songs for Quiet Hours. By the Rev. Canon R. H. Baynes.

Halleck's International Law; or, Rules Regulating the Intercourse of States in Peace and War. A New Edition, revised, with Notes and Cases. By Sir Sherston Baker, Bart. 2 vols. Demy 8vo. Cloth, price 38s.

HARDY (Thomas).

A Pair of Blue Eyes. New Edition. With Frontispiece. Crown 8vo. Cloth, price 6s.

The Return of the Native. New Edition. With Frontispiece. Crown 8vo. Cloth, price 6s.

HARRISON (Lieut.-Col. R.).

The Officer's Memorandum Book for Peace and War. Third Edition. Oblong 32mo. roan, with pencil, price 3s. 6d.

HARTINGTON (The Right Hon. the Marquis of), M.P.

Election Speeches in 1879 and 1880. With Address to the Electors of North-East Lancashire. Crown 8vo. Cloth, price 3s. 6d.

HAWEIS (Rev. H. R.), M.A.

Arrows in the Air. Crown 8vo. Second Edition. Cloth, price 6s.

Current Coin. Materialism— The Devil—Crime—Drunkenness— Pauperism—Emotion—Recreation— The Sabbath. Third Edition. Crown 8vo. Cloth, price 6s.

Speech in Season. Fourth Edition. Crown 8vo. Cloth, price 9s.

Thoughts for the Times. Eleventh Edition. Crown 8vo. Cloth, price 7s. 6d.

Unsectarian Family Prayers. New and Cheaper Edition. Fcap. 8vo. Cloth, price 1s. 6d.

HAWKER (Robert Stephen).

The Poetical Works of. Now first collected and arranged with a prefatory notice by J. G. Godwin. With Portrait. Crown 8vo. Cloth, price 12s.

HAWKINS (Edwards Comerford).

Spirit and Form. Sermons preached in the parish church of Leatherhead. Crown 8vo. Cloth, price 6s.

HAWTREY (Edward M.).

Corydalis. A Story of the Sicilian Expedition. Small crown 8vo. Cloth, price 3s. 6d.

HAYES (A. H.).

New Colorado and the Santa Fé Trail. With map and 60 Illustrations. Crown 8vo. Cloth, price 9s.

HEIDENHAIN (Rudolf), M.D.

Animal Magnetism. Physiological Observations. Translated from the Fourth German Edition, by L. C. Wooldridge. With a Preface by G. R. Romanes, F.R.S. Crown 8vo. Cloth, price 2s. 6d.

HELLWALD (Baron F. von).

The Russians in Central Asia. A Critical Examination, down to the present time, of the

HELLWALD (Baron F. von)—
continued.

Geography and History of Central
Asia. Translated by Lieut.-Col.
Theodore Wirgman, LL.B. Large
post 8vo. With Map. Cloth,
price 12s.

HELVIG (Major H.).

**The Operations of the Ba-
varian Army Corps.** Translated
by Captain G. S. Schwabe. With
Five large Maps. In 2 vols. Demy
8vo. Cloth, price 24s.

Tactical Examples : Vol. I.
The Battalion, price 15s. Vol. II. The
Regiment and Brigade, price 10s. 6d.
Translated from the German by Col.
Sir Lumley Graham. With numerous
Diagrams. Demy 8vo. Cloth.

HERFORD (Brooke).

**The Story of Religion in
England.** A Book for Young Folk.
Crown 8vo. Cloth, price 5s.

HINTON (James).

Life and Letters of. Edited
by Ellice Hopkins, with an Introduc-
tion by Sir W. W. Gull, Bart., and
Portrait engraved on Steel by C. H.
Jeens. Second Edition. Crown 8vo.
Cloth, 8s. 6d.

**Chapters on the Art of
Thinking, and other Essays.**
With an Introduction by Shadworth
Hodgson. Edited by C. H. Hinton.
Crown 8vo. Cloth, price 8s. 6d.

The Place of the Physician.
To which is added Essays on the
Law of Human Life, and on the
Relation between Organic and
Inorganic Worlds. Second Edi-
tion. Crown 8vo. Cloth, price 3s. 6d.

**Physiology for Practical
Use.** By various Writers. With 50
Illustrations. Third and cheaper edi-
tion. Crown 8vo. Cloth, price 5s.

**An Atlas of Diseases of the
Membrana Tympani.** With Descriptive Text. Post 8vo. Price £6 6s.

**The Questions of Aural
Surgery.** With Illustrations. 2 vols.
Post 8vo. Cloth, price 12s. 6d.

The Mystery of Pain.
New Edition. Fcap. 8vo. Cloth
limp, 1s.

HOCKLEY (W. B.).

Tales of the Zenana ; or,
A Nuwab's Leisure Hours. By the
Author of " Pandurang Hari." With
a Preface by Lord Stanley of Alder-
ley. 2 vols. Crown 8vo. Cloth,
price 21s.

Pandurang Hari ; or, Me-
moirs of a Hindoo. A Tale of
Mahratta Life sixty years ago. With
a Preface by Sir H. Bartle E.
Frere, G. C. S. I., &c. New and
Cheaper Edition. Crown 8vo. Cloth,
price 6s.

HOFFBAUER (Capt.).

**The German Artillery in
the Battles near Metz.** Based
on the official reports of the German
Artillery. Translated by Capt. E.
O. Hollist. With Map and Plans.
Demy 8vo. Cloth, price 21s.

HOLMES (E. G. A.).

Poems. First and Second Series. Fcap. 8vo. Cloth, price 5s. each.

HOOPER (Mary).

**Little Dinners : How to
Serve them with Elegance and
Economy.** Thirteenth Edition.
Crown 8vo. Cloth, price 5s.

Cookery for Invalids, Per-
sons of Delicate Digestion, and
Children. Crown 8vo. Cloth, price
3s. 6d.

Every - Day Meals. Being
Economical and Wholesome Recipes
for Breakfast, Luncheon, and Supper. Second Edition. Crown 8vo.
Cloth, price 5s.

HOOPER (Mrs. G.).

The House of Raby. With
a Frontispiece. Crown 8vo. Cloth,
price 3s. 6d.

HOPKINS (Ellice).

**Life and Letters of James
Hinton,** with an Introduction by Sir
W. W. Gull, Bart., and Portrait en-
graved on Steel by C. H. Jeens.
Second Edition. Crown 8vo. Cloth
price 8s. 6d.

HOPKINS (M.).

The Port of Refuge ; or,
Counsel and Aid to Shipmasters in
Difficulty, Doubt, or Distress. Crown
8vo. Second and Revised Edition.
Cloth, price 6s.

HORNER (The Misses).
Walks in Florence. A New and thoroughly Revised Edition. 2 vols. Crown 8vo. Cloth limp. With Illustrations.
Vol. I.—Churches, Streets, and Palaces. 10s. 6d. Vol. II.—Public Galleries and Museums. 5s.

Household Readings on Prophecy. By a Layman. Small crown 8vo. Cloth, price 3s. 6d.

HULL (Edmund C. P.).
The European in India. With a MEDICAL GUIDE FOR ANGLO-INDIANS. By R. R. S. Mair, M.D., F.R.C.S.E. Third Edition, Revised and Corrected. Post 8vo. Cloth, price 6s.

HUTCHISON (Lieut.-Col. F. J.), and Capt. G. H. MACGREGOR.
Military Sketching and Reconnaissance. With Fifteen Plates. Second edition. Small 8vo. Cloth, price 6s.
The first Volume of Military Handbooks for Regimental Officers. Edited by Lieut.-Col. C. B. BRACKENBURY, R.A., A.A.G.

HUTTON (Arthur), M.A.
The Anglican Ministry. Its Nature and Value in relation to the Catholic Priesthood. With a Preface by his Eminence Cardinal Newman. Demy 8vo. Cloth, price 14s.

INCHBOLD (J. W.).
Annus Amoris. Sonnets. Fcap. 8vo. Cloth, price 4s. 6d.

INGELOW (Jean).
Off the Skelligs. A Novel. With Frontispiece. Second Edition. Crown 8vo. Cloth, price 6s.
The Little Wonder-horn. A Second Series of "Stories Told to a Child." With Fifteen Illustrations. Small 8vo. Cloth, price 2s. 6d.

Indian Bishoprics. By an Indian Churchman. Demy 8vo. 6d.

International Scientific Series (The).
I. **Forms of Water:** A Familiar Exposition of the Origin and Phenomena of Glaciers. By J. Tyndall, LL.D., F.R.S. With 25 Illustrations. Seventh Edition. Crown 8vo. Cloth, price 5s.

International Scientific Series (The)—*continued.*
II. **Physics and Politics;** or, Thoughts on the Application of the Principles of "Natural Selection" and "Inheritance" to Political Society. By Walter Bagehot. Fifth Edition. Crown 8vo. Cloth, price 4s.

III. **Foods.** By Edward Smith, M.D., &c. With numerous Illustrations. Seventh Edition. Crown 8vo. Cloth, price 5s.

IV. **Mind and Body:** The Theories of their Relation. By Alexander Bain, LL.D. With Four Illustrations. Tenth Edition. Crown 8vo. Cloth, price 4s.

V. **The Study of Sociology.** By Herbert Spencer. Tenth Edition. Crown 8vo. Cloth, price 5s.

VI. **On the Conservation of Energy.** By Balfour Stewart, LL.D., &c. With 14 Illustrations. Fifth Edition. Crown 8vo. Cloth, price 5s.

VII. **Animal Locomotion;** or, Walking, Swimming, and Flying. By J. B. Pettigrew, M.D., &c. With 130 Illustrations. Second Edition. Crown 8vo. Cloth, price 5s.

VIII. **Responsibility in Mental Disease.** By Henry Maudsley, M.D. Third Edition. Crown 8vo. Cloth, price 5s.

IX. **The New Chemistry.** By Professor J. P. Cooke. With 31 Illustrations. Fifth Edition. Crown 8vo. Cloth, price 5s.

X. **The Science of Law.** By Prof. Sheldon Amos. Fourth Edition. Crown 8vo. Cloth, price 5s.

XI. **Animal Mechanism.** A Treatise on Terrestrial and Aerial Locomotion. By Prof. E. J. Marey. With 117 Illustrations. Second Edition. Crown 8vo. Cloth, price 5s.

XII. **The Doctrine of Descent and Darwinism.** By Prof. Oscar Schmidt. With 26 Illustrations. Fourth Edition. Crown 8vo. Cloth, price 5s.

XIII. **The History of the Conflict between Religion and Science.** By J. W. Draper, M.D., LL.D. Fifteenth Edition. Crown 8vo. Cloth, price 5s.

International Scientific Series (The)—*continued.*

XIV. Fungi; their Nature, Influences, Uses, &c. By M. C. Cooke, LL.D. Edited by the Rev. M. J. Berkeley, F.L.S. With numerous Illustrations. Second Edition. Crown 8vo. Cloth, price 5*s.*

XV. The Chemical Effects of Light and Photography. By Dr. Hermann Vogel. With 100 Illustrations. Third and Revised Edition. Crown 8vo. Cloth, price 5*s.*

XVI. The Life and Growth of Language. By Prof. William Dwight Whitney. Third Edition Crown 8vo. Cloth, price 5*s.*

XVII. Money and the Mechanism of Exchange. By W. Stanley Jevons, F.R.S. Fourth Edition. Crown 8vo. Cloth, price 5*s.*

XVIII. The Nature of Light: With a General Account of Physical Optics. By Dr. Eugene Lommel. With 188 Illustrations and a table of Spectra in Chromo-lithography. Third Edition. Crown 8vo. Cloth, price 5*s.*

XIX. Animal Parasites and Messmates. By M. Van Beneden. With 83 Illustrations. Second Edition. Crown 8vo. Cloth, price 5*s.*

XX. Fermentation. By Prof. Schützenberger. With 28 Illustrations. Third Edition. Crown 8vo. Cloth, price 5*s.*

XXI. The Five Senses of Man. By Prof. Bernstein. With 91 Illustrations. Second Edition. Crown 8vo. Cloth, price 5*s.*

XXII. The Theory of Sound in its Relation to Music. By Prof. Pietro Blaserna. With numerous Illustrations. Second Edition. Crown 8vo. Cloth, price 5*s.*

XXIII. Studies in Spectrum Analysis. By J. Norman Lockyer. F.R.S. With six photographic Illustrations of Spectra, and numerous engravings on wood. Second Edition. Cloth, price 6*s.* 6*d.*

XXIV. A History of the Growth of the Steam Engine. By Prof. R. H. Thurston. With numerous Illustrations. Second Edition. Crown 8vo. Cloth, price 6*s.* 6*d.*

XXV. Education as a Science. By Alexander Bain, LL.D. Third Edition. Crown 8vo. Cloth, price 5*s.*

International Scientific Series (The)—*continued.*

XXVI. The Human Species. By Prof. A. de Quatrefages. Third Edition. Crown 8vo. Cloth, price 5*s.*

XXVII. Modern Chromatics. With Applications to Art and Industry, by Ogden N. Rood. Second Edition. With 130 original Illustrations. Crown 8vo. Cloth, price 5*s.*

XXVIII. The Crayfish: an Introduction to the Study of Zoology. By Prof. T. H. Huxley. Third edition. With eighty-two Illustrations. Crown 8vo. Cloth, price 5*s.*

XXIX. The Brain as an Organ of Mind. By H. Charlton Bastian, M.D. With numerous Illustrations. Second Edition. Crown 8vo. Cloth, price 5*s.*

XXX. The Atomic Theory. By Prof. Ad. Wurtz. Translated by E. Clemin-Shaw. Second Edition. Crown 8vo. Cloth, price 5*s.*

XXXI. The Natural Conditions of Existence as they affect Animal Life. By Karl Semper. Second Edition. Crown 8vo. Cloth, price 5*s.*

XXXII. General Physiology of Muscles and Nerves. By Prof. J. Rosenthal. Second Edition, with illustrations. Crown 8vo. Cloth, price 5*s.*

XXXIII. Sight: an Exposition of the Principles of Monocular and Binocular Vision. By Joseph Le Conte, LL.D. With 132 illustrations. Crown 8vo. Cloth, price 5*s.*

XXXIV. Illusions: A Psychological Study. By James Sully. Crown 8vo. Cloth, price 5*s.*

XXXV. Volcanoes: What they are and What they Teach. By Prof. J. W. Judd, F.R.S. With 92 Illustrations on Wood. Crown 8vo. Cloth, price 5*s.*

JENKINS (E.) and RAYMOND (J.).

The Architect's Legal Handbook. Third Edition Revised. Crown 8vo. Cloth, price 6*s.*

JENKINS (Rev. R. C.), M.A.

The Privilege of Peter and the Claims of the Roman Church confronted with the Scriptures, the Councils, and the Testimony of the Popes themselves. Fcap. 8vo. Cloth, price 3*s.* 6*d.*

JENNINGS (Mrs. Vaughan).
Rahel : Her Life and Letters. With a Portrait from the Painting by Daffinger. Square post 8vo. Cloth, price 7s. 6d.

Jeroveam's Wife and other Poems. Fcap. 8vo. Cloth, price 3s. 6d.

JOEL (L.).
A Consul's Manual and Shipowner's and Shipmaster's Practical Guide in their Transactions Abroad. With Definitions of Nautical, Mercantile, and Legal Terms; a Glossary of Mercantile Terms in English, French, German, Italian, and Spanish. Tables of the Money, Weights, and Measures of the Principal Commercial Nations and their Equivalents in British Standards; and Forms of Consular and Notarial Acts. Demy 8vo. Cloth, price 12s.

JOHNSON (Virginia W.).
The Catskill Mountains. Illustrated by Alfred Fredericks. Cloth, price 5s.

JOHNSTONE (C. F.), M.A.
Historical Abstracts. Being Outlines of the History of some of the less-known States of Europe. Crown 8vo. Cloth, price 7s. 6d.

JONES (Lucy).
Puddings and Sweets. Being Three Hundred and Sixty-Five Receipts approved by Experience. Crown 8vo., price 2s. 6d.

JOYCE (P. W.), LL.D., &c.
Old Celtic Romances. Translated from the Gaelic by. Crown 8vo. Cloth, price 7s. 6d.

KAUFMANN (Rev. M.), B.A.
Utopias; or, Schemes of Social Improvement, from Sir Thomas More to Karl Marx. Crown 8vo. Cloth, price 5s.

Socialism : Its Nature, its Dangers, and its Remedies considered. Crown 8vo. Cloth, price 7s.6d.

KAY (Joseph), M.A., Q.C.
Free Trade in Land. Edited by his Widow. With Preface by the Right Hon. John Bright, M.P. Sixth Edition. Crown 8vo. Cloth, price 5s.

KENT (Carolo).
Carona Catholica ad Petri successoris Pedes Oblata. De Summi Pontificis Leonis XIII. Assumptione Epiggramma. In Quinquaginta Linguis. Fcap. 4to. Cloth, price 15s.

KER (David).
The Boy Slave in Bokhara. A Tale of Central Asia. With Illustrations. Crown 8vo. Cloth, price 3s. 6d.

The Wild Horseman of the Pampas. Illustrated. Crown 8vo. Cloth, price 3s. 6d.

KERNER (Dr. A.), Professor of Botany in the University of Innsbruck.
Flowers and their Unbidden Guests. Translation edited by W. OGLE. M.A., M.D., and a prefatory letter by C. Darwin, F.R.S. With Illustrations. Sq. 8vo. Cloth, price 9s.

KIDD (Joseph), M.D.
The Laws of Therapeutics, or, the Science and Art of Medicine. Second Edition. Crown 8vo. Cloth, price 6s.

KINAHAN (G. Henry), M.R.I.A., &c., of her Majesty's Geological Survey.
Manual of the Geology of Ireland. With 8 Plates, 26 Woodcuts, and a Map of Ireland, geologically coloured. Square 8vo. Cloth, price 15s.

KING (Mrs. Hamilton).
The Disciples. Fourth Edition, with Portrait and Notes. Crown 8vo. Cloth, price 7s. 6d.

Aspromonte, and other Poems. Second Edition. Fcap. 8vo. Cloth, price 4s. 6d.

KING (Edward).
Echoes from the Orient. With Miscellaneous Poems. Small crown 8vo. Cloth, price 3s. 6d.

KINGSLEY (Charles), M.A.
Letters and Memories of his Life. Edited by his WIFE. With a Steel engraved Portraits and numerous Illustrations on Wood, and a Facsimile of his Handwriting.

KINGSLEY (Charles), M.A.—
continued.

Thirteenth Edition. 2 vols. Demy
8vo. Cloth, price 36s.
  ₄ Also the ninth Cabinet Edition
in 2 vols. Crown 8vo. Cloth, price
12s.

All Saints' Day and other
Sermons. Second Edition. Crown
8vo. Cloth, 7s. 6d.

True Words for Brave
Men: a Book for Soldiers' and
Sailors' Libraries. Eighth Edition.
Crown 8vo. Cloth, price 2s. 6d.

KNIGHT (Professor W.).

Studies in Philosophy and
Literature. Large post 8vo. Cloth,
price 7s. 6d.

KNOX (Alexander A.).

The New Playground : or,
Wanderings in Algeria. Large
crown 8vo. Cloth, price 10s. 6d.

LACORDAIRE (Rev. Père).

Life : Conferences delivered
at Toulouse. A New and Cheaper
Edition. Crown 8vo. Cloth, price 3s. 6d.

LAIRD-CLOWES (W.).

Love's Rebellion : a Poem.
Fcap. 8vo. Cloth, price 3s. 6d..

LAMONT (Martha MacDonald).

The Gladiator : A Life under
the Roman Empire in the beginning
of the Third Century. With four
Illustrations by H. M. Paget. Extra
fcap. 8vo. Cloth, price 3s. 6d.

LANG (A.).

XXXII Ballades in Blue
China. Elzevir. 8vo. Parchment,
price 5s. •

LAYMANN (Capt.).

The Frontal Attack of
Infantry. Translated by Colonel
Edward Newdigate. Crown 8vo.
Cloth, price 2s. 6d.

LEANDER (Richard).

Fantastic Stories. Trans-
lated from the German by Paulina
B. Granville. With Eight full-page
Illustrations by M. E. Fraser-Tytler.
Crown 8vo. Cloth, price 5s.

LEE (Rev. F. G.), D.C.L.

The Other World ; or,
Glimpses of the Supernatural. 2 vols.
A New Edition. Crown 8vo. Cloth,
price 15s.

LEE (Holme).

Her Title of Honour. A
Book for Girls. New Edition. With
a Frontispiece. Crown 8vo. Cloth,
price 5s.

LEIGH (Arran and Isla).

Bellerophôn. Small crown
8vo. Cloth, price 5s.

LEIGHTON (Robert).

Records and other Poems.
With Portrait. Small crown 8vo.
Cloth, price 7s. 6d.

LEWIS (Edward Dillon).

A Draft Code of Criminal
Law and Procedure. Demy 8vo.
Cloth, price 21s.

LEWIS (Mary A.).

A Rat with Three Tales.
New and cheaper edition. With
Four Illustrations by Catherine F.
Frere. Crown 8vo. Cloth, price 3s. 6d.

LINDSAY (W. Lauder), M.D., &c.

Mind in the Lower Animals
in Health and Disease. 2 vols.
Demy 8vo. Cloth, price 32s.

LLOYD (Francis) and Charles
Tebbitt.

Extension of Empire Weak-
ness ? Deficits Ruin ? With a
Practical Scheme for the Reconstruc-
tion of Asiatic Turkey. Small crown
8vo. Cloth, price 3s. 6d.

LOCKER (F.).

London Lyrics. A New and
Revised Edition, with Additions and
a Portrait of the Author. Crown 8vo.
Cloth, elegant, price 6s.

LOKI.

The New Werther. Small
crown 8vo. Cloth, price 2s. 6d.

LORIMER (Peter), D.D.

John Knox and the Church
of England : His Work in her Pulpit,
and his Influence upon her Liturgy,
Articles, and Parties. Demy 8vo.
Cloth, price 12s.

John Wiclif and his
English Precursors, by Gerhard
Victor Lechler. Translated from
the German, with additional Notes.
2 vols. Demy 8vo. Cloth, price 21s.

Love's Gamut and other
Poems. Small crown 8vo. Cloth,
price 3s. 6d.

Love Sonnets of Proteus. With frontispiece by the Author. Elzevir 8vo. Cloth, price 5s.

LOWNDES (Henry).
Poems and Translations. Crown 8vo. Cloth, price 6s.

LUMSDEN (Lieut.-Col. H. W.).
Beowulf. An Old English Poem. Translated into modern rhymes. Small crown 8vo. Cloth, price 5s.

MAC CLINTOCK (L.).
Sir Spangle and the Dingy Hen. Illustrated. Square crown 8vo., price 2s. 6d.

MACDONALD (G.).
Malcolm. With Portrait of the Author engraved on Steel. Fourth Edition. Crown 8vo. Price 6s.
The Marquis of Lossie. Second Edition. Crown 8vo. Cloth, price 6s.
St. George and St. Michael. Second Edition. Crown 8vo. Cloth, 6s.

MACKENNA (S. J.).
Plucky Fellows. A Book for Boys. With Six Illustrations. Fourth Edition. Crown 8vo. Cloth, price 3s. 6d.
At School with an Old Dragoon. With Six Illustrations. Second Edition. Crown 8vo. Cloth, price 5s.

MACLACHLAN (Mrs.).
Notes and Extracts on Everlasting Punishment and Eternal Life, according to Literal Interpretation. Small crown 8vo. Cloth, price 3s. 6d.

MACLEAN (Charles Donald).
Latin and Greek Verse Translations. Small crown 8vo. Cloth, price 2s.

MACNAUGHT (Rev. John).
Cœna Domini: An Essay on the Lord's Supper, its Primitive Institution, Apostolic Uses, and Subsequent History. Demy 8vo. Cloth, price 14s.

MAGNUS (Mrs.).
About the Jews since Bible Times. From the Babylonian exile till the English Exodus. Small crown 8vo. Cloth, price 5s.

MAGNUSSON (Eirikr), M.A., and PALMER (E.H.), M.A.
Johan Ludvig Runeberg's Lyrical Songs, Idylls and Epigrams. Fcap. 8vo. Cloth, price 5s.

MAIR (R. S.), M.D., F.R.C.S.E.
The Medical Guide for Anglo-Indians. Being a Compendium of Advice to Europeans in India, relating to the Preservation and Regulation of Health. With a Supplement on the Management of Children in India. Second Edition. Crown 8vo. Limp cloth, price 3s. 6d.

MALDEN (H. E. and E. E.)
Princes and Princesses. Illustrated. Small crown 8vo. Cloth, price 2s. 6d.

MANNING (His Eminence Cardinal).
The True Story of the Vatican Council. Crown 8vo. Cloth, price 5s.
Marie Antoinette: a Drama. Small crown 8vo. Cloth, price 5s.

MARKHAM (Capt. Albert Hastings), R.N.
The Great Frozen Sea. A Personal Narrative of the Voyage of the "Alert" during the Arctic Expedition of 1875-6. With six full-page Illustrations, two Maps, and twenty-seven Woodcuts. Fourth and cheaper edition. Crown 8vo. Cloth, price 6s.
A Polar Reconnaissance: being the Voyage of the "Isbjorn" to Novaya Zemlya in 1879. With 10 Illustrations. Demy 8vo. Cloth, price 16s.

MARTINEAU (Gertrude).
Outline Lessons on Morals. Small crown 8vo. Cloth, price 3s. 6d.

Master Bobby: a Tale. By the Author of "Christina North." With Illustrations by E. H. Bell. Extra fcap. 8vo. Cloth, price 3s.6d.

MASTERMAN (J.).
Half-a-dozen Daughters. With a Frontispiece. Crown 8vo. Cloth, price 3s. 6d.

McGRATH (Terence).

Pictures from Ireland. New and cheaper edition. Crown 8vo. Cloth, price 2s.

MEREDITH (George).

The Egoist. A Comedy in Narrative. 3 vols. Crown 8vo. Cloth.

⁕ Also a Cheaper Edition, with Frontispiece. Crown 8vo. Cloth, price 6s.

The Ordeal of Richard Feverel. A History of Father and Son. In one vol. with Frontispiece. Crown 8vo. Cloth, price 6s.

MERRITT (Henry).

Art - Criticism and Romance. With Recollections, and Twenty-three Illustrations in *eau-forte*, by Anna Lea Merritt. Two vols. Large post 8vo. Cloth, 25s.

MIDDLETON (The Lady).

Ballads. Square 16mo. Cloth, price 3s. 6d.

MILLER (Edward).

The History and Doctrines of Irvingism; or, the so-called Catholic and Apostolic Church. 2 vols. Large post 8vo. Cloth, price 25s.

The Church in Relation to the State. Crown 8vo. Cloth, price 7s. 6d.

MILNE (James).

Tables of Exchange for the Conversion of Sterling Money into Indian and Ceylon Currency, at Rates from 1s. 8d. to 2s. 3d. per Rupee. Second Edition. Demy 8vo. Cloth, price £2 2s.

MINCHIN (J. G.).

Bulgaria since the War. Notes of a Tour in the Autumn of 1879. Small crown 8vo. Cloth, price 3s. 6d.

MOCKLER (E.).

A Grammar of the Baloochee Language, as it is spoken in Makran (Ancient Gedrosia), in the Persia-Arabic and Roman characters. Fcap. 8vo. Cloth, price 5s.

MOFFAT (Robert Scott).

The Economy of Consumption; an Omitted Chapter in Political Economy, with special reference to the Questions of Commercial Crises and the Policy of Trades Unions; and with Reviews of the Theories of Adam Smith, Ricardo, J. S. Mill, Fawcett, &c. Demy 8vo. Cloth, price 18s.

The Principles of a Time Policy: being an Exposition of a Method of Settling Disputes between Employers and Employed in regard to Time and Wages, by a simple Process of Mercantile Barter, without recourse to Strikes or Locks-out. Demy 8vo. Cloth, price 3s. 6d.

Monmouth: A Drama, of which the Outline is Historical. Dedicated by permission to Mr. Henry Irving. Small crown 8vo. Cloth, price 5s.

MOORE (Mrs. Bloomfield).

Gondaline's Lesson. The Warden's Tale, Stories for Children, and other Poems. Crown 8vo. Cloth, price 5s.

MORELL (J. R.).

Euclid Simplified in Method and Language. Being a Manual of Geometry. Compiled from the most important French Works, approved by the University of Paris and the Minister of Public Instruction. Fcap. 8vo. Cloth, price 2s. 6d.

MORICE (Rev. F. D.), M.A.

The Olympian and Pythian Odes of Pindar. A New Translation in English Verse. Crown 8vo. Cloth, price 7s. 6d.

MORSE (E. S.), Ph.D.

First Book of Zoology. With numerous Illustrations. New and cheaper edition. Crown 8vo. Cloth, price 2s. 6d.

MORSHEAD (E. D. A.)

The House of Atreus. Being the Agamemnon Libation-Bearers and Furies of Æschylus. Translated into English Verse. Crown 8vo. Cloth, price 7s.

MORTERRA (Felix).

The Legend of Allandale, and other Poems. Small crown 8vo. Cloth, price 6s.

MUNRO (Major-Gen. Sir Thomas), K.C.B., Governor of Madras.
Selections from His Minutes, and other Official Writings. Edited, with an Introductory Memoir, by Sir Alexander Arbuthnot, K.C.S.I., C.I.E. Two vols. Demy 8vo. Cloth, price 30s.

NAAKE (J. T.).
Slavonic Fairy Tales. From Russian, Servian, Polish, and Bohemian Sources. With Four Illustrations. Crown 8vo. Cloth, price 5s.

NADEN (Constance W.).
Songs and Sonnets of Spring-Time. Small crown 8vo. Cloth, price 5s.

NEWMAN (J. H.), D.D.
Characteristics from the Writings of. Being Selections from his various Works. Arranged with the Author's personal approval. Third Edition. With Portrait. Crown 8vo. Cloth, price 6s.
⁎ A Portrait of the Rev. Dr. J. H. Newman, mounted for framing, can be had. price 2s. 6d.

NICHOLAS (Thomas), Ph.D., F.G.S.
The Pedigree of the English People: an Argument, Historical and Scientific, on the Formation and Growth of the Nation, tracing Race-admixture in Britain from the earliest times, with especial reference to the incorporation of the Celtic Aborigines. Fifth Edition. Demy 8vo. Cloth, price 16s.

NICHOLSON (Edward Byron).
The Christ Child, and other Poems. Crown 8vo. Cloth, price 4s. 6d.
The Rights of an Animal. Crown 8vo. Cloth, price 3s. 6d.
The Gospel according to the Hebrews. Its Fragments translated and annotated, with a critical Analysis of the External and Internal Evidence relating to it. Demy 8vo. Cloth, price 9s. 6d.
A New Commentary on the Gospel according to Matthew. Demy 8vo. Cloth, price 12s.

NICOLS (Arthur), F.G.S., F.R.G.S.
Chapters from the Physical History of the Earth. An Introduction to Geology and Palæontology, with numerous illustrations. Crown 8vo. Cloth, price 5s.

NOAKE (Major R. Compton).
The Bivouac; or, Martial Lyrist, with an Appendix—Advice to the Soldier. Fcap. 8vo. Price 5s. 6d.

NOEL (The Hon. Roden).
A Little Child's Monument. Small crown 8vo. Cloth, price 3s. 6d.

NORMAN PEOPLE (The).
The Norman People, and their Existing Descendants in the British Dominions and the United States of America. Demy 8vo. Cloth, price 21s.

NORRIS (Rev. Alfred).
The Inner and Outer Life Poems. Fcap. 8vo. Cloth, price 6s.

Notes on Cavalry Tactics, Organization, &c. By a Cavalry Officer. With Diagrams. Demy 8vo. Cloth, price 12s.

Nuces: Exercises on the Syntax of the Public School Latin Primer. New Edition in Three Parts. Crown 8vo. Each 1s.
⁎ The Three Parts can also be had bound together in cloth, price 3s.

OATES (Frank), F.R.G.S.
Matabele Land and the Victoria Falls: A Naturalist's Wanderings in the Interior of South Africa. Edited by C. G. Oates, B.A., with numerous illustrations and four maps. Demy 8vo. Cloth.

O'BRIEN (Charlotte G.).
Light and Shade. 2 vols. Crown 8vo. Cloth, gilt tops, price 12s.

Ode of Life (The).
Third Edition. Fcap. 8vo. Cloth, price 5s.

OF THE IMITATION OF CHRIST. Four books. Demy 32mo. Limp cloth, price 1s.
⁎ Also in various bindings.

O'HAGAN (John).

The Song of Roland. Translated into English Verse. Large post 8vo. Parchment antique, price 10s. 6d.

O'MEARA (Kathleen).

Frederic Ozanam, Professor of the Sorbonne: His Life and Works. Second Edition. Crown 8vo. Cloth, price 7s. 6d.

Henri Perreyve and His Counsels to the Sick. Small crown 8vo. Cloth, price 5s.

Our Public Schools. Eton, Harrow, Winchester, Rugby, Westminster, Marlborough, The Charterhouse. Crown 8vo. Cloth, price 6s.

OWEN (F. M.).

John Keats. A Study. Crown 8vo. Cloth, price 6s.

OWEN (Rev. Robert), B.D.

Sanctorale Catholicum; or Book of Saints. With Notes, Critical, Exegetical, and Historical. Demy 8vo. Cloth, price 18s.

An Essay on the Communion of Saints. Including an Examination of the "Cultus Sanctorum." Price 2s.

PALGRAVE (W. Gifford).

Hermann Agha; An Eastern Narrative. Third and Cheaper Edition. Crown 8vo. Cloth, price 6s.

PANDURANG HARI;

Or, Memoirs of a Hindoo. With an Introductory Preface by Sir H. Bartle E. Frere, G.C.S.I., C.B. Crown 8vo. Price 6s.

PARCHMENT LIBRARY (The).

Choicely printed on hand-made paper, limp parchment antique, price 6s. each; vellum, price 7s. 6d. each.

Shakspere's Sonnets. Edited by Edward Dowden, Author of "Shakspere; his Mind and Art," &c. With a Frontispiece, etched by Leopold Lowenstam, after the Death Mask.

English Odes. Selected by Edmund W. Gosse, Author of "Studies in the Literature of Northern Europe." With Frontispiece on India paper by Hamo Thornycroft, A.R.A.

PARCHMENT LIBRARY (The) —*continued.*

Of the Imitation of Christ. By Thomas à Kempis. A revised Translation. With Frontispiece on India paper, from a Design by W. B. Richmond.

Tennyson's The Princess : a Medley. With a Miniature Frontispiece by H. M. Paget, and a Tailpiece in Outline by Gordon Browne.

Poems : Selected from Percy Bysshe Shelley. Dedicated to Lady Shelley. With Preface by Richard Garnet, and a Miniature Frontispiece.

Tennyson's "In Memoriam." With a Miniature Portrait in *eau forte* by Le Rat, after a Photograph by the late Mrs. Cameron.

PARKER (Joseph), D.D.

The Paraclete: An Essay on the Personality and Ministry of the Holy Ghost, with some reference to current discussions. Second Edition. Demy 8vo. Cloth, price 12s.

PARR (Capt. H. Hallam).

A Sketch of the Kafir and Zulu Wars: Guadana to Isandhlwana, with Maps. Small crown 8vo. Cloth, price 5s.

The Dress, Horses, and Equipment of Infantry and Staff Officers. Crown 8vo. Cloth, price 1s.

PARSLOE (Joseph).

Our Railways : Sketches, Historical and Descriptive. With Practical Information as to Fares, Rates, &c., and a Chapter on Railway Reform. Crown 8vo. Cloth, price 6s.

PATTISON (Mrs. Mark).

The Renaissance of Art in France. With Nineteen Steel Engravings. 2 vols. Demy 8vo. Cloth, price 32s.

PAUL (C. Kegan).

Mary Wollstonecraft. Letters to Imlay. With Prefatory Memoir by, and Two Portraits in *eau forte,* by Anna Lea Merritt. Crown 8vo. Cloth, price 6s.

PAUL (C. Kegan)—*continued.*
Goethe's Faust. A New Translation in Rime. Crown 8vo. Cloth, price 6s.
William Godwin: His Friends and Contemporaries. With Portraits and Facsimiles of the Handwriting of Godwin and his Wife. 2 vols. Square post 8vo. Cloth, price 28s.
The Genius of Christianity Unveiled. Being Essays by William Godwin never before published. Edited, with a Preface, by C. Kegan Paul. Crown 8vo. Cloth, price 7s. 6d.

PAUL (Margaret Agnes).
Gentle and Simple: A Story. 2 vols. Crown 8vo. Cloth, gilt tops, price 12s.
*** Also a Cheaper Edition in one vol. with Frontispiece. Crown 8vo. Cloth, price 6s.

PAYNE (John).
Songs of Life and Death. Crown 8vo. Cloth, price 5s.

PAYNE (Prof. J. F.).
Fröbel and the Kindergarten System. Second Edition.
A Visit to German Schools: Elementary Schools in Germany. Notes of a Professional Tour to inspect some of the Kindergartens, Primary Schools, Public Girls' Schools, and Schools for Technical Instruction in Hamburgh, Berlin, Dresden, Weimar, Gotha, Eisenach, in the autumn of 1874. With Critical Discussions of the General Principles and Practice of Kindergartens and other Schemes of Elementary Education. Crown 8vo. Cloth, price 4s. 6d.

PELLETAN (E.).
The Desert Pastor, Jean Jarousseau. Translated from the French. By Colonel E. P. De L'Hoste. With a Frontispiece. New Edition. Fcap. 8vo. Cloth, price 3s. 6d.

PENNELL (H. Cholmondeley).
Pegasus Resaddled. By the Author of " Puck on Pegasus," &c. &c. With Ten Full-page Illustrations by George Du Maurier. Second Edition. Fcap. 4to. Cloth elegant, price 12s. 6d.

PENRICE (Maj. J.), B.A.
A Dictionary and Glossary of the Ko-ran. With copious Grammatical References and Explanations of the Text. 4to. Cloth, price 21s.

PESCHEL (Dr. Oscar).
The Races of Man and their Geographical Distribution. Large crown 8vo. Cloth, price 9s.

PETERS (F. H.).
The Nicomachean Ethics of Aristotle. Translated by. Crown 8vo. Cloth, price 6s.

PFEIFFER (Emily).
Quarterman's Grace, and other Poems. Crown 8vo. Cloth, price 5s.
Glan Alarch: His Silence and Song. A Poem. Second Edition. Crown 8vo. price 6s.
Gerard's Monument, and other Poems. Second Edition. Crown 8vo. Cloth, price 6s.
Poems. Second Edition. Crown 8vo. Cloth, price 6s.
Sonnets and Songs. New Edition. 16mo, handsomely printed and bound in cloth, gilt edges, price 5s.

PIKE (Warburton).
The Inferno of Dante Alighieri. Demy 8vo. Cloth, price 5s.

PINCHES (Thomas), M.A.
Samuel Wilberforce: Faith —Service—Recompense. Three Sermons. With a Portrait of Bishop Wilberforce (after a Photograph by Charles Watkins). Crown 8vo. Cloth, price 4s. 6d.

PLAYFAIR (Lieut.-Col.), Her Britannic Majesty's Consul-General in Algiers.
Travels in the Footsteps of Bruce in Algeria and Tunis. Illustrated by facsimiles of Bruce's original Drawings, Photographs, Maps, &c. Royal 4to. Cloth, bevelled boards, gilt leaves, price £3 3s.

POLLOCK (Frederick).
Spinoza. His Life and Philosophy. Demy 8vo. Cloth, price 16s.

POLLOCK (W. H.).
Lectures on French Poets.
Delivered at the Royal Institution.
Small crown 8vo. Cloth, price 5s.

POOR (Laura E.).
Sanskrit and its kindred
Literatures. Studies in Compara-
tive Mythology. Small crown 8vo.
Cloth, price 5s.

POUSHKIN (A. S.).
Russian   Romance.
Translated from the Tales of Belkin,
&c. By Mrs. J. Buchan Telfer (*née*
Mouravieff). Crown 8vo. Cloth,
price 3s. 6d.

PRESBYTER.
Unfoldings of Christian
Hope. An Essay showing that the
Doctrine contained in the Damna-
tory Clauses of the Creed commonly
called Athanasian is unscriptural.
Small crown 8vo. Cloth, price 4s. 6d.

PRICE (Prof. Bonamy).
Currency and Banking.
Crown 8vo. Cloth, price 6s.

Chapters on Practical Political Economy. Being the Substance of Lectures delivered before
the University of Oxford. Large
post 8vo. Cloth, price 12s.

Proteus and Amadeus. A
Correspondence. Edited by Aubrey
De Vere. Crown 8vo. Cloth, price 5s.

PUBLIC SCHOOLBOY.
The Volunteer, the Militia-
man, and the Regular Soldier.
Crown 8vo. Cloth, price 5s.

PULPIT COMMENTARY (The).
Edited by the Rev. J. S. Exell and
the Rev. Canon H. D. M. Spence.

Genesis. By Rev. T. White-
law, M.A.; with Homilies by the
Very Rev. J. F. Montgomery, D.D.,
Rev. Prof. R. A. Redford, M.A.,
LL.B., Rev. F. Hastings, Rev. W.
Roberts, M.A. An Introduction to
the Study of the Old Testament by
the Rev. Canon Farrar, D.D.,
F.R.S.; and Introductions to the
Pentateuch by the Right Rev. H.
Cotterill, D.D., and Rev. T. White-
law, M.A. Fourth Edition. Price
15s.

PULPIT COMMENTARY (The)
—*continued.*
Numbers. By the Rev. R.
Winterbotham, LL.B. With Homilies
by the Rev. Prof. W. Binnie, D.D.,
Rev. E. S. Prout, M.A., Rev. D.
Young, Rev. J. Waite, and an In-
troduction by the Rev. Thomas
Whitelaw, M.A. Price 15s.

Joshua. By the Rev. J. J.
Lias, M.A. With Homilies by the
Rev. S. R. Aldridge, LL.B., Rev.
R. Glover, Rev. E. de Pressensé,
D.D., Rev. J. Waite, Rev. F. W.
Adeney, and an Introduction by the
Rev. A. Plummer, M.A. Second
Edition. Price 12s. 6d.

Judges and Ruth. By Right
Rev. Lord A. C. Hervey, D.D., and
Rev. J. Morrison, D.D. With Ho-
milies by Rev. A. F. Muir, M.A.;
Rev. W. F. Adeney, M.A.; Rev.
W. M. Statham; and Rev. Prof. J.
R. Thomson, M.A. Second Edition.
Cloth, price 15s.

1 Samuel. By the Very Rev.
R. P. Smith, D.D. With Homilies
by the Rev. Donald Fraser, D.D.,
Rev. Prof. Chapman, and Rev. B.
Dale. Third Edition. Price 15s.

Ezra, Nehemiah, and
Esther. By Rev. Canon G. Rawlin-
son, M.A.; with Homilies by Rev.
Prof. J. R. Thomson, M.A., Rev.
Prof. R. A. Redford, LL.B., M.A.,
Rev. W. S. Lewis, M.A., Rev. J. A.
Macdonald, Rev. A. Mackennal,
B.A., Rev. W. Clarkson, B.A., Rev.
F. Hastings, Rev. W. Dinwiddie,
LL.B., Rev. Prof. Rowlands, B.A.,
Rev. G. Wood, B.A., Rev. Prof. P.
C. Barker, LL.B., M.A., and Rev.
J. S. Exell. Fourth Edition. Price
12s. 6d.

Punjaub (The) and North
Western Frontier of India. By an
old Punjaubee. Crown 8vo. Cloth,
price 5s.

Rabbi Jeshua. An Eastern
Story. Crown 8vo. Cloth, price
3s. 6d.

**RAVENSHAW (John Henry),
B.C.S.**
Gaur: Its Ruins and In-
scriptions. Edited with consider-

RAVENSHAW (John Henry), B.C.S.—*continued.*

able additions and alterations by his Widow. With forty-four photographic illustrations and twenty-five fac-similes of Inscriptions. Super royal 4to. Cloth, 3*l*. 13*s*. 6*d*.

READ (Carveth).

On the Theory of Logic : An Essay. Crown 8vo. Cloth, price 6*s*.

Realities of the Future Life. Small crown 8vo. Cloth, price 1*s*. 6*d*.

REANEY (Mrs. G. S.).

Blessing and Blessed ; a Sketch of Girl Life. New and cheaper Edition. With a frontispiece. Crown 8vo. Cloth, price 3*s*. 6*d*.

Waking and Working ; or, from Girlhood to Womanhood. New and cheaper edition. With a Frontispiece. Crown 8vo. Cloth, price 3*s*. 6*d*.

Rose Gurney's Discovery. A Book for Girls, dedicated to their Mothers. Crown 8vo. Cloth, price 3*s*. 6*d*.

English Girls: their Place and Power. With a Preface by R. W. Dale, M.A., of Birmingham. Third Edition. Fcap. 8vo. Cloth, price 2*s*. 6*d*.

Just Anyone, and other Stories. Three Illustrations. Royal 16mo. Cloth, price 1*s*. 6*d*.

Sunshine Jenny and other Stories. Three Illustrations. Royal 16mo. Cloth, price 1*s*. 6*d*.

Sunbeam Willie, and other Stories. Three Illustrations. Royal 16mo. Cloth, price 1*s*. 6*d*.

RENDALL (J. M.).

Concise Handbook of the Island of Madeira. With plan of Funchal and map of the Island. Fcap. 8vo. Cloth, price 1*s*. 6*d*.

REYNOLDS (Rev. J. W.).

The Supernatural in Na- ture. A Verification by Free Use of Science. Second Edition, revised and enlarged. Demy 8vo. Cloth, price 14*s*.

Mystery of Miracles, The. By the Author of "The Supernatural in Nature." Crown 8vo. Cloth, price 6*s*.

RHOADES (James).

The Georgics of Virgil. Translated into English Verse. Small crown 8vo. Cloth, price 5*s*.

RIBOT (Prof. Th.).

English Psychology. Second Edition. A Revised and Corrected Translation from the latest French Edition. Large post 8vo. Cloth, price 9*s*.

Heredity : A Psychological Study on its Phenomena, its Laws, its Causes, and its Consequences. Large crown 8vo. Cloth, price 9*s*.

RINK (Chevalier Dr. Henry).

Greenland : Its People and its Products. By the Chevalier Dr. HENRY RINK, President of the Greenland Board of Trade. With sixteen Illustrations, drawn by the Eskimo, and a Map. Edited by Dr. ROBERT BROWN. Crown 8vo. Price 10*s*. 6*d*.

ROBERTSON (The Late Rev. F. W.), M.A., of Brighton.

The Human Race, and other Sermons preached at Cheltenham, Oxford, and Brighton. Second Edition. Large post 8vo. Cloth, price 7*s*. 6*d*.

Notes on Genesis. New and cheaper Edition. Crown 8vo., price 3*s*. 6*d*.

Sermons. Four Series. Small crown 8vo. Cloth, price 3*s*. 6*d*. each.

Expository Lectures on St. Paul's Epistles to the Corinthians. A New Edition. Small crown 8vo. Cloth, price 5*s*.

Lectures and Addresses, with other literary remains. A New Edition. Crown 8vo. Cloth, price 5*s*.

An Analysis of Mr. Tenny- son's "In Memoriam." (Dedicated by Permission to the Poet-Laureate.) Fcap. 8vo. Cloth, price 2*s*.

The Education of the Human Race. Translated from the German of Gotthold Ephraim Lessing. Fcap. 8vo. Cloth, price 2*s*. 6*d*.

Life and Letters. Edited by the Rev. Stopford Brooke, M.A., Chaplain in Ordinary to the Queen. I. 2 vols., uniform with the Sermons. With Steel Portrait. Crown 8vo. Cloth, price 7*s*. 6*d*.

ROBERTSON (The Late Rev. F. W.), M.A., of Brighton—*continued*.

II. Library Edition, in Demy 8vo., with Portrait. Cloth, price 12*s*.
III. A Popular Edition, in one vol. Crown 8vo. Cloth, price 6*s*.

The above Works can also be had half-bound in morocco.

*** A Portrait of the late Rev. F. W. Robertson, mounted for framing, can be had, price 2*s*. 6*d*.

ROBINSON (A. Mary F.).
A Handful of Honey-suckle. Fcap. 8vo. Cloth, price 3*s*. 6*d*.
The Crowned Hippolytus. Translated from Euripides. With New Poems. Small crown 8vo. Cloth, price 5*s*.

RODWELL (G. F.), F.R.A.S., F.C.S.
Etna : a History of the Mountain and its Eruptions. With Maps and Illustrations. Square 8vo. Cloth, price 9*s*.

ROSS (Mrs. E.), ("Nelsie Brook").
Daddy's Pet. A Sketch from Humble Life. With Six Illustrations. Royal 16mo. Cloth, price 1*s*.

ROSS (Alexander), D.D.
Memoir of Alexander Ewing, Bishop of Argyll and the Isles. Second and Cheaper Edition. Demy 8vo. Cloth, price 10*s*. 6*d*.

SADLER (S. W.), R.N.
The African Cruiser. A Midshipman's Adventures on the West Coast. With Three Illustrations. Second Edition. Crown 8vo. Cloth, price 3*s*. 6*d*.

SALTS (Rev. Alfred), LL.D.
Godparents at Confirmation. With a Preface by the Bishop of Manchester. Small crown 8vo. Cloth, limp, price 2*s*.

SALVATOR (Archduke Ludwig).
Levkosia, the Capital of Cyprus. Crown 8vo. Cloth, price 10*s*. 6*d*.

SAMUEL (Sydney Montagu).
Jewish Life in the East. Small crown 8vo. Cloth, price 3*s*. 6*d*.

SAUNDERS (John).
Israel Mort, Overman : A Story of the Mine. Cr. 8vo. Price 6*s*.

SAUNDERS (John)—*continued*.
Hirell. With Frontispiece. Crown 8vo. Cloth, price 3*s*. 6*d*.
Abel Drake's Wife. With Frontispiece. Crown 8vo. Cloth, price 3*s*. 6*d*.

SAYCE (Rev. Archibald Henry).
Introduction to the Science of Language. Two vols., large post 8vo. Cloth, price 25*s*.

SCHELL (Maj. von).
The Operations of the First Army under Gen. von Goeben. Translated by Col. C. H. von Wright. Four Maps. Demy 8vo. Cloth, price 9*s*.
The Operations of the First Army under Gen. von Steinmetz. Translated by Captain E. O. Hollist. Demy 8vo. Cloth, price 10*s*. 6*d*.

SCHELLENDORF (Maj.-Gen. B. von).
The Duties of the General Staff. Translated from the German by Lieutenant Hare. Vol. I. Demy 8vo. Cloth, price 10*s*. 6*d*.

SCHERFF (Maj. W. von).
Studies in the New Infantry Tactics. Parts I. and II. Translated from the German by Colonel Lumley Graham. Demy 8vo. Cloth, price 7*s*. 6*d*.

Scientific Layman. The New Truth and the Old Faith : are they Incompatible? Demy 8vo. Cloth, price 10*s*. 6*d*.

SCOONES (W. Baptiste).
Four Centuries of English Letters. A Selection of 350 Letters by 150 Writers from the period of the Paston Letters to the Present Time. Edited and arranged by. Second Edition. Large crown 8vo. Cloth, price 9*s*.

SCOTT (Leader).
A Nook in the Apennines : A Summer beneath the Chestnuts. With Frontispiece, and 27 Illustrations in the Text, chiefly from Original Sketches. Crown 8vo. Cloth, price 7*s*. 6*d*.

SCOTT (Robert H.).
Weather Charts and Storm Warnings. Illustrated. Second Edition. Crown 8vo. Cloth, price 3*s*. 6*d*.

Seeking his Fortune, and other Stories. With Four Illustrations. New and cheaper Edition. Crown 8vo. Cloth, price 2s. 6d.

SENIOR (N. W.).
Alexis De Tocqueville. Côrrespondence and Conversations with Nassau W. Senior, from 1833 to 1859. Edited by M. C. M. Simpson. 2 vols. Large post 8vo. Cloth, price 21s.

Seven Autumn Leaves from Fairyland. Illustrated with Nine Etchings. Square crown 8vo. Cloth, price 3s. 6d.

SHADWELL (Maj.-Gen.), C.B.
Mountain Warfare. Illustrated by the Campaign of 1799 in Switzerland. Being a Translation of the Swiss Narrative compiled from the Works of the Archduke Charles, Jomini, and others. Also of Notes by General H. Dufour on the Campaign of the Valtelline in 1635. With Appendix, Maps, and Introductory Remarks. Demy 8vo. Cloth, price 16s.

SHAKSPEARE (Charles).
Saint Paul at Athens: Spiritual Christianity in Relation to some Aspects of Modern Thought. Nine Sermons preached at St. Stephen's Church, Westbourne Park. With Preface by the Rev. Canon FARRAR. Crown 8vo. Cloth, price 5s.

SHAW (Major Wilkinson).
The Elements of Modern Tactics. Practically applied to English Formations. With Twenty-five Plates and Maps. S.cond and cheaper Edition. Small crown 8vo. Cloth, price 9s.
. The Second Volume of "Military Handbooks for Officers and Non-commissioned Officers." Edited by Lieut.-Col. C. B. Brackenbury, R.A., A.A.G.

SHAW (Flora L.).
Castle Blair: a Story of Youthful Lives. 2 vols. Crown 8vo. Cloth, gilt tops, price 12s. Also, an dition in one vol. Crown 8vo. 6s.

SHELLEY (Lady).
Shelley Memorials from Authentic Sources. With (now first printed) an Essay on Christianity by Percy Bysshe Shelley. With Portrait. Third Edition. Crown 8vo. Cloth, price 5s.

SHERMAN (Gen. W. T.).
Memoirs of General W. T. Sherman, Commander of the Federal Forces in the American Civil War. By Himself. 2 vols. With Map. Demy 8vo Cloth, price 24s. *Copyright English Edition.*

SHILLITO (Rev. Joseph).
Womanhood: its Duties, Temptations, and Privileges. A Book for Young Women. Second Edition. Crown 8vo. Price 3s. 6d.

SHIPLEY (Rev. Orby), M.A.
Principles of the Faith in Relation to Sin. Topics for Thought in Times of Retreat. Eleven Addresses. With an Introduction on the neglect of Dogmatic Theology in the Church of England, and a Postscript on his leaving the Church of England. Demy 8vo. Cloth, price 12s.

Church Tracts, or Studies in Modern Problems. By various Writers. 2 vols. Crown 8vo. Cloth, price 5s. each.

Sister Augustine, Superior of the Sisters of Charity at the St. Johannis Hospital at Bonn. Authorized Translation by Hans 1harau from the German Memorials of Amalie von Lasaulx. Second edition. Large crown 8vo. Cloth, price 7s. 6d.

SKINNER (James).
Cœlestia: the Manual of St. Augustine. The Latin Text side by side with an English Interpretation, in 36 Odes, with Notes, *and* a plea *for the* Study *of* Mystic Theology. Large crown 8vo. Cloth, price 6s.

SMITH (Edward), M.D., LL.B., F.R.S.
Health and Disease, as In- fluenced by the Daily, Seasonal, and other Cyclical Changes in the Human System. A New Edition. Post 8vo. Cloth, price 7s. 6d.

Practical Dietary for Families, Schools, and the Labouring Classes. A New Edition. Post 8vo. Cloth, price 3s. 6d.

Tubercular Consumption in its Early and Remediable Stages. Second Edition. Crown 8vo. Cloth, price 6s.

Songs of Two Worlds. By the Author of "The Epic of Hades." Sixth Edition. Complete in one Volume, with Portrait. Fcap. 8vo. Cloth, price 7s. 6d.

Songs for Music.
By Four Friends. Square crown 8vo. Cloth, price 5s.
Containing songs by Reginald A. Gatty, Stephen H. Gatty, Greville J. Chester, and Juliana Ewing.

SPEDDING (James).
Reviews and Discussions, Literary, Political, and Historical, not relating to Bacon. Demy 8vo. Cloth, price 12s. 6d.

STAPFER (Paul).
Shakspeare and Classical Antiquity : Greek and Latin Antiquity as presented in Shakspeare's Plays. Translated by Emily J. Carey. Large post 8vo. Cloth, price 12s.

St. Bernard on the Love of God. Translated by Marianne Caroline and Coventry Patmore. Cloth extra, gilt top, price 4s. 6d.

STEDMAN (Edmund Clarence).
Lyrics and Idylls. With other Poems. Crown 8vo. Cloth, price 7s. 6d.

STEPHENS (Archibald John), LL.D.
The Folkestone Ritual Case. The Substance of the Argument delivered before the Judicial Committee of the Privy Council. On behalf of the Respondents. Demy 8vo. Cloth, price 6s.

STEVENS (William).
The Truce of God, and other Poems. Small crown 8vo. Cloth, price 3s. 6d.

STEVENSON (Robert Louis).
Virginibus, Puerisque, and other Papers. Crown 8vo. Cloth, price 6s.

STEVENSON (Rev. W. F.).
Hymns for the Church and Home. Selected and Edited by the Rev. W. Fleming Stevenson.
The most complete Hymn Book published.

STEVENSON (Rev. W. F.)—*continued.*
The Hymn Book consists of Three Parts :—I. For Public Worship.—II. For Family and Private Worship.—III. For Children.
** Published in various forms and prices, the latter ranging from 8d. to 6s. Lists and full particulars will be furnished on application to the Publishers.

STOCKTON (Frank R.).
A Jolly Fellowship. With 20 Illustrations. Crown 8vo. Cloth, price 5s.

STORR (Francis), and TURNER Hawes).
Canterbury Chimes ; or, Chaucer Tales retold to Children. With Illustrations from the Ellesmere MS. Extra Fcap. 8vo. Cloth, price 3s. 6d.

STRETTON (Hesba).
David Lloyd's Last Will. With Four Illustrations. Royal 16mo., price 2s. 6d.

The   Wonderful   Life. Thirteenth Thousand. Fcap. 8vo. Cloth, price 2s. 6d.

Through a Needle's Eye : a Story. Crown 8vo. Cloth, price 6s.

STUBBS (Lieut.-Colonel F. W.)
The Regiment of Bengal Artillery. The History of its Organization, Equipment, and War Services. Compiled from Published Works, Official Records, and various Private Sources. With numerous Maps and Illustrations. 2 vols. Demy 8vo. Cloth, price 32s.

STUMM (Lieut. Hugo), German Military Attaché to the Khivan Expedition.
Russia's   advance   East-ward. Based on the Official Reports of. Translated by Capt. C. E. H. VINCENT. With Map. Crown 8vo. Cloth, price 6s.

SULLY (James), M.A.
Sensation and Intuition. Demy 8vo. Second Edition. Cloth, price 10s. 6d.
Pessimism : a History and a Criticism. Demy 8vo. Price 14s.

Sunnyland Stories.
By the Author of "Aunt Mary's Bran Pie." Illustrated. Small 8vo. Cloth, price 3s. 6d

Sweet Silvery Sayings of Shakespeare. Crown 8vo. Cloth gilt, price 7s. 6d.

SYME (David).
Outlines of an Industrial Science. Second Edition. Crown 8vo. Cloth, price 6s.

Tales from Ariosto. Retold for Children, by a Lady. With three illustrations. Crown 8vo. Cloth, price 4s. 6d.

TAYLOR (Algernon).
Guienne. Notes of an Autumn Tour. Crown 8vo. Cloth, price 4s. 6d.

TAYLOR (Sir H.).
Works Complete. Author's Edition, in 5 vols. Crown 8vo. Cloth, price 6s. each.
Vols. I. to III. containing the Poetical Works, Vols. IV. and V. the Prose Works.

TAYLOR (Col. Meadows), C.S.I., M.R.I.A.
A Noble Queen : a Romance Indian History. New Edition. With Frontispiece. Crown 8vo. oth. Price 6s.

Seeta. New Edition with frontispiece. Crown 8vo. Cloth, price 6s.

Tippoo Sultaun : a Tale of the Mysore War. New Edition with Frontispiece. Crown 8vo. Cloth, price 6s.

Ralph Darnell. New Edition. With Frontispiece. Crown 8vo. Cloth, price 6s.

The Confessions of a Thug. New Edition. With Frontispiece. Crown 8vo. Cloth, price 6s.

Tara : a Mahratta Tale. New Edition. With Frontispiece. Crown 8vo. Cloth, price 6s.

TENNYSON (Alfred).
The Imperial Library Edition. Complete in 7 vols. Demy 8vo. Cloth, price £3 13s. 6d. ; in Roxburgh binding, £4 7s. 6d.

TENNYSON (Alfred)—continued
Author's Edition. Complete in 6 Volumes. Post 8vo. Cloth gilt ; or half-morocco, Roxburgh style :—

VOL. I. **Early Poems, and** English Idylls. Price 6s. ; Roxburgh, 7s. 6d.

VOL. II. **Locksley Hall,** Lucretius, and other Poems. Price 6s. ; Roxburgh, 7s. 6d.

VOL. III. **The Idylls of** the King (Complete). Price 7s. 6d.; Roxburgh, 9s.

VOL. IV. **The Princess, and** Maud. Price 6s.; Roxburgh, 7s. 6d.

VOL. V. **Enoch Arden,** and In Memoriam. Price 6s. ; Roxburgh, 7s. 6d.

VOL. VI. **Dramas.** Price 7s. ; Roxburgh, 8s. 6d.

Cabinet Edition. 12 vols. Each with Frontispiece. Fcap. 8vo. Cloth, price 2s. 6d. each.

CABINET EDITION. 12 vols. Complete in handsome Ornamental Case. 32s.

The Royal Edition. With 25 Illustrations and Portrait. Cloth extra, bevelled boards, gilt leaves. Price 21s.

The Guinea Edition. Complete in 12 vols., neatly bound and enclosed in box. Cloth, price 21s. French morocco or parchment, price 31s. 6d.

The Shilling Edition of the Poetical and Dramatic Works, in 12 vols., pocket size. Price 1s. each.

The Crown Edition. Complete in one vol., strongly bound in cloth, price 6s. Cloth, extra gilt leaves, price 7s. 6d. Roxburgh, half morocco, price 8s. 6d.

. Can also be had in a variety of other bindings.

TENNYSON (Alfred)—*continued.*

Original Editions :

Ballads and other Poems.
Fcap. 8vo. Cloth, price 5s.

The Lover's Tale. (Now for the first time published.) Fcap. 8vo. Cloth, 3s. 6d.

Poems. Small 8vo. Cloth, price 6s.

Maud, and other Poems. Small 8vo. Cloth, price 3s. 6d.

The Princess. Small 8vo. Cloth, price 3s. 6d.

Idylls of the King. Small 8vo. Cloth, price 5s.

Idylls of the King. Complete. Small 8vo. Cloth, price 6s.

The Holy Grail, and other Poems. Small 8vo. Cloth, price 4s. 6d.

Gareth and Lynette. Small 8vo. Cloth, price 3s.

Enoch Arden, &c. Small 8vo. Cloth, price 3s. 6d.

In Memoriam. Small 8vo. Cloth, price 4s.

Queen Mary. A Drama. New Edition. Crown 8vo. Cloth, price 6s.

Harold. A Drama. Crown 8vo. Cloth, price 6s.

Selections from Tennyson's Works. Super royal 16mo. Cloth, price 3s. 6d. Cloth gilt extra, price 4s.

Songs from Tennyson's Works. Super royal 16mo. Cloth extra, price 3s. 6d.

Also a cheap edition. 16mo. Cloth, price 2s. 6d.

Idylls of the King, and other Poems. Illustrated by Julia Margaret Cameron. 2 vols. Folio. Half-bound morocco, cloth sides, price £6 6s. each.

Tennyson for the Young and for Recitation. Specially arranged. Fcap. 8vo. Price 1s. 6d.

Tennyson Birthday Book. Edited by Emily Shakespear. 32mo. Cloth limp, 2s. ; cloth extra, 3s.

** A superior edition, printed in red and black, on antique paper, specially prepared. Small crown 8vo. Cloth extra, gilt leaves, price 5s. ; and in various calf and morocco bindings.

Songs Set to Music, by various Composers. Edited by W. G. Cusins. Dedicated by express permission to Her Majesty the Queen. Royal 4to. Cloth extra, gilt leaves, price 21s., or in half-morocco, price 25s.

An Index to "In Memoriam." Price 2s.

THOMAS (Moy).
A Fight for Life. With Frontispiece. Crown 8vo. Cloth, price 3s. 6d.

THOMPSON (Alice C.).
Preludes. A Volume of Poems. Illustrated by Elizabeth Thompson (Painter of "The Roll Call"). 8vo. Cloth, price 7s. 6d.

THOMSON (J. Turnbull).
Social Problems; or, an Inquiry into the Law of Influences. With Diagrams. Demy 8vo. Cloth, price 10s. 6d.

THRING (Rev. Godfrey), B.A.
Hymns and Sacred Lyrics. Fcap. 8vo. Cloth, price 3s. 6d.

TODHUNTER (Dr. J.)
A Study of Shelley. Crown 8vo. Cloth, price 7s.

Alcestis : A Dramatic Poem. Extra fcap. 8vo. Cloth, price 5s.

Laurella; and other Poems. Crown 8vo. Cloth, price 6s. 6d.

Translations from Dante, Petrarch, Michael Angelo, and **Vittoria Colonna.** Fcap. 8vo. Cloth, price 7s. 6d.

TURNER (Rev. C. Tennyson).
Sonnets, Lyrics, and Translations. Crown 8vo. Cloth, price 4s. 6d.

TURNER (Rev. C. Tennyson)—
continued.

Collected Sonnets, Old and New. With Prefatory Poem by Alfred Tennyson; also some Marginal Notes by S. T. Coleridge, and a Critical Essay by James Spedding. Fcap. 8vo. Cloth, price 7s. 6d.

TWINING (Louisa).
Recollections of Workhouse Visiting and Management during twenty-five years. Small crown 8vo. Cloth, price 3s. 6d.

UPTON (Major R. D.).
Gleanings from the Desert of Arabia. Large post 8vo. Cloth, price 10s. 6d.

VAUGHAN (H. Halford), sometime Regius Professor of Modern History in Oxford University.
New Readings and Renderings of Shakespeare's Tragedies. 2 vols. Demy 8vo. Cloth, price 25s.

VILLARI (Prof.).
Niccolo Machiavelli and His Times. Translated by Linda Villari. 2 vols. Large post 8vo. Cloth, price 24s.

VINCENT (Capt. C. E. H.).
Elementary Military Geography, Reconnoitring, and Sketching. Compiled for Non-Commissioned Officers and Soldiers of all Arms. Square crown 8vo. Cloth, price 2s. 6d.

VYNER (Lady Mary).
Every day a Portion. Adapted from the Bible and the Prayer Book, for the Private Devotions of those living in Widowhood. Collected and edited by Lady Mary Vyner. Square crown 8vo. Cloth extra, price 5s.

WALDSTEIN (Charles), Ph. D.
The Balance of Emotion and Intellect: An Essay Introductory to the Study of Philosophy. Crown 8vo. Cloth, price 6s.

WALLER (Rev. C. B.)
The Apocalypse, Reviewed under the Light of the Doctrine of the Unfolding Ages and the Restitution of all Things. Demy 8vo. Cloth, price 12s.

WALTERS (Sophia Lydia).
The Brook : A Poem. Small crown 8vo. Cloth, price 3s. 6d.

A Dreamer's Sketch Book. With Twenty-one Illustrations by Percival Skelton, R. P. Leitch, W. H. J. Boot, and T. R. Pritchett. Engraved by J. D. Cooper. Fcap. 4to. Cloth, price 12s. 6d.

WATERFIELD, W.
Hymns for Holy Days and Seasons. 32mo. Cloth, price 1s. 6d.

WATSON (William).
The Prince's Quest and other Poems. Crown 8vo, Cloth, price 5s.

WATSON (Sir Thomas), Bart., M.D.
The Abolition of Zymotic Diseases, and of other similar enemies of Mankind. Small crown 8vo. Cloth, price 3s. 6d.

WAY (A.), M.A.
The Odes of Horace Literally Translated in Metre. Fcap. 8vo. Cloth, price 2s.

WEBSTER (Augusta).
Disguises. A Drama. Small crown 8vo. Cloth, price 5s.

WEDMORE (Frederick).
The Masters of Genre Painting. With sixteen illustrations. Large crown 8vo. Cloth, price 7s. 6d.

Wet Days, by a Farmer. Small crown 8vo. Cloth, price 6s.

WHEWELL (William), D.D.
His Life and Selections from his Correspondence. By Mrs. Stair Douglas. With Portrait from a Painting by Samuel Laurence. Demy 8vo. Cloth, price 21s.

WHITAKER (Florence).
Christy's Inheritance. A London Story. Illustrated. Royal 16mo. Cloth, price 1s. 6d.

WHITE (A. D.), LL.D.
Warfare of Science. With Prefatory Note by Professor Tyndall. Second Edition. Crown 8vo. Cloth, price 3s. 6d.

WHITNEY (Prof. W. D.)
Essentials of English Grammar for the Use of Schools. Crown 8vo. Cloth, price 3s. 6d.

WICKSTEED (P. H.).
Dante : Six Sermons. Crown 8vo. Cloth, price 5s.

WILKINS (William)
Songs of Study. Crown 8vo. Cloth, price 6s.

WILLIAMS (Rowland), D.D.
Stray Thoughts from the Note-Books of the Late Rowland Williams, D.D. Edited by his Widow. Crown 8vo. Cloth, price 3s. 6d.

Psalms, Litanies, Counsels and Collects for Devout Persons. Edited by his Widow. New and Popular Edition. Crown 8vo. Cloth, price 3s. 6d.

WILLIS (R.), M.D.
Servetus and Calvin : a Study of an Important Epoch in the Early History of the Reformation. 8vo. Cloth, price 16s.

William Harvey. A History of the Discovery of the Circulation of the Blood. With a Portrait of Harvey, after Faithorne. Demy 8vo. Cloth, price 14s.

WILLOUGHBY(The Hon. Mrs.).
On the North Wind— Thistledown. A Volume of Poems. Elegantly bound. Small crown 8vo. Cloth, price 7s. 6d.

WILSON (Erasmus).
Egypt of the Past. With Chromo-lithographs and numerous Illustrations in the Text. Crown 8vo. Cloth.

WILSON (H. Schütz).
The Tower and Scaffold. A Miniature Monograph. Large fcap. 8vo. Price 1s.

Within Sound of the Sea. By the Author of "Blue Roses," "Vera," &c. Third Edition. 2 vols. Crown 8vo. Cloth, gilt tops, price 12s.
*** Also a cheaper edition in one vol. with frontispiece. Price 6s.

WOLLSTONECRAFT (Mary).
Letters to Imlay. With a Preparatory Memoir by C. Kegan Paul, and two Portraits in *eau forte* by Anna Lea Merritt. Crown 8vo. Cloth, price 6s.

WOLTMANN (Dr. Alfred), and WOERMANN (Dr. Karl).
History of Painting in Antiquity and the Middle Ages. Edited by Sidney Colvin. With numerous illustrations. Medium 8vo. Cloth, price 28s. ; cloth, bevelled boards, gilt leaves, price 30s.

WOOD (Major-General J. Creighton).
Doubling the Consonant. Small crown 8vo. Cloth, price 1s. 6d.

WOODS (James Chapman).
A Child of the People, and other poems. Small crown 8vo. Cloth, price 5s.

Word was made Flesh. Short Family Readings on the Epistles for each Sunday of the Christian Year. Demy 8vo. Cloth, price 10s. 6d.

WRIGHT (Rev. David), M.A.
Waiting for the Light, and other Sermons. Crown 8vo. Cloth, price 6s.

YOUMANS (Eliza A.).
An Essay on the Culture of the Observing Powers of Children, especially in connection with the Study of Botany. Edited, with Notes and a Supplement, by Joseph Payne, F.C.P., Author of "Lectures on the Science and Art of Education," &c. Crown 8vo. Cloth, price 2s. 6d.

First Book of Botany. Designed to Cultivate the Observing Powers of Children. With 300 Engravings. New and Cheaper Edition. Crown 8vo. Cloth, price 2s. 6d.

YOUMANS (Edward L.), M.D.
A Class Book of Chemistry, on the Basis of the New System. With 200 Illustrations. Crown 8vo. Cloth, price 5s.

YOUNG (William).
Gottlob, etcetera. Small crown 8vo. Cloth, price 3s. 6d.

www.ingramcontent.com/pod-product-compliance
Lightning Source LLC
Chambersburg PA
CBHW021341110726
47900CB00005B/1567